I ♥ ROGUES

D1013790

I ♥ ROGUES

Bertrice Small
Thea Devine
Jane Bonander

BRAVA

Kensington Publishing Corp.

http://www.kensingtonbooks.com

BRAVA BOOKS are published by

Kensington Publishing Corp.
850 Third Avenue
New York, NY 10022

Copyright © 2003 by Kensington Publishing Corp.
"Zuleika and the Barbarian" copyright © 2003 by Bertrice Small
"All the Secret Pleasures" copyright © 2003 by Thea Devine
"The Bedroom Is Mine" copyright © 2003 by Jane Bonander

All rights reserved. No part of this book may be reproduced in any form or by any means without the prior written consent of the Publisher, excepting brief quotes used in reviews.

All Kensington titles, imprints and distributed lines are available at special quantity discounts for bulk purchases for sales promotion, premiums, fund raising, educational or institutional use.

Special book excerpts or customized printings can also be created to fit specific needs. For details, write or phone the office of the Kensington Special Sales Manager: Kensington Publishing Corp., 850 Third Avenue, New York, NY 10022. Attn. Special Sales Department. Phone: 1-800-221-2647.

Brava and the B logo Reg. U.S. Pat. & TM Off.

ISBN 0-7582-0419-1

First Kensington Trade Paperback Printing: December 2003
10 9 8 7 6 5 4 3 2 1

Printed in the United States of America

CONTENTS

ZULEIKA AND THE BARBARIAN

Bertrice Small

PROLOGUE

Many centuries ago, there existed an ancient kingdom known as Dariyabar, which sat on the edge of the southern desert in the center of the road known as Silk. Its sultan was a good man with three strong sons, and a beautiful daughter who was called Zuleika.

My name is Fatimah. I am a storyteller by trade, and I sit just within the gates of fabled Baghdad telling my stories. Hear now, gentle listener, the tale of the princess Zuleika, and the barbarian, and of how together, although at the time he did not realize it, they save Dariyabar from the evils that threatened to engulf and destroy it.

Even the girl known as Sheherizade does not know this narrative, but I swear by all the gods known and unknown that it is true.

Chapter One

"You would give me to the barbarian for his harem?" said Zuleika, Princess of Dariyabar, disbelieving.

"It is the practical solution to our problem," her cousin, Haroun, said. "Your father, the sultan, agrees." He was a man of medium height with a too beautiful face, dark blue eyes, and curly black hair.

"I thought you loved me! It has been planned since our shared childhood that we marry," Zuleika responded.

"But it is no longer necessary that I marry you, dear Zuleika," he told her. "Your brothers are all dead. I am the only male heir your father has. Even without you I shall be the next sultan of Dariyabar."

"I never realized what a snake you are, Haroun," the princess replied, her voice suddenly cold. The Gods! What a fool she had been!

"You see, cousin," he continued, "I have the throne, and I shall be able to keep my favorite, Golnar, which I could not have done if I had married you. I need a more complaisant wife. I have chosen the vizier's daughter, Bahira. She is a pretty little thing, and will do precisely what she is told. You have never done what you are told, Zuleika, unless, of course, it pleased you to do so. I cannot have a wife who would attempt to rule Dariyabar through me. I need a wife who will be loyal, and never criticize. Bahira will suit me admirably."

"Have you told her *that* yet, Haroun?" Zuleika asked him dryly. Bahira was her best friend. They were like sisters. Haroun was very mistaken if he thought Bahira a meek little ewe sheep who would follow her lord and master without question. She must find a way to protect her friend!

"The time is not right yet for me to announce my choice of a wife. Not until you are safely ensconced within the camp of the barbarian, Amir Khan. I suspect he will be quite pleased to have the sultan's daughter for his new plaything, cousin." Haroun smiled broadly.

"But not as his wife?" Zuleika probed.

"This is not a negotiation we are having with Amir Khan," Haroun said. "You are a *gift*. One does not put conditions on a gift."

"You are a fool, Haroun, if you believe that by giving Amir Khan the sultan of Dariyabar's daughter he will pack up his armies and go away. Do you think he has been besieging us for three years so he might be given the gift of a woman?"

"They say that Amir Khan is an intelligent man. Surely by now he has come to realize he cannot take the city. Without the city, the rest of Dariyabar is useless to him. We make a great public presentation to the khan of the princess Zuleika, Sultan Ibrahim's only surviving child. A peace between us is inevitable under such a circumstance. We give him the means of saving face. He can depart without embarrassment, or shame. After all, cousin, no one has ever successfully besieged Dariyabar."

Zuleika swept her cousin a low bow. "I bow, Haroun, to your clever plan," she told him. Then she turned and left him in the sultan's gardens, knowing as she went that he wore a smug smile upon his too-handsome features. He was a fool! And she would make certain that he did not follow her father as ruler of Dariyabar. But she must work quickly for Haroun, she now realized, was a ruthless man. As soon as he had gotten rid of her, and made Bahira his wife, her father's very life was in jeopardy.

The sultan was a beloved ruler who had brought Dariyabar great prosperity by encouraging a ship-building industry that built merchant vessels that traversed the known world buying and selling luxury goods of every kind. They traded in ivory, gold, silk, and slaves, among other things. Their ships carried fine oils, wines, olives and grains. There was no one in Dariyabar who did not have a home, or food in his mouth each day, or warm clothing and shoes in the rainy season. Children were schooled to their abilities so they might be of use to Dariyabar one day, no matter the circumstances of their birth, or their parents' path in life.

But the sultan had married his only wife late in life because of this deep devotion to his homeland. It had been ten years before his sultana had borne children. But she had then birthed four in the next eight years. Sultan Ibrahim was now in his eighth decade of life. He had watched proudly as his three sons, Cyrus, Asad, and Jahi, had each in their turn sallied forth from Dariyabar at the head of their troops to defend their homeland. But each in his turn was slain, and returned upon their shields. Now he was left to mourn with his surviving child, for the sultana had died giving birth to that last babe, his daughter, Zuleika. The sultan drew his wool shawl about his narrow shoulders, and sighed.

His only male heir was his much younger half-brother's son, Haroun. Sultan Ibrahim had raised this nephew almost from birth for both his half-brother and his wife had disappeared from the palace one night, and were never again seen. It was a great mystery. Sultan Ibrahim had always planned for Haroun to wed his daughter, Zuleika, but now Haroun said that was impossible. Zuleika must be given to Amir Khan as a peace offering. Surely his nephew had Dariyabar's best interests at heart. Hearing a footfall, the old man looked up to see his daughter entering the garden courtyard.

Zuleika went to her father and knelt before him, taking his hands in hers and pressing them to her heart. "Good day, my father," she said sweetly to him.

"Get up, my daughter, and come and sit with me," the sultan said in his reedy voice. "Haroun has spoke with you, I can tell, for your eyes are stormy no matter that your mouth smiles at me."

Zuleika laughed, rose gracefully, and sat by her sire's side. "Haroun is not fit to rule Dariyabar, father," she began. "You know in your heart that his only interest in our land is the riches it can bring him. He will ultimately drive the people to misery." She sighed. "I will do what you desire of me, father. However, for my sake, as well as for the prestige of Dariyabar, I beg you that I go to Amir Khan as his wife, not his concubine. I am your daughter, and the daughter of a princess. I am not some slave girl!"

"Haroun says you are a gift, and we cannot attach conditions of any kind to a gift," the sultan said in a voice that indicated his confusion over the matter.

Zuleika realized then and there that it was useless to argue the matter further with her father. Haroun had convinced him of what he must do, and being a male it was his word that would prevail over hers despite the fact her father loved her. Her facile mind was already forming a plan of action. "It will be as you wish, my father," she told him meekly. "But would you permit me a boon?"

"I will give you whatever you desire, my daughter," the sultan said, eager to please Zuleika under these circumstances. He had to trust his heir's judgment in this matter, and yet he was not certain he was really doing the right thing.

"Other than my servant, Rafa, I would take one person with me when I leave Dariyabar, father."

"You may have whomever you desire, my daughter," the sultan promised her. "You have my word on it. Who would you take?"

"I am not certain yet," Zuleika lied smoothly. "I shall tell you on the day that I leave." She leaned over and kissed his cheek. "You have not yet told Haroun about Kansbar, have you?"

"No," her father said.

"Do not," Zuleika implored the old man. "Until we can be

certain that Haroun's motives are pure, we must not put Kansbar into his hands. Promise me that, father! Swear on my mother's memory!"

"I pledge you silence on Jamila's memory," the sultan vowed to his daughter. "I know you are right in this, Zuleika."

"Thank you, father," the girl said, then arose, and kissing his cheek again she left him with his memories and his thoughts. Hurrying to her own quarters she entered, saying to her servant as she did, "I am betrayed, Rafa. I am to be given to Amir Khan as a peace offering!" Her eyes met those of her best friend, Bahira. "And Haroun has decided to take you for his wife because you are meek and mild."

"*Me?*" Bahira looked astounded. She was a plump, pretty girl with dark auburn hair and blue eyes. "I never thought he even noticed me, but I should not marry Haroun if he were the last man on earth!"

"And your father approves of this perfidy?" Rafa demanded, outraged. "My poor master! He is old, and confused. Prince Haroun takes shameful advantage of him."

"Father takes his word over mine only because he is a man," Zuleika said, almost bitterly.

"What are you going to do?" Bahira asked.

"First you must tell me if you are certain that you will not have Haroun?" Zuleika replied. "Think carefully, Bahira. If my plan fails, then you could be the sultana of Dariyabar."

"And if your plan succeeds?" Bahira wanted to know.

"I will be the sultana," Zuleika said with a smile.

"And Haroun?" Rafa asked, her black eyes curious.

"He will not be the sultan," was all Zuleika would say.

"I will take my chances with you," Bahira told her friend.

"Good! I have asked my father for Rafa and one other person to go with me to the barbarian's encampment. He swore I might have anyone I desired. Haroun will not approach your father until after I am gone. I intend asking the sultan for you, Bahira. He has given his word, and will not take it back no matter Haroun's protests. That way I can keep you safe from my cousin." She reached out and took her friend's hand, and the hand of her servant. "Will you both trust me to bring us safely back to Dariyabar? I will, you know."

They both squeezed her hand in response.

"Good," Zuleika told them. "Now let us go and see what Kansbar will show me, provided he is in a mood to cooperate."

Without being asked, Rafa scurried across the room to a tall ebony wood cabinet. Opening it, she drew out a concave vessel, and bringing it to her mistress set it upon a low table. It was a bowl, wide, round, and almost flat in design. It was oddly plain, having no decoration upon it at all, neither carving nor bas-relief. It was dull in color, appearing to be made from some base metal. Rafa and Bahira sat about the low table on red silk cushions. Zuleika knelt before the bowl.

"Great Kansbar, guardian of Dariyabar, and supreme genie of the golden bowl, come forth, I beg you, and speak with me," she said.

The bowl filled with clear crystal water.

"Please, Kansbar, we are in danger, and need you," Zuleika pleaded politely.

The dull bowl suddenly shone itself a bright and shining gold.

"We are at your mercy, and await your august presence," Zuleika murmured.

Suddenly a face appeared on the smooth surface of the water. It was a male face, ageless, and his head was topped by a cloth-of-gold turban in the front of which was set a large pigeon's-blood ruby. Black eyes looked out upon the trio, curious, and perhaps just a trifle irritated at being disturbed. "It must be great danger, my princess, that you are so deferential to me," the genie said. "What has happened, and how may I serve you?" His voice was deep, and like thunder.

"I am to be given to the khan as a gift," Zuleika said. "My cousin, Haroun, has betrayed us. I fear when I am gone he will see my father dead so he may rule Dariyabar."

"He is the male heir," Kansbar said.

"You would serve him?"

"I did not say that, my princess. I said he was the male heir," the genie responded. "I know your cousin's worth even as I know yours Now, how may I serve you today?"

"Show me Amir Khan," Zuleika said.

"It is done," Kansbar said as he disappeared from the surface of the water, which grew dark again.

And then the liquid grew quite light, and there before them was a man. He was taller than any man Zuleika had ever seen. His body was perfect, and in absolute proportion. He was well-muscled, with quite graceful hands and feet. His head was shaven, and from his smooth skull fell a single swath of black hair, dressed with narrow gold bands. His face was beardless. He had high cheekbones, a long straight nose with flaring nostrils, a generous mouth, and dark brown eyes that mirrored his intelligence.

"The Gods!" Bahira breathed aloud. "He is gorgeous, Zuleika! I should far rather have *him* between my legs than Haroun the Handsome."

"He is mine," Zuleika said, quietly admiring the curve of his buttocks as he turned. He was dressed only in a loincloth.

Suddenly Kansbar's face reappeared upon the surface of the water. "Have you seen enough, my princess?" he demanded.

"Yes," she answered him. Then she turned to Rafa and Bahira. "Leave me," she said. "I need to speak with Kansbar alone." When they had withdrawn, Zuleika said to the genie, "I would meet Amir Khan privately when none are about. No one must know that I do this. And I would be clothed in moonbeams when we meet."

The genie smiled sardonically. "Do you mean to seduce him, my princess?" he mocked her gently.

"If I must, but I think not," she replied. "Haroun would send me as a gift, a concubine. It is an insulting gesture to us both. If I must take this man, then it must be as his wife. This is why I need to speak with him, Kansbar."

"Look at me, my princess," the genie said, and after their eyes had met for a long minute he continued, "I see what it is you will say to him, and he should see reason, my princess, for he is not a foolish man."

"How can you be certain?" she asked.

"I do not spend all my time in this bowl," Kansbar said sharply. "While I am bound to serve Dariyabar, I need only come when I am called. *Tonight!* You will go to him tonight, for there is no time to waste, my princess. At the midnight hour I will send a gentle fog across the city and the khan's encampment. All will sleep but for you and Amir Khan alone. You will find his command tent in the very center of his camp. The moon will clothe you and light your way. No one will challenge either your coming or your going. My spell will only hold to the dawn, however."

She nodded. "Thank you, Kansbar," she told the genie.

He nodded at her in acknowledgement, and then both the genie and the water in the bowl disappeared, while the round vessel again took on a dull sheen with no hint of gold at all. Zuleika arose, and taking the bowl replaced it back in the cabinet. She rejoined Bahira and Rafa in her small private walled garden.

"What mischief do you plan?" Rafa asked her, suspicious.

"None," Zuleika assured her.

"I think I shall remain with you tonight," Bahira said.

"No," Zuleika told her. "You will rouse my cousin's suspicions if you do. Particularly in light of what he has told me today."

"But what if he speaks to my father?" Bahira asked.

"I have already told you that he will not until I am gone, and in the khan's embrace," Zuleika replied. "You need have no fears unless we force Haroun to a premature action. Play the quiet maiden for now, Bahira. Can you not imagine the look on Haroun's face when I snatch you from beneath his nose?" She laughed.

Bahira laughed too. "He may be handsome, but I have always thought there was something slimy about your cousin," she admitted. "He is like one of those creatures who sometimes appear in the garden and leave a trail of muck behind them." She shivered. "I would kill myself before I married such a man!"

"He thinks you would be obedient, and not object to Golnar, or thwart her authority in his harem," Zuleika noted.

"They say Golnar has magical powers," Bahira remarked. "Do you think it is true?"

"She is an odd creature," Zuleika replied. "I cannot imagine what Haroun sees in her. I find her too-pale hair, skin and eyes repellent."

"I should not like to share a harem with her," Bahira said. Then she stood up from the marble bench where she had been seated, and stretched. "If I am going home, I had best leave now. It is almost sunset, and I prefer my litter traversing the streets while it is still light." She bent, and kissed Zuleika's cheek. "I will be back tomorrow."

"I may have some interesting news for you then," the princess of Dariyabar answered her best friend. And when Bahira had gone, Zuleika said to Rafa, "I think I shall bathe after I have had my evening meal."

Rafa bowed low. "I shall bring your food now," she said, and went off to fetch it for her mistress.

Zuleika sat quietly, letting the peace of the early evening and the fragrance of the flowers soothe her. At the far end of her garden she had a view of the blue sea beyond a low wall. There was no need for a high wall, for that end of the sultan's palace sat upon a steep cliff. The sun now set to the west in a magnificent display of color. Zuleika liked to watch the sunset every day, for no two were alike. Tonight the sky above was a rich blue, streaked with glorious pink and peach clouds edged with gold. The sun itself blazed scarlet as it sank into its bed of orange and gold with just the thinnest line of pale green. As the colors muted in crimson and tangerine, she noted a bright diamond star directly above her. Rafa's voice broke into her thoughts and Zuleika turned with a smile.

"Your meal awaits, my princess," Rafa said, and she smiled too, knowing her mistress's love of the sunset. "It is especially beautiful this evening, isn't it?" she noted.

Zuleika nodded, and then rising, followed the older woman back through the colorless gossamer draperies that separated her quarters from the gardens. "What have you brought me? I find I am ravenous tonight."

Rafa chuckled. "You cannot tell me that you do not plan some mischief, my princess. You are always extra hungry when you do." She seated the girl at her table. "See for yourself."

Zuleika's violet eyes swept over the table, and then with a grin she began to eat. There were chunks of lamb upon a skewer with tiny whole onions, and bits of melon that had been brushed with olive oil and roasted over a slow fire. There was a plate of warm flat breads, and a dish of yogurt that had been strained through a piece of silk, and then mixed with an apricot puree.

"Will you drink wine tonight, my princess?" Rafa asked.

"Nay. I will have pomegranate juice," came the reply.

Rafa's eyebrow raised itself just slightly as she poured the required beverage from the silver pitcher. Something was indeed afoot, that Zuleika would not have her usual cup of wine with her evening meal. She placed the pomegranate juice by her mistress's right hand. If Zuleika did not wish to tell her what she was up to, there was nothing she could do, but she still worried. She had raised this maiden from her birth when the poor sultana had died.

"Is it dangerous?" she probed.

"Nay, and ask me no more," Zuleika replied. "Do you think I am a fool to risk my own safety, and that of Dariyabar?"

Rafa nodded. "I worry," was all she said.

"Do not, old woman," came the command, and the princess turned back to her meal with enthusiasm.

"Because you tell me," Rafa said with a wry smile.

"Because I tell you," Zuleika nodded.

Rafa chortled. "I will see that your bath is prepared," she told her mistress.

And when the princess had finished her meal, and bathed, she lay down to sleep. She would awaken at the proper hour, she knew. And when she opened her eyes again and arose, she looked at the water clock and saw it was the midnight hour. With a smile she slipped a pair of kid slippers upon her feet. Rafa lay sleeping soundly on a mat at the foot of her bed. A soft smile touched Zuleika's face. She loved Rafa as she would have loved her mother had the sultana Jamila lived. Taking up a dark cloak from a cedar chest, the princess slipped from her apartments.

Outside her doors the guards slumbered, leaning upon their lances. Everyone she passed within the palace slept. She walked through a small door in the tightly shut palace gates. The city was silent. There was not even the barking of dogs, or the howling of felines at the bright full moon. Zuleika moved swiftly through the quiet streets, now coming to the closed and barred city gates. Again she made her way through a small door within the barrier, stepping out into the country-side beyond. There, but a quarter of a mile ahead of her, lay the camp of their enemy. Zuleika walked more swiftly now, and reaching the throng of tents she stopped momentarily to get her bearings.

Amir Khan's tent would be in the center of the encampment, the genie had said. Then as if a puzzle had revealed itself, Zuleika saw the proper path to take. She moved forward, and made her way to the magnificent pavilion with its multi-colored pendants now at rest in the still night air. As every-where else, the guards were asleep before their campfires. Zuleika moved past the entrance of Amir Khan's tent, saying as she did so, "Good evening, my lord."

He looked up, startled at the sound of the woman's voice. "Who are you?" he asked, moving away from the table where he had been studying several maps. "And how did you manage to gain entry? My guards are usually not so lax, but if you are an assassin I warn you that my dagger tip is poisoned. If I touch you with it, you will die almost instantly."

The princess let her cloak fall from her shoulders. She was garbed in the sheerest garment that appeared to have been woven by spiders out of moonbeams. "I am Zuleika of Dariyabar, Amir Khan," she said quietly. "I have not come to assassinate you, but rather to parley with you."

"Your father has offered you to me as my concubine," he answered. His dark brown eyes roamed slowly over her visible form. She was probably the most beautiful creature he had ever seen, with her long ebony hair, her heart-shaped face and the unflinching violet eyes now observing him boldly. He felt a tingle in his loins. Just looking at her made him lustful.

"It is my cousin Haroun's idea to offer you the princess of Dariyabar, not my father's. But my sire is ancient, and no longer strong. His will has been weakened by his many years. He wants only quiet days, and peaceful nights. Haroun actually believes that you will go away if I am given to you. He thinks that you have come to realize Dariyabar is impregnable. He assumes the gift of its princess will allow you to withdraw while saving face, the sultan's only child now in your possession."

"What do you think?" he queried her, curious.

"I think you will not go away," Zuleika began. "You have not been besieging my city for three years for spoils, my lord. You need a window on the sea, and Dariyabar can give you one. But the city is indeed impregnable. We have never in our known history fallen."

"So you have come to dissuade me from having you, princess? Seeing you, I do not think I could now deny myself the pleasure of your body," Amir Khan told her.

A faint blush touched her cheeks, but then she continued, "I can help you gain your objective, my lord, but I want something in return for my aid. Tell my father you will not accept me as a concubine, but rather you wish to take me for your wife. I know you have no wife."

"Why do I need one?" he asked her, amused. She was tall for a female, but he still topped her by almost a foot, he considered.

"You do not need just any wife, Amir Khan. You need this wife. *You need me.* I am the key that can open the gates of Dariyabar to you. And I shall do it without further bloodshed, but for one man."

"Prince Haroun," he said.

"Aye, my cousin. He is an evil man, and will destroy my land if he is allowed to follow my father to the throne. If you take me for your wife; if you slay Haroun; it is you who will be the next sultan of Dariyabar. And you will be followed by the son I shall give you, insuring that my father's blood remains in the line of descent to follow. Haroun encouraged my father and my brothers in this war against you, my lord. I suspect he would have cajoled my father to battle were he not so old, and feeble. As it is, Haroun remained safe within the walls of the city while my brothers marched out to defend Dariyabar, losing their lives in the process. Now he would rid himself of me, and you as well. He would take my best friend, Bahira, daughter of our vizier, Abd al Hakim, to wife, against her will. He chooses Bahira because he believes her a ewe sheep who will allow his favorite to continue to control his harem. He will bleed the people of Dariyabar to fill his own coffers, and my people will suffer."

"Why should I not just take you for my concubine, and then continue my siege?" the barbarian khan asked Zuleika.

"If all you desire is my body, my lord, it is yours to take now," she told him. "But I believe you would rather have your window on the sea. Is taking me to wife so high a price to pay?"

She roused him in a way in which he had never been stirred before. Her very presence was kindling a fire in his loins. His fingers closed gently about her slender throat. "I could have my way with you, princess of Dariyabar, and force your secrets from you one by one." The dark eyes blazed down at her, his handsome face stern. His strong fingers tightened just slightly.

Her lips curved into the hint of a mocking smile. "No, Amir Khan, you could not," she told him in a soft, assured tone. "You could take my body, but there is nothing that could pry my secrets from me if I did not wish to share them. Not passion. Not torture. Besides, if you should harm me then Kansbar will destroy you." Reaching up, she removed his hand from her throat. "You must not bruise me, my lord, lest I be asked questions that I shall not be able to answer."

"Who is Kansbar? *Your lover?*" He was shocked to hear the jealousy in his own voice, and he put an arm about her, pulling her close in order to reassert his dominance over her.

Again, her mouth twitched with her amusement. "Kansbar is the genie of the Golden Bowl. He is the guardian of Dariyabar. After my brothers were slain, my father gave the bowl to me as it was expected that Haroun and I would wed. My cousin does not even know the bowl exists. Kansbar, will be to your advantage if you wed me. He is a very powerful genie, and I will bring the bowl with me as part of my dower."

"If I agree to your proposal, princess, then you must give me your vizier's daughter for my general, Sabola. Such an alliance will make my position stronger."

"As his wife?" she queried.

"Agreed!" he said. "Now tell me, how it is you were able to leave your palace and walk into my encampment without raising any alarm?" He pushed her gown off her shoulders, his hands caressing the soft, silky skin.

"Kansbar has put a spell upon all of our little world this night but for you and for me," she explained. She shrugged her garment off, and it dropped to the floor of his tent.

He felt his breath catch in his throat. "Are you a virgin?" he asked her. Her breasts brushed against his broad chest, and he admired their perfection, not to mention the exciting contrast between his pale gold skin and her creamy ivory flesh.

"Of course I am a virgin, but I have been taught all the ways of pleasing a man, Amir Khan." Her hand reached beneath his sand-and-white striped robe. She fondled his rod with surprisingly skilled fingers. "You are very big," she noted. Then her hands moved to undo his robe so she might see his body as he was seeing hers. When she had succeeded she moved back slightly, saying, "You are very beautiful for a man, Amir Khan. You are not overly handsome like my cousin, but rather you are manly. I believe that you will arouse me when the time is right between us."

"Why not now?" he asked her, drawing her back against him, one big hand roughly fondling her breasts. By all the Gods! They were like the plumpest of summer peaches, and just filled his palm with their delicious ripeness.

"Patience, my lord Amir Khan. One should never hurry too quickly along roads to paradise, I have been told."

"*Give me your lips!*" his deep, rough voice grated out to her.

Zuleika raised her head up to meet his kiss, and the sensation that exploded within her took her by surprise. His mouth was hard, yet it was soft. It demanded, but oh, so sweetly. Her lips seemed to part of their own volition. His tongue plunged into her mouth seeking her tongue. Again she was overcome by feelings that threatened to overwhelm her. *So this is passion,* noted the small part of her brain still functioning. It was really quite breathtaking.

He lifted his leonine head from hers. "You kiss well for a novice," he told her, and Zuleika laughed aloud.

"I expect you kiss very well for a lover," she observed.

"You have never been kissed before? How is that possible?" he demanded of her, astounded. Surprised.

"I told you, I am a virgin. I was taught to practice kissing upon a sheet of beaten gold, my lord Amir Khan. This is the first time I have ever been kissed back. It is quite pleasurable."

Now it was he who laughed, and the sound was deep and rich. It sent a delicious shiver down her spine. "A sheet of beaten gold," he said. "Not silver? Or copper? Why gold?"

"I am a princess," she responded simply.

Suddenly his hand was smoothing her soft dark head. "Zuleika of Dariyabar, you are a conundrum I shall enjoy both exploring and solving," he told her. He was shocked by his great desire for her, but he also had the most incredible need to protect her. She was that rarest of women, strong, yet fragile too.

"I can feel your lust against me," she said in a soft voice. "Let me ease it for you, my lord Amir, as I am obviously the cause of your discomfort." Then she slipped from his tender embrace, and fell to her knees before him. She took the ruby-eyed head of his love lance between two fingers of her hand, holding it straight. Then she began to lick its length with slow, deliberate strokes of her tongue. "I shall sup upon your juices," she told him.

He closed his dark eyes. His temples were pounding in rhythm with his heart, and all of his pulses. When she took him into the warm cavern of her mouth, almost swallowing him, suckling strongly upon him, he wanted to scream with the incredible pleasure that she was giving him. He had never permitted a woman this privilege of his body, yet he could not have made her cease even if he wished it. *And he didn't.* Wave after wave of delight washed over him until his juices finally exploded, and she swallowed them almost greedily, retaining his flesh in her mouth until he finally softened slightly. His legs felt like water. Amir Khan was amazed that he did not collapse like some maiden, for he felt weak with his satisfaction. For a moment he could not speak.

Zuleika arose to her feet, reaching out first to pick up her delicate garment which she restored to her lush body. She licked just the tiniest pearl of his juices from the corner of her mouth, smiling. "I can see I have managed to put you at your ease once more, Amir Khan. Your juices are quite refreshing, as I had been told they would be."

"You never did that before either?" he asked, reaching for his own striped robe, and putting it on again.

"Of course not," she returned with a smile. "Bahira and I were taught the art of using dildos made of some magical material that grew hard and bigger as we sucked upon it. The juices within were always sugar water. Your juices are creamy, and slightly flavored with salt. They are very stimulating. Now, shall we conclude our bargain, Amir Khan?"

"I will take you to wife," he said, "and as you yourself have said, you will be the key that opens Dariyabar for me. And your vizier's daughter will wed with my general, Lord Sabola."

"And you will destroy my cousin, Haroun," she reminded him.

"Agreed. I agree to it all, Zuleika of Dariyabar! But you must know something before we conclude our compact. Once you are my wife, and Bahira is Sabola's wife, you are both bound to obey us in all things. Do you understand me?"

"Of course," she replied. "Wives are meant to obey their lords and masters, Amir Khan. Is that not the way of the world?"

"Will you attempt to rule Dariyabar through me, Zuleika?" he asked her bluntly.

"I will offer you the benefit of my advice, my lord Amir, and nothing more. Whether you choose to accept my advice is up to you." She smiled prettily at him, and her teeth were very white.

He had to laugh. "You are not very subtle," he told her.

"I will be a good wife to you, my lord. I know that my first duty is to give you a son. I will do it as quickly as I can," she swore. Then she took up her cloak, and drew it about her. "Kansbar's magic will not hold past the dawn, and the night wanes, my lord Amir. Come to my father's palace beneath a flag of truce today. He will not, despite my cousin, refuse you. And you must insist we be wed as quickly as possible. Do not allow Haroun to delay our marriage while he considers ways to thwart you. He is not particularly intelligent, but he has the slyness of a dishonest peasant. Both he and his favorite, Golnar, are wicked. They would stop at nothing to gain Dariyabar.

That is why you must act quickly. Will you trust me in this, Amir Khan?"

"In this matter I shall heed your advice, Zuleika of Dariyabar," he told her. "Meeting you tonight has been both a surprise and a delight."

She gave him a final quick smile, and then disappeared through the entry of his tent into the moonlit night. Curious, he moved to watch her go. Her shadow passed swiftly through the maze of tents until he could see it no more. He stepped back into his pavilion and poured himself a goblet of wine. What had just happened here? Was it real, or had he imagined it all? No. His male member was still tingling from her bold attentions. Zuleika of Dariyabar had indeed been in his tent tonight.

He would take her to wife. Aye, he would! He had no wife. He had barely had time for any woman, particularly in the last three years. She was beautiful. She was clever. And she would give him Dariyabar! But she was right when she said her cousin, Haroun, would attempt to stop them. Haroun, who had encouraged his cousins to take up arms against Amir Khan, thereby insuring their demises while he remained within the safety of his city's walls to become his uncle's only male heir. The man was a coward, and he was a bully.

But Zuleika was also right when she said he had a peasant's cleverness. Choosing the vizier's daughter as his prospective wife was indeed a sly move. The khan chuckled to himself. General Sabola was his best friend. They had been raised together in the camp of his own father, The Great Khan. Sabola would be reluctant to have a bride foisted upon him, but by the Gods! If this maiden, Bahira, was as sensual as was the princess, Sabola would have no cause for complaint. Suddenly Amir Khan was overcome with a feeling of exhaustion. Was it natural, or was it the work of the genie, Kansbar? It mattered not. He lay down, and fell into a deep slumber.

When he awoke, strangely refreshed, he heard the sounds of activity in his encampment. His servants were immediately there bringing him his morning meal. He had barely begun it when Sabola arrived to share it with him. He was almost as big as Amir Khan, smooth-shaven, with the powerful frame of a bull. His dark hair was cropped very short. His brown eyes were intelligent. He sat down at his lord's table, and then his jaw dropped at the words issuing forth from the Khan's mouth.

"We are going to be married, old friend," Amir Khan said with a chortle. "Both of us! I shall have the princess of Dariyabar to wife, and you shall take the vizier's fair daughter as your mate." Having said it, the khan began to eat heartily.

"I slept the sleep of the dead last night, Amir," Sabola said.

"Of course you did," the khan noted. "A spell was placed upon the city and our camp by the genie whose task it is to watch over Dariyabar. All slept but for Zuleika, princess of Dariyabar, and me." Then the khan told his best friend everything that had transpired between him and the princess.

"How can you be certain it is not a skillful trap hatched by this princess and her cousin, Haroun?" Sabola asked, suspicious.

"It isn't. The princess hates her cousin. She realizes that it is he who was responsible for her brothers' deaths. Having finally understood his true character, she is determined he not follow her father as sultan of Dariyabar. By marrying her I gain a legitimacy as the sultan's heir. Zuleika is the key to Dariyabar for us as long as she is my wife. The vizier's daughter binds us ever closer if you wed her."

Sabola nodded. "If she is as skilled as your princess, my friend, I shall not be unhappy. I don't suppose we might share our women now and again?"

"Of course we will share them," the khan replied. "After we have had their virginities of them, we shall spend a night of pleasure and passion together with our wives. Have we not always shared out women? Zuleika will obey, and her friend as well."

"I suppose we must bathe if we are to marry today," Sabola considered. "We will wed them today, won't we?"

The khan nodded. "I think it best we do, if we are to thwart Prince Haroun. I will send a messenger with a flag of truce and a message for the sultan that I wish to meet with him. I shall say nothing of what I want, lest Prince Haroun read the message first and realize what we are about." He looked to a servant. "Fetch my scribe," he instructed him.

The scribe came. The message was dictated. The messenger was dispatched to the palace of Dariyabar beneath a flag of truce. He returned to say that the sultan would receive Amir Khan in the late afternoon.

Sabola nodded. "The die is cast," he said.

Amir Khan nodded. "Soon, Dariyabar will be ours," he said.

Chapter Two

Zuleika awoke after only three hours of sleep, but she felt as refreshed as if she had slumbered the entire night away. She listened to the birds singing out in her garden, a sense of great peace upon her. She had been kissed, but more important she had begun to put into practice all she had been taught about being a woman. She could not wait to share this with Bahira. She had found kneeling before Amir Khan, his wonderfully large manhood at her mercy, quite stimulating. The memory of it sent a flash of raw desire racing through her veins. His hands as he had lightly fondled her breasts had been exciting too. She realized that she could barely wait to have him atop her, his love lance eager to sheathe itself deep within her. She had been so tempted last night, but she had managed to push her own lustful thoughts from her mind for there was other business to conclude. "Rafa," she called to her servant.

"Yes, my princess?" the servant said, instantly appearing by her bedside.

"Fetch me my morning meal, and see what gossip you can gather while you go about your duties," Zuleika instructed the woman.

Rafa smiled a sly smile. "So, whatever you wanted to do you have now accomplished. Will you tell me?"

"Not yet," Zuleika replied, "but I believe I have saved us all. Send a slave girl for Bahira. She is to say the princess desires her companionship today."

Rafa bowed, and then hurried off while Zuleika's mind wandered back to her barbarian lord. He was so very big. When she had laid her head upon his hairless chest, a clean male scent had assailed her nostrils. His skin was so beautiful, taut over his muscular arms and legs, but smooth and soft beneath her lips. Yet so very masculine. He reeked of brute strength, and power. It had frankly thrilled her. She could barely wait to find herself in his arms once again. Her longing was almost palpable, an suddenly restless, she arose from her bed. She shed the flimsy garment she had slept in, and walking through her bedchamber entered her private bathing room. Pouring a thin stream of a creamy liquid soap into a large sea sponge, she stepped into the shell-shaped indentation in the marble floor, and gave herself a quick wash. Her breasts tingled as she touched them, her nipples puckering. She laughed to herself, realizing that she had again been thinking of Amir Khan, and the big warm hand that had so gently cupped her breasts, each in its turn. Zuleika rinsed herself off beneath a stream of water pouring from the mouth of a goldfish spout. Then coming from the shell basin she stepped down into the warm, scented pool. She floated about, relaxed, her long black hair streaming behind her like dark seaweed.

Would he come today? she wondered. He was a barbarian, yet she believed he was intelligent enough to understand everything she had told him. Would he ask for the princess of Dariyabar for his wife, and not accept her as his concubine? She knew her visit to his encampment had surprised him, even as her direct speech had. He had been more than interested by the magic she possessed through the genie, Kansbar. Her upper teeth worried her lower lip. She wanted him to come today!

Zuleika heard Rafa returning from her errand with the meal, and, it was to be hoped, some useful gossip. She came forth from the perfumed pool, twisted the water from her heavy dark hair, and dried herself on a fine heavy drying cloth made of cotton imported from a land to the southwest. Wrapping the cloth about herself, and another about her head, she reentered her bedchamber saying as she came, "What news?"

"It is said that the barbarian comes into the city this afternoon beneath a flag of truce, my princess," Rafa replied, her eyes bright with her curiosity. "Did you have something to do with this?"

Zuleika smiled, but said nothing on the subject. Instead, she sat down and began eating the melon Rafa had placed upon the table. It was pale green in color, and exceedingly sweet. It almost melted in her mouth, caressing her throat as it slid down. She remembered the head of his manhood pressing against the back of her throat before she had relaxed her throat muscles, easing him deeper. She shuddered at the memory, wondering if all men's lances were as fleshy and as long as his had been. That was the difficulty with being both a princess and a virgin. So much more was expected of you than just an ordinary girl. Still Amir Khan would, she suspected, prove an excellent lover. He could not be otherwise. Finishing the melon, she reached for a small flaky crescent of bread that had been fried crisp, dipped in warm butter and honey, and then dusted with cinnamon. Wolfing it down she took another, and sipped from her goblet of pomegranate juice thoughtfully.

"What will you wear today?" Rafa demanded to know.

"Royal purple, or course," Zuleika said, "but I will not dress yet. When the barbarian is entering the city."

"The sultan has sent no word that he wishes you to be at this particular interview," Rafa answered her mistress.

"Nevertheless, I will be there. Do you think I want Haroun whispering in my father's ancient ear and ruining all my plans? Oh no! The princess of Dariyabar will be in the audience chamber when the barbarian enters it. My cousin may gnash his teeth, but my father will allow me to remain. He loves me in his own way, for I remind him of my dead mother. If Haroun attempts to thwart me, I need only bring up the memory of Jamila, and my father melts."

"You are a very wicked girl!" Rafa scolded her. "I do not know if your mother would approve of you at all."

"Perhaps she would not," Zuleika responded, "but Jamila is not here, and I am. I must do everything in my power to protect both Dariyabar, and myself."

"And the old sultan," Rafa said softly.

"My father is Dariyabar," Zuleika said. She arose from the table, and at that moment Bahira entered the princess's chamber.

"Good morning, Zuleika! I have come for all the gossip!" She plunked herself down upon a silk-covered sofa, eyes twinkling. "I had the most amazing sleep last night," she remarked innocently.

"Humph," Rafa remarked, and then she muttered, "Probably filled with lustful dreams too, Lady Bahira." She gathered up the dishes from the table, and placing them on a tray went off, saying as she shut the door to her mistress's apartments, "I will see what else I can learn."

"You slept well because Kansbar cast a spell over everyone but Amir Khan and me," Zuleika began. "I went to his encampment, for I had a proposal to offer him. He is coming into the city today beneath a flag of truce, but he will not accept me as his concubine. He will ask for me as his wife, Bahira! And you are to be married to his general, Sabola! If he is as gorgeous as Amir Khan you will never want to leave your bed. I am Amir Khan's key to Dariyabar. Together we will vanquish Haroun, and my father may continue to live out his final years in peace and prosperity. When he is gone, Amir Khan will be sultan here."

Bahira's blue eyes were thoughtful. "It seems a foolproof plan," she said slowly, "but what if Haroun objects? He is greedy and ruthless, and as we know, both cunning and resourceful. He might be willing to let me go to a barbarian as wife, but not you, I think."

"He will have no choice," Zuleika said smugly. "The barbarian lord does my father honor by offering to wed me, and not just accept me into his harem. Sultan Ibrahim is old, and he is forgetful, but his pride is still intact. I shall be in the audience chamber this afternoon, and you must be with me. I shall dress us both in the finest robes that I have, Bahira. We will impress the barbarians, for they have surely never seen our like."

"What is *he* like? Amir Khan," Bahira asked.

"He is a beautiful man, if indeed such a word can be used to describe a man. His body is magnificent, and when his lust for me became obvious I took his manhood in my mouth, and soothed it. It was much, much better than those dildoes we have practiced on all our lives."

"What were his juices like?" Bahira leaned closer to her friend, her eyes wide with curiosity.

"Hot, creamy and salty," Zuleika replied.

"And he caressed you?" Bahira's breath quickened.

"His hands were all over my breasts," Zuleika responded. "I cannot wait until we lay together, and really make love!"

"Tell me about his body," Bahira begged.

"He is taller than any man I have ever seen. His chest is broad, and hairless. His waist tapers into his hips, which are narrow. When he turned I could see his buttocks were tight, and deliciously rounded. The nipples on his chest are perfect circles with deep rose-colored peaks. His skin is the palest gold in color, and while the flesh is firm, it is soft. His arms and his legs are muscled, and big, yet nicely formed. I thought his feet and hands graceful despite their size. The curls around his shaft are as black as the horsetail of hair that leaps from his shaven skull. I already desire him greatly."

"Is his face a handsome one?" Bahira wondered.

"Yes, but not like Haroun. Haroun is almost pretty, but Amir Khan's face is strong and masculine. His eyes are dark, and his nose very straight, and his mouth big like the rest of him. When he speaks, his voice is both deep and rough. I find him exciting."

"Did you see his general, Sabola?" Bahira queried.

"Nay, I did not, but I have yet to see an ugly barbarian," Zuleika noted. "As I walked to and from the city I saw their guards sleeping, and their features were very pleasing to my eye."

Rafa returned with more information regarding the impending visit of Amir Khan. The barbarian would arrive with his general. Here Zuleika and Bahira exchanged a look that Rafa did not miss, but she continued on. They would come with but a dozen of their men. The gates to the city, however, were to remain open while the khan was within its walls.

"And my father agreed?" Zuleika was surprised.

"Prince Haroun convinced the sultan that the khan may be the enemy, but he is, like the sultan, a man of honor," Rafa said.

"And where, I wonder, did he get that idea?" Zuleika remarked. "What hour is he to arrive?"

"Three hours past the noon hour, my princess," Rafa responded.

"Good," Zuleika said. "Then there is time for us to prepare ourselves, for Bahira is coming with me, Rafa. She will wear the emerald green robes, for the color flatters her. I shall have the robes that match my eyes. Royal purple brings out the softness in my skin tones." She unwound the toweling from her hair, and a slave girl hurried up to brush the princess's tresses dry.

"Such foolish vanity!" Rafa snorted, but she began to fetch all that would be required so she might dress her princess and the vizier's lovely daughter. The two gowns were carefully laid out, along with matching slippers, jewelry, and headdresses. The two girls lay down to rest upon a wide sofa, cuddling companionably in each other's arms. When they awoke, slave women brought them fresh apricots, green grapes, and purple plums to eat. When they had finished, silver basins of warm scented water were brought so they might refresh their hands, faces and mouths.

Their hair was dressed by the slave women. Zuleika instructed them to weave her long black hair with tiny strands of pearls. Bahira's auburn tresses were pulled into a single horse's tail with slim braids on either side of her face. Their hair done, the two girls were dressed. Their gowns were simple in design, but extremely elegant. They wore nothing beneath. Each had a low open neckline. Zuleika's was a teardrop, and Bahira's was square. The gowns fit snugly beneath their breasts, and were designed with bejeweled bands set into the rich cloth beneath their bosoms. The broad sleeves had cuffs to match. Bahira sparkled with emeralds, diamonds, and pearls. Zuleika glittered with amethysts, diamonds, and pearls. Their nubile bodies were visible beneath the sheer fine silk of the garments.

A slave girl entered the princess's apartments, and hurrying up to Rafa whispered something in her ear. Rafa nodded, then she turned to Zuleika. "The barbarian is entering the city with his escort," she told her mistress.

Zuleika nodded, and said to Bahira, "We must hurry to the audience chamber so that if Haroun objects there is time to convince my father that our presence is necessary," she said.

Bahira bobbed her head in agreement. "I can't wait to see the look on Haroun's face," she giggled.

Together the two girls hurried through the sultan's palace, finally arriving at the great audience chamber. It was a large room with a domed ceiling decorated in sheets of beaten gold, as were the walls. The marble pillars in the chamber were smooth dark crimson. A floor of the same material was flecked with gold. It was the audience chamber of a powerful man. Ibrahim Sultan was already seated upon his throne, a high-backed bench of pure gold studded with multi-colored jewels and a striped satin cushion beneath him. It was set upon a black marble dais with two steps. Next to it on the right was a three-legged silver stool topped with a white velvet cushion fringed with gold.

The elderly sultan was garbed all in white and gold, an aigrette with a large diamond sprouting forth from his cloth-of-gold turban. To his left stood Prince Haroun, garbed all in black, but for a cloth-of-silver turban decorated with a pigeon's-blood ruby. Zuleika quickly seated herself upon the stool, and a slave set a red silk cushion down for Bahira next to the stool, and slightly behind it.

"You should not be here!" Haroun said sharply.

"Why not?" Zuleika demanded to know. "You would give

me to this barbarian as his concubine. Should he not at least see what you offer him before he decides whether to accept, or reject it?"

"Why is Bahira here?" was Haroun's next question, his eyes openly admiring the vizier's daughter.

"Do you expect me, the princess of Dariyabar, to sit in the royal audience chamber unattended?"

"Would not a slave girl do? Haroun asked.

"Bahira is my friend, and as curious as I am about these barbarians, and no, a slave girl would not suit me! How dare you even suggest such a thing! I am the princess of Dariyabar, and the vizier's daughter should attend me. Is that not right, father?" Zuleika turned her face up to her father's and smiled.

The sultan's eyes twinkled. He stroked his silvery beard thoughtfully, and then he said, "Yes, my daughter, you are absolutely correct. I permit you and Bahira to remain."

"Thank you, father," Zuleika said in a soft voice, but her eyes mocked her cousin, Haroun.

"Thank you, my lord," Bahira added, her eyes modestly lowered.

Haroun smiled, pleased by Bahira's response. Then he licked his lips, anticipating the pleasure the vizier's daughter would give him when he took the beautiful girl to wife.

The trumpets sounded outside the great doors to the sultan's audience chamber. The portals were flung wide to admit Amir Khan and General Sabola, along with their escort. They marched directly to the foot of the sultan's throne, and then the khan saluted the elderly ruler, his right arm, fist clenched, striking his broad chest in respectful salutation.

"Greetings, Sultan Ibrahim. I am Amir Khan, and he who accompanies me is my general, Sabola. We thank you for your invitation. Perhaps we can now settle this matter between us peacefully."

"There can be no peace between us as long as you continue to besiege our city," Prince Haroun said quickly, rudely usurping both the sultan and his grand vizier, Abd al Hakim, before either might speak. "You will never take Dariyabar, Amir Khan! No one has ever captured this city in a siege. We are at an impasse. But we respect you, Amir Khan, and so that you may withdraw without shame, we offer you our own princess Zuleika as your concubine. She is, as you can see, a beautiful young woman, and she is a virgin, though well trained in the amatory arts as are all the young women of Dariyabar." Haroun's dark eyes swept the barbarian lord. A handsome, if rough-looking fellow he thought. His cousin could certainly not complain.

Zuleika waited eagerly for what was to come. Amir Khan looked impressive in his tight black leather breeches. He wore a wide jeweled belt about his supple waist. The buckle was fashioned of engraved ivory banded in silver. His massive chest was oiled but bare.

"*He's magnificent,*" Bahira murmured so that only Zuleika heard.

"*So is his companion,*" the princess breathed softly, her violet eyes inspecting Sabola as discreetly as she dared. "*His polished metal breastplate adds a nice military touch, don't you think?*"

"*He is built like a bull,*" Bahira whispered.

"I will accept the sultan's gift, but only on one condition," Amir Khan replied to Prince Haroun.

"A condition? You would dare to make conditions with Dariyabar?" Haroun said indignantly. "Are you a peddler then, to attempt to bargain with us, Amir Khan?"

The khan ignored Haroun's insult, instead saying in a quiet voice that was somehow heard by all in the great hall of audience, "My general, who has mounted and maintained this campaign we have fought against you, must also be compensated lest he be dishonored. Give me the princess's companion, she who wears green silk and sits now by her mistress's side. She is, I believe, Bahira, daughter of the sultan's grand vizier, Abd al Hakim, a worthy prize for General Sabola. We will take these two women back with us to Khanistan."

Haroun was surprised by the request, and felt the briefest moment of regret, but then he said, "It is agreed. My uncle, the sultan, will make it so, Amir Khan." The Gods! He had looked forward to the little blossom, Bahira, in his bed. He would have treated her well. The vizier would have then been in his power. Now he must find another bride, but no matter.

"Are you in agreement, my lord Sultan?" the khan asked gently of the white-bearded old man. He watched cynically as Haroun bent to whisper in his uncle's ear. He could see the sultan was not really pleased with what was transpiring, but finally he nodded.

"It is agreed, Amir Khan. You will have my daughter, Zuleika, as your concubine, and General Sabola shall have Bahira for his."

The startled blue eyes of the vizier's daughter met the furious violet eyes of the princess of Dariyabar, but Zuleika knew better than to voice her outrage at this betrayal in her father's presence. What had made the khan deceive and mislead her? Was he really so stupid that he had not understood her proposal? She swallowed hard, as her anger threatened to burst forth and overwhelm her.

"We will return to our encampment with our prizes now, with the sultan's permission, of course," Amir Khan said, bowing.

Again the sultan nodded.

Now Zuleika spoke up. "What of my servants, and my possessions?" she asked boldly.

"I am not prepared to host a gaggle of females," the khan replied sternly. "You may share a servant between you. She will come tomorrow, and bring all your possessions with her. Is that agreeable, my lord?" He looked directly at Haroun.

"Indeed," Haroun nodded, smiling broadly. "I shall send Rafa to you, cousin, and you, vizier, will see that your daughter's things are packed up for Rafa to carry as well."

"Then it is settled," Amir Khan said in his deep, rough voice. He looked directly at Zuleika. "*Come, woman!*" he commanded her.

"Where is my litter?" Zuleika demanded. "Surely you do not expect me to walk like some slave woman!" *Come, woman?* He dared to address her as if she were nothing? Ohhh, he would pay for his words, and for his deceit! She glared angrily at him from her silver stool.

So she had a temper, the khan considered, amused. He struggled to maintain himself in the face of her outrage. The plan she had presented to him last night was well thought out, but not quite perfect. He hoped she would not kill him before he could explain the strategy he had devised to compliment her cleverness. His features retained their sternness. Without another word he stepped forward, and pulling her up from the dainty stool, he threw her over his broad shoulder and began to stride from the sultan's audience chamber.

He had taken her by surprise. She had never thought that any man would act in so barbaric a fashion. *But he is a barbarian!* her inner voice shouted at her in her outrage. Her dignity was in tatters now anyway. She pounded on his back with her balled-up fists as she was taken from the audience chamber. Free of the great hall he began to chuckle, and Zuleika, outraged ever further, swore at him in rather colorful language that he had not suspected a princess of Dariyabar would know.

Sabola looked to Bahira, and held out a hand. His handsome features were serious, with no hint of humor. Bahira reached out and took the hand, startled at the jolt that almost stunned her when their fingers touched. The sudden surprise in his brown eyes told her that he had felt it too. The Gods! Bahira thought with amazement. This man is my true mate. How very odd that such a thing should be, and yet I know it is so. With a reassuring smile at her father, and the sultan, Bahira walked from the hall with the khan's general. When they reached the courtyard where the khan was now mounted upon his stallion, Zuleika seated before him, they found the khan's guards awaiting them as well.

"You are a monster!" they heard Zuleika say furiously.

"Shut your mouth, woman!" the khan replied, and then he

bent and whispered in her ear. *"I will explain when we are free of the city."*

"There is nothing you can say to me that I will believe," she hissed back at him. "You have betrayed me! You have betrayed Dariyabar!"

His big hand reached up and locked itself into her hair, thus preventing her from moving. His mouth took hers in an almost brutal kiss that left her breathless. "Be silent, Zuleika," he murmured low against her lips, "or I shall be forced to beat you. I may anyway, just for the pure pleasure of it." His dark eyes held hers.

She could not turn away from him. "You would not dare," she gasped, but she wasn't really certain.

"I am Amir Khan, my princess, and after last night there is nothing I would not dare to retain you in my possession," he told her, and then kicking his stallion lightly he finally looked away from her as they began to move off, through the palace gates and out into the city.

Sabola had mounted his own big stallion, and reaching down he pulled Bahira up with him. She nestled like a small bird in the curve of his thick, muscled arm. "You are very beautiful," he told her as they rode. "I like your blue eyes, and the red lights in your soft hair. Are you afraid?"

"Of course not," Bahira said, smiling up at him. "The moment we touched, my lord, I knew you were he for whom I have waited since my birth. I am yours, and will not question the gods in this." She gave him a sweet smile.

Sabola, the fiercest of the khan's warriors next to Amir Khan himself, felt his heart contract at her words. He had known many women in his time, but he had never loved. He had never even been certain what love was until this moment. "I will always care for you, Bahira," he told her tenderly.

"I know you will," she answered, and then she put her head upon his chest, hearing the steady rhythm of his heart beneath her ear. He was very big. She wondered if he was big all over. She suspected she would soon know.

They reached the khan's encampment, and wending their way through the tents they finally stopped before the khan's pavilion. Dismounting, the two men lifted the girls down from their horses. Zuleika attempted to strike Amir Khan, but he ducked the blow, and then yanking her over his knee smacked her bottom several blows, causing his men to burst into guffaws of laughter. He dragged her kicking and swearing into his quarters, Sabola and Bahira following behind.

When they had reached the relative privacy of the interior, Amir Khan said, "Are you going to allow me to explain without shrieking at me, or must I gag you and tie you to a tent pole?"

"There is nothing you can say to me that would explain your betrayal, you devil! I offered you Dariyabar upon a silver—nay, a golden—platter, and you have scorned it! I cannot believe you are that stupid. Are all barbarians such blockheads, my lord?"

"If I had insisted upon marrying you rather than having you as a concubine, Zuleika, it is likely I should have never left your father's audience hall alive. And if I had, my days, and yours, would have been numbered. Prince Haroun is a sly fellow, but he would have understood the threat I posed as your husband."

"So you decided that you would rather fuck me, and return to Khanistan with your tail between your legs!" she accused.

"No, I decided I should fuck you to both our pleasures, and then take Dariyabar, kill your cousin to prevent his threatening us, and lastly, marry you in your father's house with the old man by our side," he told her.

"But by dragging me in such barbaric fashion from the palace you have forced me to leave Kansbar behind, you great fool!" she cried.

"Will not your Rafa number it among the possessions she brings you?" he asked. "I assume your servant knows the secret of the bowl?"

Zuleika nodded.

"And your cousin does not know about the bowl?" he continued.

"No. I do not think so, though what my father will say to him now that I am no longer there, I do not know! Ibrahim's greatest passion, even greater than his love for my mother, is Dariyabar. Kansbar is Dariyabar's guardian. He may now tell Haroun of the genie. If my cousin gets his wicked hands on the bowl, you have no hope of gaining the city," she told him.

"Your father is old. His memory is not good. It is not likely he spoke with your cousin the moment you departed. He will mourn your going, for now all of his children are gone from him. Rafa will be here tomorrow. I will send a company of my own men to bring her safely to us. Tonight is for pleasures you and Bahira have never tasted." He smiled at her.

"I do not trust you now," she insisted. "How can I? You might have told me last night of what you planned."

"I did not know last night. I did not even know this morning, for Sabola will confirm that I told him we were to marry this day. We even bathed for the occasion, Zuleika. It was just before we were to leave for the city that it came to me that if your cousin believed everything he has planned and schemed for is coming to fruition, it will be easier to overcome him. The genie can gain the city for us, but we must together defeat Prince Haroun, my princess."

"You are, I am learning," Zuleika said, "a far cleverer enemy than I anticipated, Amir Khan. How can I be certain that if I allow Kansbar to aid you, you will not deceive and delude me once again?"

"You cannot," he said, "unless you trust me."

"What guarantees can you give me, what proof of your honor, if indeed barbarians understand honor?" she demanded.

She was a worthy opponent. She would make him a commendable wife. The children from their loins would be strong, and have integrity. Daughters as well as sons. "I have not lied to you, Zuleika," he said.

"But you did not tell me everything," she countered.

"It is a mistake I will not make again," he promised her. "It is not in my nature to lie. I am simply not used to a woman as an equal."

"I am superior to you, barbarian," she snapped, but she found she was somewhat mollified, especially when she focused on his tight leather pants. He was the most breathtaking man.

"Do you wish me to spank your round little rump again, you wildcat?" he asked pleasantly, but there was a look in his eyes that she did not like.

"I am hungry," she told him. "Do you mean to starve me, my lord? And what of my poor Bahira?"

"I am hungry, but content otherwise," Bahira said mischievously.

The khan clapped his hands, and immediately two elderly male servants appeared bearing trays of food. There was roasted lamb, and to Zuleika's surprise, fresh fish from the sea. There was a bowl of saffroned rice with plump raisins and almonds. There was yogurt, and a platter of peaches, melons, grapes, pomegranates, plums and oranges. There were small honey cakes. The khan motioned them to the pillows that were set about a low and square ebony table banded in polished brass. They sat, and their cups were filled with a sweet heady wine. They ate, and when they had finished the servants brought bowls of scented water in which to wash their hands and faces, handing them linen cloths to dry with.

"You are more civilized than I had anticipated," Zuleika said.

"Do you call all people not of Dariyabar *barbarians?*" he asked.

"Yes," she answered him simply, and he laughed.

"Why do you want a window on the sea?" she wondered.

"For trading purposes," he told her. "It is trade that brings a people their wealth. There is much in the interior lands, especially furs and gems, that are desired by those beyond your shores. And then, too, a seaport offers us the chance to easily go forth and conquer other lands that can be of value to us. I intend to build a navy."

She nodded. "You are an intelligent man, Amir Khan."

"Are you still angry with me?" he asked her.

"No, but that does not mean I trust you either," she told him candidly. Her gaze turned to Bahira, and she smiled. "It would appear that Bahira is content to give herself to your general. Sabola is a most impressive man."

"You find him attractive?" the khan said.

"Of course I do. He is. I have been taught to admire all beauty in all of its forms. So has Bahira. We have been companions and friends our entire lives."

"How old are you?" he asked.

"We are sixteen," she answered him. "We were born but two days apart. Bahira is the elder," Zuleika explained.

"And she is a virgin too?" he inquired.

"Of course," Zuleika told him.

"Good. I would have Sabola gain the same pleasures this night as I will gain from you," the khan replied. "I would have you both remove your robes for us now."

The girls' eyes met, surprised, but then they both arose, and divested themselves of their silken robes. Where Zuleika was tall, and slender but for her plump breasts, Bahira was pleasingly rounded with full breasts, full hips and thighs. They kicked their slippers off almost in unison.

"Undo your hair," the khan ordered them.

The two girls complied, laying the jewels from their tresses upon the table and fluffing out their long hair so that it showed to its best advantage. Each had hair that fell to just below their hips.

"Now you must both disrobe for us," Zuleika told the two men.

They complied without question, and Bahira could not help but admire both men quite openly.

Amir Khan said softly to his friend, "She is eager. She must be first with us, eh?"

Sabola agreed, nodding. "Your princess is so in control of herself that she will need more priming."

"We shall see that she has it," the khan said with a grin. Then he turned to the two girls. "It is known that girls who are close to one another, sisters or friends, it does not matter, toy with each other as their curiosity grows. I think it is so with you two despite your excellent education in the amatory arts. Certainly you were not satisfied with a simple tutorial in passion. Surely you have played with each other's breasts, and other succulent parts."

Neither Zuleika or Bahira said a word, but their cheeks were warm with their blushes.

"You did not learn to kiss so well, my princess, by merely pressing your lovely lips to a sheet of beaten gold. Sabola and I would be entertained now by the sight of you both kissing, and touching each other as you have undoubtedly done many times in the past."

Bahira did not hesitate. She slipped an arm about Zuleika, and kissed her mouth even as the princess began to fondle her friend's lovely full breasts. For several minutes they kissed and caressed one another, and then they fell upon the pillows embracing. Bahira was the aggressor of the pair. She laid her length atop Zuleika's, and pressed her mons hard against her friend's. Together the girls moved in rhythm, their little pants of desire quite audible, their lush bodies entwined as the two men watched and became quickly aroused by the sensuous sight of the virgin duet at play. They seemed to know exactly when to stop the girls, Sabola leaning over from where he was seated to push Bahira off the princess. The khan then pulled the princess up. His finger pushed between her nether lips, and he smiled. Then, to Zuleika's shock, he tied her to a tent pole with soft silk bonds.

"Wh . . . what are you doing?" she gasped.

"It is all right, my princess," he told her, and his big hand caressed her face tenderly. "You must not be afraid, but Bahira needs our attentions first. We will get to you soon enough. You will watch us as we play together, and then you will play with us." He kissed her lips softly, and then turned back to Sabola and Bahira.

It was disturbing, but it was also exciting, Zuleika thought. She was not at all afraid of losing her virginity, but she had never considered that she would lose it in such a manner. She focused upon Bahira and her lover, fascinated by the erotic tableau that they presented sprawled upon a coral-colored silk mattress upon a raised dais across the tent. Bahira lay between Amir Khan's long legs while he played with her full breasts and murmured in her ear, leaving little kisses upon her face now and again. Sabola slowly licked Bahira's widespread legs, murmuring with pleasure at the delicious taste of her.

Zuleika felt her heart beat faster as the man moved slowly, slowly, until his fingers pulled Bahira's lips apart, and the fleshy tongue began to lick at Bahira's most private place. Bahira's little cries of delight sent her friend's pulses pounding even harder. Zuleika's lips felt dry. She licked them several times, and then she felt the khan's eyes upon her. She met his gaze, and Amir Khan smiled knowingly. Then he bent to kiss Bahira's parted lips.

"She is marvelous," Sabola's rough voice ground out. "You must taste her before I have her, Amir. Virgin juices are always wonderful."

The two men switched places, and Bahira's cries grew greater in intensity. "Ohh, do it!" she begged. *"Please do it!"*

Sabola chuckled. "Such an eager little maiden," he murmured, and he nibbled on her ear. "Let the khan have the pleasure of your juices, Bahira. You will soon enough be impaled upon my lance."

"I want it!" Bahira gasped. *"The Gods, I want it!"*

Zuleika could barely breathe now. The sight of the two men making love to her best friend was proving incredibly arousing. Then the khan was arising from the mattress, and

Sabola's great body was covering Bahira, who moments later cried out as if in pain. Then her cries turned in an opposite direction. Amir Khan now stood behind the pole where Zuleika was tied. His hands fondled her plump breasts, and he whispered in her ear.

"Soon, my princess, you will suffer your friend's fate. Are you as eager for it as she is?" He gently but firmly pinched one of her nipples, and a thrill of excitement raced down her spine.

"*Yes!*" she managed to say, straining against her bonds.

He laughed. "We shall both have her, Zuleika, and we shall both have you as well." The tip of his tongue teased at her ear.

"But if one of us should have a child?" she asked him. "How can either of you be certain as to the babe's paternity, or don't you care, my lord?" The Gods! His hands were now on her belly, and she had begun to ache with her need for him.

"The wine Sabola and I were served had an herb in it that has destroyed the life in our seed this evening. It will revive tomorrow," he explained. "We barbarians like to share our women now and again. It is a hospitable thing to do. But we would have our sons be ours." His lips brushed the side of her neck. "You and Bahira are just too beautiful and too delicious not to share this night."

"Will you share me after we are married?" she asked him.

"Only if you desire it," he promised her.

Bahira now shrieked a cry of such intense pleasure, while Sabola roared like a lion, and the khan laughed as his best friend collapsed atop his lover.

"The Gods," Sabola said as he came to himself again. "The wench is insatiable, Amir. Come and enjoy yourself. She is ready, I have not a doubt, for more cock, eh, my beauty?"

"*More!*" Bahira demanded.

The barbarian general lay sprawled by Bahira's side as the khan mounted her, and used her fiercely until she begged him to cease. When he withdrew from her she noted that he was still hard, and she raised a questioning brow.

Amir Khan laughed again. "I would save my passion for my

princess, but you, my darling, are quite wonderful." He gave her a kiss upon her ripe, bruised lips.

The trio bathed themselves in basins of water that had been left out for them earlier. The khan arose from the silk mattress. His dark brown eyes met those of Zuleika's.

"Now, my princess, it is your turn to be fucked. Bahira is a most proficient lover. You must be even better." He went to the pole and untied her. Then he led her to the dais where both Sabola and Bahira awaited her, smiling.

Chapter Three

It was like the most incredible dream, Zuleika thought. She lay between the two men, amazed that such hardened, fierce warriors could be so tender with a woman. They bathed her body with their tongues, licking with long strokes across her torso and breasts. They turned her, and the fleshy organs moved down her back, and over her buttocks. She was rolled again onto her back. Bahira now sat cross-legged upon the mattress, an alabaster vial in her hands. The two men cupped their hands, and she poured a pale lavender cream into the upturned palms. Now Amir Khan and Sabola began to massage the fragrant cream into Zuleika's soft skin. She sighed with delight, and they smiled down at her. Their combined touch was both sensual and gentle.

"They did not teach us that men made such delicious love," she murmured, and she sighed again.

"You are not afraid then, my princess?" Amir Khan asked.

"No."

"And you will trust us to offer you pleasure such as you have never imagined?" he said. He bent and brushed her lips with his own.

"I thought I should please you," Zuleika responded.

"In time you will show me all you have been taught, Zuleika, but your first encounter with passion must be at our hands, for we are skilled in making love," Amir Khan told her.

"Having seen you with Bahira, I am convinced of it," Zuleika answered him. "Perhaps you should have sought another way to conquer Dariyabar than the one you chose."

Sabola laughed aloud. "I can see my friend will have no easy time with you, princess," he teased her. Then, he too bent to kiss her, and she found his hard mouth exciting, his lips far different than Amir Khan's. So, all men's mouths were not the same. She kissed him back, running a naughty little tongue across his lips to his surprise. His warm brown eyes met her gaze, and then he winked, leaning by her ear to whisper, "You are a very bad girl, princess."

Zuleika giggled. "I think I could be," she whispered back.

Together the two men now played with her plump breasts. They caressed the flesh, drawing their fingers across the sensitive skin. They nuzzled her. Their tongues licked at her nipples, encircling them slowly over and over again until she was squirming. Sabola's mouth closed over the nipple he had been entertaining. Bahira began to very gently nip at her other breast, alternating with little laps of her tongue, and soft puffs of blowing. Zuleika's breasts felt swollen, and almost sore with their attentions.

She felt the khan's big hand cover her mons, pressing down to send a bolt of excitement through her. His fingers brushed the pale mound of her flesh, noting its shadowed slit which was long and showed the distinct signs of moisture. He ran a finger down it, and the finger slipped between her nether lips, deep into the creamy dampness. He smiled to himself. Then he pushed a single leg up, and lowered his dark head so he might taste her at his leisure.

Her leg lay partly over his shoulder and neck. She forced her mind and her senses away from the mouths at her breasts, and when she did she almost swooned with the feeling of his mouth on her most private place. His tongue tasted, teased, and drove her to near madness. She felt a hand beneath her buttock so he might avail himself of her even more. His tongue pushed itself slowly into her love channel. She gasped audibly as it moved back and forth for a time. Then it withdrew, and he began to flick the fleshy organ over her lovebud, which responded in the most amazing way. She was overwhelmed with the sensations they were pressing upon her. The three mouths were giving her such intense pleasure.

"*Stop!* In the name of all the Gods, please stop!" she begged. "I can bear no more! It is too wonderful! I shall die!"

"No you won't," the khan said, and he was now looking into her eyes. "It is just your first time, my princess. Sabola, have her sweet juices for yourself now." Then he began to kiss her, and Zuleika's head spun with the excitement engendered by his kiss, Bahira's mouth at her breasts, and Sabola's mouth lapping at her juices.

"You will kill me!" she cried, pulling her head away from him.

"More than likely you will kill me," he replied. "Do you want my love rod deep inside you, Zuleika?" He licked at her throat and face. "I will fill you full, my princess. In your wild and virgin dreams you cannot imagine the heights we will attain together!"

"*Yes!*" she sobbed, and then she cried out as Sabola's vigorous attentions caused her little love bud to break with pleasure.

"She is ready," the general said, moving back up by her side. "Take her, my friend, and enjoy!" Then he reached out to Bahira, and began to kiss her again.

Zuleika closed her eyes. She felt Amir Khan covering her slender body with his big one. Her heart was pounding wildly. She wanted him desperately!

"Open your eyes!" he commanded her.

"I can't. Not this first time. Not until I really know," she half-sobbed. She felt the head of his lance just touching her.

"We proceed no further until you open your eyes," he growled. "I want to see your soul when I take your virginity, Zuleika! *Open your eyes for me!*"

She couldn't. She just couldn't. And then he moved ever so slightly upon her. She felt his length, eager to enter her. She felt the ruby tip just barely lodged within her, and throbbing with its need. Or was it her need? Zuleika opened her violet-colored eyes to meet those of her lover. "*Now!*" was all she said.

He smiled down at her, and slowly, slowly, slowly he began to enter her fevered body. "Wrap your legs about me now, Zuleika," he told her. He pressed forward again when she had obeyed.

It was a feeling unlike anything she had ever experienced. He filled her, and she wanted to weep with the completeness of it. "*Ohh, yes!*" she said, and then she gasped as a sharp pain knifed through her. "*Ohhh!*"

"Your virginity is gone, my princess, and now the pleasure begins in earnest," he told her. He began to thrust and withdraw. Thrust and withdraw, until Zuleika's head was spinning, and every inch of her young body both ached and resounded with the pleasure he was offering. It seemed impossible that he could go deeper, and yet with each thrust he seemed to plunge himself in further and further until she thought he would touch her racing heart. "Do you like it?" he murmured in her ear, kissing it.

"Yes! Oh, yes, my lord Amir! I like it very much!" she told him, and then remembering the lessons she had been taught she decided she would offer him a bit of enjoyment too. Forcing her own pleasure back she concentrated, and then she began to squeeze the great lance that drove itself within her.

The khan groaned, but his eyes lit with appreciation at her efforts.

They labored together for some minutes, and then Zuleika began to lose control of herself. Her heart was beating too rapidly. She could no longer focus, nor could she barely breathe. She cried out as a wave of intense enjoyment washed over her. She clung to the khan with all her strength, her nails raking down his long back. He laughed, and then he groaned, crying out as he exploded his juices into her body. He collapsed upon her, and they lay, limbs entwined, for some long minutes. Finally he rolled off her, placing a kiss upon her lips as he did so, and brushing an errant strand of hair from her pale forehead.

Zuleika blushed as he washed her free of their passion.

"Sabola must have his turn, my princess," he told her softly.

"I am ready," she said as softly.

"May I take her other virginity, my lord Amir?" the general asked. "I hesitate to go where my lord has already been, for the princess will soon be your wife, and my sultana."

"Yours is a thick tent peg, Sabola," the khan replied. "We must prepare my princess for your entry first." He looked down at Zuleika. "Do you know of what we speak?"

She nodded. "We have been taught to accept a lover in that manner, my lord, using the dildo."

"Good! We shall begin that way while you make Sabola ready," Amir Khan told her. He then accepted from the bedside basket a long, smooth ivory dildo. He dipped it into a wide-mouthed vial of thick oil that Bahira held up for him. "Take the proper position, Zuleika," he told her.

She knelt, her buttocks raised, directly over the general's groin area, taking his flaccid manhood into her mouth as she bent her head. She began to suckle upon him as the khan inserted the dildo carefully into her bottom. He was gentle, and painstakingly careful. He moved the dildo warily forward, then drew it back, working it guardedly until the entire length of ivory was sheathed within her. Sabola groaned as Zuleika's skillful lips and tongue aroused his lance to stand hard.

"*Enough!*" his rough voice finally growled.

She raised herself just enough so he might move from beneath her. Zuleika then again assumed the submissive position that was expected of her. Behind her, he moved the dildo back and forth, and then she realized that he had replaced it with his own manhood. Carefully, he pushed inside her as Zuleika arched her back and raised her buttocks high to accommodate him better. He was very big, but he was gentle, she had to admit, his big hands tightly grasping her hips. Back and forth. Back and forth. She felt her rear channel widening to accommodate him even better. He groaned suddenly and his lust exploded inside her. "You have the ass worthy of a God," he told her as he finally and reluctantly withdrew.

She was pulled again onto her back, and before she might say anything else the khan was filling her with his hot and eager love rod. *"Did you enjoy him?"* Amir Khan snarled in her ear. "Did you like it when he shoved himself into your beautiful little ass, *my princess?"* He thrust hard, and she cried out.

"'Tis your custom to share!" she replied.

"You enjoyed it," he accused her.

"It had a certain piquancy about it," she admitted. "Are you jealous, my lord? Then do not offer to share my favors with your friends again. I was trained that the sharing of one's body with another is to be enjoyed. If you make me your wife, and ask it of me, I shall never allow another to have me. *But you must ask!"*

He drove deeper and deeper into her soft flesh as if he were trying to punish her. "I will kill you!" he threatened.

"Then you will not have Dariyabar!" she taunted him, and the muscles of her love sheath tightened about him hard as she leaned forward and sank her teeth into his shoulder.

"Ohh, bitch!" he cried, and his hot juices once more flooded her interior.

"You will love me, Amir Khan, and I will love you," she told him, her tongue now soothing the shoulder she had bitten.

"The lion of Khanistan has found his lioness," Sabola said. "Marry her quickly, Amir. She is perfect for you, and her belly must be filled with your sons as soon as possible if you are to hold Dariyabar," the general chuckled. "Now, I would take my beautiful Bahira and seek my own tent, my brother. With your permission, we withdraw."

"Go! Go!" the khan said impatiently, and he turned back to Zuleika when they were gone, and said, "You are mine, and mine alone, my princess. Do you understand what that means?"

She laughed. "I understand, my lord, but I will admit the evening was a stimulating one. Will you not agree?"

"The Gods! How well Sabola knows me. I have not been

able to erase you from my mind since we met last night, Zuleika. Had he filled your love sheath with his manhood, I do not think I could have ever forced that picture from my mind. My length is the only one that shall ever fill you, my princess."

"I am content with that, my lord," she told him. "I hope that Sabola will be as generous to Bahira."

"I suspect that your Bahira will have my general fully compliant to her will by the dawn, my darling," the khan laughed.

Zuleika nodded with a smile. "My cousin, Haroun, thought her a meek little ewe sheep to be managed and directed. Now, my lord, tell me how we are to take the city?"

"Wait until tomorrow when Rafa arrives with genie and his bowl," he said. "I think your Kansbar will want a say in our plans."

"You must treat him with respect," Zuleika advised. "He is a very old genie, and sometimes apt to be impatient. When you want to dump his bowl of water into the sea you must recall his power."

"I have never met a genie before," the khan said with a smile.

But when Rafa arrived the following day from the city she brought bad news. The sultan had taken ill in the night. It was not likely that he would recover. "What will become of us among the barbarians!" she wailed piteously. "The gods curse the evil Haroun!"

"Get the bowl!" Zuleika said. "We must consult with Kansbar."

A look of horror suffused Rafa's face. "Oh, the gods! I have forgotten the bowl! Ohh, my princess, you must forgive me!" She threw herself at the princess's feet. "I was about to fetch the bowl and pack it among your possessions when the vizier and his wife arrived with the lady Bahira's things. Both of them were weeping, and it took me forever to get rid of them. I was distracted. I forgot."

Zuleika's first instinct was to order her faithful servant beheaded by the khan's guards, but instead she swallowed back her anger. "I will have to go back into the city," she said. "If my father is ill, and thought to be dying, even Haroun will not refuse me entry. Rafa and Bahira will come with me. No! Bahira must remain here," she decided in an afterthought.

"When will you return?" the khan asked her quietly.

"When my father is dead, and I have overthrown Haroun," she told him.

"You will need my help to overthrow the prince," Amir Khan said. "What if he attempts to retain you as a guarantee of his inheritance?"

"He has no power over me as long as I possess the genie," Zuleika assured him.

"Then you must fetch the bowl, but I would prefer you return to me as quickly as possible. If your father is dying you can be of no further aid to him. Is it possible your cousin poisoned him?" the khan wondered.

"Anything is possible," Zuleika agreed, "but I do not believe Haroun would have acted so swiftly, or before he has found a suitable bride to be his sultana. His favorite, Golnar, knows she will not have that position however she importunes him. But she will want to help him choose the girl. No, this is simply fate at work. But I must remain in the city as long as I can be a comfort to my father, my lord Amir."

"Then I must come with you," he responded. "It is too dangerous otherwise."

"Nonsense!" she told him. "You must remain with your men. I could not trust Haroun if he had you in his grasp. No, my lord. It is too dangerous for the khan. Rafa, however, can be our go-between, for I have now decided I shall go into the city dressed as I am, and with nothing else. I will tell my cousin that Rafa must go back and forth with changes of garments for me, for the Khan will not allow me to take my possessions from his tents. That will sound most barbaric to him, for he would not permit his women to travel without everything they own. Give me a good horse to ride, and have one of your men accompany me. Haroun will see you already value me by this."

"I will send two men with you," the khan replied, "for I do value you very much, my princess." He pulled her into his strong arms, and bending his head, found her ripe lips with his own.

She soared with the touch of his mouth on hers. For a brief moment she closed her eyes and let him become her world. It was a good feeling, and she would have wished it could go on forever, but it could not. With a reluctant sigh she drew away, reaching up to caress his cheek with her hand, a little smile on her lips. "Can I really trust you, Amir Khan? Or will you betray me once you have Dariyabar?" she asked.

"Those are questions that you must answer for yourself, Zuleika," he responded with the utmost seriousness. "There is nothing I can say that will allay your suspicions. Your heart must decide." He loosed her from his embrace. "Go now, my princess, but be careful, and be on your guard."

They brought her a beautiful golden gelding with a full black mane and an equally luxuriant black tail. The black leather saddle was decorated with bright brass studs, and turquoise. Zuleika introduced herself to the beast, murmuring softly in his ear and rubbing his soft muzzle before she gave it a kiss. Then to his surprise she mounted without any aid, springing lightly into the saddle and fitting her feet into the stirrups. She gathered the reins into her hand, smiling with her approval. "You barbarians have the finest horseflesh," she told him. "What a magnificent beast you have given me to ride, and how unfortunate he is gelded. He would breed up wonderful colts."

"His sire has," the khan told her. "And he is his sire's image. He is called Sunrise, and he is yours now. He has never before accepted a new rider. It is obvious he has been waiting for you."

Zuleika patted the gelding's slim, arched neck. "One stallion is more than enough for me, my lord," she said with a chuckle. Then she urged her horse forward, and flanked by two of the khan's men she headed back into the city.

"Can she trust you?" Rafa asked him when he had returned to the tent.

"Yes," Amir Khan said quietly. "Now go to the tent of my general, Sabola, and help the lady Bahira while the princess is gone."

Hiding her smile, Rafa departed the khan's pavilion. He was a proud man, just as the princess was a proud girl. No. Zuleika was now a woman, and obviously none the worse for her initiation into her adulthood. "Where is the tent of General Sabola?" she asked the guard at the entry to the pavilion.

"It is the one flying the blue and silver pendant, lady," the guard said politely.

"Thank you," Rafa said, and hurried toward her destination.

"Ohh, you have come at last!" Bahira said with a smile when Rafa entered. "My possessions have already been delivered. Come and help me sort through them. Who brought them? My parents? Did they weep with my loss? The general is an incredible lover. A bull! But I finally wore him out. Where is Zuleika?" The words tumbled forth excitedly from her mouth.

"I can see that you have survived your first foray into womanhood well," Rafa noted dryly. "The princess has gone back into the city. Her father took ill in the night, and is not expected to live."

"Haroun?" Bahira's big blue eyes were wide with her curiosity.

Rafa shook her head. "More than likely the loss of his last child, and the knowledge that Haroun is to inherit, and would prefer to do it sooner than later," Rafa replied.

"Is Zuleika safe?" Bahira inquired, concerned.

"The princess is more than a match for her cousin. Especially as I forgot the bowl, and she will have it with her."

Bahira's hand flew to her mouth. "Ohh, Rafa! How could you?"

"Your parents came weeping with your things just as I was about to pack it. Then the guards hurried me out before I could remember," Rafa admitted. "Do not remind me, for until my mistress returns with the bowl I shall not be content."

"She will be back in the city now," Bahira said.

And Zuleika was. The people greeted her warmly as she rode through the streets, but their eyes were worried, she could see. She dare say nothing to reassure them. It was not her place yet, and she dare not have such behavior reported to Haroun. It would but arouse his suspicions. She rode through the great open gates of her father's palace, and dismounting, told the slave to take the beast to the stables. Then she hurried inside, going directly to her father's quarters. The guards bowed, nodded, and immediately permitted her to pass.

Maryam, the slave woman who cared for her parent, came forward. "Ahh, princess, it is good you are here. Did the prince send you word?"

"Nay. It came with Rafa, and my possessions," Zuleika answered. "You have a place in my household," she reassured the slave woman.

Maryam bowed, her eyes relieved. "I will take you to him," she said, and led Zuleika into her father's bedchamber.

The elderly sultan was awake, and his eyes lit up at the sight of his sole surviving child. He was seated in a chair, viewing his gardens.

"Now, what is this?" Zuleika teased him gently. "I am gone but a few hours, and you take to your bed?" She knelt by his side.

"What is left for me to live for, my daughter?" he responded.

"*Dariyabar!*" she told him.

He shook his white head. "Nay, Zuleika. I am too ancient, and far too frail now to carry the burden of Dariyabar upon my shoulders. I long to be with your brothers, and your mother."

"Would you leave me, then? Would you deny yourself the pleasure of knowing your grandchildren?" she demanded, half-angrily.

He laughed weakly. "I have no doubt you will bear the khan

many strong sons, but you will not be here in Dariyabar, my daughter."

She was silent for a moment. One could not be certain who was listening. "Khanistan is not that far away. They are on our northern borders," she finally replied. "Do you think I should not come to visit you, my lord father?"

His gaze grew suddenly sharp as he looked at her, realizing there was much she was not saying. "*Kansbar?*" he whispered to her.

"*Safe,*" was her soft reply.

"Keep him so," the sultan said, a small smile upon his thin lips. This strong, intelligent daughter of his, he now realized, would not easily give up her heritage. "The khan treats you well?" he asked.

She nodded. "Very well. He is a man of honor, I am certain. He rules his own people well."

"And his wives treat you well?"

"He has none. *Yet,*" she replied.

"Ahh," the sultan said, immediately comprehending what it was she was telling him. "Bahira? Poor Abd al Hakim and his wife are devastated by her loss. My vizier no longer thinks kindly of your cousin."

Zuleika laughed. "Bahira has completely wrapped the khan's general about her plump little finger, my father. The vizier and his wife need have no worries about her. I shall tell them that myself."

"How long will you remain with me, my child? Will the khan permit you to stay?" the sultan asked.

"I will be with you, my father, as long as you need me," she promised him. "Now I must go to my apartments, for poor Rafa was so distracted by our sudden move she left one or two of my possessions behind."

"I will sleep now," he told her, and closed his eyes.

Zuleika moved with assurance through the palace corridors back to her own quarters. To her surprise all her furniture was gone, including the cabinet where the bowl was kept. Her heart pounded with fright at the realization, and then Haroun's favorite, Golnar, was by her side.

"What are you doing here?" she demanded rudely, her pale face suspicious. Her eyes were so light a blue that in some lights they appeared almost white.

"My father is ill. I returned to be with him. Where is my furniture? Rafa left some things behind."

"These are to be the new sultana's quarters," Golnar said.

"Oh? Has my cousin then chosen a wife?" Zuleika inquired casually.

"The vizier has a younger daughter. Her heritage is excellent, and he has decided that she will do," Golnar said.

"*Tahirah?* She is only ten years old!" Zuleika exclaimed. How predictable of Haroun. He chose the easy and quick path. Perhaps he did have something to do with her father's sudden illness.

"Yes, Tahirah. She is young enough to be trained to please the prince, and he will not have to mount her for several years. She is said to be well-mannered and obedient. She will do exactly as she is told," Golnar said smugly.

"And you will retain control of the harem," Zuleika noted. "How very nice for you, Golnar. Has Haroun approached the vizier in this most important matter yet? He will be very honored, I have not a doubt. One daughter a concubine to the khan's general, and the other the new sultana of Dariyabar!"

Golnar, who had a peasant's cunning but was not particularly intelligent, was not certain if the princess mocked her, or was admiring. She chose to believe the latter. "Yes," she said. "It is a good solution for us all. When is the khan to leave Dariyabar?"

"I have been fortunate enough to please my lord Amir Khan," Zuleika explained in a manner that Golnar would comprehend. "He has said we may remain until the situation with my father is resolved one way or another. Of course that should be no problem, as we are no longer at war." Zuleika smiled. "Now, can you please tell me where the cabinet in my quarters went? Rafa left behind my foot basin, and I must have it! It has been mine my whole life." She smiled again almost apologetically. "You know how it is with the things we use to beautify ourselves, Golnar. Do you not have something you could not do without?"

Golnar nodded. "My hairbrushes," she admitted.

"And you have such beautiful hair," Zuleika admired. "It is like spun moonlight. My hair is just an ordinary black."

"But you have always kept it nicely," Golnar responded. "It shines like ebony."

"Ohh, thank you," Zuleika gushed. Then, "The cabinet?"

"It was taken to the storage rooms in the cellars," she said.

"I will go and get it," Zuleika replied.

"Would you like to stay in the harem tonight?" Golnar offered.

"Thank you again," the princess answered her politely, "but I think I will sleep in my father's apartments. You understand?"

"Of course," Golnar said. "The sultan's condition is very delicate, or so the gossip goes."

"Yes," Zuleika murmured, forcing tears to her eyes.

"Go and fetch your foot basin, princess," Golnar advised. "And if you want the company of women, please know you are welcome in the harem. I will instruct the women to pray to the Gods for the sultan."

"I never knew you were so kind," Zuleika said softly, struggling not to laugh. "Thank you." She took one of Golnar's hands, pressing it to her heart in a gesture of politeness. Then she turned and walked slowly away. As everywhere else in the palace, she was not challenged. She entered the storerooms, and searching among the bits and pieces of furniture there finally found her ebony cabinet. She opened the doors, and sighed with relief. There was the basin. She removed it, saying as she did, "Forgive me, Kansbar." The bowl quivered in her hands. Holding it tightly she returned to her father's apartments.

"Oh good!" Maryam said. "You are back. I would like a bit of time to myself, but I did not want to leave the sultan here alone. Prince Haroun has taken all his attendants, and I alone remain."

"When did this happen?" Zuleika asked.

"Yesterday, while we were all in the sultan's hall of audience. When I returned with your father afterwards everyone was gone. When I sought an explanation I was told that the prince had ordered it. I was very afraid, princess. If I leave him, what will happen?"

"You may go and rest," Zuleika said. "I will keep watch by my father's bedside this night."

"I think the prince seeks his inheritance, princess," Maryam said in a low tone.

"I believe you are right, Maryam," Zuleika answered the old serving woman. "Haroun has never been patient, even when we were children."

"I curse the Gods that they took your brothers from us!" Maryam said passionately.

"Do not curse the Gods, Maryam. They had, I think, very little to do with it. How interesting is it that my cousin encouraged my father and my brothers to war with Amir Khan while he remained safe behind the walls of this city. The Gods allow us a modicum of freedom, Maryam. But they are there to judge us when we exchange life in this world for a life in the next. More important, the Gods know what is in our hearts. There are no secrets from them, although we may believe we are clever enough to keep our innermost thoughts from them."

Maryam sighed. "You are right, princess," she said. Then seeing the basin in Zuleika's hands she asked, "Shall I take that for you, my princess?"

Zuleika shook her head. "Nay. I will put it aside. Rafa is coming tomorrow with a change of garments for me. It is my foot basin. She left it behind. I will have her take it back to the khan's camp with her when she returns." Zuleika set the vessel aside casually. "Go now and rest, dear Maryam."

"I have fed your father, what little he would eat," Maryam said. "He is tucked in his bed, but not asleep yet, I suspect. He will be pleased to know you are here." Then she turned and left the sultan's apartments.

Haroun had not yet put in an appearance, and Zuleika knew that he was sure to do so. He would know now of her presence in the palace. He would want to appear concerned. She was eager to consult Kansbar, but it was too dangerous until her cousin had come, and then gone. The princess went into her father's bedchamber and seated herself upon a padded stool next to the elderly man.

"Kansbar?" he husked at her softly.

"I have retrieved the bowl, father."

"It must be given, by tradition, to the next sultan," Ibrahim said to his daughter.

"Not Haroun," Zuleika replied in a determined voice.

"You are strong enough to lead Dariyabar," her father replied.

"The khan is stronger, father. And more worthy. Please trust my judgment in this, though I be but a woman," she told him.

A cynical smile touched his lips at her words. "And a diplomat as well, my daughter. I know that it is you who have inherited my intellect. Your brothers were good men, but they had not, any of them, the strength or ability to rule Dariyabar. Tell me of your khan."

"He is strong, not simply of body, but of mind," she began. "His people respect but fear him as well. Not because he is cruel, rather because he is mighty. On our short acquaintance I have found him to be kind, and fair."

"Do you trust him, my daughter?" the sultan asked her.

"Yes," Zuleika answered unhesitatingly, "although I have told him that I do not."

"Why?"

Zuleika quickly explained in soft tones her visit to the khan's encampment the night before he entered Dariyabar. "But then when he came he did not ask for me as his wife, and took me for his concubine."

"He is clever," the sultan said. "He realized that if he insisted upon having you for a wife, Haroun would become suspicious, and plot his demise. Could you not see that, my daughter?"

"I did, upon reflection, my father, but he must believe he has to re-earn my trust lest he betray me ever again," she said.

"There speaks the woman in you, Zuleika," her father chided her. "How was he to communicate with you before he entered the hall of audience? The khan did the right thing. I believe that your judgment is correct. It is Amir Khan who should follow me upon the throne of Dariyabar, but there is still the matter of your cousin, Haroun."

"He must be killed," Zuleika said implacably.

"Let the genie make that decision, my daughter. I dislike having the blood of my nephew on my hands. Kansbar will do what is best for Dariyabar. You must bring him to me that I may tell him of my desires in this matter," the sultan said.

"Haroun has not yet come, father, and he will come, I know it. Let us wait until he is gone. Sleep now. I will stay by your side."

"You are not afraid of Haroun, are you, my daughter? Yet you must not be overconfident. He is a dangerous man."

"Yes," she agreed, "he is, father. But he did not realize that I was the key to Dariyabar, so great was his greed for the kingdom. That greed will cost him dearly."

"You must also beware of Golnar," her father warned.

"Why? She is a simple creature who has told me she cannot do without her special hairbrushes," Zuleika said scornfully.

"She is more to be feared than your cousin," the sultan said. "Her eunuch is in my pay, daughter. Golnar is the whip that drives your cousin, Haroun. Your cousin has no mind of his own to scheme. He is merely an avaricious fool. It is Golnar who plans and plots the strategies that will lead to Dariyabar's downfall. She is a crafty creature, far more treacherous than Haroun. He but concerns himself with satisfying his own desires for wealth, women, wine and the power she promises him will be his when I am dead."

"Why did you not tell me all this before, father?" Zuleika asked her parent, surprised by the depth of his words.

"Because you needed an ally to fight Haroun," her father said.

"I have Kansbar," the princess responded.

"It is not enough, my daughter. Dariyabar will not accept a ruling sultana. There must be a sultan, and without a viable alternative candidate you would have been helpless. That is why I allowed Haroun to believe he had convinced a senile old man to give his daughter to the enemy," Sultan Ibrahim said.

Zuleika had to laugh at this revelation. "Father, you sly fox!" she chortled.

"Old age and cunning will always triumph over youth, my daughter," he responded with a chuckle. "It is a good lesson to remember."

"I will indeed remember it," she promised him. "Now get some rest, father."

The old man closed his eyes, and Zuleika settled down by his side to watch over him. Until this night she had not fully realized what a clever man her father really was. He had spent more time trying to teach her brothers how to be rulers than being with his daughter, though it had been a useless exercise. Cyrus, Asad, and Jahi had been men of brawn, but little intellect. Zuleika came to realize that it was this that kept her father from giving in to his own desires, and joining his beloved Jamila in the afterlife. Dariyabar needed him. And the truth of the matter was that of his four children, only his daughter had the wit to rule. And in order to do that she must have a husband. He had parented his half-brother's nephew in hopes that Haroun could be molded into a ruler, but Haroun was controlled by his insatiable desires and his greed. He was worse than the sultan's sons.

And then Haroun, encouraged by his favorite, Golnar, had come up with the idea of giving Zuleika to Amir Khan.

Zuleika smiled to herself as she sat by the sultan's bedside. The old man had played his part to the hilt, nodding and agreeing with his nephew that this would be the answer to their problems. But Haroun was not defeated yet. Zuleika sighed. She wished she were back in the khan's pavilion, naked and in her lover's arms. This second night, alone and together, would have been magic. *But first things first!* Her cousin must be dealt with as quickly as possible now that her father's health was in such a precarious state. She started as two hands fell upon her shoulders.

"Zuleika, my dear and beautiful cousin, how dutiful a daughter you are," Haroun's voice murmured softly. His hand caressed her neck lightly.

She arose. "Come into the outer room, Haroun," she whispered. "I would not wake my father, and he has just fallen asleep." She knew, however, that the old man was fully awake.

In the outer room he held her in his embrace and said, "A night in the khan's camp has sent you back to us with a new lushness, my cousin. Were you well fucked last night? Did you find his barbarian ways pleasing to you?"

Zuleika smiled boldly into her cousin's face. "I was very well used, Haroun, not just by the khan, but by his general as well. They took both Bahira and me to the great bed in my lord Amir's tent, and shared our favors between them. It was very exciting. I could never have imagined such a thing, but I will admit to enjoying it." She smiled again. "You would not have shared me, and allowed me such pleasure if I had been yours, cousin, would you?" she taunted him.

His too-handsome face darkened. "You could yet be mine, *cousin,*" he replied. One arm about her waist, his other hand clamped about her breast, and he squeezed it.

Zuleika's tongue ran provocatively across her lips, and she pressed herself against him. "Do you dare to steal what is not yours, Haroun," she mocked him. "Golnar wants me gone lest I influence you instead of her. That is why she has chosen a mere child, a little girl who cannot be a true wife to you for several years, for your mate. If you take me, and keep me in your harem, *cousin,* Golnar and I will fight for supremacy. One of us will die. Even if it is I, Golnar will never forgive you, and she will find a wonderful way to revenge herself upon you. If I survive, I shall kill you myself, Haroun, and thus rule our land alone. But perhaps Golnar and I will conspire together against you, Haroun." She laughed. "If you think it is worth it, then take me now! Of course you will also have to deal with the khan, who has found my favors much to his satisfaction."

"I am well rid of you!" the prince snapped, backing away from her. "How long are you to remain with us?"

"They say it is a possibility my father is dying," Zuleika replied. "I will remain until either his health improves, or he leaves us for the afterlife."

"May he join your mother quickly, then," Haroun said nastily, "so we may be rid of both of you!"

"You are too kind," Zuleika murmured, bowing to him from the waist. "My serving woman, Rafa, will be traveling back and forth between the city and the khan's camp each day with a change of clothing for me. The khan would not let me bring anything with me, so fearful is he that I might not return," she said.

"Yet you claim to have enjoyed his lust," Haroun responded.

"Indeed I do," Zuleika said enthusiastically, "but I also find the khan's camp primitive. I am used to the elegance of our city."

"Enjoy it while you may," the prince said, and then without another word he turned on his heel and departed the sultan's apartments.

Zuleika was hard-pressed not to laugh aloud. She went to the door of the chamber, and threw the bolt that locked the door to her father's rooms. Then she went back into the sultan's bedroom, and closing that door behind her locked it as well. The draperies were already drawn across the tall arched windows. Fetching the old and dented basin, she set it on the table near her father's bed, and leaning over it said, "Kansbar, genie of the golden bowl, great protector of Dariyabar, come to me now, I implore you."

The bowl filled quickly with crystal water, and transformed itself into the beautiful vessel that it truly was. Kansbar's stern face appeared upon the surface of the water.

"Well, daughter of Dariyabar, what is it you want? I see that you have managed to retrieve me after that fool, Rafa, left me behind."

"We have much work to do, genie," the princess said.

"*Explain!*" he replied sharply.

Chapter Four

"My father is dying, Kansbar. Can you restore his health?" Zuleika asked the genie.

"If it is his time, my princess, then it is his time," the genie responded sanguinely.

"Would you have Haroun rule Dariyabar, Kansbar? You may speak with my father. He would have Amir Khan succeed him. But to make that happen we need more time. If my father dies this night, or in the next few nights to come, then Haroun will seize power here. Sultan Ibrahim must make his wishes publicly known. To do that he must be restored to his previously good health."

The waters in the golden bowl grew dark for a moment, and then light again as the genie considered the problem. "I can give your father a moon's span, but no more, my princess. It is simply not in my power. If I do, I tamper with the will of the Gods, but I have not asked them for a favor in eons. They will grant me this, I know, for Dariyabar's sake. I shall also make both you and your father impervious to poisons of any kind, for Golnar is an impatient and vengeful woman. She already sees herself ruling Dariyabar through Haroun, but she will not allow that buffoon to live long, I suspect, before she kills him and takes the power for herself through the son she will seek to give your cousin. Haroun's heir may certainly come from her wicked womb as long as his sultana is of respectable lineage."

"Golnar tells me he will seek the vizier's youngest daughter, Tahirah, who is still a child," Zuleika said.

"Ahhh," Kansbar said, "then I am right. Golnar wants to

give your cousin his heir. Pray she is not already with child, or if she is that the child is a female."

"What are we to do with Haroun?" Zuleika asked. "Should we not kill him so he may not prove a problem for us?"

"Fierce! Fierce!" the genie murmured. "You should have been your father's son! Still, you should not have his blood on your conscience. Haroun is a fool, my princess, but I believe we might allow him his life. However, I think he should live it in another place," he chuckled. "There is a land called Kava where women rule, and men are their slaves. His pretty face and randy cock would be much appreciated by the women of Kava. Of course he will, I expect, need to be retrained to know his place in their unique society," the genie said with a wicked and knowing smile. "I can arrange to send him there, my princess."

"But what if he should escape Kava, and attempt to return to Dariyabar?" she asked him.

"Kava is almost two years of travel from Dariyabar, my princess, but more important, the women of Kava have learned how to control time. For each year Haroun is in Kava, twenty-five of our years will have passed. If that does not reassure you, let me tell you that no man has ever escaped from Kava. Only a fool would want to, and while your cousin is indeed a fool, he will adjust. The women of Kava are very beautiful. They know pleasure well. After the shock has worn off, Haroun will find himself a mistress who will cherish him, and cosset him. He will live in luxury, his every need met as long as he pleases his mistress. He will quickly learn that those men who are recalcitrant find themselves in either the gem mines, or the fields behind a plow. Haroun would not enjoy that. But if the impossible happened and he did escape and find his way back to Dariyabar, he would be a very old man himself, for once he has entered Kava he remains young. But if he leaves, he will return to what he is, for he was not born of Kava. It is the perfect solution, and you will not have his blood on your hands."

"What of Golnar?" Zuleika queried.

"That is for Amir Khan to decide, my princess."

"Very well," Zuleika said. "But my father?"

"Will awaken in the morning healthy and well. He will be stronger in body and mind than he has ever been," Kansbar promised. "But in one month he will go to his bed, and not awaken again in this world. He has but thirty days in which to make his will known to the people of Dariyabar. He must bring Amir Khan into the city tomorrow, and the khan must marry you before all the people. This binds your father's blood to that of Amir Khan, and to the previous sultans of Dariyabar. Amir Khan will only co-rule with you, my princess. It is your first son who will inherit after his father, and his maternal grand-father."

"And where is Haroun in all of this?" she demanded.

"Your cousin even now is awakening to find himself in Kava," the genie chuckled, well pleased with himself. "He is among a group of slaves brought in from a nearby city to re-stock the stud pool."

Zuleika giggled. She couldn't help herself. "He will be so confused," she said. "He may even think himself mad." She sounded rather pleased by the thought, remembering how he had squeezed her breast and threatened her just a short while ago.

"He will survive after the shock has worn off," Kansbar said. "I will check on him now and again, but once he learns the lay of that particular land, and that there is no escape, he will adjust quite nicely, I am thinking. Perhaps I shall see he is given a stern mistress to start. One who will whip his bottom to train him to obedience."

"Ohh," Zuleika murmured, "the very thought excites me, genie."

Kansbar chortled. "Tell your father what I have told you, and then return in the morning to your khan." For a mo-ment he arose from the waters of his bowl, and smoothed his big hands down the sultan's frail body. "There," he said.

"Ibrahim is healed, and free from death for the next thirty days." The genie reached out and put his hand upon Zuleika's dark head. "You will be free of poisons forever, my princess," he told her. "Do not leave me behind again, however," he gently scolded her. Then he disappeared back into his bowl, the waters drained magically away, and the golden vessel once again became a plain metal container of no import.

To her surprise Zuleika fell asleep for several hours, awakening to see a thin shaft of light pushing through the curtains. She arose and opened the draperies to a glorious morning. She opened the windows, allowing the soft fresh air into the room. Then she went to the bedchamber door and unbolted it, walking through to unbolt the main door to the sultan's apartments. When she returned to her father's bedside he was awake. His color was restored, and he looked better than he had in many years. "Father!" she cried happily. "Kansbar has kept his word!"

"What have you done, daughter?" the sultan asked her. "I cannot ever remember feeling this well."

"Kansbar has restored your health for a moon's span, father. At the end of that time you will join mother in the other world," Zuleika explained. "Today, the first day of the new moon, the genie says you are to bring the khan into the city with me. We will wed, and you will declare him your heir."

"And Haroun? What of your cousin in all of this, my daughter?"

"Haroun is no longer in Dariyabar. The genie transported him in the night to a place called Kava." And then Zuleika explained.

The sultan chortled. "It is an ideal solution, my daughter. I should not like to have had your cousin's death on my hands. Lock the bedchamber door again, and summon the genie for me now."

Zuleika did as she was bid, and then placed the bowl in her father's hands.

The old sultan called, "Kansbar, genie of the golden bowl, your master, the sultan of Dariyabar, summons you to him."

The bowl immediately filled, and Kansbar was there, his voice deferential. "I am here, Master. You have but to command me, and I will do it." The turbaned head bowed.

"I thank you for the opportunity you have given me," the sultan said. "Now give me your wisdom. Is this Amir Khan the man to follow me? You are certain of this?"

"I am, royal master," the genie said. "And your blood will flow in the veins of the children he gets on your daughter, princess Zuleika. The line of Dariyabar will not be broken."

"Then so be it, Kansbar, guardian of Dariyabar," Sultan Ibrahim agreed. "I give my power over to you, to my daughter, and to Amir Khan from the moment they are bound together in marriage."

"It will be according to your will, my lord sultan," the genie replied.

"Farewell, Kansbar," the sultan said softly.

"Farewell, Sultan Ibrahim," the genie replied, and Zuleika would have sworn that there were tears in his eyes, but then he was gone, and the bowl drained of its water.

"Take the bowl out with you to the khan's encampment, and tell him of my wishes. He will take you as his wife this very day, and then I will declare him my heir before all the people." The sultan threw back the coverlet, and stepped from his bed. "The Gods! I feel better now than I have felt in years, daughter. Find Maryam, and tell her I am hungry! I want a joint of roasted kid, fresh bread, cheese, and melon for my meal! Hurry! Then go back to your khan."

Zuleika bent, and kissed her father happily. Then she left his bedchamber to find Maryam, his personal servant, entering the royal apartments. "Maryam! My father has recovered from whatever it was that was ailing him. Go and see, and then fetch him his meal. He wants roasted kid, bread, cheese and melon. I will wait for you."

Maryam hurried into her master's bedchamber, and when

she came out she was beaming with happiness. "It is a miracle, my princess! It is a miracle. It was your visit, I am certain, that has restored him. Ahh, but I have news. Prince Haroun is nowhere to be found in the palace. His bodyslave put him to bed last night, but when he went to awaken him this morning he was gone. The imprint of his head was on his pillow, but he could not be found," Maryam said. "His servants are in an uproar."

"He is probably with Golnar," Zuleika said.

"No! She swears he did not come to visit her last night," Maryam said. "She is very upset, my princess."

"I am sure she is," Zuleika said, "unless this is some plot of hers, for we all know the sort of woman she is. Tell my father. It is he who rules here, not Prince Haroun. I am ordered to return to the khan's encampment." She picked up the metal basin. "And I am to return here later today with the khan. I shall see you then, Maryam."

Zuleika moved swiftly through the marble corridors of her father's palace, and out into the courtyard. Her golden gelding was immediately brought to her, and with it were the khan's two guards, her escort. She mounted without a word, and carefully holding the bowl against her she moved off, out through the palace gates and into the city. Again the people greeted her with smiles and words of blessing. She smiled back at them, happy to know that she would soon be living amongst them one again. She found that she was excited to be returning to Amir Khan. She wondered if he would cooperate with Kansbar, but then if he refused, Kansbar would destroy him. And that would be a great shame, Zuleika considered. Amir Khan was a beautiful man with a fine cock. They would make wonderful babies together for Dariyabar.

He was awaiting her at the entry to his pavilion, a small smile upon his face. She slid easily from her gelding, even holding the bowl next to her. His eyebrows quirked. She nodded in response, and walked into his vast tent. Her heart was beating a tattoo. Just seeing his strong face thrilled her. When would he make love to her again? she wondered. It could not be too soon, she decided.

"This is your fabled golden bowl?" he asked, reaching out for it.

Zuleika drew back. "It is not yours to have yet, my lord. I must explain what the genie has said, and what he has done. Then I will summon him, and introduce you to each other."

"Very well, but come and sit, my princess," he said, taking her by the hand and drawing her down into a pile of multi-colored silk cushions. "And give your lord and master a kiss, for I find that I have missed you, Zuleika of Dariyabar. Is it possible that you may have missed me as well?" His big hand caressed and cupped her face.

"Perhaps, my lord, the longing I felt in the night was for you," she teased him. *"Amir!"* she squealed as he pushed her back into the cushions, his hand sliding beneath her gown and up to brush her thigh. "You are too bold, my lord!"

"And you, my princess, are shamelessly eager. You are wet with your desire, and ready to accept me, are you not?" His dark eyes looked down into her violet ones. Then he pushed two fingers into her love sheath, and began to move them back and forth.

"Ahh, you devil! We must conclude our business first!" she protested. "Ohhh!"

"Aye, we must," he agreed, and covered her body with his own, pushing her gown up to bare her lower body. Then his love lance was pressing into her, and she was wrapping her legs about him, and making little noises of distinct pleasure.

"Oh yes, my lord! Ohhh, yes! Oh! Oh! *Ohhh!"* Zuleika cried, pushing back at his every thrust and clinging to him.

He began to laugh with his delight in her, and her obvious pleasure in him. "I adore you, Zuleika of Dariyabar!" he cried as his juices flooded her hidden garden of love.

When once again they had come to themselves, and restored their disarrayed attire, Zuleika told the khan of the visit she had had with her father; how the genie had restored his health for a single cycle of the moon so they might wed, and the sultan might declare Amir Khan his heir. "We are to enter the city this afternoon and we will be married tonight," she explained.

"And Prince Haroun will stand by and permit this?" the khan asked. "I think not. I shall have to kill him first, and that may not prove easy, Zuleika."

"No! No! Kansbar has transported my cousin by means of his great magic to a land called Kava. There, he will live his life a slave in this society of women. Kansbar says that once he accepts this fate he will be very content. No one escapes Kava. He will never return. Already they seek him in Dariyabar, but they will not find him. Nor are there any signs of violence, for there was none. Haroun is simply gone from Dariyabar."

"Has he offspring?" the khan wanted to know. "We can leave nothing of him if we are to rule Dariyabar in peace, Zuleika."

She shook her head. "Golnar, his favorite, has seen that Haroun did not spawn children. She wanted him sultan first. She planned to have him marry Bahira's little sister, Tahirah. The child is too young to be bred, but Haroun would have had a sultana who would be accepted. Then Golnar would have birthed my cousin an heir of her womb. A sultan's first son, be his mother the sultana or a concubine, is the heir."

"A clever woman," Amir Khan noted. "I look forward to meeting her, my princess."

"*Why?*" Zuleika demanded to know. She had hardly expected this.

"One should always know one's enemy," he said quietly.

"I want her sent from Dariyabar!" Zuleika said angrily.

"We will consult the genie on the best way to manage this woman," Amir Khan told Zuleika. "Come now, my beauty, and remember you promised to introduce us."

"I do not know if I should," Zuleika said.

He laughed. "Are you jealous then, my princess? You should not be. I am yours, and yours alone," he swore.

"Golnar is very beautiful, and does not appear to be what

she really is," Zuleika said. "She will present herself to you as meek and mild, but she is evil incarnate."

"Is she really that wicked, or do you not perhaps exaggerate just a little to protect your place in my heart?" he asked her gently.

Zuleika could not believe what she had just heard from his mouth. Why was it that men could be such fools, and believe that every action or word a woman suggested had to do with them? She swallowed back her anger. "Golnar," she told him, "is far more iniquitous than you can possibly imagine, my lord Amir. When you are chosen by my father over my cousin, Haroun, when Haroun cannot be found, no trace of him at all, she will see all her plans and schemes coming to naught. That is when she will prove the most dangerous. She has an entire harem at her command, and she will use them and her own body to regain her objectives. If you believe otherwise, then I fear for Dariyabar."

"You will be my wife," he said to her in an attempt to reassure her. "But when your father crosses into the other world, I will be sultan, Zuleika. It is my will that will be law, and not yours. I have already warned you that I will not be tampered with in my rule."

"And I have promised you that I would but *advise* you. I advise you now to beware Golnar. Not because she is beautiful, and I am jealous, but because she is wicked, and will seek to destroy you. I cannot make you listen to me, my lord, but I hope that you have heard, and believed." She arose from their bed. "I must tell poor Rafa not to unpack, as we are to return to the city shortly," she said. And she left him.

Was she jealous? he wondered. He did not know her well enough to be certain, but her devotion to Dariyabar was fierce. Would her loyalty to him be as strong? Or would her allegiance to Dariyabar overcome even her fidelity to a new sultan, not of her family's blood? He could not know that until more time had passed, but by nightfall she would be his wife, and as she had so succinctly put it, she was the key that would open the gates of Dariyabar to him. The war was over, but was yet another war beginning?

Sultan Ibrahim sent out two litters. They were of sweet-smelling cedar, gilded in gold leaf. The larger and more elegant of the two had coral-colored silk gauze draperies and matching cushions edged in gold rope, decorated with gold tassels. The smaller litter's drapes and cushions were turquoise and gold. The sultan had also sent an escort of her personal guard, and his war elephants, who were dressed in bejeweled green silk covers fringed with gold beads and pearls, with matching bejeweled headpieces. There were blackamoors holding purple, rose, silver and sky blue silk parasols fringed in gold, and set upon tall ebony poles banded in silver. There were musicians in their colorful robes of stripes and brocades.

"What is all of this?" the khan demanded of Zuleika.

"My father is bringing us into the city with honor," the princess explained. "You do not come as a conqueror, but rather you enter as a welcomed friend. This way his people will more readily accept you as his chosen heir. While my cousin was not well liked, there will be questions that cannot be answered about his disappearance. Kansbar, however, will have the answers for us."

"You have yet to bring the genie forth, my princess," the khan said. "Should I not know this magical creature before I enter into Dariyabar?"

"Yes! Yes!" she agreed, and ran to fetch the battered metal bowl in which the genie resided.

"I thought you said the bowl was gold," he remarked.

"Do you believe I could have brought a gold bowl from the palace unimpeded?" she laughed. She set the basin on a low table, and invited him to sit next to her. When they were both settled she said, "Kansbar, genie of the golden bowl, great guardian of Dariyabar, come forth, I pray you."

"You are very deferential," the khan whispered to her. "I thought genies were at our service, and must obey."

"You haven't met Kansbar," she murmured with a smile.

"Where is he?" the khan inquired.

"Wait, and be patient," she said. Then, "Kansbar of Dariyabar, come to me, I beg you!"

Suddenly, before the startled eyes of the khan the bowl began to glow, and become the most shining gold he had ever seen. The dents and scratches disappeared, and it was filled with a crystal clear liquid. Then a turbaned head appeared on the surface of the water. The genie had a beautifully barbered black beard, and for someone as old as Zuleika claimed he was, his face bore no signs of age. Atop his head was the most fantastic cloth-of-gold turban with a pigeon's-blood ruby in its front folds, the like of which the khan had never seen. Black eyes stared up at them from the liquid.

"Well," Kansbar said, "what is it you wish of me, my princess?"

"I would present Amir Khan to you, great Kansbar," she replied. "I thought it only proper you meet before we enter the city."

The genie nodded. "Shortly, my lord khan, you will be my new master," he said. "I can but hope our faith in you is justified. Do you swear to rule wisely over Dariyabar?"

"I will do my best," the khan answered.

"You must do better than your best!" the genie roared. "The Gods! The Gods! Is this human no better than the fool, Haroun? My princess, have you been befuddled by passion, and a lusty cock? You are certain this man is the one?" Kansbar looked distinctly dubious.

"I will rule with justice and equanimity, Kansbar," the khan replied. "I am a human, and more I cannot promise, for I will not lie simply to placate you. I am a warrior. I expect you to advise me in matters of governance so I may be fair, and learn from your wisdom."

"He shows promise, I will agree," the genie said grudgingly in response to the khan's speech, looking directly at Zuleika.

"And he would, it seems, have a sense of honor which is more than the foolish Haroun had. Very well, I will accept him on one condition, my princess."

"What is that, mighty Kansbar?" she flattered the genie.

"My bowl must remain with you until I am certain that he can be trusted," the genie said. Now his gaze swung to that of the khan. "Will you agree, Amir Khan? Will you accept my judgment in this matter, and know that Zuleika of Dariyabar will understand when the time is right for you to have possession of me?"

"Are you not obliged to obey me when I am sultan of Dariyabar?" the khan asked.

The genie shook his head. "I am only required to obey those in the direct bloodline of Dariyabar's founder, Sultan Sinbad," he explained. "When the time comes that the princess believes you are fit to be my master, that will change, but the choice is mine, not yours."

"I have no option but to agree, then," the khan replied, "but I trust Zuleika. Shortly she will be my wife. I know she will not act against me or the best interests of Dariyabar, great Kansbar."

"No, she will not," the genie responded. "Zuleika of Dariyabar understands loyalty, and will keep faith with you, Amir Khan, as long as you keep faith with her. Listen to her, and trust her words. Now, it is time for us all to return to the city." And the genie was gone, his bowl emptied, dark and battered again.

Amir Khan didn't know whether to laugh, or not. "He is a powerful presence," the khan finally said.

It was Zuleika who laughed. "He is, but wise beyond all. My ancestor found him in a bottle by the seaside, and released him. He granted Sinbad three wishes. The third wish was that Kansbar remain as the protector of Dariyabar always, and be subject to the will of Sinbad's direct descendants until the day came that there were none, at which time the genie would choose his new master."

"So the key to Dariyabar must open two locks, and not just one," the khan observed.

Zuleika thought a moment, and then she nodded. "I suppose that you are right, my lord Amir," she told him.

"I do not know if it pleases me that you have such control over my life, Zuleika," he told her.

"Because I am naught but a woman?" she asked him.

"No, because I prefer to control my own fate, princess," he responded.

"None of us controls our own lives, though sometimes we believe that we do," Zuleika answered him wisely. "We are, all of us, in the hands of the gods, my lord. You are, I believe, meant to follow my father on the throne of Dariyabar, and you will. That I possess the golden bowl counts for little, for in time I will give it to you. But Kansbar is right when he says you are untried yet. He will, himself, I promise you, instruct me when the time is propitious for you to have the bowl. It will not really be my decision at all. I am but his caretaker by virtue of the fact that I am my father's last child."

"You have the skills of a diplomat, Zuleika," he said with a small smile. "When shall we go into the city?"

"First I must bathe," she said to him. "I scent your lust upon me, Amir Khan. I would prefer my father did not when we meet again. Can a bath be brought to me?"

"We do not have such accoutrements to offer, being an army," he said, "but we bathe ourselves in a stream behind the camp out of sight of the city, my princess. I shall call Bahira and Rafa to you, and see that the area is free of my men." He bowed to her, and then was gone from his tent.

Shortly afterwards Bahira arrived, looking slightly the worse for wear. "I have found a man who can actually tire me out," she announced with obvious pride. "Never did I dream of such a lover as General Sabola. Now, tell me what has happened." She sat down on a pile of cushions opposite her friend.

Zuleika once again told her tale of the last day; of how the genie had managed to restore her father's health for a moon cycle, but no more. The secret of Haroun's disappearance was also shared, and Bahira laughed to learn of the prince's fate.

"What of Golnar?" she asked the princess.

"Her fate will be decided later," Zuleika said.

"Then we are to go home!" Bahira clapped her hands.

"I am to wed the khan tonight. I will see that Sabola is wed to you as well, Bahira. You must have the authority of a wife, as must I, for these men will want other women, you may be certain," Zuleika said.

Bahira nodded. "Yes," she agreed. "We must be mistresses in our own homes. Then the beautiful litters and the caravan sent out from the city are our escort."

"Yes," Zuleika said.

"Come, my girls." Rafa now reentered the pavilion. "I am to take you both to the bathing pool. The khan and his general have seen that the area is cleared of others. The sooner you both bathe, the sooner we can go back into the city, and civilization."

The two young women followed Rafa from the tent and through the encampment down a small hill and into a grove of trees. There was a crystal clear stream that entered the pool, with a delicate waterfall that soared above the pond. The girls quickly threw off their robes and dove into the water, squealing at its icy cold.

"I am told there is a warm spring to your right," Rafa called.

They moved to where she pointed, and were rewarded with a flow of almost hot water. Rafa handed them soap-filled sea sponges, and they washed quickly, then swam back beneath the waterfall to rinse themselves. Then the two frolicked, laughing and splashing water on each other as they played.

"Go back to the pavilion," the khan murmured in Rafa's ear.

She turned, and cast a surprised look at him and the general.

"You will all have to bathe again," she warned them.

"We will," the khan chuckled.

Rafa shook her head. "The enthusiasm of youth is to be

most wondered at, my lord," she remarked, and then she moved back through the trees, and was gone from their sight.

The khan and his general stripped their loincloths off, and dove into the pool, startling the two young women who screamed at first, not realizing who had joined them. When they saw however that it was Amir Khan and Sabola, they began throwing water at them, laughing.

"You must not get us dirty," Zuleika protested as the khan swam next to her.

"We will bathe again, my princess," he said. "Sabola and I are filled with a wicked lust, and must satisfy it before we go into the city. You do not want us to disgrace ourselves before your father." He pulled her into his arms and began kissing her, his tongue pushing past her lips to seek her out and play.

Reaching down, she caught his engorged rod in her hand, and fondled it. "You are hard with your desire already. Men can become aroused so quickly, but women cannot. I must be stroked and caressed before I am ready to entertain this eager fellow." She gave him a little squeeze, which only served to render him harder than ever before.

He picked her up and carried her from the water. "I shall prepare you myself, my princess, but you must prepare Bahira for Sabola while she entertains his lance."

"As my lord desires," Zuleika murmured docilely.

He laid her on her back upon the mossy bank of the stream. The positions of their two companions were acrobatic in nature. Bahira squatted over Zuleika's head, revealing her secret parts to her friend, while Sabola, legs wide, stood before Bahira, placing his already hot love rod between her lips. Bahira suckled upon him, her head awash with her emotions as Zuleika foraged between her nether lips, teasing the sentient flesh. The khan prepared his lover in the same manner, but then he mounted her, slipping his great length into her hot and welcoming sheath. Bahira was swiftly in her lover's arms, taking him into her body. The moans of pleasure grew in intensity as the quartet drove themselves to nirvana, and collapsed in a heap of arms and legs with their mutual satisfaction.

"The Gods!" Zuleika finally spoke. "I do not think I can get up. That was much, much too wonderful."

"Ummm," Bahira agreed.

Both men laughed weakly.

For several minutes they lay upon the stream bank while their hearts slowed and some small strength flowed back into their limbs. Finally the khan managed to arise to his feet, pulling Zuleika up with him. Together they walked back into the water to wash the scent of their new lust from their satisfied bodies. At a distance, Sabola and Bahira joined them. The four lovers were careful not to touch too fondly or come near to each other. Bathed once again, they emerged from the water to reclothe themselves and return to the encampment. They did not speak, lest they spoil the moment. It would never again be that way for them, and they understood it.

Rafa dressed both Zuleika and Bahira in exquisite garments. The princess wore a loose-fitting gown of white silk gauze shot through with threads of pure gold. It was sleeveless, had a keyhole neckline, and was fitted beneath her firm young breasts. The skirt of the garment fell in long, narrow pleats from her bust to her ankles. Her feet were fitted with delicate gold sandals, her hair braided in a single plait with strands of tiny pearls, diamonds and sapphires. About her neck was a thin gold chain from which fell a large sapphire oval. The gemstone hung directly in the center of the keyhole neckline. In the princess's ears were great hoops of gold from which hung more sapphires, diamonds and pearls.

Bahira was garbed in very similar fashion, but where Zuleika was the sun, her friend was the moon in a gown of wispy white silk gauze shot through with threads of pure silver. The style of the garment was identical to Zuleika's. On her feet the vizier's daughter wore silver sandals. Her rich auburn hair was braided into several narrow plaits intertwined with silver chains strung with turquoise. She wore a collar of turquoise, black onyx, and red agate. Her ears sported turquoise hoops. "Am I beautiful again?" she demanded of Rafa.

"As always, Bahira, daughter of Abd al Hakim," Rafa replied with a smile. "And you, my princess, are regal as ever."

The two young women entered their litters, Rafa riding with Bahira. The procession now began to form. The khan, upon a great white stallion with a silvery mane and tail, would lead it. Amir Khan was garbed in his black leather pants and a gold breastplate. His dark horsetail of hair was intricately braided behind him so that the people might see his strong, handsome features. On his feet he wore red felt boots, showing that he was not prepared for battle, but rather a social encounter. He would lead the procession, followed by a troupe of the sultan's guards and then a troupe of his own men. Zuleika would follow in her open litter for all the people of Dariyabar to see.

"Let the musicians go before you, my lord," the princess suggested. "It makes your entry into the city even less ferocious, and more felicitous."

He nodded at her with a smile, and signaled the group of players forward. They carried pipes, and oboes, cymbals, drums, and trumpets. Immediately they began a triumphal march, and the parade began to move forward. They passed through the great iron-bound gates of Dariyabar, the musicians playing. Behind them rode Amir Khan, and to his surprise the people cheered him. Accompanying the soldiers behind him were men on horseback with drums who beat a rather fierce tattoo to remind the people that they really were warriors. Then came the princess, and the citizens of Dariyabar were driven into a frenzy of delight.

"Zuleika! Zuleika! Zuleika!" they called out her name.

From her litter the princess smiled, and waved until her arm was sore and threatened to fall by her side.

She was followed by General Sabola and another mixed troupe of soldiery. Then came Bahira's litter. On either side of the entire procession walked the slaves carrying the parasols. And finally, the great lumbering war elephants in their be-jeweled green satin coverings brought up the rear of the procession, which marched down the main avenue of the city to the great white marble palace with its gold-leafed gates and gilded towers. The khan's men were astounded by the richness of it all, and by the loyalty of the people to their princess.

In the palace courtyard the princess and Bahira, along with Rafa, exited their litters. Now they walked in procession to the great audience hall of the sultan of Dariyabar where Sultan Ibrahim awaited them, smiling broadly.

"I welcome you back to Dariyabar, Amir Khan," he said in a strong voice such as Zuleika had not heard him use in many years.

A servant ran forward to take the bridle of the khan's horse, and Amir Khan dismounted the beast and it was lead away. The khan bowed with a deep flourish. The courtiers nodded, pleased by this show of respect for their sultan, and when Amir Khan stepped forward to kiss Sultan Ibrahim's ring of office a distinct murmur of approval hummed through the hall.

"I thank the sultan for his generous welcome," the khan said. "Now I would ask one other thing of him. Give me your daughter, the Princess Zuleika, for my wife. My pleasure in her far exceeds that of a man for a mere concubine. And give my general, Lord Sabola, the daughter of your vizier, Abd al Hakim, the lady Bahira to wife as well."

"My daughter you may have to wife, Amir Khan," the sultan said, "but the lady Bahira is not my child to bestow upon your general. It is her father's choice. Come forward, Abd al Hakim, and say what you will do," the sultan commanded his vizier.

Abd al Hakim was a plump little man with a small white beard. He came forward, his red-and-silver striped robes flapping. "Her mother would know if she is happy with this arrangement, my lord sultan," the vizier said, bowing low to his master. His voice was high and reedy.

"If I get any happier," Bahira said boldly, "I shall die of it, my father. Aye, I am more than content to be this lusty man's wife."

The sultan's court erupted into laughter as this blunt statement from the vizier's eldest daughter, who had always been thought to be a meek creature, met their ears.

"So be it, then," the sultan said, a twinkle in his eye. "Bring forth the temple priests, and the marriages shall be celebrated now."

The priests, with their shaved heads and their loins wrapped in white linen cloths that fell to their ankles, came into the sultan's hall of audience. They were bare-footed. The chief priest, distinguished by a gold-and-onyx collar about his neck, signaled for the two couples to come before him. "We worship the lords of the sky, the waters, the earth, and the winds. Do you respect these gods, my children, and agree to abide always by their natural laws?"

The four voices agreed, and the four heads nodded.

"In the name of the gods, and in accordance with the laws of our world, do you take each other as mates till death parts you?"

The voices once again agreed, and the heads nodded.

A young priest stepped forward and held out a small round gold salver to them. Upon it were four small pieces of bread. The four lovers each took a piece of the bread, and fed it to their chosen mate. Two cups of sweet wine were presented. Each couple took one, and offered their mate the cup. When all four had drunk, the cups were removed.

"Two have become one now," the high priest said. "The feeding of the grain, the sip of the grape, binds you to each other in the sight of the gods. Multiply, as do all the creatures of the earth, and you shall be blessed." The high priest turned to the sultan. "It is done now, my lord Ibrahim. Is there any other way in which I may serve you this day?"

"Nay," the sultan said. "I am content to see my child wed. Come now, and let us partake of the feast that has been set out in their honor."

"You feast? You dare to celebrate when Prince Haroun is missing?" They all turned to see Golnar, who had come into the hall. *"What have you done to my good lord?"* she cried piteously, stretching out her gold-bangled arms.

The sultan signaled to his guards. "Remove the lady Golnar from the hall," he said in his strong voice. He watched impassively as she was carried, struggling, from his presence. The old man turned to his court. "I do not know where my nephew is, but none here can say I have ever borne him any malice. I am as mystified as you all are. But now is not the time to discuss or investigate this matter. This is my only child's wedding day. I will not have it spoiled! Come now into my banqueting hall," the sultan said, and they all followed him without another moment's hesitation.

Chapter Five

Golnar, Prince Haroun's favorite, had been returned most forcibly to her harem. "When my lord is sultan here you will pay for this outrage!" she screamed at the guards who none-too-gently thrust the struggling woman back into her quarters, closing the great doors to the harem firmly. Golnar shrieked with her fury, and looked about for some hapless soul upon whom she might vent her anger. There was no one. Slaves, eunuchs, and harem women were nowhere in sight. The fountain in the main chamber tinkled pleasantly, but the air was devoid of any other noise. Even the birds in the gardens beyond seemed hushed by her anger.

Taking a deep breath, Golnar calmed herself. She reached for a piece of paste candy on a nearby silver salver, and sucked upon it thoughtfully as it melted in her mouth, releasing the flavor of plum as it did so. *Where was Haroun?* How could he have disappeared at just the perfect time for his enemies? And disappeared without any trace at all? She had personally questioned Haroun's bodyslave. He was as mystified as they all claimed to be. He had put his master to bed. When he had gone to awaken him in the morning, Haroun was gone. There were no signs of a struggle. The imprint of his head was yet upon his pillow. *What had happened to her prince?*

Golnar was no fool. Haroun was gone, and suddenly Zuleika was returned into the city amid great pomp and spectacle. She was married to Amir Khan before the court. Her best friend, the vizier's daughter, was wed to the khan's general. Something was afoot, and Golnar suspected that Zuleika's husband would be appointed the sultan's heir, as Prince Haroun had so conveniently disappeared. *And the sultan.* He had been dying but two days ago. The physicians all said so. Yet now he appeared in miraculous good health. How had that happened? And then Golnar knew. *There was magic afoot here!*

She went directly to her private apartments. Her personal servants were also among the missing. So much the better, she thought, as she locked the door to her bedchamber behind her. Then she pulled the latticed shutters tight, and drew the gauze draperies over them. No one must see her. Opening the painted wood cabinet she drew out a slender alabaster vial, and setting it upon a table, uncorked it. *"Mother,"* she called. "I need you now."

Violet smoke, first little in color, and then growing darker, arose from the vial. The smoke began to take shape, and it was a beautiful woman with silver hair, and eyes like blue ice, very much like Golnar in appearance. "What is it, my daughter?" the woman said. Her voice was smoky, and yet pleasant.

"Haroun has disappeared!" Golnar cried. "And no one seems to care, mother. I think they will make Zuleika's new husband, Amir Khan, the sultan's heir. And the old man, dying but a few days ago, is suddenly restored to good health!"

Keket looked at her daughter irritably. "Of all my children," she said, "you seem to be the most hapless, Golnar. Why do you allow your humanity to overrule your mystical side? Even your father was not this unfortunate. I do not know what I shall do with you." Keket was a magical creature born of a fairy mother and a genie father. She had certain powers she used for her own amusement. "I allowed your human father to raise you. I saw that you caught Prince Haroun's eye. I taught you how to please him so mightily that you became his favorite. All that was required of you, Golnar, was that you give him a son. Now he has gone missing? Well, child, I do not know what else I can do for you, but tell me everything in detail, Golnar, not just what affects you and your comfort."

"Everything was going exactly as we planned," Golnar

whined. "The princess had been given to Amir Khan, and devastated by her loss, the old sultan took to his deathbed. Learning of it, the princess returned to the city, dutiful daughter that she is," Golnar sneered, "to sit by her father's side. But when morning came the sultan had recovered his full health and strength, *and Haroun was gone!* Zuleika returned to the khan's encampment, and later she was escorted with much pomp back into the city with the khan. There were musicians, and even the sultan's war elephants all caparisoned in their green jeweled satin. The populace threw rose petals, and shouted the princess's name over and over again. *I hate her!*"

"Do not waste your energies hating, Golnar," her mother advised. "Concentrate upon your revenge. Now continue," Keket ordered.

"There is nothing more but what I have already told you, mother. The khan asked the sultan for Zuleika in marriage, and he asked for the vizier's daughter for his general."

"I thought the lady Bahira was to be Haroun's choice for a wife," Keket said. "What happened? I can see things have been going wrong for you from the beginning."

"When the khan first accepted Zuleika as his concubine, he also asked that his general be rewarded with the vizier's daughter, Bahira."

"How did he know of the lady Bahira?" Keket asked.

"I don't know!" Golnar whined impatiently. "He just did!"

"Hmmmm," Keket said thoughtfully. "Go on."

"So when the princess married Amir Khan today, Bahira was also wed to General Sabola. They are feasting in the sultan's banquet hall even now. Mother, there is absolutely no trace of Haroun. *None!* I know that the sultan will make Amir Khan his successor; and what is to happen to me then? The princess will be Dariyabar's sultana, and she will not want me about. *What will become of me?*" Golnar wailed.

"There is magic here," Keket said slowly. "Do you have something that belonged to Haroun, daughter?"

Golnar thought a moment, and then her eyes lit up. "Yes!"

she cried. "He gave me this ring from his own finger last week." She held out her hand to display the large diamond.

Keket pulled the ring impatiently from the girl's hand, ignoring her squeal of protest. "Be silent now, and let me see what I can see." Keket looked deep into the ring, concentrating. An amused smile suddenly touched her full lips, and she began to chuckle.

"What is it?" Golnar demanded. "What do you see, Mother?"

"Someone has transported your lover to the kingdom of Kava, Golnar. It is a place where women rule. You will not see him again," Keket said. "Oh, my!" And she laughed aloud.

"Can you not bring him back?" Golnar demanded. "You have powers, mother. I want him back."

Keket looked up. "No one ever returns from Kava, Golnar, and whoever sent him there knew it. Obviously, the princess has very powerful friends. Here, look into the diamond, and see your prince."

Golnar stared hard, and then she saw Haroun. Fascinated, she watched as his bottom was whipped until it was pink and glowing. She gaped as he was then spread-eagled upon a block, and women, one after another, came to use his upstanding cock, some sucking on it, some mounting him and riding him until his mouth opened so wide Golnar could almost hear him scream. "What are they doing to him?" she gasped, looking to her mother.

"Obviously he is proving recalcitrant, daughter. He has been brought by his new mistress for public punishment at the palace of common pleasures. The women of Kava do not allow their men rebellion. Hopefully Haroun will learn obedience, for it is his only salvation. They will be more patient with him than others for he is so pretty, and his cock so randy. Eventually he will learn to be happy again, even if he does not rule in Dariyabar. And, you daughter, must now decide how to save yourself."

Golnar grew pale. "Tell me what to do, mother," she begged.

Keket smiled, and put a comforting arm about her daughter. "Do you know why I allowed your human father to have you, Golnar? Do you know why I saw to it that you caught Prince Haroun's eye? Do you know why I have advised you what to advise your prince?"

Golnar shook her head in the negative

"I did it because I want to destroy Dariyabar," Keket replied.

"But why?" Golnar was very surprised.

"Long ago," Keket began, "there were two genies, brothers. They had the misfortune to fall in love with the same young girl. One, in an attempt to gain an advantage over the other, entrapped his brother in a bottle, and threw it into the sea. After some days the bottle washed up on this shore, and was found by an adventuring prince named Sinbad, who was in the process of building this city, and this kingdom. He released the genie from the bottle, and to revenge himself upon his brother, the genie showed Sinbad the beautiful girl. One look and the prince was in love. The genie brought this girl to the prince. She loved him, and so they were wed. The other genie, learning of this turn of fate, was about to revenge himself on them all when he discovered that his magic was gone. *Stolen!* Furious at losing the girl as well as his magic, he flew into a temper, and burst into a thousand pieces. He was my father, Golnar. All my siblings since have been told this story in order that one day our family might wreak their revenge upon Dariyabar. You, and your prince, were to be my tools," Keket said.

"What happened to the other genie?" Golnar asked. "The one that helped Sinbad?"

Keket shrugged. "It doesn't matter," she said.

"If you believe that magic was involved in what has happened, mother, could not your father's brother yet be involved in Dariyabar?" Golnar questioned. "What was his name?"

"Kansbar," Keket said, and her look was thoughtful. "Golnar, my daughter, you have never been particularly clever, but perhaps in your curious innocence you have discovered something. It would take a genie with truly great magic to protect Dariyabar, to transport your prince to Kava, and to strengthen the sultan's life force. Kansbar, if it is indeed him, would have that magic because he has his brother's magic as well. I cannot fight such powers. You must outwit this genie, whoever he is, if you are to help me destroy Dariyabar and avenge your grandfather. The sultan will die within the month. Even the most powerful necromancer cannot maintain a life that has come to its end."

"But then this Amir Khan will be sultan!" Golnar began to weep.

"*You must seduce him!*" her mother said. "And then you must seduce General Sabola as well. We will make certain that both men know that the other is using you. They are certain to quarrel, particularly if you tell each of them that the other forced you. These human warriors are so noble. With luck, Amir Khan and Sabola will kill each other. Without its sultan, Dariyabar is lost. They will not listen to a woman, and so the princess will have no influence. With no one to rule its empire, Dariyabar will collapse. It is a simple and foolproof plan," Keket concluded.

"But what of this other genie?" Golnar asked.

"The genie will have no interest in you, Golnar," her mother told her. "It will be over and done with by the time anyone realizes what is happening. Even the most powerful genie cannot bring a man back to life, my daughter. Dariyabar cannot do without its sultan, and there will be no sultan." Keket smiled, and arose from the chaise where she had been sprawled. "I must leave you, Golnar. Do as I have instructed you, and destroy Dariyabar for your family. You will be well rewarded for your success, I promise you, and you shall never have to worry about yourself again." Keket bent, and kissed her daughter upon her forehead. "Farewell, my dear. Call me if you need me." She began to dissolve into a deep purple smoke that grew paler and paler until what was left of it made its way back into the alabaster vial. When she was gone, Golnar corked the vial, and lay down upon her bed to consider what her mother had told her.

It was all well and good for Keket to say she would be the instrument of Dariyabar's downfall, but she had not her mother's magic, Golnar thought. All she had ever wanted was to be the mother of Dariyabar's next sultan so she might have power. Now she was expected to seduce the khan and his general, and bring Dariyabar to its destruction? And what of this genie that had all that power, and might very well be guarding the kingdom? Haroun was gone, and was unlikely to ever return. *I need to think of myself,* Golnar considered. *I still might be the mother of the next sultan, if I can seduce Amir Khan into my bed.*

It was a tempting thought, and a little smile played about Golnar's lush lips. *I do not want to destroy Dariyabar. I want to rule it from behind the sultan's throne. Zuleika is beautiful, but I am just as beautiful. No man is ever completely content with just one woman. That is why princes and sultans have harems. Even my merchant father had a small harem.*

I must bide my time, and make certain that I am not sent from the palace. Tomorrow, I will go to the sultan and beg his forgiveness for causing such a scene today. And I will beg the princess' forgiveness too. Her heart is good, for all she is fierce and proud. Haroun always said it was so. I wonder if the feasting is over yet? She went to her windows, drew back the curtains, and opened the latticed shutters. She could hear music from the banqueting hall. They were still celebrating. She wondered if the brides and their husbands were still in the hall, or if they had retired to their nuptial beds. Yes, tomorrow she must make amends for her hysterical outburst. Golnar lay down on her bed. She thought about Haroun being whipped, and the thought was satisfying. She wished it were she who might wield that whip.

In the morning, Golnar awoke to her bodyslave knocking upon her door. Irritated with herself for forgetting she had locked the portal, she arose and opened it.

"Ohh, mistress, I was so fearful for you!" her slavewoman cried, and kissed her hand.

"Not so fearful that you disappeared last evening," Golnar snapped. "Word of my removal from the sultan's hall of audience must have traveled even more swiftly than the wind, for when I returned to the harem there was no one in evidence. The place might well have been deserted! Fearing for my life, I locked myself in my bedchamber. Go to the baths, and tell them I am ready for my morning ablutions."

"Yes, mistress," the slave replied, and scurried off.

In the baths, the slaves were silent as Golnar entered. They tended to her efficiently, and without their usual chatter. Like the prince's favorite, they had no idea what would happen now that Haroun had disappeared and the princess had returned triumphant with her khan. They dared offend no one until it was decided what was to happen.

Golnar was silent also as she was bathed, massaged, and oiled. She had to consider carefully how to remain within the palace. She was not a slave, at least. Haroun had seen her, and admired her, and asked her father for her as his concubine. Her father could not refuse, and was encouraged by his favorite wife to see that Golnar was brought to the palace as if she were a bride. The women had never particularly liked Golnar, but becoming the prince's concubine could but bring honor and glory to her husband's family. Now with Haroun gone, there was no excuse for her to remain unless she was asked. To be returned to her father's house, even with honor, was unthinkable!

She returned to her quarters, and ordered her servants to dress her carefully in sky blue silk robes. Her silver hair was dressed with small, fragrant flowers sewn to silver ribbons. Then she went to find the sultan. He was with the vizier, Abd al Hakim, but hearing she was at his door, Sultan Ibrahim told his guards to allow her to pass.

Golnar threw herself at his feet, and taking the hem of his red silk robe in her hand, kissed it.

"My lord! My lord! I beg your forgiveness for my behavior yesterday. You must understand that the great love I bear my lord Haroun precipitated my outburst. I did not realize that the princess was being wed. I am so ashamed if I spoiled her day. I hope you will forgive me, my lord sultan." She did not look at him, and kept her head bent low.

Neither the sultan nor his vizier were fools, but they were also men with daughters, and their hearts were good.

"Arise, my dear lady Golnar," the sultan said. "You have my forgiveness. I know your love for my nephew."

She stood, and there were tears in her light eyes. "Is there . . . is there any word?" she quavered in a voice filled with emotion.

The sultan shook his white head. "I am sorry, my dear. It is as if the earth opened up and swallowed him. Still we are searching every corner of the city, and the kingdom."

"Should I return to my father's house, my lord sultan?" Golnar asked him. It was a bold move, and one that could easily backfire on her.

"I have not given up hope, my child," the old man said. "Until we know for certain what has happened to my nephew, you will remain in your harem as you always have. It would not do for Haroun to come home and discover that you were missing, now would it?" He took her plump hand in his, and patted it in fatherly fashion.

"Ohh, thank you, my lord sultan!" Golnar cried, the relief in her voice palpable. She bowed low to the sultan, and asking his permission withdrew from his presence.

"Are you really unknowing of Haroun's whereabouts?" the vizier, Abd al Hakim, asked the sultan.

"I am indeed, and I expect I do not want to know," the sultan answered his old friend. "Zuleika has promised me that they have not killed him, but also that he will not return. If I sent Golnar back to her father's house now, it would appear that I knew something, and actually I do not. Nor do I wish to know."

"With your health so wonderfully restored," Abd al Hakim

said, "you will reign over Dariyabar for many more years, my lord."

"No, old friend, I will not. My health has been returned to me for but a single cycle of the moon. My miraculous restoration began on the first day of the new moon. When that moon wanes into the darkness, I will die. This I know, for the genie told Zuleika it was so."

"Then you mean to make the khan your successor," the vizier said.

"I do. Who else is there? And at least my blood will flow in the sultans that follow Amir, as will his. He is a strong man."

"If your days are numbered, my lord, when will you announce this change in succession?" the vizier wondered. "If you say it too soon, there will be those who will wonder if you yourself did not dispose of your nephew."

"I know, and since I am unique in the knowledge that when I lie down to sleep on the last day of the waning moon I shall not awaken in this world, I shall make my announcement in the week before I die."

"There will be some then who will believe that the khan has had a hand in your death when you leave us," the vizier noted.

"There will always be those who believe that every coincidence is a conspiracy, my friend. It is human nature to see plots where there are none. You have been my vizier long enough to know that."

The vizier chuckled. "Too true, my friend. Too true. And you will leave the problem of Golnar to the next sultan, then?"

Now it was the sultan who laughed. "I think it better that I do, don't you?"

"The princess will not be pleased," Abd al Hakim said.

"My daughter will manage, nonetheless. She has, by a quirk of fate, been given a good husband. He is a strong man, and while he may listen to her advice, for she is wise, he will be the sole ruler of Dariyabar," Sultan Ibrahim said.

"For now I think both our daughters will revel in their lust with these men they have wed," the vizier chuckled. "Ahhh, to be that young, and full of love's juices once again. Bahira can scarcely keep her hands from her general, and the looks that the princess casts in her husband's direction are fiery."

And they were. The entire court had seen last evening how Zuleika of Dariyabar felt about the tall barbarian now her legal mate.

She could scarcely wait to leave the hall, and several times attempted to do so, but Amir Khan had prevented her, catching her hand hard, smiling at her and murmuring, "Not yet, my princess." Finally she had decided that if she left him, he would certainly follow.

"I am going to our apartments," she whispered softly. "Come to me as soon as you can," and she nipped at his earlobe.

"I will come when I can, Zuleika. There are many men here of great importance to Dariyabar whom I must meet. You know what is to come, but they do not, and I would have them our friends," the khan told his wife. Then he turned away from her to speak with a wealthy merchant of the city.

Zuleika decided that she was offended. This was their wedding night. Their real wedding night. There would be no amusing sexual games with Bahira and Sabola. Tonight they would be together, and have the leisure to enjoy each other. *And he preferred to remain in the hall to chatter with merchants?* He would pay for that insult, she decided silently to herself. She walked slowly through the hallways of the palace to her own apartments.

Rafa greeted her, her look questioning. "Where is the khan?"

"In the banquet hall talking with the city's men of business," Zuleika responded, her tone distinctly annoyed.

Rafa considered a moment, and then she said, "He is wise to do so. When he is sultan one day, he will need their cooperation."

"Any other time but tonight," Zuleika replied. "This is our wedding night! And do not tell me that I have already tasted pleasures at his hands, that is not the point. *This is our wedding night!*"

"You are a grown woman now, my princess," Rafa said. "You will be our sultana one day. You must think of Dariyabar."

"Do not presume to tell me my duty towards Dariyabar, Rafa," Zuleika snapped. "I have done my duty toward this kingdom always and ever. *But this is my wedding night!* Go now, and leave me to myself. I do not need you to find my lonely bed."

Rafa bowed, and departed. It was always better to take Zuleika at her word when she got like this.

Alone, the princess looked about, and decided that she would bathe in her private bath. She shrugged her gown from her body where she stood. Rafa would pick it up in the morning. She walked naked to her bathing room, filled the sea sponge with fragrant liquid soap, and washed herself. Next she rinsed herself in the marble shell basin beneath the fish spigots, finally descending into her bathing pool. She felt calmer now, but she was still angry. Well, had she herself not told him she was the key to Dariyabar? He had possessed himself of the key, and now he had what he had fought for for three years. He had Dariyabar. Her father would be dead by the end of the moon's cycle. She looked through the pale cream and gold marble pillars separating her bathing room from her gardens, and saw the thin crescent in the sky.

Each day the moon grew fatter brought her closer to losing her father. Would it not have been better if he had died several nights ago? At least then he would be safely with her mother, and she would not have to bear this eternity of waiting. Ibrahim had always favored her brothers, but she knew now that her father admired and respected her even if she was a female. And he had always been good to her. It was something to remember, and it was a good memory. She floated lazily in her bathing pool, her long, dark ebony hair streaming out behind her.

But she would not be just a sultana. She knew everything that there was to know about Dariyabar, and its history. Amir Khan had to listen to her, and at least consider her advice. She would not be an ornament, or a creature to be appreciated only for the pleasure she could give him. She was far more intelligent than her brothers had been, and she was equal in intelligence to the khan. Why were men so stubborn? Sabola wasn't that difficult. He had departed the banqueting hall with Bahira early. *But Sabola is not to be the next sultan,* a small voice murmured in her head. "The Gods!" Zuleika swore. She hated that little voice, especially when it was right.

"May I join you?"

Zuleika turned her head in the direction of her husband's voice. "Have you concluded your business, my lord?" she said, half-angrily.

"I have," he calmly replied. He went about washing himself in an efficient manner, rinsed, and then dove into the bathing pool, surfacing next to her. "I am surprised that you do not understand the importance of what I was doing tonight," he began.

Zuleika's feet hit the marble bottom of the bathing pool, and she whirled about to face the khan. "I understand everything, my lord! Given the brief time we have for you to soothe the citizens of my city before my father dies, you must make the most of your time. *But this is our wedding night!* Could you not have waited until tomorrow?"

"Now, my princess," he began, almost laughing at the look of pure outrage on her beautiful face, "the opportunity was there to show the merchants and ship owners of Dariyabar that I am not a barbarian, though you have all called me thus. They needed to know that I understand the various elements that make up their great trade. That my main goal in attacking the city was merely to gain an entry to the sea and that trade. They needed to understand that I am not a monster, that I love and adore their princess," he finished with a mischievous smile.

"Do not try to wheedle me, Amir!" she grumbled at him.

"But, my princess, who else is there for me to wheedle?" he teased her, and reaching out, he pulled her resisting form against his.

"I hate you," she said, half-heartedly.

"No, you don't," he replied.

"So you love me?" she said, and began to melt at the pressure of his thighs and his belly on her thighs and belly.

"From the first moment I saw you," he confessed.

"Indeed?" she replied.

"I am an impulsive man," he told her. "You do not yet love me, my princess, but in time you will. You are a careful woman who must consider the entire issue before you will commit yourself, or in this particular case, your heart."

It startled her that he should know her so well after only three days. "You are arrogant, and you presume far too much," she responded, and pulling away from him swam to the steps of the pool and stood up, looking back at him a moment. Slowly she ascended the marble steps, the droplets of water gleaming like diamonds on her beautiful lithe body. "It is possible that I just might forgive your behavior tonight," she told him, drying herself off. "You have pleased me in the past. It is possible you may do so again, my lord."

He chuckled. "Now, my princess, who is being naughty?"

Zuleika ignored his remark, and picked up a crystal flask containing a thick pale green cream. "You will rub me with this lotion," she said, and turning, moved slowly back into her bedchamber.

He quickly dried himself with a length of toweling, and then followed her. She was already lying upon her belly. A warm breeze, scented with damask roses and lilies, blew through the silk gauze draperies that hung between the marble pillars through which he viewed a walled garden. There was the song of a nightingale coming from that garden. Straddling her, he used her delightful and provocative bottom as a seat. Uncorking the crystal vial, he watched as the pale green cream coated its sides, finally pouring itself out into his palm. He set the container aside on the ebony table. Then rubbing his two hands together to distribute the fragrant cream, he began to massage her with slow strokes of his big hands.

"Ummm, that is quite satisfactory," she murmured as those hands swept up the long line of her back and over her shoulders.

"Just satisfactory?" he mocked her. Then he continued to massage her until all the cream in his hands had been worked into her pale skin. Now he reversed his position, and poured more cream into his hand. Distributing the lotion between his hands a second time, he began to massage her round buttocks with an expertise that frankly surprised her. His supple fingers dug into her flesh.

"Ohhh, yes!" Zuleika said. She could feel her desires beginning to rouse themselves. "You have obviously done this before, my lord?"

He smiled, but said nothing, instead going on to massage each of her long legs in its turn with the spicy liquid. Now he turned about once more, pushing her wet hair from her graceful neck and pressing little kisses upon the damp skin. He poured more cream, and rubbed each of her arms, her hands and long fingers.

"*Amir?*"

"Yes, my princess?" he answered in dulcet tones.

"I think you can cease now," she said. Her voice was almost a squeak, and she could not prevent herself from wriggling about though she tried. When she had started this she had not anticipated how exciting it would be. She was quivering with her desire.

"You want me to cease now, my princess?" he replied in innocent tones. His hands slipped beneath her to seize her perfect round breasts. Then he pinched the nipples hard, enjoying her gasp of surprise as he did so. Now he stretched his length to cover her body with his own. Tenderly he nipped at the nape of her neck. "You are a wicked little tease, Zuleika," he told her.

"If you think to discourage me with your anger, you have but succeeded in arousing me." He nipped softly at her neck again.

Zuleika shuddered as tiny flames of desire began to lick at her. This wasn't turning out the way she had planned it. *"Amir!"*

For all her schooling in the erotic arts, she had no real experience other than that he and Sabola had given her. The lovely vessel that was her body was filling to overflowing with lust for him. He had heard the plea in her voice although he suspected that she had not meant it as one. He rolled off her, and then reaching out, turned her over onto her back. Her exquisitely perfect breasts rose and fell with her emotion. He gazed down at her, smiling at her closed eyes. Then his dark head bent to capture a pert nipple. He caressed it with his tongue, encircling it over and over and over again until she was moaning softly with her open longing. He moved to her other breast now while a hand fondled the breast he had just left.

Zuleika was astounded to find how sensitive her breasts were. She would not yield easily to him, however. Reaching out, she tangled her slim fingers into his thick black hair, and yanked him from her breast. "You must kiss me!" she demanded of him, and her now open violet eyes met his gaze.

He laughed softly. "With pleasure, little princess," he said, and his lips took fierce possession of hers. Their tongues fought a battle to fill each other's mouths. Hers battled his with skill and newfound cunning. She could not be subdued, and she brought quick hot fire into his loins.

She sank her teeth into his shoulder, laughing when he swore softly. She moved provocatively, whispering wickedly in his ear, *"Now, my lord, Amir! Now!"*

"No!" he said. She was the princess of Dariyabar, and key to her kingdom, but by the gods, he was the khan of khans, and he would rule her in their bed.

She thrust her pelvis up at him.

"No!" he repeated, and turning her over swiftly, he gave her several spanks on her buttocks before rolling her back to face

him. "Passion should be savored, Zuleika, and not hurried."
He shifted his body in order to put his head between her milky
thighs. His fingers pushed the tender pinkish flesh apart, and
his mouth fastened on the delicate bud of her womanhood.
Then he began to suckle upon it.

Zuleika gasped with surprise, but she was not displeased by
his actions. He was unleashing delights within her body that
sent her gasping for air. The waves of heat came quickly in ex-
plosions of rapture that caused her to consider she might be
dying. "Amir! Oh, Amir! It is too sweet. *Too sweet!*"

There was a tone in her voice that alerted him that he
might be driving her too far. She was not really that experienced in passion. He stopped, and pulling himself up again,
covered her body with his own. "Zuleika, my love! My own
true heart!" He murmured the soft words of low passion into
her little ear even as he plunged deeply into her burning flesh.
He thrust hard, slowly, slowly until she was almost weeping
in his embrace. "Tell me you love me," he murmured to her.
"Tell me!"

Her arms went about him, holding him tightly. Her breasts
flattened against his smooth chest. She pretended that she had
not heard him, and he was wise enough not to press her further.

Then together they found a perfect rhythm. Their passions
drove them higher and higher until together they finally found
a nirvana far above that of the gods. They clung to each other
in that perfect little world of exquisite rapture. And then, since
paradise is not permitted humankind, they descended in a rush
that left them both half-conscious and breathless. When they
came to themselves once again, Zuleika found herself wrapped
in Amir's arms, her cheek against his chest. Beneath the flesh
she could hear the strong beat of his great heart.

"I do love you, princess of Dariyabar," he told her.

"But you do not understand me," Zuleika said. "You love
my body, and the pleasure that we can give each other, but do
you respect me as an intellect, Amir? Can you listen to my

judgment, and weigh it carefully before making a decision? I do not know if I can be satisfied just to be a trophy for you."

"What would you be, then?" he asked quietly.

"If you are to rule Dariyabar successfully, Amir, then we must be equal partners. I need no public acclaim, but what do you really know of my country but that you wanted it because it provided Khanistan with a window to the sea, and beyond? You have no great cities in your land, Amir. Your people live a different life than mine live. You cannot make decisions for Dariyabar based simply on your own experience. You need mine as well."

"We are herdsmen and warriors, it is true," he agreed, "but does not common sense apply equally on the steppes as well as in the city, Zuleika?"

"If you are dealing with cattle, perhaps," she said with a smile, "but you cannot treat the merchants of Dariyabar as you would your cattle, Amir. I will gladly teach you the language of diplomacy that you will need to be a good sultan. My father rarely made a decision that he did not consider in private first. I have learned much from him."

"Yet he favored his sons over his daughter," the khan said shrewdly.

"Yes," she admitted, "he did, but it did not keep him from despairing over Cyrus, Asad and Jahi. Like you, they were warriors. My father has in the past year come to rely upon me, and upon Abd al Hakim, Bahira's father. You must do the same, Amir."

"I had thought to make Sabola my vizier," he said.

She shook her head at him. "Nay, keep Bahira's father as your vizier. You need Sabola to lead the armies. You will not be content to sit here in Dariyabar. You will go forth, this time across the sea, to find and conquer new lands. You need Sabola by your side. Besides, he has no real administrative experience in the government of any country."

He nodded. "You are indeed clever, my wife," he told her.

"And I will come to love you, Amir," she said softly.

He smiled down into her violet eyes. "I think you probably will," he replied.

"So arrogant," she laughed up at him.

"So haughty," he chuckled down at her.

"You spanked me before," she said, remembering.

"I did," he answered her with a grin. "You were being most recalcitrant, and I must be master in our bed, princess of Dariyabar."

Suddenly she was astride his chest, and laughing at the look of surprise upon his face. "And I shall be mistress!" she told him.

His look grew serious, and then he said, "Yes, Zuleika, my princess of Dariyabar, you shall, for I can love no other."

"It is a grave vow you make, my lord," she answered him.

"I know," he responded. "Trust me always, Zuleika, and I swear that I shall never fail you. Believe in me, my darling, and I will trust in your judgment though it be difficult for me to accept the council of a woman. I shall, nonetheless, for I adore you!"

Her look was equally sober. "Do not say these things to me, Amir, if you cannot keep your promises. I will forgive much in you, but never will I forgive betrayal. As I will be loyal to you, so must you be loyal to me."

He drew her down into his embrace. "Then we are agreed, my darling princess of Dariyabar. I shall love you always, and be ever faithful." His lips brushed hers softly. "What vow will you make me?"

She smiled now into his dark eyes. "That I will always be faithful to you, my lord. *And that I will love you too.*" Then she kissed him passionately, and Amir Khan knew in that instant that he had found a treasure beyond all price.

Chapter Six

For centuries Kansbar, the genie who protected Dariyabar, had considered who his enemy might be. An enemy who worked subtly and skillfully to destroy all that his first master, Prince Sinbad, had built. Now he knew. Keket, his own niece. She had been but an infant when his brother had entrapped Kansbar in his bottle and thrown it into the sea. Unfortunately, like her father, Keket believed what she chose to believe, neglecting the truth that stared her directly in the face. *And Golnar was her daughter.* Keket would not take lightly that chosen child's betrayal.

Poor Golnar. Her heritage was as much magic as it was human, but other than love potions, elixirs, and creams to preserve her great beauty, she knew nothing, nor did she understand. Her human heritage would eventually take over entirely. Golnar wanted power. Knowing she could gain it by using her body, she was fully prepared to do so. Not to destroy Dariyabar, but to have it for herself. She was quite a simple creature. He had long ago sworn to protect this kingdom. They were bound together as one entity. He would not fail in his duty even if it meant using this foolish child of his vengeful niece to gain the victory. But, he would protect Golnar from her mother's wrath. The girl was more to be pitied than scorned.

Kansbar had the ability to appear outside of his bowl, and now he did so, almost filling the bedchamber where the princess and her husband lay sleeping, their arms about each other. For a brief moment he allowed himself to be touched by the sight of them, but then his voice boomed out, "Awake, Zuleika and Amir! Awake!"

His voice fiercely penetrated their dreams. The couple awoke, sitting up against the pillows and staring surprised at him.

"Kansbar, I do not believe I have never seen you outside of your bowl," Zuleika remarked. "You are a most impressive genie."

"You have grown too used to thinking of me as small, my princess. The time has come for you to see that my power, as well as my great size, are related. What you see is but half the size I can attain, for your chamber constricts me. My lord Amir, are you quite awake now?"

"Will you always disturb us at our slumbers, Kansbar?" the khan asked, half-amused.

"Only in moments of danger, my lord khan," the genie replied respectfully, "and danger is near, in the presence of Golnar."

"Do you see?" Zuleika demanded of her husband. "Did I not warn you that the bitch would be a thorn in our heel?"

Kansbar actually laughed, and the sound shook the very rafters of the chamber. "You are jealous, my princess. You should be. The wicked wench means to seduce the khan, and bear his heir, thus supplanting you and any child you would have. I have discovered this night that Golnar has a magical heritage which might help her in her nefarious plot, had I not learned of it."

"I will kill her myself!" Zuleika declared. "I will slit her throat from ear to ear! Then I will drink her blood!"

Again, Kansbar laughed. "Which is stronger, my princess? Your desire to protect Dariyabar, or your jealous love for the khan?"

"*Both!*" Zuleika cried, but she blushed at her bold admission.

The genie chuckled knowingly. "For now, you love him more," he told her, "but that will pass. You will never, I know, betray Dariyabar. It is *your* son who will inherit one day. *Your blood, the blood of Sinbad* that will flow in the veins of future sultans of Dariyabar."

"And my blood," the khan interjected.

"Oh, yes, mighty khan, your blood as well, but not the blood of Golnar, daughter of my niece who is half-genie, and half-fairy. Hear now my story, for it has been many centuries since I have told it, or anyone has known of it, or remembered it. Long ago my brother fell in love with a mortal princess, but she was afraid of him. She did not love him in return. This princess begged my help and I gave it to her, keeping her safe from my brother. He, however, mistakenly believed that I too was in love with this fair mortal. He thought that if I was no longer in his way, the princess would love him. So he entrapped me in a bottle, threw it into the sea, and imprisoned the princess in his palace. The gods, however, were with me. I floated within a relatively short time up onto this shore where I was found and released by Prince Sinbad. I offered him three wishes in exchange for my freedom."

"I have always wondered what he wished for," Zuleika interrupted.

Kansbar actually smiled with the memory. "He was a most unusual mortal. For his first wish, he asked me to build him a city right there upon the seashore. I did. His second wish was for a fleet of merchant ships, for he knew that wealth and prosperity were the key to his city's success. I granted him his desire, and waited anxiously for his third wish. I expected him to ask for gold, or other riches in abundance, but instead he requested that I remain always as the guardian of Dariyabar, keeping it safe from its enemies and remaining a friend to his descendants. I could not refuse him. I am bound by my sacred oath, an oath all genies take when their powers are granted to them.

"I realized, however, that my prince must take a wife, and sire an heir. In his dreams I brought him the princess that my brother coveted. They fell in love. So I transported her on a magic flying carpet from my brother's palace to Dariyabar, where they were married, and lived happily ever after. But my brother, still believing that I had stolen the princess for myself, complained to the Great Genie, who is lord over us all. The Great Genie listened to his tale, and then asked for mine. When he learned that my brother had imprisoned me in a bottle and thrown it into the sea, the Great Genie became enraged. It is against our own laws to act against a fellow genie in so cruel a manner. To punish my brother, the Great Genie took back his powers. My brother, embittered, told our family that *I* had stolen his powers after escaping from the bottle in which he had imprisoned me. My niece, Keket, who is half-fairy, grew up believing this. It is her daughter, Golnar, raised in her mortal father's household, who is to be the instrument for my brother's family's revenge in the manner in which I have told you."

"Then Golnar must die," Zuleika said.

"No," Kansbar replied. "She is my own blood. I cannot allow it, but instead, listen to my plan. The khan will appear to fall into her trap. He will go to her bed, and when he has had his pleasure of her, Sabola will follow him, *and then* one hundred hand-picked men from the khan's troops will enjoy Golnar's favors. Neither the khan nor his general will conceive a child with her. That, I promise you both. But Golnar will indeed bear a child from that night of lustful delights and diversions. Whose child it is she will never know, but it will not be either the khan's, or his general's.

"And after that night she will be sent from Dariyabar as wife to a merchant of Samarkhan. She will seduce him. He will believe the child is his. He is childless, and will welcome a son or a daughter to bear his name. Golnar wants but riches and power, unlike her mother, who seeks revenge. I shall give this daughter of my niece what she so desperately desires, and protect her from Keket."

"But will your niece be satisfied that you have thwarted her, Kansbar? Will she be content to leave Dariyabar in peace at last?" the khan asked the genie.

"In the matter of my niece," the genie answered, "I must go to the Great Genie, and seek his advice. Keket and her daughter are the last of my brother's descendants."

"I don't know why my husband must allow himself to be seduced by that wretched girl," Zuleika grumbled, glaring at the protector of Dariyabar. "Why not just send her off with this merchant?"

"Golnar must be disabused of any notion that her child can rule Dariyabar," the genie said. "She is a sensual female. Once she has attained her goal, or believes she has, it will not be difficult to introduce her to a night of a hundred lovers," the genie said.

"Nonsense! You seek to break her spirit, Kansbar! You seek to convince her that she has entertained so many randy cocks that she cannot be certain who her child's sire is! You want her grateful to have a rich merchant as a husband. You will, I have not a doubt, point out to her the advantages of giving this man a son, and ruling his household. You will appeal to her vanity, her greed, and her lust for power. But why do you need my husband and Sabola for your plan?" Zuleika demanded.

"She must be lulled into complacency, my princess, and only the khan can do that. I am sorry, but it must be as I have told you if we are to succeed."

"We might watch together from a balcony while my soldiers use her," the khan suggested softly, licking the delicate curve of his wife's dainty ear. "You would like that, Zuleika, wouldn't you? You will see your revenge against this bold creature, and enjoy it." He kissed the ear.

"Yes," Zuleika murmured softly. "Yes! I should enjoy seeing her take a thousand cocks into her lover's bower." Her violet eyes were alight with the thought, and the khan realized that he had not considered that his wife had a streak of cruelty in her, but she did. Or was it merely her jealousy?

The genie's dark eyes met those of the khan. Kansbar smiled knowingly, as if he could read Amir's thoughts. "Complete this thing swiftly," he told the man who would soon be his master. "Have it done before Sultan Ibrahim leaves this earth." Then he was gone in a puff of smoke, and a faint rumble of thunder.

"I hate this plan!" Zuleika said.

Amir Khan pushed her back amid the pillows. His big lean body covered hers, and he pushed his hard rod into her love sheath slowly. "But you will obey, my beautiful wife, because it is for Dariyabar, will you not?" He had been very aroused picturing in his mind's eye the clever genie's plan. He moved on his wife and, her eyes closing, she moaned with the pleasure his entry and subsequent actions were giving her.

"Yes, my lord," she murmured her promise.

He thrust hard and quickly into her willing body. "Yes, my lord, and *my master!*" he growled.

She tightened her muscles about his length, feeling a burst of satisfaction when he groaned in response. "I hear, and I obey, *my lord and my master,*" she whispered in his ear, biting down upon the lobe.

"*Bitch!*" he hissed, moving more swiftly upon her.

Her nails raked down his long back. Her slim legs wrapped tightly about his waist. She was soaring. "Ahh, you devilish barbarian, I am yours! Do not stop! *Do not stop!*"

And together they found nirvana.

In the morning, Amir Khan explained to his general the plan that the genie had devised. The general grinned wolfishly.

"While I surely love my wife," he said, "I shall not object to having a little taste of that princely treasure. Do you want me to choose the others? What criteria would you have?"

"Those who are loyalest, most deserving, and especially those with big cocks. Let us give Golnar an experience she will not soon forget. One that will sustain her on the long nights she will have with her elderly merchant," the khan chuckled. "Do not, however, pick men who are cruel to their women. I do not want her harmed. Just well satisfied."

Sabola laughed. "After a night such as she will have, I expect she will be very well satisfied," he chortled. "When shall this event take place, my lord khan?"

"Tonight," Amir Khan replied. "The sooner, the better. I do

not want to give Zuleika time to reconsider this matter any more than she already has. Nor will Bahira be pleased, I expect. So let us get it over and done with quickly, before our wives cause difficulty. I trust the genie, for he has guarded Dariyabar for centuries. While he feels a certain loyalty to his niece's child, his own loyalties to Dariyabar are greater. Of this I am certain."

"Then I will go now to choose the men who will join us," the general said, and left the khan.

Amir went almost immediately to Golnar's harem, entering it unchallenged, for it was he would rule after the sultan's death. The guards at the doors to the harem were aware of it. The eyes of the two dozen or more women were immediately upon him. He smiled at them, and said, "You need have no fear, ladies. You will all be well taken care of, I promise you. Where is the lady Golnar?"

An older servant came forward. "She is in her own chamber, my lord khan. Shall I take you to her?"

"Lead on," he replied, and followed the woman across the main room of the harem, down a narrow hallway to its end, where the servant opened a door and beckoned him inside. Golnar was seated upon a marble bench having her long silvery-blond hair brushed by a slave girl. "Your tresses are the most beautiful color I have ever seen, Golnar," the khan told her with a smile. Then he took the brush from the slave, dismissing her and the older woman. "Let me brush your glorious hair, lady."

"*I knew that you would come,*" Golnar whispered when they were at last alone. She leaned her head back to meet his dark gaze.

"Did you?" His tone was amused. He set the brush down next to her upon the bench. "Why?"

"I saw how you looked at me in the hall, my lord. Do you desire me, my lord? Prince Haroun always said I was the most desirable of women. He said he had never seen a girl as beautiful as I am."

"My wife is beautiful," the khan noted.

"But her passion is for Dariyabar, my lord. It will never be as great for you as it is for Dariyabar," Golnar murmured, and then she turned so she might brush his lips with her own. "If you were my lord and master, I should think of none other but you." Her pointed little pink tongue flicked out, and around the shape of his mouth. "If I were yours, my lord, you would be my very reason for existence."

Her perfume was lush and heavy. Her words were tempting in their meaning. He realized in that moment what a truly dangerous woman Golnar was. Any small guilt that had niggled at the back of his mind was now dispelled. He would enjoy taking her, then allowing Sabola and their men to have their pleasure of her. He put an arm about her supple waist, and pulled her close. "I will be sultan when Ibrahim dies," he said. "He has already told me that whatever I desire in Dariyabar is mine, Golnar. I need not even ask. My wife is passionate, and a most satisfying lover; but a man of my stature craves variety. I think that your prince will not return, Golnar."

"I believe, my lord, that you are correct," Golnar answered him. Her heavy, thick gold eyelashes brushed her cheek, feigning modesty. "Do you think you might *crave* me, my lord?" she murmured softly.

In reply he stood up, and his hands fastening about her waist, he lifted her so that she was standing upon the marble bench. "Remove your garment, Golnar."

For a moment she looked at him, surprised.

"Obedience is the first trait I look for in a lover," he told her. "When I command you, you will obey."

"Yes, my lord," Golnar replied, and loosening the ties on her garment she let it drop.

He walked slowly about the bench, observing her carefully. She was small, and well-rounded, but exquisitely well proportioned. "Put your hands beneath your breasts, and display them to me," he said.

Immediately she obeyed, slipping her hands beneath her full

bosom and lifting her breasts for his viewing. Haroun had never treated her like this, she thought, excited. Haroun had been soft. This man was a dominant conqueror.

Reaching out, he pinched a nipple hard, and she squealed. He smiled, almost cruelly. "Remove your hands from your breasts. Use them to draw your nether lips apart, Golnar, that I may view your hidden assets," he ordered her.

She was again shocked, but quickly complied, catching her breath sharply as a single finger reached out, first to touch her love bud, and then begin to rub it assertively. Her eyes glazed as the pad of his finger began to obtain the desired effect. "Oh, my lord," she gasped, "how good it is. *Yes! Ohh, yes!*"

Now the khan pushed his fingers between her nether lips, and thrust three of the digits deep into her love sheath, moving them swiftly back and forth until Golnar's legs began to shake. Immediately he withdrew the fingers, licking them slowly and deliberately until no trace of her juices were left. "You will receive me tonight," he told her, and then turning abruptly, he left her.

Golnar fell to her knees upon the hard marble bench. She would be bruised, she knew, but she could not have dismounted the bench if she had tried. Never in all of her life had a man been so assertive with her. Men had lusted after her from the time she grew breasts. Her father's first wife feared that her sons would commit incest with their half-sister, so beautiful was Golnar. Men had always wanted her. Her beauty had ruled them, but not this man. This was a man who took what he wanted, *and he wanted her.* She would conceive his child this very night, and one day rule Dariyabar through her son.

Golnar called for her women. She must be prepared, and perfect for the khan when he came to her bed this night. She laughed aloud to think of the proud princess of Dariyabar who would one day have to give way to Golnar's son, the heir to the kingdom of Dariyabar. Then Golnar thought of her mother, Keket, and how angry she would be to learn that her daughter had betrayed her. But she would tell her mother that it would be better to destroy Dariyabar through Golnar's son. Certainly her mother could relish the thought of her grandson working to ruin the kingdom founded by the evil genie, and Prince Sinbad. And perhaps before that happened, her mother would die. Genies and fairies did not live forever, although mortals believed that they did.

Golnar's women came, and she excitedly told them that the khan would come to her bed this night. She must be perfectly prepared. They immediately set to work to make her even more beautiful than she already was. She was bathed. All superfluous hair was removed from her body. Her toenails and her fingernails were pared, and filed smooth. She was massaged with thick scented cream so that her lush body was soft and perfumed. Her love sheath was readied, an elderly woman flushing it out with perfumed water, and massaging her genitals and vulva with sweet oil. Her long hair was washed, and brushed dry, and then rubbed with silk until it took on the shine and texture of the material. Her teeth were cleaned, and her breath made sweet. She ate nothing lest she stink from her food, drinking but sips of iced water.

And then a servant came to say that the lady Golnar was to be conveyed to another apartment where she would await her lord and master. Her servants were overcome with excitement. Golnar herself was almost weak with the anticipation. She was tempted to tell her mother, calling her forth from the flask, but she refrained. She would tell her afterwards that she had stolen the khan from his wife. She climbed into the litter that had been sent for her, and allowed herself to be conveyed to her destiny, smiling benignly at her women as she was taken away.

The chamber to which she was brought was large and square. It had pale pink marble walls and a colonnade of delicate carved columns that rose to a balcony enclosing the entire room. The top of each pillar was gilded where a sheaf of feathers had been carved. There was but one piece of furniture in the room. Set in its center was a cream-colored marble dais upon which rested a great square bed, with neither a head nor a foot. It was covered in black silk.

"You are to give me your robe, lady, and await your master there," the servant said, pointing.

At first she was loath to disrobe before a male servant who was not a eunuch, but then she remembered that the khan demanded immediate obedience to his will. This was his order, and she would not question it. She removed her single gauze garment, and handed it to the man. He bowed without looking at her, and departed the room. Golnar set about arranging herself in the most pleasing position that she could imagine, for first impressions were very important. She did not have long to wait. He entered almost immediately. He was naked, and he was magnificent.

He gazed at her, a slightly amused smile upon his lips, and then he said in a hard voice, "Prepare my cock for its entry, Golnar."

She arose from the bed in a graceful fashion, and knelt before him to take his manhood into her mouth. She began to suckle upon him. When he was finally hard she licked his great length, and her facile little tongue encircled the head of his lance, staring into its single eye. "You are ready, my lord," she finally said. She could hardly wait to have him pierce her and fill her sheath. She arose, and then fell back upon the bed, her legs spread wide for him.

Again the tiny amused smile touched his lips, but did she detect scorn? No! That was impossible. He covered her dainty body with his own big one, and began to ream her fiercely. She had expected a little more delicacy, but then he was a barbarian, and he was having a quite marvelous effect upon her. "The Gods! The Gods!" she half-screamed as the first wave of pleasure began to overcome her. And then suddenly her mouth was filled with another cock. She gulped, and gasped.

"Do not bite him, or I shall flay the skin from your pretty bones, Golnar," the khan warned her. "We barbarians enjoy sharing our women, as I know you have been told. Now suckle

General Sabola as nicely as you did me, and he will fuck you as well. I could see that you were a woman who could use more than one sturdy cock, and tonight, my pet, you shall have a full hundred or more cocks fill this hot little maw of yours before the dawn tints the eastern skies."

She couldn't be hearing him aright, Golnar thought, and putting his words from her mind she concentrated upon tightening her vaginal muscles about his rampaging cock. He groaned, and she was pleased, but then he loosed his juices, and she was not ready. She cried out with her frustration, but the khan was rolling away from her, and his general was mounting her, thrusting and withdrawing, thrusting and withdrawing. She gasped with undisguised pleasure, realizing even as she did that with both men using her she would never know who her son's sire was, but suddenly Golnar didn't care, and then a third cock was being put into her mouth. She sucked eagerly upon it, her eyes going past the general's broad shoulder to the line of tall barbarians now entering the room.

They encircled the bed, and cheered their general onward. His passion peaked, and he leapt off Golnar, saying as he did so, "A bag of pearls to the first man who can make her come!" And the bed suddenly sagged with the weight of the men piling upon it, pulling Golnar this way and that in their quest to make her admit to her passion.

"Come, men," the khan called to them. "Take her in turn. Each of you has been well rewarded this night to follow in the path of not just a prince of Dariyabar, but in the path that Sabola and I have blazed for you. How many of you could have ever attained such noble cunt? Treat her well. I will not have her mistreated."

Now the barbarian soldiers grew more orderly, and once again lined up to take their turn with Golnar. They took her in every way that they could in the hours that followed. Some in an ordinary manner. And the first to breach her in a place that Golnar had never expected to entertain a manly cock elicited a shriek of surprise from her that caused those waiting their turn to laugh.

"She's a virgin here!" the young man with the slender manhood now well lodged in Golnar's bottom cried, delighted.

"Plug her well, lad, for others will surely follow you," one older soldier said, grinning.

And they did. Golnar could scarcely contain herself when she was taken at both ends by two young soldiers who first twisted her legs about and over their bodies, one fucking her hot cunt while the other took her bottom, his big hands squeezing her breasts as he grunted and thrust his manhood within her. Her lips became bruised with the kisses of her other lover. And her cries of delight echoed throughout the chamber as, one after another, the chosen soldiers of the khan took their pleasure with the lost prince of Dariyabar's favorite.

From the balcony above, Zuleika watched the erotic and compelling scene below her. Her violet eyes were alight with excitement, and her breath came in quick little pants. She had never considered watching as another woman was used by man after man. And particularly so many men.

"Are you enjoying the spectacle, my princess?" her husband asked, coming up behind her, pressing his big body against her as she leaned over the balustrade viewing the lustful activity below. His hands slipped around her to cup her breasts, and he tore away the slight fabric covering them, tweaking her nipples wickedly as he did so.

"It is thrilling," she admitted to him. "And Golnar seems none the worse for wear considering all the cocks that have so far probed her. Nor does she seem distressed by those to come." She ground her round buttocks into his groin teasingly.

The big hands squeezed her breasts, and he whispered in her ear, his breath hot and noisy, "You are going to be fucked, wife!"

"*Am I?*" she murmured back.

"Yes!" he groaned at her. His hands tore away the delicate fabric of her skirt. He bent her forward, and for a moment

Zuleika thought that she would fall into the mass of soldiers below, but her husband's strong hands grasped her hips as he thrust eagerly into her womanly sheath, moving himself back and forth until their cries mingled with those of Golnar and her lovers.

It was the most exciting thing she had ever done. Her own sheath was well ploughed even as she watched Golnar receiving the very same treatment. When he finally withdrew from her, he was yet hard. He took her in his arms and pushed her up against the marble wall of the balcony, commanding her to put her legs about his waist as he once more thrust into the hot swamp of her sex, groaning and straining with his need for her. Finally he was satisfied, but Zuleika could no longer stand, so her husband carried her from the balcony above the carnal room below to their own chamber, where she fell into a deep sleep. When she awoke she wondered if it had been a dream, but the khan assured her that it was not. And there was no way that Golnar could claim any child conceived the previous night was that of Amir Khan. They might have remained abed but for the shrieks that suddenly erupted from the harem.

Suddenly, the sky over the city of Dariyabar grew black with storm clouds. Lightning flashed, and great peals of thunder erupted. The palace itself shook and the sea beneath it roiled, its waves crashing over the sea walls angrily.

"Get the bowl!" the khan called to his wife.

Zuleika climbed on still-shaky legs from their bed, and fetched the golden bowl, calling to Kansbar as she did. The genie appeared quickly, but not within his bowl, rather within the room, part of him outside in the garden. His face was grim. "What is happening?" Zuleika begged him. "It sounds like the furies have been loosed in the city."

"My niece has obviously learned of her defeat, and is not taking it well," the genie said. He suddenly shrank to mortal size. "Come! We must save the poor foolish Golnar from her wrath." He ran from the chamber with the princess and the khan behind him.

The women of the harem were cowering in a single corner of the apartment when they entered it. Kansbar went directly to Golnar's quarters, entering them, and saying as he did, "Keket, daughter of Ja'fa, cease your rage, I command you!"

Keket whirled about, her beautiful face dark with anger. "Who are you to dare to order me about?" she demanded to know of him.

"I am your uncle, Kansbar, the genie of Dariyabar," he told her. "Why have you sought to destroy this kingdom?"

"You have stolen my father's magic," Keket cried, "and by doing so you rendered him mortal, and he died long before his time. I have vowed to revenge myself upon your creation, this kingdom of Dariyabar! And so I would have, had it not been for this lustful creature I spawned from the seed of a mortal. Even you, uncle, must be disgusted by her overwhelming humanity!"

"I did not steal Ja'fa's magic, niece. The Great Genie took it from him as punishment for his crimes, which were many. It was not just his attempt at vengeance upon his brother, a fellow genie, but against many others in the world of magic. My brother was a wicked man, Keket."

"I do not believe you!" she cried.

"I see that, like your father, you believe only what you wish to believe. You must be punished for your destructive behavior. Your magic is taken from you at the order of the Great Genie, and the Fairy Queen. You are henceforth mortal. Treat your daughter well, and perhaps she will take you in in your old age, for you are, Keket, an old woman now," Kansbar said.

"Noooo," Keket shrieked as she saw the look of horror upon Golnar's beautiful face. She looked down and saw her hands had grown withered and spotted. "Noooo!" she cried again, and then to their surprise Keket swelled up and burst into a thousand tiny pieces that disintegrated as they exploded into the air.

"What has happened to my mother?" Golnar cried.

"Amazing!" Kansbar said with admiration. "Somehow she

managed to destroy herself before all the magic drained from her soul. Can you but imagine what she might have accomplished if that force had been used for good? My poor niece." He shook his head. Then he turned to Golnar. "You are my brother's last descendant, Golnar, but you are more mortal than magic. You have conceived a child during your orgy last night, but it is neither the khan's nor his general's. It is the offspring of a common barbarian soldier. But because you are my brother's grandchild I will save you from your shame."

"*How?*" The query was short and sharp. Golnar gazed hard at the genie, who now seemed to be growing in size once again.

"First you must promise me that this quest for vengeance has ended with your mother's demise," the genie said.

"It was never my battle," Golnar said sullenly. I just wanted the wealth and power that the mother of Dariyabar's sultan would have, had I been that fortunate."

"I will give you wealth and power on a smaller scale," the genie said, "but you must leave Dariyabar in order to obtain it."

"*How?*" Again, the question was direct.

"There is a merchant of Samarkhan who has been here in the city for a year, but is now preparing to return to his home. I will make you his wife, Golnar, and give him the power to mount you most lustily for a brief time. He will believe the child you bear his own. It will be his only heir, for he has no others. He will treat you like the queen you sought to be. He is rich, and will, I promise you, grow richer with the passing years. That will be my gift to you, daughter of Keket. Will you accept it?"

She did not hesitate, but nodded in the affirmative. "I will, Great Uncle Kansbar, for that is your name, is it not? My mother told me that it was your name."

"It is," the genie said, so large now that he practically filled the entire room.

"May I take my possessions with me to my bridegroom? All the beautiful things that Prince Haroun gave me? And may I take my servants as well? A woman should not go to her husband without her servants and her possessions."

"I can see how well you loved my cousin," Zuleika murmured dryly at Golnar's pronouncement.

"I loved him every bit as much as he love me," Golnar responded. "Do you know where he is, princess?"

Zuleika nodded.

"Then you must surely know by now he has adjusted himself to his new surroundings, and has found himself another woman to love," Golnar said almost bitterly.

"At least you are free, and will have an honorable estate," the princess replied in return. "Poor Haroun will be a slave for the rest of his life. *But at least Dariyabar is now safe!*"

And that, gentle reader, is the end of my tale. The princess and her barbarian lived happily for many years, and had many children. As for Dariyabar, it was created by magic, and one day it disappeared without a trace, in the same manner. To this day, no one knows what really happened, for nothing remains of it by the sea on the edge of the southern desert along the road known as Silk.

ALL THE SECRET PLEASURES

Thea Devine

Chapter One

London, 1820

This much was known about Lady Corinna Woodholme—that she was the daughter of an honorable, and that she had grown up in the Cotswolds in a rather unconventional household since her mother had died when she was very young. That her father had had an understanding with his neighbor, Baron Charlesworth, that their children would marry, and that latterly, Corinna decided that a baron's son was neither wealthy enough nor well born enough for her, and elected instead to marry an earl who was older, more moneyed, and much more worldly, and made few demands on his young and beautiful wife; in point of fact, he fully expected they would eventually have children, but he died unexpectedly when they were in Italy the second summer of their marriage, and the Lady Corinna became a widow at an unconscionably young age.

Nor did she return to England any time soon after that. Her father had died in the interim, and she had sold the family home through her husband's lawyers, for she wanted no reminders of the past intruding on her present, nor had she any need for it at that point.

And as was proper, only after the requisite period of mourning did she ease back into the public eye; soon enough, it seemed, there were sightings of Lady Corinna throughout Paris and its environs now and again, at the opera, the theater, the spas, and on the arm of one dashing young suitor or another.

Lady Corinna, it was whispered, was living the Continental life. It *sounded* impossibly exotic and romantic. And just a little *risqué*. Such a young widow, after all. So well-positioned. Money to spare and spend—the earl had well taken care of her, his having no other heirs, and of course what came from her father—and, well—things were just a little more *lax* over *there* anyway, as everyone knew.

Although she hadn't quite gone round the bend, she knew well enough to have a proper chaperone and she maintained a proper and elegant household wherever she was, and she was said to be kind and considerate in every way, on the whole.

She hadn't entirely lost her wits, although sometimes she wondered exactly what she was doing. Passing time, perhaps. Trying to eke out an existence of some interest since her husband's death.

The gossips said she was bored with life on the Continent. They said that though she was conversant in French and Italian, and moved in the best circles, she had run through and tossed aside every worthy paramour, and a dozen more fortune hunters, and just out of boredom, she felt compelled to return to England—but really, the gossips said, she had come to seek fresh blood.

They said . . . she did not wish to remarry, that she was solely looking for a *man*—whatever that *meant* . . .

"Oh, poof—*they*—" She dismissed them all as she always did, with the wave of one hand, to her ever-present chaperone. "What do *they* know, after all? They live to feast on the bones of everyone else's lives, because theirs were bleached dry years ago. Pale desiccated things. I never listen to *them*. I can and will do as I please, as I always have done since I was a girl."

The words resonated . . . *since I was a girl* . . . and she stopped for a moment to consider the phrase.

Since I was a girl.

She felt older than her years, suddenly. She hadn't been a girl in forever. She'd married too young, and had been widowed too soon, and she'd led the life of a worldly woman for far too long—she'd barely been out of leading strings when she'd married . . . or so it seemed.

There was nothing Woodholme did not provide for her in those two glorious years of marriage, including a deep abiding *affectionate* love, which, while she could not return it with the intensity that he felt, made her feel cherished and safe, feelings which she could and did return in kind.

When he died, she felt as if her whole world had fallen away and nothing would ever be the same. It took no little time after she came out of mourning for her to realize that, and that there were men who adored a woman of experience whom they would not be expected to many, and that those men were solely seeking women who understood how to play.

And of course, there were also the men who associated with certain women merely to gain countenance in certain social circles.

Which was all to the good for her. She did not want to make any commitment to any man after Woodholme. It was too painful, she could never stand such a loss again; and then, after she'd gotten out and about and taken on some light flirtations with a battalion of eager young men, she decided she had just as soon have the sex and have done with idea of marriage altogether.

She loved sex. Dear Woodholme, with his patience, and the caring way in which he had initiated her into its mysteries—she had never met a man his equal since; she didn't want to. It was much easier to maintain control than fall wildly in love with someone who would ultimately disappoint her.

And they all did. It was one reason she finally did decide to return to England: the field of eligible bachelors had fairly dried up.

Shriveled up.

She'd taken them all on and found them wanting. Too much dash and flash. Too many compliments and not enough concupiscence. She was, at the end of her five year sojourn, tired of them all.

At which point, the idea of some fresh British blue blood began to seem very appealing.

"You are still a girl." This from Fanny Blakeney, her traveling companion and chaperone, who was twice her age, a widow of many years standing, who had been living cheaply on the Continent, and seeking a *situation* when Corinna found her and hired her to be her companion and her buffer. "And you mustn't think that all these years abroad have made you any the wiser. You are still a fool for love, my dear, and the trail of broken hearts you will have left here will be the stuff of legend for years after you are gone."

"Nonsense," Corinna said placidly, staring out the window of the carriage that was taking them from the inn where they had spent their first night off the boat train, into London. "I'm merely happy to be out of the way of fortune hunters and obnoxious toadies."

"As if there were no such animals in the whole of London," Fanny murmured.

"They will have better manners about it," Corinna said cynically. "Appearance is everything, is it not? A subtle approach would be refreshing, for a change."

And scary, the more she thought about it. It had been many years since she'd last been in London, and now she was opening Woodholme's townhouse in Regent's Park and she hadn't the slightest idea what to expect.

What she wanted, on one level, was to immure herself there, and to walk in anonymity on the streets of London and reacquaint herself with all its delights and diversions.

But that would hardly be possible. She knew the intricacies of the *ton*. There wasn't a matron in Town who wouldn't know that she had returned, and who didn't consider her a formidable foe and competition for every sweet young thing on the marriage mart this coming season.

She ought to have just gone up into the country to hibernate, until early next winter when Town would be empty and she could have everything to herself.

No. It would make no difference in the end: it would be the same circus, no matter when she took up residence in London.

She was used to it: Woodholme's widow must always be the subject of gossip and innuendo. It wouldn't matter what she did, or where she might choose to hide. They would find her out and talk about her anyway, even if she did nothing.

So she might as well do *something*. Or at least, that was how her thinking had gone when she'd made the decision to return to England.

But as the carriage came closer and closer to the outskirts of London, she felt an incipient panic. She hadn't been among these people in years. They played different games by different rules that were more lenient, formal, and, conversely, more stringent. Her behavior had to be exemplary because it was Woodholme's name she would be flaunting, and that meant something in England, if it did not in France.

And her own family's name as well.

No. She couldn't allow herself to think like that. It was perfectly permissible to do as one chose as long as one was careful and circumspect.

And well-chaperoned.

And besides, all anyone knew was that political circumstances had forced her return, hers among a hundred others seeking asylum from the threat of war.

There was nothing to worry about. Her life would go on as it always had, smooth and unmarred by any financial concern, and filled with the excitement of her one and only amusement for the past three years: the hunt to find the perfect lover.

What would life have been like without servants? As silent as elves, they opened houses, stoked the heat, changed the sheets, prepared a repast for a tired traveler, did everything they could think of to ensure her comfort, and kept everything running in an entirely unobtrusive way so that she had nothing to think about but the welcoming warmth of the house on Regent's Park as she entered its doors for the first time in five years.

This, however, was Fanny's first visit to London altogether

in many years, and Corinna was captivated all over again seeing the city and Woodholme's townhouse through Fanny's eyes.

Her mouth rounded, and she stood stock-still in the entryway, while she turned in a perfect circle taking in the details: the high ceiling with a subtle frieze picked out in gold; the rich wine color of the foyer walls; the elegant walnut tables; the polished marble floor; the staircase that seemed to wind its way to heaven; the glimmer of candles in glass sconces up and down the walls; and the butler standing by deferentially, waiting for Corinna s command.

"Oh, dear lord," Fanny breathed. "I had no idea . . ."

"This is hardly extravagant," Corinna murmured, but she knew that by Fanny's lights it was even more so than their luxurious apartments in Paris, or the sweet cottage she had leased in the Italian countryside. "Come, take off your coat. Chittenden tells me there's a fire in the library, and tea will be forthcoming in a moment."

And of course the library seemed even more grand to Fanny as she seated herself gingerly on one of the two brocade-covered sofas that fronted the fireplace, and looked around in awe at the floor-to-ceiling windows shrouded in matching fabric, and the marble fireplace with its gold-leaf mantel-to-ceiling mirror framed in classical motifs.

"This is too much," she whispered. "I didn't know . . ."

"Here is the tea," Corinna said. She had some sympathy for Fanny's dismay; had she not felt it herself when she had first come as a bride to this townhouse? It had been way more opulent than anything she had ever known, even growing up in the well-to-do confines of her home in the Cotswolds.

Of course, she understood perfectly how Fanny felt. It was grand beyond grand, but she was so accustomed to it now that she had to remind herself how it must look to a visitor. To someone who had made do with so much less.

To her, it was home.

Home . . .

The thought hit her right in the heart. Home.

Had France ever felt like home? No, Paris had been a playground to distract her from her loss, nothing more, nothing less.

This was home. Where she belonged. She felt the full shimmering sense of it settle into her bones, into her mind and her heart as she lifted the teapot to pour.

Home.

Alone. In this big house. Not to mention Woodholme's country house—oh! The pain of her loss threatened to swamp her.

No! She held it back forcibly. Don't think about that. Think about the possibilities. New life. New blood. New love . . .

Yes, new love. Nothing permanent, just the thrill of the chase, and the capitulation to the pulse-pounding moment of inevitable surrender . . . yes . . . fertile new ground to plow—

. . . new secrets, new life, new sex—and a new chance to bloom, to flower, to sow . . .

The invitations had come to Regent's Park thick and fast, even before her return. It was the end of December, after all, and the Little Season was almost about to begin, and Town was thin of company and so whoever of the *crème de la crème* was available was automatically issued an invitation.

Especially one whose reputation preceded her. They all wanted a look at Woodholme's widow, they all wanted to be the first to relay the telling tidbit: was she beautiful, branfaced, accomplished or shy? Did she dress well, was she shabby, was she intelligent or sly?

There were a list of details to consider: her youth, her countenance, were her clothes custom-made, was she plump or slender, elegant or countrified, and how did she speak, and in what manner did she dress her hair?

And if Corinna didn't care about any of that, Fanny certainly did.

"And indeed, this is precisely why you chose me as your companion—and guide," she scolded gently, as she went through the accumulated invitations over tea in the days following their arrival. "This is no easy thing, walking back into these elevated social circles, and expecting that not a quizzing glass would be turned upon you. My dear, you will provide enough line-space for a week's worth of *Tattlers* and more. It is of prime importance to pick where you will make your *entree*, and how you will dress, always remembering the limits of what is proscribed for a widow five years out of mourning."

"Already I am bored," Corinna said. "And tired."

"It will get worse," Fanny predicted. "You are the *on-dit* of the moment, my dear. There's no help for it. You are too young, too tragic and too beautiful; every rake from here to Gretna will be in pursuit before you can snap your fingers."

"My widow's portion notwithstanding," Corinna murmured with a touch of irony. "It is safer to keep them all at arm's length, because how can one ever know?" But she knew the answer to that; she could never know unless she were to attract a man of equal wealth and station, and then everything she had would become his.

And how could she even consider such a thing after five years of glorious independence and freedom? No, her way was the best. Dally and discard, and never become so attached to a *man* that you gave away your heart.

Or your fortune.

And at that, she wasn't even certain she was ready to begin the game all over again.

"This is what we do know," Fanny interpolated gently. "The Appersons are giving a dinner in a week's time to which they request the pleasure of your company. Now, they were great friends of Woodholme, were they not? What could be more appropriate? A small dinner, good conversation with old friends . . . it is perfect: let *them* disperse the particulars who have always had Woodholme's best interests at heart . . . this will do nicely, Corinna, this is perfect—do say yes."

"It's all of a piece," Corinna said, feeling a streaming irritation. "One or the other event—there is no difference to me."

Wasn't there? She was not, in truth, so indifferent as she tried to appear. She had to make her grand entrance somewhere. The Apperson's dinner was as good a place as any. The company would be small, select, discreet. There would be music, cards perhaps. Nothing socially strenuous. Old friends, catching up, easing the way for another old friend to reenter their world.

It was the perfect venue. Fanny's instincts were, as always, spot on. So she couldn't understand why she felt so restless and out of sorts. It was too soon, perhaps? Did she really need more time to become acclimated?

No. She could handle anything. She always had.

She poured Fanny another cup of tea. The fire burned bright, and its warmth suffused the room, radiated through her body.

She never wanted to leave here. She was home. At last—*home*.

"Tell them yes," she murmured. "Tell them I can't wait to take my pleasure with them . . . no, tell them that of course I accept their kind invitation. That I'll be absolutely delighted to come."

Chapter Two

It was said he was like snow, substantial when you looked at him, and melting away at a touch. That Simon Charlesworth wanted no attachments, commitments, or emotional ties. His sole entertainment was to flirt and fly, settling on no one flower, but leaving no petal unfurled.

He was a great favorite of the *ton,* sought-after, personable, and wealthy. Not to the point of ostentatious display, but certainly with enough money to command all the niceties of life.

These past two or three seasons had shown him that a perfectly eligible man, be he peer or landowner, was a treasure beyond price, and that a personable man would be competed over on every level, in every realm.

It was rather fun, actually, after years of penury and prudence, to take his place among those the most sought after, season after season. He reveled in it and had garnered a reputation as *the elusive one.*

Ah, Simon Charlesworth, they whispered, so charming, so handsome, so courteous, so not there.

Or they said, *elusive* is here, picking his way through the innocent flowers, flitting here and there like a bee, sipping the nectar and buzzing away.

And they said, once he mated, he would die.

It amused him, as he stalked through the ever-bending field of sweet innocence, the virginal best that society had to offer, because one could die of boredom as surely as expiring from the exigencies of marriage.

There had been hardly an interesting one among them season to season: there were the artless ones, the bold ones, the self-assured ones, the brassy ones. The ones who allowed liberties, and the ones who were too coy.

And never, in these two last elevating years, had he found a one he would even remotely consider calling his wife.

There was always something to deter him, something that turned him off and away at the very moment it looked as he might pursue the object of his attentions that further step.

It never happened. Thus, he was ever "elusive," and the *ton* waited with baited breath to see what the next installment in his romantic life would bring.

Even he didn't know, as he prepared for the journey into London that wintry December day shortly after he heard the news that Corinna Woodholme was returning to London.

This bit of gossip, delivered by a friend and confidante who promptly spread the word, had the opposite effect on him than the *ton* had imagined it would, and they were watching oh-so-closely.

As well he knew.

He had been waiting for this moment. He hadn't planned to have it happen yet. No matter how he tried to avoid it, there was no getting away from it: he needed a wife, he needed heirs, and now that Corinna Woodholme was finally back in London, it was time to put his plans into action.

It was time. He was tired of waiting, tired of flirting and kowtowing to whims of the missish mermaids who floated around, throwing out lures, waiting to be caught.

No. This was the year, it was time to cut the chaff from the chase. He didn't need to do much to accomplish that, either. He just let it be known to the very same friend who had brought him the news of Corinna's return, that he was a serious man who seriously wanted to set up his nursery, and this season, he was seriously in search of a wife.

Which he had timed perfectly to coincide with Corinna's return. The news would most certainly bring the old story of his proposal to her to the attention of the gossipmongers once again.

Perfect.

Though he wondered how many even knew of the abortive match that had been agreed upon between his father and Corinna's. It was such a long-ago little Cheltenham tragedy, and he had gotten well over it after Corinna's defection with her worldly old earl.

But those things rose up like bubbles in a cauldron. He wouldn't need to do anything: everyone would most assuredly keep him well apprised of Corinna's comings and goings. In fact, he was counting on it.

So whatever the wealthy wily Lady Corinna was up to, he was not in the least worried. The word would get to her soon enough that *he* was busy looking for a wife.

"And so here we are," Fanny said brightly as they were helped from the carriage at the Apperson's door. "You look lovely, not in the least widow-ish, but not disrespectful either. That dove gray color is perfect, and the touches of lavender are deliciously subtle and just right. Come, Corinna, you should not be in the least nervous."

"I'm not nervous," Corinna said, "just wondering how I shall be received."

"Like family, I'm certain—these are Woodholme's friends; they cannot be other than delighted to have you here tonight, if they went to all the trouble to invite you. And anyone else's feelings are of no moment."

But they had been dining out on stories about her for the last few years, Corinna thought mordantly. She wondered what they expected, how they thought she would look and how they expected her to behave for someone who had been living rather *loosely* on the Continent all this time.

She had forgotten how constrained English society was, how many rules had to be observed, how much formality there was, while behind the curtains everyone flirted and played.

But then perhaps that was a good thing, the thing that weeded out the *poseurs* from the possibles.

It was just a little dinner, after all. There wouldn't be too many people, and her hosts would slide her into the assemblage in the wink of an eye and she would feel right at home again.

She handed the majordomo her gray fur-lined pelisse and walked into the parlor as the butler announced her name.

Conversation stopped. Everyone turned to look at her, stopped in mid-motion like players in a tableau. The silence beat in her ears like a drum. A dirge. *Boom, boom, boom,* and then suddenly, Lady Apperson came forward, her hands outstretched—"Corinna, my dear, oh, you look so beautiful tonight, come in, come in . . ." and suddenly the room went into motion again, several people crowded around, people whom, perhaps, she had known before she married Woodholme, some of them his friends, and so changed in the ensuing years, of course she wouldn't recognize them.

And a few with whom she wanted to become reacquainted again in this new phase of her life, and so she greeted them all warmly, requested their names, and thus so easily was pulled into the conversation in the parlor and back into the niceties of the social life of London.

There were perhaps ten or a dozen people there, a slightly larger party than she had envisioned, but she had no trouble at all summoning up conversation and answering the well-meant questions as to the state of her health, and her feelings about returning to England.

After twenty minutes of this, she made her way to the tiring room to wash her face and have Fanny tuck in her hair.

"Such a lovely party," Fanny murmured. "Such an elegant house. And how do you feel?"

"Strange," Corinna said. "I know this, and yet I know it not. It will take some getting used to, and I have found already it is a good thing to keep your own counsel on a number of inflammatory subjects, and just nod and smile sweetly when addressed. As any well-bred, simple-minded woman should."

She stood up and surveyed herself in the mirror. "Thank you, Fanny. That will do nicely. I hope they will serve dinner soon. I am quite hungry."

She pulled aside the curtain into the foyer, and stopped still. There, his back to her, was a very tall gentleman dressed in the most austere black, who had just handed off his cape to the majordomo.

Her heart started racing. Broad shoulders, dark well-kept hair. Clothes that looked molded to his body. She recognized the cut of the clothes, the elegance of the fit. And the highly polished boots. And, thank heaven, he had an excellent leg.

Here was someone elegant, rich, virile . . . she bit her lip. She wasn't ready, she wasn't, and here he came, walking into her life, into a *reception room,* as if she had conjured him there.

Her next conquest . . . the next *man* in her life—the thought made her catch her breath, and washed her body with a telling heat. She knew that feeling, she had missed it, she craved it—so much, she almost swooned.

She pressed back against the curtains just to watch him, pleased with the grace of his movements, his posture, the precise and kind way he spoke to the servants.

She still couldn't quite see his face. She didn't want to. Just for the moment, he was her anonymous lover, perfect in every way.

The butler led him to the parlor.

She heard a flurry of footsteps, Lady Apperson's voice too far away to make out the words, then she saw him disappear into the parlor. Heard murmurings of welcome.

If she just stayed where she was, she didn't have to know anything more about him. He would remain forever the incomparable, the model, the ideal. He didn't have to kiss her or touch her for her to know: he was the most sublime man she would ever know—peerless and ever superb.

"Corinna?"

Dear Fanny. "Yes, dear."

"They've announced dinner."

"Of course." She stepped into the hallway, torn between wanting to see the stranger wholly and fully, and wanting to just leave him to her fantasies and go straight home.

Fanny pushed her gently toward the parlor.

Everyone had risen and they were waiting on her. She stood framed in the doorway, a vision in lavender and dove gray, strong and beautiful, as radiant and feminine as the sun.

"Ah, there you are, my dear," Lady Apperson cooed. "We're just going in to dinner and here comes your knight errant—you remember Simon Charlesworth, do you not? Were you not neighbors not so long ago? Here he is—he will escort you to dinner."

Simon . . . the man in the hallway—

The earth shifted—or maybe it was the floor beneath her feet—as Simon walked toward her with that lion grace of his, bowed, and offered his arm, all without a word.

But he didn't need to say a thing. It was all in his dark sparking eyes. He hadn't nearly forgotten her. He wouldn't have forgotten anything.

He held her chair and she sat, murmuring a polite thank you. And became suddenly aware that everyone was covertly watching them.

Lady Apperson's dining room with its golden hangings and heavy mahogany furniture suddenly became suffocating; between the smoke from the candles, and the smoke in Simon's gaze, Corinna felt as if she were in a boxing ring and going down for the count.

This was a moment to be chewed over after this party, when all present would venture their opinion to anyone with half an ear who had even a remote interest in her or Simon's affairs.

And that would be everyone, she calculated swiftly. She felt it in the air, even as they bent to begin the first course. They were all watching, listening, speculating.

She could imagine them the next day. *Did you hear? Simon Charlesworth and Corinna Woodholme at the same dinner party and she barely spoke five words. Imagine. After all this time. Still disdaining him. You would think . . . but then, I wonder if she knows . . .*

Now *her* imagination was going haywire. What ought she know about Simon? He was quite striking now, really elegant and refined. Dressed expensively and well, and still had that dangerous look in his eye, the same one as when she had refused to marry him all those years ago.

She picked up her soup spoon. This was infernally awkward; Lady Apperson ought to have known better. She slanted a look at Simon to find him staring at her.

And everyone else avidly watching them.

Now what? Would he not even talk to her to give the gloss of civility to whatever it was thought their relationship had been?

Well, if he wouldn't, she would. She felt a tearing irritation with the whole situation. It was just Simon, after all, and not the dashing knight of her dreams that she fantasized in the foyer.

And she knew him too well to harbor any idea of taking *him* as a lover.

She put down her spoon emphatically. "So tell me about *your* life these five years past, Simon."

He tipped his spoon at her. "Very good, Corinna. Excellent polish." He looked around at all the eager faces, cocked an eyebrow, and everyone busily went back to eating.

"But there is nothing to tell," he said smoothly. "My father passed on, I took over the estates and by dint of some luck and sheer hard work, I have made the family situation what it should always have been, and now I am seeking a wife."

The little buzz of conversation stopped dead, as if everyone had had one ear trained on *their* interchange.

She felt a jolt at the words. *Seeking a wife. I am . . .* well, of course—why should she feel any shock about the matter? He was a perfect and finely turned out gentleman, with better resources than previously, his family honor and wealth restored, if she read him aright, and of course he would want . . . a wife.

What man didn't want a wife?

"A wife," she said faintly in response to that neatly encapsulated summary of five years of a life lived on the knife edge of ruin. "I see."

What woman didn't want a husband?

Well—she didn't, for one, but that was no reason he ought not seek a wife . . .

She picked up the spoon, shocked to find her hand was trembling.

"It's time," he said. "Time to think about my legacy and my heirs, and a companion to share my life."

They sipped the soup for a moment.

"I would suppose," Simon continued, "that after five years, and what was by all accounts a most successful marriage, you too would be thinking in that direction, my lady."

Every ear pricked up.

"I am thinking of nothing more than how delicious is the soup," Corinna said tartly. And to Lady Apperson, "most excellent soup, ma'am."

"A family recipe," Lady Apperson murmured, keeping the comment brief in the hope that she and Simon would resume their shuttlecock conversation and they could all listen.

"Well, a marriage is very much like a soup," Simon said, stirring his portion thoughtfully. "Many ingredients stewed to a fine boil that cooks to your taste and cools down enough to savor over time. An apt comparison, would you not say, Corinna?"

"Unless it be overcooked, undercooked, too salty, spicy, watery or too tasteless altogether," she retorted without thinking.

The guests' eyes lit up with glee.

"Well, of course. It does take a prudent hand to control all the elements of a perfect soup," Simon said, his voice suspiciously bland. "To know when to bring it to the boil, and when to let it simmer, when to use a little spice and when to leave things alone."

"Indeed, Simon—a *woman's* hand . . ."

"Oh, do you think so, my lady? Now I would have said a man's hand . . ."

". . . which does not rock the cradle nor cook the soup," Corinna said sweetly. "So we all know to whom a well seasoned, nourishing and savory soup is to be credited."

"And likewise, a marriage?" Simon asked politely.

"My dear Simon—he who seeks a wife surely needs no recipes from me."

"No, just your fine hand stirring up the pot, as usual," he muttered.

A dark silence fell. The servants unobtrusively removed the soup course. The gentlemen sipped their wine. Lady Apperson looked around the table and then directed her bright, heightened gaze at Simon.

"So tell us, Simon—what is this new permutation about a wife?"

He shrugged. "I've had enough of the sport and play. It is time."

"To make soup?" Lady Apperson asked archly.

"To make babies," he said bluntly.

Corinna choked. . . . *make* . . . Instantly she saw it, Simon in bed with some simpering young thing, *making* babies. This Simon in bed, not the Simon she had known, the dangerous and provoking man she didn't know, the one who was exciting her far beyond what she wanted to feel for him or any man.

The problem was, she knew him better than most, and she could see that some things, under the veneer of elegance and polish, had not changed.

But still—*making* babies . . .

Lady Apperson bit her lip. "Perfectly understandable," she said with a straight face. "One must ever be vigilant about making babies."

"Exactly. And there comes a time a man must . . . do what a

man was meant to do," Simon said, taking the thought and running away with it. "And so, I'm *fully* prepared to . . ."

"Indeed," Lady Apperson interpolated. "I think we have the *whole* picture, Simon. Ah, here is the second course . . ."

And with the fish course, the conversation veered pointedly away from babies and the mechanics thereof. For which Corinna was inordinately grateful. Not that anyone didn't want to hear more or wouldn't be gossiping about it five minutes after they returned home.

But for the moment, the talk was intermittent, placid, and centered on politics and the theater, and she needed do nothing else but concentrate on the excellent dinner, and Simon beside her, raising a shuddering excitement in her breast.

Curiously, in the course of conversation, he did not ask to extend the acquaintance.

She found herself not a little piqued by that. Simon was, after all, her childhood playmate, the one to whom she was closer than close when growing up, and someone who had done her the honor of wanting to marry her.

She had never borne him any ill feeling, and she would have thought he would be happy to see her back in England at last. As she would him. As she was happy to see him, broad shoulders, expensive clothes, excellent leg and all.

Dear Lord, when had he become so dangerously enticing?

But that didn't matter; she knew him too well, and for far too long, and could not consider him anything but an old friend.

Didn't want to. Reluctantly went with the ladies into the parlor as the men poured their brandy. Looked over her shoulder to see him lifting his snifter, making a comment to Lord Apperson, utterly oblivious to her hot seeking gaze, ignoring her utterly as if he didn't even know her.

She hated him.

She wanted him.

Simon???

No. She wanted him to want *her* still.

She couldn't stop thinking about him as Lady Apperson led the genteel discussion of whether hostilities would affect fashion, and what exactly *was* the mode in Paris these days?

She was forced to speak then, because she was the exotic creature from the Continent and had all those details at her fingertips, but all she wanted to do was ruminate on why Simon would not want to call on her.

Even if he were seeking a wife, that had nothing to do with anything.

She couldn't stop thinking about it, about him. About the moment she first saw him in the foyer, when she hadn't known who he was.

Incomparable, she had thought him. *The perfect, unknown lover.*

And he turned out to be the person she knew best of all. He must come to call on her, he *must.*

And yet, how could she broach such a thing without seeming forward, *bold,* Continental . . . ?

Lady Apperson saved her the trouble. "My dear Corinna," she said as the majordomo was handing everyone his coat at leave-taking, "you are receiving, are you not, now you've opened the house at Regent's Park?"

"Indeed I am," she answered gratefully, "and would be happy indeed to greet old friends—" she slanted a look at Simon, "—and new—in the afternoon. Do come visit soon, Lady Apperson, and let me reciprocate for this lovely dinner."

"Delighted," Lady Apperson said. "There you go. Here's your carriage. Fanny is waiting."

Corinna pulled her cape tightly around her shoulders. She had done all she could reasonably do. She stepped out into the cold starry night air, which suddenly seemed fresh, sharp, and tinglingly alive with possibilities.

Chapter Three

"I've never seen the like of it," Lady Apperson said in a confidential tone as she settled in to take tea with Corinna late one afternoon a week later. "How determined is our Simon. My dear—everyone is talking about it. Elusive has now become obtainable—Simon truly means it. He will have a wife by the end of this very season."

"So of course he has not a moment for an old friend," Corinna murmured. "I had wondered but here we have the explanation . . . he is that busy, chasing after the idea of a wife."

Lady Apperson eyed Corinna over the rim of her cup. "When a man decides, Corinna, he cannot make it happen quickly enough. Did not the earl snap you up the moment he—?" She stopped abruptly. "I'm so sorry, my dear; I didn't mean to bring up Woodholme's memory. It is far more amusing to gossip about Simon. Let us just say the word has gotten out about his intentions . . ."

Exactly, Corinna thought caustically, the *word*, flailed to a froth by the guests at the dinner party . . . so much that did Simon find success, Lady Apperson might well take some of the credit.

But that was uncharitable of her. She herself had not been out since the Apperson's dinner party; she had had an ample number of callers who had taken Lady Apperson's lead, but not a word from Simon. Not a note, not an overture, not an apology for his cavalier treatment of her . . .

But what had she expected? She had treated him badly those many years ago, and had not been all that cordial at the dinner table the week before, truth to tell.

And old memories died hard, as she herself knew. And age did not always confer wisdom nor time salve over old wounds.

"Stirring up soup," she said lightly.

"Well, exactly," Lady Apperson said.

"Nonetheless, sometimes a man needs dessert," Corinna murmured.

Oh, but did she really mean that? She wanted no attachments, not yet. Why was she feeling so prickly about the whole thing? She had no claims on Simon, none at all, except that of an old friend.

A *dear* old friend.

So why was she thinking about him so much? Why was her mind so occupied by her first breathtaking view of him that night, before she knew who he was, when a man could be perfection in the eye of the beholder, and all things were possible?

She shook off her restiveness. Simon ought to have called on her. It was excessively bad of him not to have called. She didn't deserve *that,* even if she had refused to marry him.

"A man must calculate the ingredients," Lady Apperson went on, "make sure everything is . . . symmetrical."

"Indeed, a man doesn't like rough edges, or uneven pieces," Corinna mused. "Anything he chooses must be the freshest available, nothing old, stale, soggy or misshapen for him. I quite see how it is with Simon. He must definitely tend his soup to obtain the best result. And you have the right of it: it is never too soon to start once a man makes up his mind."

So there. That was all there was to it: Simon was worlds too busy to attend to old friends. She would see him now and again at a musicale, a dinner party, at Almack's eventually, should she secure a voucher, and it would be the same as it had at Lady Apperson's dinner: badinage overriding bad feelings that simmered beneath nonetheless.

Fine. *Put Simon out of your mind.*

"Oh, this season promises to be the best in recent memory," Lady Apperson went on gleefully. "It will be so much fun to watch Simon brought to his knees."

* * *

And *that* was an image that positively possessed her. Simon on his knees. The Simon of the broad shoulders and well-turned leg who was the darling of the *ton*. The worldly, weathered and wealthy Simon who reeked of danger and sensuality. The one who made virginal hearts flutter and who was as elusive as the wind.

That Simon.

Corinna was hearing a lot about *that* Simon as Woodholme's old friends began to call. Too much about *that* Simon, she was beginning to think.

He was a flirt and a tease. He had a look in his eyes that no woman could resist. His kisses were so treasured that whomever he had kissed never told, for he valued discretion above anything.

Ha! Corinna thought agitatedly, she could tell them all about Simon's boyhood and fumbling kisses, and many other things. But she wouldn't stoop that low.

When had Simon become such a lover?

STOP IT!

He was the talk of the town.

"A very stable man in the matter of running his estates, Corinna," another caller confided. "You never would have guessed it would be so, all those years ago. Put everything on a profitable footing not two years ago, he did. His father almost wasted it all away. Would that he had lived to see how successfully Simon recouped all he lost."

"Truly," Corrina said dutifully. "He would have been so proud." He would have gotten in the way more likely, a man who was stuffed with his own importance, so certain his way was the right way, and who never listened to anyone's advice. Poor Simon.

Not so poor now . . .

"And then," another caller told her, "there were a good half dozen young things who thought he might offer for them last year. Elusive is not the word for him. He got out of all of that with a wink and smile, and somehow everyone still thinks highly of him. Well, they will be right back in the fray this year, wading through the new crop of showy flowers vying for his attention. My lady, I must say, you are well out of all of that."

"Indeed I am," Corinna agreed. Here was the exact right person to spread her message. "I would not be in their shoes for any money. I have had my turn; I want for no more—my marriage was full, loving and Woodholme was the best companion in the world. I shall never find his like in this life again. And I am determined to honor his memory in that way."

There. Lavinia Linley would tell everyone now—Corinna was not looking for a husband. She would be content to sit on the sidelines, secure in the fond remembrances of her deceased husband.

Was that clear to Lavinia?

"You are exactly right, my lady. You would be hard put to find a man as fine and noble as was Woodholme. So you thinking only to . . . ?"

Perfect. Lavinia would relay this entire conversation in all the right quarters. "To resettle myself in London, and partake of the season's entertainments from the vantage point of a woman who is past her first blush, and seeks nothing more than to reacquaint herself with old friends and make a new life here. Nothing more."

"Of course," Lavinia said suddenly, "someone did mention that your father and Simon's had had some agreement that you two would wed all those years ago."

Crunch . . . Corinna felt like someone had squeezed her heart. This of course was the true reason for Lavinia's visit, then. "Did they?" she murmured. "How very odd. Why ever would anyone talk about that when everyone knows Simon is looking for a wife?"

"Well. You were to have been . . ."

"My dear Lavinia—no one was to have been anything. How young were we at the time? Our fathers cooked up this notion.

Nothing ever happened. Who would even remember it after all these years?"

"You," Lavinia said pointedly.

"Well, of course I would. But why would you?" Oh, that was rude, and bordering on something even more violent. And she had wanted so much for Lavinia to be on her side in the matter of her expressed intentions.

"It wasn't me," Lavinia said righteously. "It was mentioned in passing only."

"And away like the wind, I hope."

"The merest breath of a mention, and of course, no one will ever hear a word about it from *me.*"

"Thank you, Lavinia. And I truly appreciate your apprising me of it. It is good to be aware of what people are saying."

"Exactly," Lavinia said, as she made ready to take her leave. Corinna could see her already making a mental list of everything they had discussed, everything she would share with her next best friend in absolute confidence.

So be it. She could share the moon, for all Corinna cared. Lavinia probably would. But it still would not be enough to make Simon come.

The next event was a card party—for about fifty—or perhaps a hundred—of Lord Balter's best friends, with tables set up all around the lower floor of his commodious townhouse in Belgrave Square.

There were a half dozen games of whist, several more of vingt-et-un, and faro in the upper hallway . . . and Corinna couldn't decide which or whether to partake of the play, as she wandered through the crowd dressed in the mauve silk which Fanny had insisted upon because, "it will be such a crush that in the end you will be happy you are wearing something light as air."

Fanny was right in that: within the hour, the atmosphere had become constricted from the warmth of so many bodies milling around in a fairly limited space.

But more than that, it was Simon who fanned the heat in the room, striding in as if he owned the world, utterly commanding everyone's attention, and then making himself agreeable to whatever young lady was nearest to hand, propelled by mothers who wanted to get a foot in the door before the season went into full swing.

Corinna eyed them all with some skepticism. It was easy to see which of them had any backbone at all, and which would be lumps of clay.

Simon needed a woman with a spine, and these chits were hardly women anyway, with no strength of will at all, and barely any conversation except to say yes and no, and do you think so my lord?

Corinna shuddered. She was never that young, she could not have been. And watching this display, she was coming to think that the absence of a mother had been a prime contributor to her becoming a person with some character and decisiveness.

Surely Simon was aware of all that—but watching him, as young ladies in yellow and blue flower dresses fawned over him, she wasn't certain that any man didn't need someone to point out the proper direction when his mind was so befuddled, he was drowning in his own soup.

It made perfect sense. And she could posit that to him, did he but desire to continue their childhood friendship and call upon her, which he already should have properly done.

Truly. It had nothing to do with his shoulders or the look in his eyes.

Nevertheless, she found she did not like watching him escort this and that flittering young thing to the various tables to view the play and discuss the finer points of vingt-et-un.

There was thankfully a welcome distraction in that dinner was served as well, which provided an opportunity for less frenetic conversation; there was also lively wagering at the tables, and on the side, about Simon and who he would spend the most time with this night, and what her chances were of engaging him to that extent at the next party.

It made Corinna grit her teeth. Even here, Simon was the one whispered about, speculated about, and watched covertly as he went from room to room, spending his charm like silver coins among the sweet and simpering.

Thank heaven there weren't that many. A half dozen of them, perhaps, to whom he devoted his attention equally. Escorting one into the dining room, getting another something to drink, having a bit of conversation with the third . . . she had to admit he did it handsomely, with a kind of irresistible air of rakish charm that, if one looked closely, one might perceive was coated in irony.

Surely the insipidity must be wearing. Surely a few moments with a dear old friend would be welcome.

She wished it weren't so, that he would approach her, but apart from acknowledging her presence in passing when she arrived, it was quite obvious that was not going to happen.

He looked so good to her. And he was a known commodity. Maybe.

She considered him for a moment as he came toward one of the butterflies with a glass of ratafia.

She knew him. They had been neighbors, they'd consorted together for as long as she could remember. He was older than she, and he had been like a brother to her, teaching her to ride, to dance, to do her sums, to mind her manners. To kiss.

She'd practiced her incipient feminine wiles on him, and he had never let her get away with a thing. He'd been indulgent and strict, and it had never occurred to her as she was growing up that he might want her as a wife. Or that her father and his were conspiring to make it so.

And when it was broached, she found it inconceivable. He was her friend, her confidant, her brother. He had never touched her, only kissed her on the lips in that respectful, seeking way of a new lover, that aroused nothing in her breast, and then, he never kissed her as often as she might wish, and most times on the cheek or forehead.

The whole thing was, she could never see Simon Charlesworh as her fantasy husband, and she hadn't wanted his kisses or his hand in marriage. And he had to have known it. She'd been so certain at the time that it was plain as pudding.

And so she had pursued what she wanted, a wealthy worldly much older man, and had spent two contented years with him in an affectionate, loving, instructional marriage that, while it lacked a certain glorious excitement, provided her with all the other things she thought she had wanted.

What had she mourned when Woodholme died? Companionship. A presence in her life. A wise advisor. A guiding hand.

And so, after five years, a feeling of abandonment, a consuming loneliness, and a massive waste of time filling up her life with meaningless and useless flirtations, she had come home . . . to what, she hadn't known, until the Apperson's dinner party.

At which point, she had veered utterly off-balance. And watching Simon now, she felt that transcending moment of anticipation wash over her again.

It mattered not that he sought a wife; he was still the anchor of her childhood and her former life, and she needed him—now.

But it wouldn't do to approach him. That was the most frustrating part . . . the proscribed dance between a man and a woman. She must not look like she was in pursuit, especially because her reputation had preceded her.

No, she must mind her manners, and she must wait until he came to her. So the only thing she could do was to engage in a game of cards, which supposedly was the purpose of her attendance at this party in the first place, and so, having decided that, she moved toward a table that was just disbanding.

Someone set a fresh deck of cards on the table, and someone behind her pulled out her chair, and when she turned to say thank you, she saw it was Simon and he was taking his place beside her as a fourth.

He raised an eyebrow. "Don't lead out of turn, Corinna. Lady Balter and I are to partner. I believe you are acquainted with Mr. Talvaney?"

She wasn't, but she acknowledged him in her flirtatious way, and Lady Balter, who had just joined the table.

"I believe Talvaney has the deal," Lady Balter said. "Call the play, if you would."

"Short," Mr. Talvaney said and began dealing the cards, the first to Simon, until all were gone but the last, which he laid face up on the table.

From then on, the play became intense, terse and tight; it immediately became obvious that she and Simon were pitted against each other, and neither would give over.

"Misdeal," Simon said at one point.

"Misdeal?" Corinna murmured, deliberately, to provoke him.

"New deal," Talvaney interpolated.

"Revoke," Simon said.

"Misspoke?" Corinna queried.

"Abandon hands," Talvaney said sternly, tossing his cards face up on the table. Lady Balter followed suit.

"Abandon plans?" Simon said lightly. "Yes, I'm conversant with that maneuver—not a sophisticated play, that. Leaves a man hanging in the wind. What were you saying, Talvaney?"

Talvaney cleared his throat. "New deal, Simon."

Simon shot a look at Corinna. "Is it?"

"Only the cards liable to be called," Corinna said softly, "which seem not to be the ones I ever hold."

"Cut the pack," Talvaney said dampeningly.

Simon cut. "We will play out the hand," he said, his dark and lively gaze fixed on Corinna.

"Will we?" she murmured, taking up her cards.

The trump card was laid on the table, and honors were called: two for three, four for four, and the game began in earnest.

"We have made book," Talvaney announced after ten minutes of intense play.

"We seem to mesh excellently well—in cards," Corinna said. "The remaining six points will flow to us as simple as syrup."

"I think not, my lady," Simon said resolutely. "Lady Balter and I are but one trick short of book, and closing in fast."

A moment later, he took the next trick and murmured, "And now we are even."

"Oh, I think not," Corinna said sweetly, as she took the deal. "Don't be so eager, Simon. One wouldn't know what to think."

"But I know what to think," he retorted, "we are adversaries, after all," and he aggressively led with an ace.

"Oh, I am in the soup now," Corinna moaned theatrically, and the play turned almost cutthroat from that moment, to the point where other guests began to gather around to watch and wagering began, *sotto voce,* as to which partners would make the seven points first.

Simon felt brazen; Corinna was confident, and between the two, the air became hot, steamy, combative.

Corinna did not even know why it must be, but she knew she and Talvaney must win. There was no other course—for her pride alone.

But then, on one level it was no contest—she had spent a good portion of her social life playing cards in Paris. She was cool under pressure, and not easily distracted by an adversary's win.

And though Simon easily matched her in *sang-froid,* he did not have the advantage of honing his skills continually.

In the end, she and Talvaney prevailed after a half hour more of play, and they were applauded as they quit the table, and money surreptitiously changed hands.

And that, Corinna determined, was the departure point.

"Cards on the table," she said as Simon politely escorted her back to the dining room. "I do wish you would call that we might talk over old times."

"Playing out of turn, Corinna?" Simon said. "The old times are past and gone, my lady, but—I would be delighted to pay my respects to the earl's widow."

Corinna smothered a comeback and straightened her shoulders. At least he would come. He said he would come. "I should be delighted to see you," she said, striking a formal note in her tone. She gave him her hand, suddenly aware that people were watching, people would gossip.

He was so tall, taller than she remembered, his hand was so warm, his eyes glinty with amusement because he was perfectly attuned to what was happening around them.

The dance must be done. She must have no recognition of improprieties at all—there were none, really. An old friend would be calling upon an old friend, albeit one old friend had had to make the request.

He bowed and relinquished her hand, properly waiting as her carriage was sent for. And then she had to leave and she watched over her shoulder as the carriage pulled away, watched as Simon most assuredly returned to the game.

And she knew exactly which game she meant—and it wasn't cards.

Chapter Four

Waiting heightened the anticipation. But it wasn't as if she sat around staring out the window, wishing and hoping. Rather, she shopped, she visited Lady Apperson, she walked with Fanny to the lending library, she rode sometimes in the morning, or had a carriage ride, took tea with acquaintances on invitation, and in the course of all this, heard more about Simon's comings and goings than she wished to.

And that was because Simon was not coming to visit *her*, and time was speeding by: Parliament would be in session within a fortnight or so, and the season would spin into full swing, and Simon would be so busy at that point with mamas wooing him and hostesses claiming him every night for their own specific entertainments that he would have no time for anything or anyone else.

And that didn't even take into account the time he must spend dancing attendance at Almack's or time he would want to spend with his friends at the clubs.

Oh, it was too frustrating, that he would not call. And while Fanny's company was bracing for her fine-tuned knowledge of the ins and outs of society, it was not stimulating intellectually, and not at all equal to having a paramour dangling after her. So even though she was having a much finer time during this renaissance return to England than she ever could have anticipated, Corinna still felt something was missing.

But once in a while, she found spending an afternoon reading a book was a very welcome respite. And so, of course it was on one of those cold dismal rainy afternoons in March, when she was lounging in a plain woolen house dress, her skirts wrinkled, her hair untidy, and deeply immersed in a novel, that Simon chose to come.

Fanny answered the door at his brisk ring, and gently inquired who was calling, and elicited all manner of information from him in her sweet unassuming way as Corinna listened with burbling amusement. She could just picture Simon charming Fanny, the lioness at the door; Fanny who was perfectly aware of the niceties of dealing with new friends and old, and who would never commit any solecism that could redound on Corinna.

Thank heaven for Fanny. Fanny would bar the gate, and she wouldn't have to see Simon when she was not at perfect pitch.

And then she heard Fanny, charmed beyond redemption say, "Please go into the parlor, Mr. Charlesworth. I'm sure she will be so happy to see you," and she froze, suppressing every instinct to just jump up and flee.

No, she was at point: she must receive Simon, who appeared at the instant on the threshold and left her no other choice. She set aside her book, rose from her chair, and moved toward him, her hands outstretched, with all the dignity of a queen.

"My dear Simon, I'm so happy to see you—come by the fire and sit."

She led him to one of the two sofas on either side of the fireplace and immediately rang for tea. It would give them something to do. If they were sipping, they couldn't have much conversation beyond the conventional pleasantries, not yet; and they couldn't say things, perhaps, that she didn't want to hear.

Besides which, she was just not at her best at the moment; this wasn't nearly the scenario she had envisioned for their next meeting, and she felt at a distinct disadvantage, and she didn't like the feeling at all.

"Well, my lady, I must tell you," Simon began easily, "I was well and truly whipsawed the other night, and it took me this long to come to terms with it."

It was the perfect thing to say, designed to disarm and charm.

And she was. Charmed and disarmed. Dear heaven, when had he learned such flirtatious repartee?

She bent her glimmering gaze on him, and said dismissively, "Oh, poof. Believe me when I tell you that I have sat at dozens of such tables over the past few years, and that win was solely a credit to long hours on hard chairs with inept partners."

"You are too good," Simon murmured.

"Am I?" she whispered, leaning closer, just as Fanny barged into the room with the tea tray.

"Here we are," she sang out. "I was certain Mr. Charlesworth would be hungry and perhaps appreciate some small cakes and sandwiches."

"Hungry I am indeed," Simon said, slanting a look at Corinna who was unselfconsciously tucking away several stray strands of hair.

Fanny poured, making small talk. Corinna sipped, happy for the diversion. She was not a little put out with Simon, she thought, watching him. He looked too good, too handsome, too . . . perilous. He ought to have sent round a note asking when he might come. These five minutes already had her toppling off balance and she didn't quite know how to deal with it. Or whether Simon's comment had another level, another meaning.

Or whether this was the moment to find out.

Certainly not with Fanny chattering away. Fanny had been well and truly seduced already. And was being punctiliously proper. Which made Corinna feel like grinding her teeth.

But finally Fanny comprehended that she could not in good manners intrude on their conversation any longer, and Corinna leaned back in her chair, sipping her third cup of tea, lukewarm on her lips, feeling a momentary relief as Fanny withdrew.

But now what?

"This has been most refreshing," Simon said at length, "but as you know, I am seeking a wife, and so to spend any appreciable time with you might give rise to the notion of impropriety."

"Would it?" she asked gently. "How so? Old friends that we are . . ."

"No," Simon said sharply, emphatically. "We are not old friends, my lady. We are old adversaries who do not know quite how to get on with each other at this awkward moment. We could never have been just *friends,* given that we could have been married, or—" he paused and slanted a look at her, "even possibly lovers . . ."

Yes—thank the fates he had brought it up—even so soon. She wasn't prepared, she wasn't, but sometimes one had to grab for the ring even if it was likely one would miss.

"We still can," she said softly, before she thought it through.

He went very still. "My lady?"

She met his dark gaze. Now . . . oh now—she must present it in a way that made sense to him, and to her, because her response to him made no sense to her at all.

But to choose the right words, to find the way to present it without seeming like a piece of amoral baggage—? All her years away, and all her experience, had not prepared her for that.

"It is very simple, Simon. You are on the hunt for a wife. I surely do not want another husband. But I find that I miss the intimacy of a male relationship, and so here we both are, neither encumbered at the moment, old—adversaries—who have known each other since childhood, who used to deal with each other extremely well . . . and, well—you have needs, and . . . I—"

"Indeed yes, my lady; the gossips have been having a field day with *you* . . ."

"And *you,*" Corinna shot back.

He considered that for a moment, and *her,* with her blazing eyes, high color and utterly natural beauty as she spoke her mind without constraint. But she had always been blunt and to the fore with him.

Most especially the day she had refused him. And there was about to be a day of reckoning for that.

"Indeed, my lady, we are a pair. Gossip-fodder of the first vintage."

"Then we ought to take advantage of it, since they will talk about us in any event," she said, "if you feel the *need* as strongly as do I."

"The need, Corinna? My wife-to-be will provide the necessary surcease for my *need*."

Of course she would, and he was to be commended for thinking that way, Corinna thought instantly. It pleased her—it *should* please her; it showed his character, his restraint. His grasp of the niceties of the chase. And what was due his intended bride.

But not for long. "And until then?" Corinna asked softly.

"I am fully able to control my impulses," Simon said.

"Of course you are," she agreed instantly. "But the season has not even begun, you have seen the best of the eligible in Town already, and I daresay there is not a one among them you would ask to be your wife tomorrow."

"Not a one, my lady?"

"Truly, Simon, let us not play speculation with each other. It will take time. Finding this wife, I mean. You would be cheating yourself if you thought differently."

"And so, you are suggesting that as I begin my search to find a wife, I should, with the other hand, be taking my ease with you?"

Corinna blinked and flushed. There was candor for you. It sounded bald and ugly put that way. It sounded impossibly shameless and abandoned . . . it didn't sound like her, and yet it was exactly like her and precisely what she wanted.

And it demanded no less honesty from her. This was the do-or-die moment, and she didn't even know if he prized that kind of plain-speaking. It struck her that she knew nothing about *this* Simon at all, and she felt a certain shuddery excitement at the idea of finding out.

"That is what I'm suggesting," she said at length, her voice low, her fingers stiff around the teacup. She felt a little brazen to be broaching the arrangement; but there was no time for the usual contredanse with him. This might be his one and only visit to her, and so she had to burst out, before he could be swallowed by the pack. Or she could even formulate a more palatable plan.

This impromptu strategy, however, had nothing to recommend it, if the expression on his face was any indication, and much calculated to turn him away from her forever. She saw instantly that she had handled the whole thing abysmally, but there was no help for it now.

"But my dear Corinna, we don't even know if we should suit."

"Lovers need not suit, they need only to be willing," Corinna retorted.

"Well—" he murmured, looking a little thunderstruck, "obviously you are more conversant with the matter of lovers' needs than I."

Well, now what? she wondered, a little taken aback. Perhaps she was. And perhaps that might be to her credit. Still, this was her reputation, after all. She could not in good conscience spoil his expectations. She wasn't sure she wanted to. After all, she only wanted the sex, and what he wanted, besides a wife and a vessel in which to spend his seed, didn't enter into the picture at all.

"Well," she murmured, "be that as it may, it is obviously much less torturous to find a . . . companion in certain other situations, it seems. I should not need to roll hoops to convince you, so perhaps—even though it might help you to have the practice—" oh, and it nearly killed her to say it, "we should not, as you say, suit and I should look elsewhere."

Help him—to have the practice?? Heaven help him altogether . . . he thought, grimly. What the devil did she think he had been doing all these years besides learning to plow fertile ground of one sort or another?

"On the other hand," he drawled, "one could be *willing*, seeing as one does have *needs.*"

Corinna stared at him. Willing was enough. Willing was all that was needed. And did she not feel relieved that he felt so? "Well then, we are finally on common ground." She looked at him expectantly. He stared back.

"Surely you have some idea what next to do," she said impatiently.

"I have many ideas I would put into *practice,*" Simon said blandly, a statement that made her heart start pounding. "But somehow it doesn't seem right to just throw you on the floor."

Yes it does . . .

But it was time to give over control of things to him. "What does seem right then?"

"Let us just—practice this—"

A kiss—a lightly-pull-her-forward, touch-her-lips, barely-there kiss that sent little darts of pleasure ticking her very vitals.

His hands were warm on her shoulders, her sense of him behind her closed eyes so all-pervasive, so enveloping, she just wanted to lean into his body and let him devour her.

But instead, he pulled away very, very slowly, so that she felt the warmth, the texture, the fullness of his lips, and she opened her eyes. The expression on his face was inscrutable, but she didn't care—she wrapped her arms around his neck and pulled him to her again.

"Oh, but I'm very *out* of practice, my lady—"

"Then you do need my help," Corinna breathed against his lips.

". . . kissing you," he added in a husky whisper and swooped in on her mouth so expertly that she almost fainted from the shock of the first contact.

He didn't have a wife yet, she thought dizzily, as she opened her mouth to him and he devoured her. Oh yes, oh this . . . she had so missed this—being enfolded, consumed, burning, learning . . . her bones felt like they were melting . . . There was still time—time for everything, time to make love and time for lust, time to explore every secret pleasure . . .

"Ahem," Fanny said, her voice slightly rusty.

Corinna pulled out of the kiss, her lips a mere fractional inch from Simon's. "Yes, Fanny?" Her voice sounded foggy, blurred with her mounting excitement, and the ever-enchanting rill of desire.

"It's time," Fanny said gently.

"Time . . . ?" Hadn't she just been thinking about time? Time . . . there was never enough time.

"For Mr. Charlesworth to—"

"You're exactly right," Simon said, easily relinquishing his hold on Corinna, apparently having recovered his wits far more easily than she. "I was *just* taking my leave, as it happens."

"I thought so," Fanny said complacently, and discreetly withdrew.

Corinna put out her hand as Simon rose. He took it, and pulled her to her feet. "My lady?"

"Must you?"

"Engagements tonight, Corinna. No backing out."

"Of course." When she dearly wanted him to stay. But she mustn't forget that men were different creatures than women when it came to *needs.* She could have kissed and cuddled the whole night, but for him, a card game somewhere into the wee hours must take precedence.

"And we shall meet again—when?"

"Ah, that is for me to know," he murmured, as he left her. "And for you to discover. I *will* see you soon, my lady, most willingly."

She still felt as if she were in a fog, fighting her way out of Simon's ravishing kisses to some kind of rationality.

Discover, he'd said. What did he mean, discover? Oh, there was still such a way to go before there would be any assuaging of *needs,* she thought longingly. And she already wanted more of his kisses.

She wondered if she could stand the wait.

* * *

"Well, Simon?"

Simon looked up from the chessboard where he was studying his next move, in a game that had lasted well into the three hours since he and Richard had arrived at Richard's townhouse after a night at Heeton's.

"Well, what?"

"Have another brandy, old son," Richard, Viscount Cawley, said, holding out a snifter. "Come, it will loosen your tongue, and you have to admit I've been damned patient waiting on your leave to hear about the outrageous Lady Woodholme. But by God, I will know what transpired between you and that termagent before this hour has passed."

Simon took the goblet, and held it to the light. Excellent color, scent, body . . . but then everything about Richard was of the first and finest body. He was that kind of man, in heart, character and conscience.

"Here is the long and short of it," he said finally, "my lady is still vain, stubborn, selfish, willful, and has no qualms about speaking her mind. But she is also older, wiser—one hopes, more seasoned, and still—" his voice grew soft, "incredibly beautiful."

Richard joined him at the table, swept a knowledgeable glance over the playing pieces, set down his snifter, moved his bishop and sat back. "And?"

Simon studied the counter-move for a long moment. "Nothing has changed." He edged out Richard's bishop with his knight.

"Umm—bold move, my friend. One of many these days, I take it." Richard swiped the knight with his queen.

"Take it how you will. Nothing has changed." Simon blocked the piece with the second knight. "The knight still protects his queen, circumstances notwithstanding."

"So I see." Richard bent over the board and considered the predicament of his queen. "And you've been so summarily successful in eluding her."

"Exactly," Simon said with no small degree of satisfaction lacing his voice. "Precisely the strategy: the queen coming in pursuit, and the knight stalemating her every time."

"So it seems that you have . . ." Richard conceded, studying the possible next move. "Hmmm. Of course, there are always rooks and pawns to stave off an attack."

"Oh indeed, and one can always allow himself to become a pawn, knowing to a fault just what risk he is taking."

"Really? Is that the end game?"

"Richard, Richard, Richard," Simon chided. "You know the end game. You've known it for years."

"And if the queen is captured?"

"I will do everything in my power to win her back."

Richard laughed. "While you are seducing every virgin from here to Gretna in the process? Those mothers will kill you, Simon. They are man-eating tigresses. You have no idea."

"Then you must distract them, Richard."

"But I've vowed not to marry from the common crowd, as you well know. Unless of course, it's a paragon like my lady Corinna."

Simon looked at him sharply. This was a joke, was it not? He couldn't tell. Richard had never been the darling of the marriage-minded mammas. He disdained them all year after year, eschewing Almack's, evading the tiger-mothers, searching for someone wonderful, waiting patiently for her to cross his path.

But Corinna? Still, how could he help wondering about her, after listening to Simon rave on about all the negative and positive attributes of the beauteous and exasperating Lady Corinna all these years?

Simon had never once considered it—that a best friend could become a best adversary, a competitor, a winner.

"Take your shot, if you must," he said, keeping his voice neutral.

Richard moved a pawn between the queen and Simon's knight. "It's merely a warning, my friend. You never know who might come from the corner and trip you up. The one least expected could knock you right off your seat."

"Excellent advice, my dear Cawley—I will keep it at the forefront of everything I plan to do. From now on, I will think five steps ahead instead of two . . ." He took Richard's pawn with a rook and looked up at him with an air of disingenuousness. "And make sure anyone who tries to storm the castle drowns in the moat."

Chapter Five

Later, she felt as if she had dreamt the whole encounter.

"Tell me truly, Fanny—was Simon really here?"

Fanny sighed. "Oh yes, he was, my lady. *Such* a nice man."

"Fanny! He got to you too . . . he could seduce a house cat, I swear."

"He is a very fine figure of a man, and well-regarded, my lady, in case you had not heard."

"His pursuit of the ladies notwithstanding . . ." Corinna said acridly.

"Oh no, my lady. He is considered to be very fair and equitable with all the young ladies. They do like him. As do I . . ." Her tone muted in coy approbation.

"Oh, poof," Corinna muttered. "What has he got to recommend him but a pair of broad shoulders, several thousand a year and that look in his eye?"

"In some quarters, my lady, that would be more than enough."

But Corinna knew that, though she still couldn't see a one among those currently to hand who would make a suitable wife for Simon. However, not every blooming virgin was yet in town.

Meantime, she had hoped to see Simon at the next succeeding event, an evening of music at the home of Lord and Lady Luscombe. Here too it was as much a crush as everywhere else in the high-ceilinged ballroom, but this night, only the lightest refreshment was to be served. The guests were led to chairs set out in symmetrical rows, and servants discreetly brought drinks as commanded before and during the performance.

It was one of Corinna's favorite entertainments because she did not have to make small talk, or be involved with anyone she didn't wish to. It was an opportunity to be seen, to be kind and courteous, to renew old acquaintances still further, or—if she chose—to not talk to anyone extensively at all.

But above all, she had thought it would be the next time she would see Simon, and that did not prove to be the case.

The depth of her disappointment shocked her, and she tried to shake it off. It was too soon to feel this urgency, and especially after only one kiss. It was too much to want it this keenly, this acutely. It felt almost painful, and yet, it hadn't been but a day or two since she had seen him.

Kissed him.

No, since he had agreed to . . .

What exactly *had* he agreed to?

To be willing . . .

She caught her breath. *Willing*—

She looked around at the flower girls as everyone milled in the reception room at the end of the performance. Who among them was willing? Who among them could stand toe to toe with any of the lofty bachelors on the prowl this season?

She could have done, had she not pursued Woodholme with such single-mindedness. She could have been among them, all those years ago, showing them how, and leading the way.

No pretensions now. Or ever. She had always gone after what she wanted, and what she wanted was Simon, *right now,* and he was nowhere around.

She bowed and spoke to a dozen people as she made her way to her hosts to relay her appreciation for the evening; and by the time she got to the door, her carriage was already in front of the townhouse.

She climbed in dispiritedly; the footman closed the door, enveloping her in a surprising darkness, and she was summarily pulled down onto the seat and her hands tied behind her with rapid expertise as a disembodied voice whispered in her ear. "Shhhh, my lady—shhhh. There is nothing to fear . . ."

Simon? Her heart started pounding wildly as she put up a vain little struggle against his strength. A moment later, those same expert hands wound a blindfold over her eyes, and then turned her toward him, wound his arms around her, and pulled her up hard against his body.

"Who are you?" she breathed, all-consumed with a combination of uncertainty and excitement, helplessness and potency, because he *had* come, and her desire and his willingness were powerful enough to *make* him come.

She could feel his heart pounding, feel the radiating heat of his body, his broad chest against which she lay.

"Call me . . . call me your shadow lover, my lady. During the day, I am a proper man seeking a proper wife, but by night, I am your lover in the shadows, dominating your body, demanding your sex, where no one can see . . ." He crushed his mouth on hers, ravaging hers with his tongue, seeking, sliding, boring into the wet heat of her, and then pulling away to whisper against her lips: "I will always take you in darkness. You will never know when I will come. But I *will* come . . . and I promise *you* will come—if you can accept those terms."

Could she? A lover in the shadows whom no one would ever know. Their every encounter in the darkness with her bound and open to him, her sex a siren call to his mastery of her body? Had she bargained for this when she had enticed him into willingness? This suddenly had become a level of sensuality that was terrifying and galvanizing all at the same time. So easy to be seduced by it. She wanted to willingly submit to it.

His lips and tongue were even now making a trail of hot wet persuasion across her lips and on her tongue, cajoling her, seducing her, sucking her in.

The utter mystery of the dark enfolding her, binding her, so that what he willed became her desire to feel, to experience, to know.

Was she willing? Her senses, whipped to a frenzy just by this one dark encounter, clamored for more. Her body shuddered with anticipation, her every nerve ending quivering, seeking, needing him to touch, stroke, fondle, anywhere, any part of her body that he wanted.

And every part of her was clothed, bound, constrained.

She could barely swallow, barely say a word, she was so aroused by just his words and her own helplessness against his potent strength.

"That was what you wanted, wasn't it, my lady?" He swiped her lips again with his tongue. "A lover in the shadows to fill you up with his manhood and his seed? One you don't have to see, or be attached to, or even speak to—just a willing body and a hard penis, isn't that just what my lady needs?" He nipped her lower lip. "Thus my lady's shadow lover is born, of a wish, a whim and a willingness . . ." He kissed her then, that crushing, consuming kiss. ". . . to lie down in the darkness with the need and the lust—"

"Yessss . . ." it was barely a breath against his ravaging lips. "Yes. Yes. Yes. I want *more* . . ." In the darkness. The voluptuous anticipation, the not knowing where and how he would touch her, kiss her, feel her. *If* he would caress her and arouse her. If he felt the same uncontrollable lust for her as she felt at this moment on the precipice . . .

He was a stranger this night, she knew him not, and it was well that she would surrender her body to this dark stranger whose kisses made her body feel boneless, made her soaking wet with need, and whose hot probing tongue right now was her whole sensual world.

She was not aware of the carriage movement, or of time passing, only his insistent hot tongue and the darkness and his heat, and suddenly, suddenly, his hand slipping beneath her cloak, cupping her breast. And then he was sliding that hand up to her gauzy neckline, and tearing the fragile material, so he could slip his hand into her bodice and masterfully surround her hard peaking nipple with his two fingers.

Everything in her body liquefied as she felt him squeeze her nipple—she surrendered to the darkness, the kiss, and his expert fondling of her nipple as the carriage drove on and on and he drove her on and on with his insistent fingers and his hot tongue, and he succumbed to the dark lure of her sex and her power, even as she yielded her naked nipple to him.

In the dark and bound by him and to him, her shadow lover, she took his terms, took his lust and his desire, and bound him thereby to her.

And so they lay, his fingers playing with her nipple, his tongue idly playing with hers, as the carriage meandered through the dark endless streets and finally drew up to her townhouse.

She was wet, hot, swollen with need. "Come in with me."

"No, my lady. On this I am adamant—your shadow lover can never be seen. Nor can you be seen bound and blindfolded by your lust and my desire. No, my lady, this is solely and only for us, in the darkness, in the shadows . . . Next time, my lady. Until next time—"

She felt him ease away from her, felt as bereft as if he had been torn from her body, felt the bonds around her wrists loosening to her dismay; she ripped them off in a frenzy, and then her blindfold.

But, as quick as she was, she was too late—somehow, like a shadow, he had merged with the darkness and slipped into the night.

The hunger to have him again raged in her like a fever. Never in her wildest imagination had she pictured such a scenario: herself bound and blindfolded and at his mercy in the dark. And yet, she felt the power of such a subversion as well. Her will drove his desire, and her submission to his need was the prize.

She knew she need only say no, and the thing would be over. And that just escalated her excitement that much more. She never thought to experience such a voluptuous response, such a wildfire of need; she had never wanted anyone more.

Until next time . . .

But only he knew when next time would be. That was the game. And her part was to feast on the memory of his words, his kisses, and his fingers on her breast. On the unfurling of her body, and feelings long suppressed, glorying in the luxury of her sex.

From this, it could only be barely a step into her bed. Into the lust and heat and nakedness of his possession of her. The pure yearning for it made her aching and hot with longing.

She couldn't catch her breath for thinking of it. She wanted him in her bed, now. No one had ever made her this lustrous and wet and squirming with desire.

For one unseemly moment, she wished she were a man, she wished she could roam the streets, choose a body and fuck whom she would.

But that would be such a quick release, over and done in a breath. Nothing like this heart-pounding need, this lush, languid, breathless yearning, this fantasy-crazed imagining of what would happen, how it would be.

She knew some of it already. It would be in the dark. She would be unable to see, blindfolded, perhaps; bound, maybe, and all that by *her* leave for her pleasure . . . with her body taut and tight waiting for that first invasive caress that would send her spiraling out of control.

She felt out of control already thinking about it, her body taut and quivery with the rending craving for it, and in her mind, always suspended in that voluptuous moment before submission.

Dear heaven . . . next time.

She must wait until next time.

Whenever next time would be . . .

Difficult to get through the day now, with the thought of *next time* flirting on the edge of her consciousness like sin. She felt like stripping away her dresses and waiting, naked and vibrating, every impediment removed, just to be ready for him, available to him.

But then, she would be in daylight, and he had made it very clear: their assignations must always be in the dark.

Who had devised these terms?

She almost couldn't bear to leave the townhouse. But the daylight hours were for living her daily social life; the night alone was for her descent into unbridled lust.

She had never reckoned on that. Or her flaming response. She had thought it would be a neat coupling. He would come to her, he would kiss her and come to her bed, he would perform on her with a smooth elegance, and leave her in the morning.

But this—this opulent loss of every impulse, this velvety desire to be sucked into his lust . . . oh, this was something wholly stunning—and on some level, wholly known, and too real, as if it had always been close to the surface, and she had never chosen to acknowledge that part of her.

This was a greedy carnality that fed on itself and was devouring her in the process.

She needed for it to be next time.

She slept now in the sheerest of nightgowns, made of fine lawn, and utterly transparent. He could tear it off. He could burrow beneath.

He would come. Every night, she dreamt he was in the shadows, watching her in her sleep, as consumed as she with the hunger for possession.

The waiting was intolerable. And yet, she could do nothing else.

Until she was awakened one night to find her arms spread apart and bound in slings, her eyes covered once again, and the sense of the presence of her shadow lover at the foot of her bed.

"My lady . . ." his voice was low, and throbbing with that ineffable male lust.

"You have been a shadow truly," she whispered, deep in the dark of her imagination as she felt him climb on the bed and straddle her legs. "Nowhere could I grasp you."

"You feel me now—" He ran both hands up either leg, pushing her nightgown up toward her thighs, and then stroking her with long cupping movements all over her legs.

And so he was taking her, quick, fast, no preliminaries—
she didn't care. She writhed, she moaned, she canted her
hips in invitation for him to caress her bottom. She felt succulent, pliant, thick as clotted cream as he moved his hands
all over her legs and closer and closer to the prime point of
her body.

His hands were relentless, every which way she turned and
wriggled, his hands were there, sliding all over her, hot, provoking, pushing her legs further apart as he caressed them, and
stroked the outer lips of her cunt.

Keeping her hands away, her shadow lover in the dark, as
his hands came closer and closer to the pleasure point.

And then, she twisted her hips one way, and her torso the
opposite way, and suddenly, he penetrated her, his fingers deep
in the hot satin between her legs and crease.

She almost drowned in the sumptuous surge of pleasure
from feeling his fingers inside her. Her body went tight, taut,
stretched to accommodate him, easing his way into her secrets
in the dark.

And he rode her this way, twisting his fingers deep inside her,
pushing and probing her darkness, her pleasure, her holes. And
she didn't stop him; she could have pulled her arms out of the
slings, she could have embraced him, but instead she embraced
the violent pleasure of his invasive fingers exploring the depths
of the most private parts of her.

She rode his fingers, sinking deep into the lavish darkness of
this lustrous sensual ravishment, her hips undulating urgently
as she sought the hardness of his fingers and the depth of his
penetration.

In the dark. Everything was heightened by the dark and his
total possession of her nakedness. She wanted him to root
there forever, just like that, deep, dark, hard, twisting, moving,
stroking, both ways. It was like a wave, rippling front to back,
rising and falling, dark plummy waves of pure creamy pleasure, clotting one sensation on another until she almost could
not bear the feeling.

And then it broke, thick, luscious, whipped high and hard against his finger, deep in the dark pleasurable places between her legs.

And even then she still rocked against him, draining every last feeling from her body. "More . . ." she whispered.

"How hungry is my lady?"

"As hungry as a shadow. No substance. Must ever be fed."

"Your shadow lover can provide you with the sustenance you crave, my lady."

"Then I must have it."

"And I will give it to you—when your way is eased."

She heaved up her body so that his hold on her slackened. "I have eased your way. I want it now."

"As you wish, my lady." He stripped away his trousers and positioned himself so she could take his penis easily in her mouth. "And now my lady . . ."

"This is no shadow," she murmured, as he rubbed himself against her face, and slowly inched his bulbous head between her lips. Oh yes, this. It aroused her all over again, to feel him like this, in the dark. Just the tip of his penis, so thick and pliant, luscious . . . "Ummm . . . thick . . ." She enclosed the tip with her mouth and began sucking eagerly . . .

He drowned in the wave of her sensual sucking—it would not take long, not with her lapping tongue rolling all around his shaft, as if she were feeling every inch of him; not with her rhythmic sucking on the very pleasure point of his being.

This was a Corinna he never could have conceived of—a sensual creature of the night, already opened, alluring, naked, willing, yearning for *him* . . . and he was gone—

Gone—over the edge and into the lust of the sensual sounds as she pulled and sucked the cream out of him, a blast of pure wanton culmination that spewed into her mouth and down her neck, to pool sticky and thick between her breasts—pulsing, throbbing, ejaculating every last drop . . .

Gone . . .

"Simon . . . ?" But she knew—her shadow lover was no

longer in the room, leaving her on the skirling edge of pleasure, and covered in his cream.

And yet, later—he wondered. She was so well schooled, Corinna. So easily aroused and brought to point. Positively panting to live in his dark fantasy of lust. Well versed in the obverse ways of obtaining pleasure. Begging for his sex.

He hadn't expected to have such a hard time merging the old Corinna of his dreams with the new.

But it wasn't as if she had come upon this carnal knowledge out of the blue. There had been the earl. Not a man to brook foolish virgins.

Corinna had caught his eye—deliberately, one might say—and it was over. He was not a man, at his age, to be denied. He would have wanted to savor every last inch of her silky body. He would have taken her as he would, teaching her to please him, in all the ways a man might invent.

She could not have been in love with him. That Corinna had known nothing about love. But two years under the earl's tutelage—who knew what preferences the earl might have had? Who knew what Corinna had done to accommodate him?

It was not for him to speculate. Two years of marriage with a lusty older man could yield a world of experience that Simon had yet to imagine.

To say nothing of other lovers Corinna might have had.

The feckless Corinna he had loved as a boy existed no longer. She *was* a woman now, with all the passion and lust that a woman should desire, and last night had been a voluptuous surprise that he was not over yet, even while he was ruminating over the nature of her experience.

But to dwell on that was suicidal. It was enough to be her shadow lover, which was all she wanted him to be.

Until, of course, he found a wife . . .

Chapter Six

Now he knew everything, he knew her weakness and her desire, and every part of her body that was open to him, he knew.

Corinna stared at her reflection in the mirror the next morning and wondered if she looked any different. It didn't seem to her that there was a change, but deep inside, in all the secret pleasurable places he had touched her body, she knew there was.

She rubbed her chest where he had spilled his seed. Her skin felt softer, did it not? *She* was softer, like tallow—thick and malleable with this burgeoning lust she couldn't seem to contain.

She had taken a lover and given him everything, in the dark, and she was melting for him already between her legs not hours after he finger-fucked her so thoroughly.

What kind of woman was she?

The kind of woman who had a lover and no commitments, no constraints, and utter sensual freedom. The kind of woman she had long ago determined she would be.

And counting the hours until her shadow lover would return?

She understood her impatience—it had been far too long since she had had a paramour, and his expert use of her body was too new, too delicious; she wanted to savor it and she wanted more of it, and more. Even the thought of it aroused her to a fever pitch.

It had not been like that with the others . . .

But she had not given over her body so freely and fluidly before. Ever. Not even to Woodholme . . .

No!—never say so . . .

Yes—that was the truth of it. And that the idea of a shadow lover excited her beyond coherence.

But there was yet another day to get through—and still he might not come.

"What shall we do today?" she asked Fanny the next morning over a of pot of hot chocolate and a plate of scones.

"I do believe my lady needs to refresh her wardrobe. The invitations are coming thick and fast, and while you bought enough dresses in Paris to outfit an army, they might just be a little too *avant* for some occasions. If you take my meaning."

"You want to go to the dressmaker," Corinna translated dryly. "So, who is the *modiste* of the moment?"

Fanny wriggled her eyebrows. "Miss Wytch—and only a favored few are among her clients. She is as selective as a patroness, and no less haughty. Suffice to say, I cannot tell you how I came by her name—or any of this information. There is even a secret word."

"Oh, my word . . ." Corinna murmured. "Well then, of course we are obligated to go." At least it would be a distraction. It would take her mind off of the night, the feelings, the sex.

"Exactly, my lady."

They set off an hour later, and had not a little trouble locating Miss Wytch's establishment in Mayfair, which proved finally to be on the upper level of a highly unobtrusive building, with no signage or anything to indicate that a dressmaker was in business there.

Fanny not only delighted in her knowledge of this, but also in the fact that she had got the password, and because of that, Miss Wytch would, accordingly, receive them.

Miss Wytch proved to be as tied back, starched up and stiff-necked as an arbiter of taste should be. She examined Corinna from every angle, grudgingly allowed that she was "well formed," took copious measurements of her nearly nude body, and held up swatches of a rainbow of colored fabrics to deter-mine her appropriate colors, all in aid of manufacturing "a style for my lady that is wholly, completely and suitably her own."

And all Corinna had to do was to put herself into Miss Wytch's hands, money no object, and in several weeks—barring the immediate need for one exquisite ball gown—just at the onset of the season, in fact, she would be utterly transformed.

Corinna looked at the bill and felt well and truly transfigured by the amounts written thereon. But she agreed that Miss Wytch should proceed as they had discussed, and with that, she left Fanny to the details, and descended to her waiting carriage.

One step up and in, with the help of the footman, and instantly she was pulled into the dark magical world of her shadow lover, the blindfold deftly slipped over her eyes and his strong arms enfolding her tightly against the hardness, the heat of his body.

And then he fit his mouth slowly and deliberately against hers, taking her tongue, hot, demanding, utterly powerful, totally irresistible. She wrapped her arms around him, slipping into his wet sensual world, every nerve ending thickening with desire.

This—yes, this. Just like this.

The carriage jerked forward, bearing them away. He brought her more tightly against him, deepening the kiss. In the dark, she had nowhere else to go but to focus on the every nuance of the kiss, her every heightened sense, the sinuous wetness between her legs.

The kiss went on forever, a kiss without end. She allowed herself to touch his face, to feel the texture of his skin, to feel the strength of his jaw, the erotic tenseness of his body.

All that, in one long heated kiss.

How many miles in that kiss?

She broke for just an instant, her lips a breath away from his. "How—?"

He ran the back of his hand against her cheek. "Does it matter?"

She touched his firm lips with her fingers. "No. Wait—
Fanny? You—? Miss Wytch . . . ?"

He nipped at her lower lip. "I will never tell."

"So discreet, Simon. I do like that about you."

"I hope there will be other things you like as well, my lady."

"There are," she whispered, "I will," and she gave herself up
to his kiss. It was all she needed—just his mouth teasing her,
caressing her, taking her in the dark, where her desire was mag-
nified and sharpened to the knife edge of anticipation.

All he wanted was her kiss.

Was it an hour—two—that they drove around London in
her carriage, in the dark, with her lost in the vast hot world of
his kisses? It never stopped, not the carriage, not his kisses, not
her squirming need to make him touch her, make him take her
against the squabs, against all common sense and reason.

It was dark after all, and she needed more, truly more; her
body twisted and turned, as she tried to entice him into the lust
of possession.

He never gave in. He didn't caress her in any sensual way; he
just held her and kissed her and felt her body wholly dissolve
against his in the dark.

And then suddenly he pulled his mouth from hers, set her
away from him as the carriage stopped, and in that one befud-
dling instant, he was gone.

She ripped the blindfold from her eyes, but the light was too
piercing for her to follow him. He was gone as suddenly as a
shadow, into the shadows, and into the dark world of her
imagination and desire.

The next event she attended was a ball not two nights later.
Two nights of ruminating and yearning and in her heart of
hearts delighting in this sensual game that Simon played so excellently well.

But it was time to come to point. She couldn't take much
more of this lustrous foreplay without some kind of culmina-

tion. Her body felt like a tightly strung wire—at perfect pitch and ripe and ready to play.

But, she thought as she entered the ballroom at Wofford House and looked around at the assemblage, could the green girl Simon would choose for his wife even appreciate the finer points of his elegant seduction? He had honed his skills too finely. He needed no practice on her. She was embarrassed to even have suggested it.

He needed a wife, and his skills and her needs had no place in that equation.

It was best not to think that way, in any event. But she couldn't help it, because the ballroom was full and wall-to-wall with sweet young flower girls in their first bloom, all dewy and delicate, clothed in silk, challis, gauze and guile.

The seasonal assault had begun and the Wofford ball was the opening salvo. Perhaps it was as well that she had paid Miss Wytch, at Fanny's urging, that much extra to provide an exclusive gown, made up of rose-colored silk crepe overlaid with blond lace dyed to match, for this first real event of the season.

It was a crush beyond all crushes. Everyone had come to Town for this event. One could barely move, let alone breathe. Procuring a drink was impossible. Having any conversation beyond nodding to acquaintances was impractical. And there wasn't a breath of fresh air to be had anywhere in the cavernous and crowded room.

There seemed to be music playing somewhere as well, but the goal of most of the guests was solely to see and be seen and gird for the seasonal competition.

So Corinna was relieved finally to come upon Lady Apperson, who in her good-natured way, invited Corinna to stay with them and comment on the milling crowd.

"For we are taking bets on which of the vestals Simon might choose," she told Corinna gleefully. "They have all paraded by at one point or another, for to a certainty, they had strict instructions to circulate and be seen by one and all. So it has become a most diverting game. Perhaps you would like to play?"

Would she? No, there were just some instances where it was better to keep her own counsel. And this was dangerous ground anyway, given her shadow lover.

"Oh, I think not. It will be more amusing to hear your opinions in the matter who know him all that much better than I," she said finally, with, she hoped, disarming tact.

Lady Apperson sent her a sharp look. "Perhaps you are right. But certainly your opinion about the girls themselves must have some merit. How they comport themselves, their beauty, their dress—we will have at least that valuable commentary from you, Corinna. You cannot back out. It is the only sport of the evening."

"And seeing old friends back to town," Corinna murmured. "Surely there is some value there."

"It is a blessing and a joy," Lady Apperson agreed. "And here comes a dear old friend now, a man who never sets foot into anything resembling a social situation on pain of death. And yet here he is."

She gave him an arch look, which gave Corinna a moment to assess him. He was tall, elegant and austere. Older than the dandies and heirs who were milling around and greeting friends. A little too worldly, she thought, maybe very wise. It was in his eyes, his very frank pale blue gaze that settled on *her* as he awaited an introduction.

Lady Apperson took the hint. "Corinna—this is the usually absent Richard, Viscount Cawley. Richard, Lady Corinna Woodholme."

They bowed in acknowledgement and then Lady Apperson dug in. "So, Richard—are you here to lend support to Simon's ongoing quest?"

He kept his eyes on Corinna. "It has vast amusement value, I'm sure you'll agree. Nevertheless, he is serious in his intentions."

"Well, now we have it from the one man who should know.

Richard is Simon's dearest friend, of course, and were it not for this folly of Simon's, we would not see him in public of a whole season, let alone one hour this night."

"Perhaps I have changed, and wish to put my affairs in order as well," Richard said lazily. "Or—" He peered through his quizzing glass at the crowd. "Or perhaps I was bored and looking for some entertainment. Having forgotten, of course, how chaotic these events can be."

Lady Apperson smiled at him. Richard would forget nothing, and well she knew it. "But then, here comes Simon," she said lightly. "He has such pretty manners, don't you think, Corinna? Every demoiselle commands equal attention with equal *politesse*. No one could suppose that he favored one above the others."

"Yes," Corinna said, "he's very good at it." But having proper manners and never overstepping the bounds of propriety did not win a man a wife, she thought. There would hardly be any time at all to get to know a girl as it was. They would all have invitations everywhere, and if they had a fortune and were fortunate, they would be sought after by more than one eligible *parti*. How could Simon make any kind of informed choice with such limitations, and the further constraint of the watchful eye of a chaperone? It was daunting, to say the least.

"But surely there are no odds-on yet?" she added.

"Oh, I'm not up on the betting books. Richard would know."

"I will say only that money has been laid down here and there, but it's early days yet," Richard said in that offhanded way of his. "Not everyone has looked over the crop yet. That will effect a signal change once the eligible have been parsed out. Ah, Simon . . ."

"What are *you* doing here?"

"You see," Lady Apperson murmured.

"Tripping with great caution around the ballroom," Richard said lightly. "I haven't done that in years. I find it—edifying, and the perfect confirmation that all my past instincts have been right on the money."

"And yet you are here," Simon said, his tone slightly threatening.

"Could not stay away as you begin your pre-marital adventure, my friend."

"Corinna—" Simon turned to her and ignored his comment altogether.

"Simon." What else was there to say? The comedy of it all was that no one really wanted to make conversation. Every one of them was scanning the crowd, looking for the flower girls, seeking the one who stood out, who was the most magnetic, elegant, intelligent, beautiful—all the graces a man could wish to possess in a wife—so to push Simon in that direction.

It took Simon no time to leave them in search of that very one, and for Richard to sequester Corinna apart from Lady Apperson and her company.

"So my lady, it seems you have so easily renewed your acquaintance with Simon."

"Indeed," she said—carefully. "It seems as if the years just fell away."

"That must be very comfortable, considering how it might have been."

"I had not thought it would be," she admitted. "As you must know, we did not part on amicable terms."

"That is understating it," Richard said, "but I am aware of the circumstances."

"I assumed so, if you are Simon's friend."

"Well. Good," Richard said. "Now we can be friends as well."

She felt a ripple of something—awareness, an undercurrent. Richard was not so innocuous as he looked. Nor had he been bosom-bows with Simon before the debacle of her refusing his offer of marriage. So what did Richard really know?

"It is done," she said lightly, giving him her hand. "And so now—tell me, how goes Simon's search for a wife?"

"You tell me."

She shrugged. "I only know he is the talk of the town."

"I'm afraid his virtue in wishing to find a wife is far out-weighed by the *ton*'s curiosity about you, my lady. Do you not wish to find a husband?"

Ah, plain-speaking. Corinna slanted a look at him. Yes, he was a one who would not tolerate dissembling. He didn't need anyone, only himself, and so the frivolous gossipmongering about everyone's love life could not concern him, except inso-far as it affected his friends. He was above all that, and she had the gleeful thought that it might be great fun to find the woman who could bring him to his knees.

But she had other fish to fry. And surely they must be of one mind that Simon's interests were paramount. So she answered him candidly and with the intent of shocking him, "No, I do not wish to have another husband. I wish solely to have sex."

Her response had the desired effect. He choked, and she am-plified further, "You need not offer yourself, my lord. I have found a suitable lover who makes me very content."

"Have you? I'm so sorry."

"Now, my lord. It is ever thus. You may wish and want and then take action—while a woman of my circumstance must hope and wait, and expire of need and desire. I infinitely prefer things this way—in my control, with no constraints and no husband to ride roughshod over me."

"I see," he murmured, feeling a deep pang of regret. She, of anyone he had ever met, made him yearn—just for a moment—for female companionship. She was bright, sharp, elegant, beautiful. Experienced. Experience had some merit, if it had been obtained within the bounds of matrimony.

But he must stop thinking like this. She had a lover. Simon must be told.

"Oh, and Richard—" she touched his arm, "I just had the best idea." She had—and talking with Richard had precipi-tated it. It made such sense. She could even enlist his aid, given how removed he seemed to be from the social situation. "I will help Simon find a wife."

Richard looked thunderstruck, and she went on, elaborating

on the thought, "It will be simple as stones . . . he will have the benefit of my impartial assessment of whichever worthy damsel catches his interest. It's a most excellent idea, and you must help me convince him. There is no one among his friends who can be as objective as I."

Richard choked again. "How true," he murmured. "It will be my pleasure, my lady. I agree—it is a most excellent plan."

Within two hours, Simon was bored to tears. The level of insipidity among the flower girls was at a new low, he thought, and he was ragingly impatient to have the evening over with.

And he knew why, too. *Corinna* . . . whom he'd left with Richard, which might have been the biggest mistake of his life.

But the niceties must be done. The gossips were watching. Never too long with one girl. Visit with friends. Pay obeisance to the patronesses of Almack's because his attendance there must be secured.

With all of that, it was with much relief that he saw Richard on the edge of the crowd, *not* conversing with Corinna, and doing what Richard did best—watching everything with a supercilious eye.

He made his way toward him, stopping every step of the way to greet some acquaintance, eager match-making mother, or just-arrived-in-Town friend.

It was wearing to say the least, to find the right word or tidbit to keep up his end of the conversation. Richard, at least, was bracing and refreshingly raw sometimes and didn't require a man to run a constant commentary.

He looked, actually, a little disturbed, and his attention, Simon was puzzled to see, was focused wholly on Lady Corinna who was deep in discussion with some acquaintances on the opposite side of the room.

"She is still quite alluring," Simon greeted him, following his gaze.

"Just enchanting," Richard said caustically. "I now have it

on good authority she does not seek to remarry, but would rather just have sex."

"An admirable desire," Simon said, a little stunned that Richard had elicited this information in about five minutes' acquaintance. No one else could have apprised him of Corinna's wishes but Corinna herself and that seemed a little too forthcoming, even for Corinna, and even if she always spoke her mind.

Richard turned to look at him, his expression grave, as if he were going to impart some disastrous news and did not know quite how to spare him. "Well, dash your hopes, my boy. There's a lover."

Simon didn't look at all distraught. "Of course there is, you dolt. *Me.*"

Richard sent him an awed look. "By God—you *are* up to the rigs . . ." He wouldn't have thought it, but Simon was a deep one, and full of surprises since he'd remade his family fortune and come to Town. Talking of wives, taking lovers, planning a *coup* . . . wait till he heard the rest of it.

"There *is* one other thing—" he added, and broke off abruptly.

Why tell him, after all? There were just some things Simon didn't need to know.

Especially when it would provide such rare entertainment.

"Forget that," he said, waving it off. "There's nothing else."

The thought tickled him. The whole idea was exquisitely delicious. The man who professed to be seeking a wife had taken as his lover the woman who had refused to be his wife, and now wanted to help him choose a wife.

This was so choice. A bear would come out of hibernation just to watch the fun. And he himself would give a fortune in coin just to see Simon's face when Corinna offered him her *objective* help in finding a wife.

Chapter Seven

She knew he would come this night. There was something about the look in his eyes, that mocking reckless look that deepened and became more dangerous as the evening wore on and he got worn out.

It was the first full exposure of this season's white lilies to the exigencies of operating in the *ton,* and they were all scared to death of committing any solecisms. So they were like puppets, manipulated by their rapacious mammas behind the closed doors of the tiring room, and barely coherent when spoken to.

And this was only the beginning. Corinna remembered it well, Simon had forgotten how onerous it was, and taxing to the best manners of the best men. They were all in the same retinue—men of position looking to mate and marry, and carrying their standard into the moated walls of Almack's and the most sought-after events of the season.

Of course he would come. He needed surcease from the rigors of the evening. He'd made no choices, singled out no one dewy bud, and so he was hers for the evening—for the night.

When, the night? He would come, she had no doubt. She lay in a fever of anticipation until she finally drifted into sleep.

And only then did her fantasy begin. She awakened in darkness, the blindfold over her eyes, her wrists harnessed, to the feeling of something wet and hot laying her legs upward, licking, nipping, sucking the tender flesh between her legs.

Inch by inch her shadow lover worked his way upward with his tongue until with one heated swoop, he embedded himself in her cleft and began sucking her there.

Now she was wide open and vulnerable to him. In the dark, she could imagine, wholly feel, every lick and flick of his tongue as he dug it into her labia and the honey that flowed there.

He held her legs spread so wide apart that she felt as if there was no part of her between her legs that wasn't open to him. And she had no other choice but to ride his probing tongue as he burrowed it deep and hard into her.

He kept coming at her and coming at her, his insatiable tongue stroking and sucking at her woman flesh, and the distended nub of her desire.

The pleasure was sharp, deep, and incandescent. She felt as if her body was sending off explosive flares as he pulled at her clit with his lips and tongue, and then—like a cannon, the spasms hit her—*boom, boom, boom*—one after the other, crackling all over her body, and jolting her deep between her legs.

And then she had to get away. She couldn't take anymore. She felt raw and sated. Over—she was too naked, too open. She twisted her body wildly away from his possession, and he pulled her back and buried his head in her pubic hair and inhaled her scent.

She pulled her hands from the harnesses, removed the blindfold, and stabbed her fingers in his hair. Thick lovely hair. Thick lovely pleasure. She wanted more. They lay like this for a long, long time, and then he slowly crept up beside her.

"It was a hellacious night. I need your kisses."

"Take them . . ." Her voice was hazy, clotted with satiation and burgeoning need as she realized he was naked, he was lusciously hard, and he meant to take her tonight.

He eased his mouth onto hers with a long low groan. Now he was home. This was a woman, eager, aware, knowledgeable about her body, her needs, her desire.

He lost himself in her mouth, in feeling the lean silky line of her body, barely clothed under her gauzy nightgown. Her nipple, so tight and hard and responsive under the fragile material, as he tweaked it back and forth with his thumb just to feel her body arch tightly, ferociously against him.

Her naked legs, long and shapely, made to wrap around his hips, to pull him more deeply inside her. Any minute now, he would plumb deep, deep, deep into her hot honey.

He nudged her leg, pushing it wide, and rolled over onto her pliant body. She melted into him, spreading her legs wider, canting her hips and enticing him in.

This was the moment, in the dark. She felt him probing her slit, felt the first push of possession, and then his penis, in the full, lush pleasure of penetration.

She caught her breath—it had been too long, too long . . . he was so big, thick, all-encompassing as he plowed his penis deep into her feminine core.

And then they lay, with him cradled between her legs, rocking gently, his hips undulating to push himself still deeper, his mouth tight against hers as she made pleasurable little sounds at each incremental thrust.

Perfect. Nothing could be more perfect. She was tight, hot, wet. He couldn't get deep enough inside her. He wanted deeper—right to the hilt, and if he could cram himself into her still more, he would. It just wasn't enough, this penetration. He wanted his balls inside her too and even that wouldn't be enough.

And then she wrapped her long legs tightly around his hips and the pleasure boiled up inside him, thick, creamy, volcanic, a spew away from swamping her in the flood-tide of it, drowning her in it.

Losing control. He hadn't yet moved in her, or stoked her naked body to a fever pitch. But she was there already, feeling his lust for her naked body right to her soul, right between her legs. No words were needed—and every word was needed—but not yet, not yet . . .

If one word was uttered, he would blow. He could barely concentrate on her kisses and the fluttery little back of the throat sounds she made as he insinuated his length deeper still.

Shadow lover no more. But she was now his naked lover, utterly bare to his lust, his need, his penis. Wet and willing. Open and honey hot to take him as deep and hard as his penis could go.

Who wouldn't want to fuck this perfectly wanton and willing body? Who wouldn't want to soak her cunt, her nipples, her body with his semen?

Just that thought—his cream oozing between her legs, smeared hot and thick on her hard pointed nipples . . . and he erupted like a gun-blast, pouring himself into her, hot and replete.

Her shadow lover, no longer an abstraction . . . dear lord, how she had missed this—the closeness, the kissing, the naked feeling of skin against skin, the scent, the sex. The unbelievable sex, raw and real and pleasurable beyond sanity.

From Simon. Her long-ago, who could have known he would be so excellent in bed, Simon. So amazing to believe. Oh, but she believed it because those spasms of pleasure had shaken her to the core.

Thank goodness, she did not have to deal with this after the morning, because she didn't know what she would have done. It just wasn't possible to live a normal life with such lust lurking around every corner.

Thank heavens Simon was seeking a wife. A wife would calm him down and ease him away from his wild ways. And give *her* just enough time to enjoy him before he must get an heir.

It was perfect, because she didn't think she could live day to day in such tumultuous need. His being her shadow lover was enough. And the fact he would leave well before morning. That was the best part. The perfect part. The way she had envisioned it when she planned her return to England.

Of course, she could never have predicted Simon would be her lover, but those were the surprises that made life so delightful. And she really did well and truly want to help him find a wife. He would be endlessly grateful to her for the suggestion.

"Simon—?" she shook him gently.

"Ummmph?"

"*Simon*—listen . . ."

"I listened. I know all your secrets."

"Shhh. That's not what I want to tell you."

"Oh . . ."

"I had the best idea today."

"That's good." He shifted his body so that he covered her again.

She wriggled away from him. He was too hard again, too hot; and she knew where that would go, but that was later. "I'm going to help you find a wife."

He pulled her back. "Ummm?"

"I'm going to help you . . ."

He bolted upright. ". . . help me—find a *wife?*"

"Exactly—who better? I can be utterly impartial, totally objective. And who has your best interests at heart?"

"My mother?"

"*Simon*—"

"You will *not* interfere," Simon said, his tone just this edge of dangerous.

"You'll see," Corinna said, snuggling down next to him, not for a moment thinking that she was using her body to seduce him to the plan. "It will be perfect. I will find you just the girl of your dreams, and you will be beholden to me forever."

The only thing he felt beholden to was the fact he was the only one in her bed right now. But leave her on the loose a few weeks more, and there might well be a line outside her bedroom door.

Find him a wife . . . dear heaven. First she thought he needed practice, and now she would aid in his quest to find a wife. He had found the wife he wanted many long years before, and he wanted only for her to realize it.

He had planned his strategy oh-so-carefully, on hearing the news of her return. Let her come home. Let her attend the intimate dinner parties that preceded everyone's return to Town. Let her hear about his desire to find a wife. Let her become curious, and then, at the proper moment, put himself in her line of sight and let her see what he had made of himself.

And then, withdraw. Let her be piqued by the fact he had not a moment for her until finally she must ask him to come. He knew she would, but it still had been a risky plan at best.

He never could have predicted *she* would broach the suggestion they be lovers to *him,* but that was so much the better. And last night's coupling had been wild beyond imagination.

And so, she now must help him find a wife.

It defied explanation. Unless she really *was* wholly wedded to the idea that she would not marry and truly only wanted the sex. But he couldn't—wouldn't—believe that. She was so young yet, still of childbearing years. She must, in some deep curled up place, want a child, a husband, a home, love . . .

Love . . .

He had loved *her* forever, it seemed. And those years that she had been abroad now seemed so long ago. Perhaps he couldn't have loved her then the way he did now. Perhaps he had been too young, too rash, too untempered at the time. Had too little to offer and too much to do.

Sometimes fate took a hand and steered you the way you were meant to go, and brought back to you the thing you were most meant to have.

No one else would have her, she was the wife he sought, the one he loved. And so he would sit back, fuck her until she couldn't live without it, and let her help him find a *wife.*

Lady Apperson was the source: she knew everyone and everything, and she for certain knew the names and virtues of every paper white girl who had come this season upon the scene.

And she wasn't loath to share the information with Corinna, all in aid of helping Simon find his wife.

"I will not, at the outset, tell you my feelings," she told Corinna one afternoon over tea. "You must approach this mission with no one's opinion swaying your impressions of these girls."

"Exactly my thought. Though these last several evenings, I have not seen any evidence that Simon is leaning toward any one of them with any favor."

"Still too early. And a man must size up his competition and decide where his chances lie. An honorable wouldn't want to pursue a duke's daughter if there is a prince in the offing. That way is disaster—to a man's worth and sense of self. Simon will approach this with the same forethought and logic with which he recouped his father's fortune. You will see."

But what Corinna saw was Simon in social situations operating with unfailing courtesy and good humor, and not a nod to single out any of the girls who were obtaining town bronze and flirtatious repartee faster than the gossip spread about them.

And then, there was Richard. For a man who had not presented himself in society for many years, he seemed suddenly very ubiquitous.

"And why not?" he asked of Corinna. "Simon is my dearest friend; I have concerns for whatever decision he might make. And then, in looking after his interests, I have had the great good fortune of making a new friend, whose opinions and sensibilities match mine, and with whom I can share a good piece of gossip or a candid observation."

"Exactly what kind of friend is she to you?" Simon demanded, hearing Richard's version of what he had said to Corinna.

"Should it matter—if you are indeed seeking a wife?"

"Damn it all, Richard, you know intimately what my plans are."

"Well, until you act on them . . . my lady is fair game."

He had been warned—weeks before and now this night. It was up to him to tie Corinna to him so tightly she would never think of wanting another.

Damn it, there was no time. And she was too busy vetting potential wives. And enjoying it too much, too.

"Well, here we have Miss Heath," Corinna said of the newcomers at dinner one night. "She is no beauty, is well dressed, has two thousand a year to offer her prospective husband, and a family history of many siblings four generations back. I do believe she has a half dozen brothers. You will not want for an heir with her. She would breed well and fast, Simon."

"She does not attract me," Simon said grimly.

"My lady Worsley, perhaps. Let us look. Well, she is quite lovely, beautifully dressed, well-mannered . . ."

"Pale as a ghost, ethereal as a shade. If I kissed her, she would scream and die."

"*Simon . . .*"

There was no talking to her. "Let us leave off and enjoy the dinner."

Except he didn't enjoy the dinner. Richard was too attentive to Corinna, and Miss Heath was too interested in him.

"You will have all the mothers frothing at the mouth at the thought of one of their daughters snagging *you*," Simon told Richard bluntly at a rout the succeeding week. "Look at them buzzing around. I do believe you have lost your mind."

"Nonsense. I have found a friend, and never knew how delightful these proceedings could be when you have a beautiful and intelligent companion with whom to share the absurdities."

Simon gnashed his teeth.

"Here is Lady Barkham," Corinna said. "Now let me think—what did Lady Apperson tell me about her? Ah, yes. Daughter of an earl, has a nice presence for one so young. Beautiful dress—I do believe it is one of Miss Wytch's creations—so she is well-funded. And becomingly modest.

Well, at least she doesn't blush when a man speaks to her. Simon! Here is a girl with potential."

"She is too thin, too coming, in spite of her seemingly modest airs."

"You are too particular," Corinna said, stamping her foot. "Time is wasting and there are too many others eager to make a choice."

"I can wait."

But he couldn't, because Corinna was attracting too much attention herself. Even Fanny mentioned it.

"Oh, pooh. I am too beyond the pale for anyone to have any interest in me."

"Excepting my lord Richard, and Simon, of course. Oh, and that earl—Bothwick, was that his name?"

"Oh, he was chasing every green girl under the age of seventeen, Fanny. Give over. He could have no interest at all in me."

"No, only to engage you in conversation for a good twenty minutes."

"I have no idea what we talked about." Nor did she care. She was having an amazingly good time at these events, even though she had removed herself from contention.

She supposed it was because Richard was there, providing an ongoing commentary on the foibles of the *ton*, and comically avoiding any mother hell-bent on introducing him to her particular flower girl.

Because finding a wife for Simon was proving to be hard work. And it was difficult to separate her shadow lover from the man who would be a husband and father, and she hadn't expected that at all. So she was glad he hadn't fixed on anyone yet; she still wanted him in her bed.

He came to her again that night, insinuating himself into her room as she slept, always as she slept, so that she would be enfolded in the dark, the shadows, and he could do with her body what he would.

Eat her, suck her, play with her, bring her to point. Always to point, always to the lush, sumptuous, back-bending crackling point . . . and she never knew just when he would come. She would feel him massaging her feet, her legs, playing with her nipples, his tongue in her mouth, his fingers invading her cunt . . . he couldn't get enough of her cunt, the heat, the wet, the thick honey essence of her . . . he lived in her cunt, night by night, burrowing his penis deep and dark into her hole, stretching her to the limit, and then pushing still more.

In the dark, in the shadows, naked, hot, breathless, kisses, thick wet kisses, voluptuous, opulent, her cunt soaked with his come, his penis still jutting in the thick cream of his come, hot, hard, lusting for more.

Hours in her bed, with every inch of the potent power of his penis focused between her legs.

Where she wanted him. Naked and over the moon to fuck her.

So how she could divorce the pleasure of this from the need to find him a wife, she could not understand.

"So, here comes Miss Gibney. Here is a prize—Simon, are you listening?"

"I see her," Simon said stoically.

"Is she not delightful? So petite, so perfectly formed. Everyone staring at her. What do we know of her? Oh, she is the one—much money, little pedigree. But one can overlook such things, can one not, Simon? Thank heaven she has beauty to recommend her, and pretty manners, it would seem."

And she was so tiny, he would split her in two in bed, Simon thought caustically, but he wasn't about to say so.

"Money can soothe over many faults," Corinna was saying. "I believe her father is prepared to pay for the right suitor."

"You are too well-versed in everyone's business," Simon said trenchantly. "It is not a pretty trait."

"But how else can I help you?" Corinna asked, stung.

"I have specifically asked that you do not."

"Well, you cannot mean that, Simon. I am the perfect one to give advice. Tell him, Richard, am I not?"

"You are the perfect one to be linked with Richard when

you may well wish not," Simon said, a hint of anger seeping into his tone.

"Nonsense. Nobody takes Richard's appearances in society seriously. He has chased off every hopeful mother, and they are talking about it even now."

"Plotting strategy, you mean."

Corinna ignored that. "And as well, Simon, everyone knows I am not looking for a husband. I have made that plain and clear."

"Everyone knows women are contrary, you mean," Simon contradicted her. "And that when she says no, she might well mean yes."

"Well, I don't, and everyone knows it. So do you now consider Lady Darfield. No. Do not. I have only just taken a good look at her. Could she be more prune-faced? It's as if she didn't wish to find a husband at all . . . *Simon* . . . don't walk away—for heaven's sake." She turned to Richard. "Did you ever see anyone so singularly uncooperative?"

Richard shrugged. "It may be there is no one here to his taste."

Corinna considered this for a moment and nodded. "You may be right. Well, it means I must dig in my heels and try harder." She slanted a look at him. "Don't you think?"

You don't want to know what I think . . . "Whatever you think best," he said, keeping his voice neutral. He knew what was happening, and he didn't want it to be so. But in that one lingering moment, he knew he was half in love with her, and he wished that all that energy and determination were focused solely on him.

Chapter Eight

Corinna awakened the next morning after a night of hard-riding coupling, satiated and serene, languidly stretching her naked body and inhaling the scent and residue of her shadow lover thick on her skin.

He could not stay away. Every exigency of seeking a wife was set by the board with his voracious possession of her. If she wished for anything, it was that he were free solely to be her lover. But he was a man, and must look for a wife, and set up his nursery, and she would do anything she could to help him.

So with all that, things could not be better, she thought, shivering deliciously. Things were wonderful, in fact, and everything was working out just the way she had hoped. Better than she could have imagined actually, because now she had gained so many new friends, she had the perfect lover, and she had a purpose.

And she had no constraints, and no restrictions, and she could do whatever she wanted. And she had a great ally in Lady Apperson in their mutual desire to see Simon married off this season.

And then, there was darling Richard with his caustic wit and his *touch me not* air. Richard came calling so often that Lady Apperson wanted to know if anything were up in that direction. But Corinna could hardly think about Richard in a romantic way when her body still resonated from the previous night's coupling with Simon. And what was Lady Apperson thinking, anyway?

They were both there to take luncheon with her this rainy afternoon, and to plot strategy for this evening's event, since

Simon was so intent on being so willfully obtuse. But then, why should that surprise her? This was the very reason she had offered to help him, the ungrateful wretch.

Still, there wasn't a one among the ladies they had so far seen that he could stand for more than thirty seconds. He had every excuse—too young, too fidgety, too thin, too heavy, too poor, too blithery, too fair . . .

She was out of patience with him, and she said so, roundly, adding, "Are you not as frustrated as I am, Richard?"

"Oh no, my lady. I'm enjoying this rondo enormously."

"Rondo?" Lady Apperson asked, perplexed. And then her brow cleared. "Oh!" She sent Richard a thoughtful look. "Oh . . ."

"Well, we must do something. Time is wasting, and all the good girls will be snapped up and gone before Simon can make a move. So . . . what should we do?" She looked at them both brightly. "Oh, come. Who is new this evening? Who has not yet been seen?"

"You," Richard drawled.

"Oh, pooh—I am out of contention as you well know. I like my situation, and my independence, too well. And I am well chaperoned."

"Oh indeed—no one could crash your bed," Richard murmured, and Corinna looked at him sharply.

"Not unless I wanted him to," she retorted, her tone warning him not to pursue this thought further. But it made her stop long enough to wonder just how much Richard knew. And just what Richard might really want of this friendship.

No. She had set the boundaries. No one could mistake her intent. It was Simon's future they were there to discuss.

Lady Apperson watched this interplay with an eagle eye, comprehending suddenly with a blinding clarity everything that had not been evident before, and then she picked up the train of thought just as if they were in the midst of a conversation. "Well yes, actually, there is among the ladies this evening a newcomer, a Miss Hounslow. I don't know much about her—yet—but perhaps she will prove to be interesting enough to fix his interest."

And if she wasn't, Lady Apperson thought, he ought to pretend, because nothing would jar Corinna's complacency better than a good dose of jealousy. And now she knew which way the wind blew, she thought, she must in good conscience advise him thus.

And as for Richard—well, let that wind whistle where it might. Richard could take care of himself. And if he were falling in love with Corinna, so much the better. Simon could use a good dose of lover's jealousy himself.

So here it was, two weeks into the season and Simon had not made his move, was content to let Corinna labor under the delusion he was looking for a wife, and Richard was getting very tired of the game.

He had warned Simon, his conscience was clear in that regard, and certainly Simon had seen how well Corinna and he got along, and if that had not galvanized him, then—well—he had had fair warning, and it was time for Richard to make his play.

The thing he did not know was whether Simon still shared her bed. He hated that thought, just hated it. And it wasn't something he wanted to confirm at the moment. Nor compete with. So he was better not knowing.

And in any event, that was all about to change. Simon's Corinna, about whom he had heard for all these many years, was now fair game, and ripe for a lover who would take her in hand and marry her. No games. No delusions. Richard was a man who knew what he wanted, and even on this short acquaintance, Corinna was *it*.

Meantime, Lady Apperson sought out Simon. "I truly don't comprehend what game you are playing with my Lady Corinna, but I'm warning you now, Richard is in it for real, and you need to raise the stakes and incite some response from her or you will lose her forever."

"I'm sorry—what are you talking about?" Not that he could feign ignorance for more than one minute. Lady Apperson was as sharp as a shard and nothing got by her for long.

"I am talking about this ridiculous charade you are enacting when it is perfectly clear to anyone who has half a brain that it is Corinna you want—*still*—and Corinna you will lose if you don't *do* something."

"And what do you suggest I do?" Simon asked with dangerous silkiness.

"Make her jealous," Lady Apperson said promptly. "For real. This seeking-a-wife protocol cannot play itself out without your making a choice. If you had made one already, perhaps things would have come to a head sooner than this. But now you have Richard playing counterpoint, and fast falling in love with her, and the two together—who do not play by the rules and who are already laws unto themselves—will cut you out faster than the patronesses at eleven."

Well, he had planned for that very thing. When the moment was ripe, he had been going to make a choice, just to see how it would sit with Corinna. But now she must force his hand and he would be leading from a weakened position.

What was that but a challenge? What was dear Richard but the smallest obstacle? He had still held one winning card—he was her lover and the one in her bed.

He took note of Miss Hounslow in a most provocative way. She at least was interesting—she had milky-white skin and red hair, and there was an air about her that reeked of the country, but in a way that was enticing rather than off-putting.

She was enjoying herself, for one thing. And the whole evening was not do-or-die for her. She wasn't desperate for a husband, and so she was magnetic in how she dealt with the people she met.

She was no milk-and-water-miss, *and* she was rather lovely.

The kind of girl it made sense he might be attracted to. Or that Corinna would think it made sense.

So he made a point to show Miss Hounslow some attention, while watching Richard and Corinna out of the corner of his eye. And later, Corinna accosted him, saying, "It seems you need no help from me after all."

"Was my interest that pronounced?"

"Only to those of us who have been waiting for this moment."

"I count that as everyone in the room," Simon said.

"She is very beautiful," Corinna said generously.

"I hoped you would think so. But do not try to make a cake out of some flour and salt. There are many other ingredients to be added to mixture before it bakes."

"Soup and cake," Corinna murmured, feeling a little disquieted. "All that heat required to make the raw ingredients into something palatable . . ."

"You will like her," Simon said, taking note of her diffidence. "She is not a flower girl. Quite the opposite, in fact. Do let me make the introduction . . ."

"No, I think not." *Why* was she feeling so fretful? This was perfect: Simon had found someone beautiful who seemed to have a half brain in her head. This was just what she wanted for him. To meet someone.

Because after all, meeting someone was not the same as marrying her. That would take time—they would have a courtship and a long engagement and then they had to call the banns.

All that time had to pass, so she could still have him while his lady-love waited for the moment they would marry and then *she* would have him.

And after?

She caught her breath. In all this seeking-a-wife business, and in all their voracious lovemaking, she had never really thought about *after.*

After was beyond forever at this point. Not to be thought of or considered in any real time.

But now, in the person of Miss Hounslow, it was not. It was

sooner than forever, it could be real, Simon might well marry her, and Corinna would no longer have his sex.

Oh dear lord . . . she felt breathless at the thought. Like she would just collapse from the thought. No more sex with Simon. And sooner than later now, with Miss Hounslow of the milky skin and lively eyes.

No, she was reading too much into it: there was still time. Mustn't rush it. They'd only just met, and there were several possible other suitors buzzing around the redoubtable Miss Hounslow like bees around honey. It might not be Simon who won her hand after all.

The tightness in her chest eased. It was just an evening out, after all. He would come to her tonight, she was certain.

Maybe not, if he were too enamored of Miss Hounslow. She knew how that went: he would go home, and he would want to spend the after-hours thinking about Miss Hounslow. How she looked, the inviting shimmer in her eyes only for him, what they said, what they really meant, how soon he could see her again . . .

Her breath caught again. No. Her imagination was galloping away and on no evidence whatsoever, other than Simon had spent a few minutes in conversation with her, and had had a very favorable impression.

There. She took a deep breath. Now she felt better. And besides, he wasn't even anywhere near Miss Hounslow at the moment.

"Miss Hounslow is quite the sensation tonight," Richard said quietly in her ear. "It won't take the rest of the month before someone engages to marry her. Perhaps it will be Simon. He seemed particularly attentive."

Corinna swallowed bile. Richard was either being malicious or making idle gossip, and either at the moment was untenable. "She seems a cut above the usual innocents," she said finally. "Like she has some wit and intelligence. She is exactly the kind of girl Simon should seek."

"I think so too, because that then takes him away from the pursuit of anyone else."

She looked at him sharply, and then chose to misunderstand. "But there hasn't been a lily girl who even measures up to this one country-bred vestal. Not a big field to chase, if one chooses to be really candid about it."

"There's always *you*," Richard said. "Any number of eyes are on you, Corinna my dear. Including mine."

"Oh, don't do this, Richard. Don't. I'm perfectly content as things are . . . I have no interest in setting up my nursery—I'm too old, in any event, and I have become set in my ways. I am my own mistress, I can do as I will, have the companionship I choose, and all without the nonsense that goes with a lasting commitment. Why would anyone in my position choose otherwise?"

Did the words ring hollow? Richard was too astute.

"Because finding the ideal sensual companionship is a treasure beyond price, and at that moment, you will want to make it yours forever."

She couldn't help it—her gaze skewed right to Simon, and she knew Richard saw it.

But Simon was conversing with Miss Hounslow, and suddenly she felt very vulnerable, and she was aware Richard saw it, because he leaned into her body, blocking that view, and he whispered in her ear, "Simon is otherwise engaged, Corinna. So think it over—and let *me* be your lover—no—let me be your husband."

Richard was too close, too intimate, too tight with Corinna, and Simon felt himself steaming up like a train engine, imagining every prurient thing Richard could be whispering in her ear.

Things a lover would say in the shadows, in the night. Things he couldn't even begin to think about saying to the delightful and virginal Miss Hounslow, with all her wit and countenance, even if he were to consider her as a wife.

Enough of this. No, not enough, because Corinna was looking just a little stricken and not at all like she wanted to hear whatever Richard had to say. Nor had her gaze moved an inch away from him and Miss Hounslow. So perhaps the strategy was profiting him.

But to what avail? Corinna's deep distress? That had hardly been his intent; he had thought in fact that the mere discussion of a possible wife would turn her feelings from friendship to something deeper. And if not that, then their stormy lovemaking, night after night, had to have touched her deeply and at a level where she could not abide the thought of him with someone else.

Fine. He had reckoned without taking into account the *laissez-faire* years she had spent on the Continent, where such things were common and merited barely a passing glance.

A lover here, a lover there—it meant nothing, it was a way to pass the time, perhaps, and make life interesting, especially for a widow who was in comfortable circumstances and thought not to breed or marry ever again.

All of that had been made plain, of course, but he was ever a romantic, waiting for his moment, and now it had come, he was talking with Miss Hounslow and Richard looked about to eat the shell of Corinna's ear.

If he so much as grazed it with his lips or tongue, Simon would kill him. Period.

Who ever thought Corinna would cause so much sensation? But then, she had underestimated her value as both entertainment for the *ton,* and as an eligible and beautiful young widow of some wealth.

Who would not be interested in her in either regard?

Lady Apperson had the right of it: he had the advantage, and he was wasting time.

No more smokescreens. Corinna was *his,* whether she knew it or not, and now it was time to make it known. Things had come to a head, and he had to play his one leading card: he was the one in her bed, the one between her legs. It was time to make her know it—time for the lustiest, most potent, and powerful seduction of Corinna . . . all the secret pleasures, all for Corinna, in the shadows, in the dark, this very night.

Chapter Nine

Corinna was so disturbed by Richard's proposition and Simon's attentions to Miss Hounslow, she could hardly sleep that night.

Simon had found all the ingredients for making soup. The perfect Miss Hounslow with her shimmering eyes and sweet knowing smile was the perfect spice for his matrimonial concoction. Perfectly young, of perfect age to bear children, and perfectly full of the liveliness and wit to keep him reasonably interested and on his toes.

Oh, but in bed . . . ? Simon in bed with Miss Hounslow, rooting between her legs?

She couldn't bear the thought—she wouldn't think about it, that or Richard's headlong and ridiculous proposition that had come like a bolt of lightning out of nowhere . . .

What was he thinking?

Where was Simon? With Miss Hounslow? Touching her? Kissing her? Learning *how* to love her and want her?

She jumped out of bed and began pacing agitatedly.

Why should she care? Becoming this involved with a lover had not been her plan. No, the plan had been to care about nothing except her own comfort, her own pleasure. Why should she toss that out the window just because Simon had found a potential mate, or because Richard had some ridiculous notion he wanted to be more to her than a friend?

Well, she shouldn't. She was losing perspective. And she was letting Simon and Richard turn her whole world upside down, as men always did, when she had vowed she would never allow that to happen.

There. Now she was thinking right. Richard would get over his brainstorm, and Simon would eventually ask for Miss Hounslow's hand and she would happily dance at his wedding.

The perfect ending for the perfect couple . . .

Was he perfect?

Perfect in the way that mattered most—

She must stop thinking about Simon and sex . . .

But perhaps that was the sticking point: the thought of any other woman in his arms, beneath his lustily pumping body . . .

No no *no* . . .

Every fiber of her being cringed. Sex was ever a person's downfall, and the hard lesson she was learning from this was that one should never take as a lover a man one had known since childhood because it was just impossible to let go.

Unknown and capricious men were so much easier to relinquish because invariably they had traits and habits that began to grate, they were in love with themselves, their interest inevitably waned, or hers did, and *voila*—gone, and the thing was done.

This was something else altogether.

Someone should have warned her.

And she had the awful feeling that tonight Simon would come—*she did not want him to come*—and given the circumstances, she would have no choice but to end everything, unreasonably soon.

He came. Soft as a cat, he came into her room, almost as if Fanny had opened the door and *welcomed* him in, he came. One moment she was alone in her bed, the next he was there, a length of shadow limned in the candlelight, he was there, and Corinna had not one word to say.

He took a step toward her.

She found her voice. "Stay." She sounded hoarse, rusty. Angry.

"Why?" He sounded soft, coaxing. Aroused.

"Miss Hounslow. So this—our liaison—must end." There,

admirably brief, to the point, exactly what she wanted, with no mincing of words.

"Why?" He sounded amused.

"My dear Simon, don't be dense, and don't play me for a fool. Miss Hounslow is a likely candidate to be your wife, and you cannot in good conscience diddle around with a paramour while you are courting her."

"But we are of exactly the same mind, my dear Corinna."

She looked at him suspiciously. "How so?"

"For one thing, I am not courting her. My dear lord, I have only just met the chit. And for another, my conscience likes diddling around with *you*. That I will not give up. So the choice has been made—Miss Hounslow loses."

"That's ridiculous. You must consider her."

"Why must I?"

"You want a wife."

"So I do. Indeed I have publicly said so. What about you?"

He threw that question at her so off-handedly, so fast, she barely heard it. "So you must . . . *what?*"

"What about *you?*"

Corinna bolted out of the bed. "Don't you do that, Simon Charlesworth. *Don't* say that, don't do that, don't ask— *don't* . . . I won't listen to you. I told you the rules. I told you how it must be. You cannot change things now. I don't want it, do you hear me? I don't want to be married, not to Richard, not to you, not to *anyone*—"

He let her rage for a moment. "Why not?"

"*What?*"

"Why not?"

"Because. Because sex is more fun and there's no responsibility. Because men are beasts, they get control of everything, and it's much better if they don't get control of your heart and they have to exert themselves to give you pleasure . . ."

"It's no hardship, Corinna."

She sank back onto the bed. "Don't be funny. I hate this. Miss Hounslow will be perfect for your soup."

"Ummm . . . but I'm looking for more unusual ingredients. It's my nature to seek something not in the common way—a woman of some little experience, for example," he heard her faint whimper, and he went on relentlessly, "who takes great pleasure in my handling of her body, who opens herself willingly to me, who takes me deep between her legs and urges me to press and pound for more. Whose kisses are as intoxicating as wine; whose cunt tastes like honey; whose lust is as bottomless as mine . . . does that sound like the prosaic Miss Hounslow?"

"I do not wish to marry. I will not have sex with you. Go away."

"Of course you'll have sex with me. You're waiting to have sex with me. You're dressed to have sex with me. You might just as well lie down and spread your legs . . ."

He was not wrong. His words liquefied her body even as she denied her need. And it would always be this way, she thought. She could never refuse him. She wanted his sex too much, too often, she was too greedy.

"I would mount *you*," she said suddenly, not a position many men preferred.

"As my lady wishes," he murmured, as he walked toward the bed and slowly disrobed. "The deeper I can take you the better."

She shuddered with anticipation as she pulled forward a chair and motioned for him to sit, while she admired the way the candlelight sculpted the hollows in his body, and elongated his thick jutting manhood so it looked almost impossible to enfold.

She shivered at the thought. How did one take that bone-hard muscle and insert it into her body? She canted her hips as she climbed onto the chair, and grasped his throbbing penis and angled it perfectly between her legs.

And then she sank into his hardness, down and down, his hands on her hips, guiding her, down still more until her pubis nestled against his and she felt him so rooted in her, she could not move, and neither could he, he was that close to drenching her with his seed.

He wound himself around her—his arms, his lips, touching, stroking, kissing her, his hips as always seeking to drive his shaft deeper within her. It was just never enough. Never. That was the secret pleasure—that he could never get enough, and seeking that surcease would keep him in her arms forever.

She was so pliant . . . so open; he loved her seat on his penis, the depth to which he could push it in her hole. And he loved the freedom he had to move his hands everywhere, to explore every part of her, between her legs, into her crease, stroking her anus, her nipples, and the particularly sensitive sides of her breasts; and she loved his handling of her buttocks as well, her body writhing as he caressed her there, and as he wriggled his fingers to feel her succulent clit.

He almost wanted to suck her senseless there. The impulse was so intense—he wanted that clit, those nipples, her hot tongue . . . he wanted—a thousand orgasms on her body was what he wanted, all of it now, that moment, and that still would never be enough . . .

He felt the first spurt of his come, and he vigorously controlled it as he took every liberty he wanted with her naked body. Every inch was his, every lush pleasure point was his, and he meant to keep her in thrall in this luscious position as long as he could stand it.

And every time she moved, he put his hands on her hips, and settled her cunt more tightly on his penis.

Don't move, don't move . . . just leave me jammed up inside you . . .

Perfect. Holding her bottom, perfect. Spreading her buttocks and stroking her there, perfect. Keeping her hot honey cunt centered on his penis—perfect . . .

Her squirming need to move, to undulate . . . perfect because then he could pull her back even more tightly onto his bulging shaft. He could keep her like this forever, enfolding his penis in her tight hot cunt-kiss.

"What were you saying?" he whispered against her lips.

"I love sex, I want sex, and *only* sex . . ." she breathed.

"I can do that. I could do more . . ."

"No. I want to spend the whole night embracing your penis like this."

"Let's do that," he murmured, seeking her lips. "Hold my penis rooted between your legs like this the whole night."

"Can you hold on?"

He thought about it for one second. One second too long. His body seized up, he whispered, "Absolutely—" and he came, in one long volcanic spew he came, and he took her over the edge with him.

She looked too happy, Richard thought the next night as Corinna made yet another entrance into another ballroom for yet another rout that would be such a crush nothing could be accomplished. So obviously Simon had got to her, got into her last night, which answered his question as to whether Simon still shared her bed.

He hated knowing that, he hated the crowds, he hated the insipid misses parading before him and sending him coy looks as they made their too-obvious entrances. He hated everything about the season at this point, and he would have retired to his study to read a good book already, but for Corinna.

Delicious, delightful, acerbically acute Corinna who would not listen to one protestation of love.

She might be the wisest woman in the world, he thought. Because she had to have refused Simon too. Corinna knew what she wanted. She wanted a lover. She had chosen Simon, but she could just as well have chosen him.

Maybe it really was a question of marriage, Richard thought. Maybe Simon hadn't asked her. Or maybe it was a moment for public display where she would have to make a choice. He wondered if that would up the stakes. If, on that level, he were that much of a gambling man.

He just hadn't expected Corinna. But that was what several seasons abroad did to a woman—cut and polished her to a rare finish and made her more precious than diamonds. That was the thing, for him, about Corinna. Even on such limited acquaintance it was obvious she was worlds above any woman he had ever known. Worlds away from the spoiled and spiteful miss who had spurned Simon and run off to find an earl. Worlds more intelligent, witty, beautiful, practical. Plainspeaking. Experienced.

God, he'd soon be singing paeans to her; he was that besotted already. Or was it that he just wanted to cut out Simon?

Ah, Corinna. Her eyes all alight, her skin glowing, a room-tilting smile at the ready, her gaze seeking, seeking—Simon.

"So will you many me?" he drawled as he strolled up beside her and took her arm.

"Will you not ask me?" she answered in kind.

"No," he said. "I will not *not* ask you. I deserve you. You most assuredly need and deserve someone like me."

"I need—" she stopped abruptly. "I need not to be importuned; it doesn't suit you, Richard."

"You are too right about that," he said agreeably. "But I am also not a one who takes an out-of-hand *no* gracefully."

"You are too spoiled, then."

"You are too kind."

She smiled at him. "I do like you, Richard."

"And whom do you love?"

"I do not give my heart." But she knew that was not true, and she turned her face away from him so that he did not read the lie in her eyes.

"Well, it is yet another chaotic event. We will hear no music, will have no meaningful conversation, and in the end, return home as drained as if we had put in the effort all evening."

"It is of course the sole reason we put up with all of that," Richard said. Put up with any of it, he thought irritably, when he could be home and comfortable, and be rid of this intrusive and gnawing need to make Corinna his own.

Everything had been about Corinna from moment he'd met her. And with her ongoing refusals, all the season events had begun to pall. He wanted resolution. He wanted love, he wanted companionship, and he wanted sex, and all of that with a woman of spirit who was witty and worthy.

In short, Corinna.

Who had not yet either been asked by or said yes to Simon. So there was still one last gamble. One last chance before he retired and licked his wounds.

He moved away from Corinna and made his way to the podium where the orchestra was playing, and where he presented a most commanding figure as he held up his hands. "Ladies and gentlemen—" his voice boomed over the music, the gabble and gossip, and the noise, and the crowd quieted as if it were one person, taking one deep disbelieving breath to see a most private person up on a very public and visible stage.

". . . ladies and gentlemen . . ." he stepped off the stage and started making his way toward Corinna, who looked horrified. "Corinna—Lady Woodholme . . ."

". . . will you marry me?" Another voice, commanding and overriding Richard's, from the opposite side of the room.

Simon.

Corinna whirled to see him coming toward her as well.

"Will you marry *me?*" Richard asked, not to be deterred, following Simon's words in a similarly commanding way, but a beat behind.

Oh, this was the worst, Corinna thought frantically. She wanted to sink into the floor; she wanted to render herself invisible, but the crowd had made a passageway from either side of the room as Richard and Simon paced toward her, and the crowd waited with baited breath to see what she would say, whom she would accept.

The silence was deafening after the arcing noise, and all eyes were on her.

"I have expressly told both of you—I do not wish to marry," she said desperately.

"And yet we each wish to marry *you*," Simon said. "Who will you choose?"

Everyone was watching. She couldn't get away. "You know what I choose."

"And you know what I choose," Simon and Richard said simultaneously.

Immediately a murmur rippled through the crowd. Corinna knew what it was—they were making bets. It was ever thus: they cared only about being the first with the best news, or holding the winning hand, the trumping wager.

"Perhaps it might do to have a contest," Richard said.

"There will be no contests," Corinna pronounced immediately.

"We will each kiss Corinna."

There was a smattering of applause.

"We each will *not*," Corinna said. "I will not kiss anyone—" She looked around at the crowd, at Richard, at Simon, at the Misses Hounslow, Heath, and the ladies Worsley and Darfield who were hovering around the edge. Perfectly good ladies, all, worthy of being kissed, and loved, and asked for their hands in marriage.

Richard would do well with any of them, if he truly wanted to be married. And Simon—

Simon . . .

She licked her lips. "—unless the other ladies in search of a husband will kiss them too."

A titter went up, and then a wave of voices, an undercurrent of excitement. Why not? Why not? Every man in search of wife should kiss the paper white lilies who wished to be married. It made such sense. Separate the chaff immediately, and go from there.

Bets were made surreptitiously. Money changed hands. The flower girls were pushed forward to the center of the room to one side, and the eligible gentlemen to the other, almost as if they were lining up for a reel.

"A kissing reel, one after the other . . ." Richard said.

"Come—some music—step lively . . . my Lady Hounslow—you will begin . . ."

Miss Hounslow stepped forward, meeting the very young and nervous Lord Penderfield midway, and lifting her face for his smacking kiss. Then they each moved in the opposite direction in time to the music, to buss each succeeding candidate clumsily, expertly or chastely on the lips.

The onlookers clapped, watching as the candidates on either side then diminished and retired to the sidelines, until only Corinna, Richard and Simon were left.

"Corinna, you must take your turn," Richard said, "and you will be mine."

He moved toward her, reaching for her, and it didn't take three steps but Simon was directly in front of him, challenging him.

"Touch her, and I will kill you."

Everyone heard. The music stopped. Everyone stopped dead in his tracks. Richard stared at Simon. Simon stared back, daring him to do something he might regret.

"Well then," Richard said finally. He knew how to be a good loser in any event, and how to retain Simon's friendship as well. "'Tis as I had planned: to evince enough interest in my lady to finally provoke Simon to jealousy and to action. And here we have every visible evidence of it. But what does my lady say?"

Corinna sent him an irritated and speaking look. "I would choose kiss Simon."

"And do you *choose* Simon? We all are witnesses."

And so she was cornered. And if she said no, she would not lose him, certainly, but the *ton* would pressure him anyway on his expressed determination to find a bride.

So he could not yield, and she could not back down.

If she said yes, she would be committing to something more than just a shadow lover coming to her in the night. She was so torn. A shadow lover was a perfect thing, in and out, and gone, leaving her wallowing in cream and satiety. A shadow lover didn't interfere, could have no say in her affairs, would not share her bed if she didn't wish it, would not require anything of her but that she be naked for him.

And something more was something more. A husband. A partner, a companion, a lover . . . and two with different temperaments and personalities living as one, none of which mattered in bed, in the shadows.

A lover was so easy. Something more could mean clashes, pain, sorrow . . .

. . . *losing Simon to a woman who might treasure him more* . . .

It was no one's business what might be her choice.

"*I* am going home," she said, because there was nothing else she could say, and she wheeled around and marched toward the doors, her posture as ramrod straight as a general's.

The music started up. The crowd began milling around, to talk over this last scene, and Richard turned to Simon to say, "Well, I tried . . ."

But Simon was already gone.

She stamped into the reception room out of all patience with everything and everyone. It was time to return to the Continent, where things were easier and men were less difficult, less demanding. She'd had quite enough of the Richards and Simons of society. And enough of the cackling hens who even now were chewing over the evening's events, and embellishing them probably to the point where she, Corinna, would become such an object of attention that she could not go out for a month.

"Oh you *are* in a temper," Fanny murmured, taking her pelisse.

"You can have no idea. I do not wish to see anyone of the male gender in this house—*forever* . . ." Corinna said angrily, pulling off her jewelry as she stamped up the stairs.

Enough of them all. Sex was not worth it, this public embarrassment and demand that *she* make choices. What had Richard been thinking? How smooth he was, shifting it all altruistically onto the notion he was trying to push Simon to some kind of declaration and her into some kind of acceptance . . .

MEN!

She was not so easily prodded and pushed, and Richard and Simon would discover that soon enough. It wanted only some planning—she needed to mend what had been unraveled this night.

Simon had better not be lurking in the shadows . . .

And he wasn't. He was sitting, naked, in her bed.

She stopped short on the threshold, almost tripping on the ledge.

"Go away."

"Come here."

Lord, he was so seductive—so naked, so hard, so enticing, with his legs angled and spread and his penis jutting up at her.

"The answer is no." She could resist. She tossed her headdress onto a nearby chair. That chair. The one where she had mounted him and sunk onto him, into him . . . *stop it!!!*

"Let me give you a home truth, Corinna. The answer is yes. Because in the same way that I concocted this ridiculous plan to get you back, you deliberately and calculatedly returned to England to find me."

"Never.

"Because your marrying the earl was a horrible mistake, wasn't it?"

She sat down on the chair—that chair—and kicked off her shoes. "He was a dear and kind man and treated me well, and left me with the wherewithal to do as I please. What more can a woman want of a husband?"

"A shadow lover," Simon said immediately. "A real lover. Real love. A partner. A life you build together. A home. Children . . ."

"I am too old," Corinna said instantly, insistently.

"You aren't."

They stared at each other.

Corinna's children—the thought, which had never quite entered his consciousness when he thought of marrying her, hit him in the gut.

Simon's children—the thought was like honey, slowly seeping into her consciousness, so she could almost feel a baby in her arms.

She wasn't too old, really.

"Say yes, Corinna. It will be an adventure, every bit as exciting as all the secret pleasures we've explored in bed."

She rolled down her stockings. "I am thinking on it."

"You came back for *me* . . ."

"I didn't." She shrugged out of the sleeves of the gown. "I thought you were married, frankly."

"How overjoyed you must have been then . . ."

"That you ignored me? I think not."

"It worked," Simon said smugly.

"You were busy making soup, Simon."

"Yes, and finally it has come to a consistency to be savored," he said. He grasped his penis and waved it at her. "Come to me, Corinna. Taste what we will make together. Let us simmer into something so delicious that it will feed us for the rest of our lives."

"I'm tired of this soup," Corinna said, naked now. "I need something to *eat.*" She climbed up onto the bed, and enclosed his penis head in her mouth and gave it a good hard pull. "An excellent bone to flavor things," she murmured around his penis tip as she licked and sucked at it.

This she could not give up. No matter what she might obtain in the future, this she wanted, she needed—his sex—*now*, and yes, before he chose elsewhere, his love.

"Yes, then," she whispered, licking him avidly up and down his thick shaft. "My answer is yes, Simon. But only because I think I could be nourished just by *this* for the rest of our lives."

THE BEDROOM IS MINE

Jane Bonander

Prologue

Twin Hearts, California
New Year's Eve, 1879

Tugging mercilessly at his stiff collar, Ross spat out a vile oath, then strangled the urge to swear again. He hated getting trussed up like a turkey. Might as well put a damned noose around his neck and hang him from the nearest tree. One was as uncomfortable as the other.

He pulled cold air into his lungs, savoring it. And savoring the brief quiet. Except for the distant battering of the surf against the rocks, there was no sound he wanted to hear. He let the ocean sounds soothe him as he tried to block the noise that filtered out from inside his sister and brother-in-law's house.

He leaned against the porch railing and closed his eyes, allowing himself to think about Trudy and how much he wanted to slip into her warm bed and between her lusty white thighs. He swore again, getting hard just thinking about it.

He took a long, angry pull on his cigarette as he stood in the shadows, listening to the shallow laughter of those inside as they prepared to ring in the New Year.

He called himself ten kinds of a fool for letting Samantha drag him to one of her shindigs again. Unfortunately his younger sister could wrap him around her little finger and she knew it.

The back door opened, allowing a stream of light to wash across the porch.

"Ross Benedict, are you hiding out here?" The voice was filled with pique.

"You know damned good and well I'm hiding out here, Sam." Ross flicked away the cigarette he'd been smoking, the ash dying the moment it hit the grass.

She shut the door behind her and pulled her shawl around her shoulders. "Aletha Carmody is looking everywhere for you."

He didn't like the teasing tone of her voice. "Aletha Carmody has a face that would stop a clock and a voice like a whining hound."

Sam sputtered an exasperated sound. "Oh, I thought she'd be perfect for you. Really I did."

Reaching into his pocket, Ross dragged out his tobacco pouch and a piece of paper. As he rolled himself another cigarette, he retorted, "Just like you thought Olive Hornsby would be perfect for me last year? And Hortense Cobb the year before that?"

Samantha sighed. "Olive Hornsby married Elias Rhodes last May, Ross. They're expecting a baby sometime after the first of the year. That could have been *you*."

He lit his cigarette and visibly shuddered at the thought of bedding the scrawny, pale Olive Hornsby. "Well, thank the bloody hell it wasn't." He took a drag on the cigarette, then stamped it out beneath his boot—perhaps a bit harder than was necessary. He could feel Sam's eyes probe him through the darkness.

"All I want is for you to be as happy as I am."

There was a wistfulness in her voice that he forced himself to ignore. It wasn't . . . *natural* for a man to tie himself down to one woman. He didn't understand how men did it. Of course, if he ever discovered that Derek, his brother-in-law, had cheated on Sam, he'd twist the man's balls until they came off in his hand, then make him eat them.

"And the only way I can possibly be happy is to be married?" He was incredulous. After all these years, she still didn't get it. He loved the bachelor life.

"Well, of course." Her voice had the ring of false innocence to it. She nodded toward the door. "Aletha is probably wondering if you've skedaddled back to your cabin in the woods."

Ross snorted. "If she's thinking that, she's smarter than I've given her credit for. And speaking of the cabin, Sam, when are you going to let me buy you out?"

She brushed her hand across his shoulder. "Not any time soon. And I refuse to talk business on New Year's Eve. Once I sell you my share, I'll have nothing left of Mama and Papa's."

He smiled in the darkness, sensing her sadness. Although she was a married woman, she was still his little sister. "It's not as if someone you don't know is living there, Sam."

"I know, I know. Oh," she wailed on a soft sigh, "don't remind me of them, Ross. It makes me sad, and I don't want to be sad tonight. We're having a party. Come." She tugged on his arm. "Aletha is waiting for you."

He cursed again, resisting her pull. "She spent the entire night hanging on my arm, tittering and giggling like a dull-witted child. How in God's name do you expect me to put up with something like that? And the *questions*. Hell, Sam, she bombarded me with questions. 'Do you like children, Ross? You'd be such a wonderful father,'" he mimicked in a simpering voice. "'Do you like cherry tarts, Ross? Why, I make the best cherry tarts in Twin Hearts.' And she kept squeezing my arm, saying, 'My, my, aren't you the strong one? I'll just bet you could lift little ol' me up with one hand. Oh, but that beard.'" He clucked foolishly. "'Doesn't all that facial hair bother you, Ross?' Then she lets out this godawful whinnying giggle. It grates on me like a saw on a anvil. Besides," he groused, "I like my beard."

Samantha laughed quietly beside him. "You mean you wouldn't shave off your mustache and beard for a very special woman?"

"Hell would freeze over before I did." He'd grown accustomed to his beard and would feel naked without it.

He suddenly felt her eyes questioning him through the darkness. "What is it?"

"How about a little friendly wager, brother, dear?"

"Like what?" he asked, skeptical.

"I'll bet that if the right woman came along and asked you to shave, you'd do it."

He didn't like the sound of that. "Gambling isn't ladylike, Sam."

"Afraid you'll lose?"

He sensed her cocky, self-assured smile. "Hell, no, and I'll prove it. Name the terms."

"I'll bet you . . ." She paused and tugged at his beard. "I'll bet that a year from now, you'll have no beard or mustache, and it will be because of a woman." She sounded ridiculously triumphant.

"And if it doesn't happen?"

"Well," she began, "then, I promise on a stack of Bibles that I won't ever try to marry you off again."

He guffawed, unable to help himself. "You couldn't stop meddling in my life if your own depended on it."

"I'm serious, Ross. Cross my heart."

"Yeah, I know. You cross your heart with one hand, and the other is behind your back with its fingers crossed."

"Oh, don't be gutless, you big boob. Do we have a deal or not?"

He chuckled at her persistence. "Sure. Hell, why not?"

The door opened, and Derek stepped onto the porch. "What are you two doing out here? Ross, Aletha Carmody is looking everywhere for you. And Samantha," he added, pulling his wife into his arms, "it's almost midnight. My arms are empty without you. I don't want to miss my New Year's kiss."

"Oh, dear heart," she said, her voice filled with love, "you can kiss me anytime and all the time."

"But we had our first kiss on New Year's Eve, sweet lips, and I plan on kissing you on this night every year for the rest of our lives."

Ross would have gagged had the man not been his brother-in-law. Christ! Did men really talk this way to women?

"Oh, all right, you silly goose. Anyway, I've missed you too, and I'm cold." She cuddled against him and waited for him to open the door.

"Come along, brother, dear," she called over her shoulder. "Aletha is waiting for you." Her voice was filled with gentle mocking.

Ross grunted. With great reluctance, he turned to follow her inside, feeling like a lamb being led to the slaughter. Never again, damnit. Never again! This was the last time he'd ever let Samantha set him up. Hell, he liked his life just the way it was. Responsible to no one but himself. He neither wanted nor needed some damned woman trying to fit him into her own personal little mold. Crowding his space. Constantly cleaning and fussing around the cabin. He shuddered at the thought.

Next year would be different. Sam's little New Year's Eve party would occur without him. If she tried to wiggle out of her promise not to meddle again, he'd just ignore her and the women she threw at him. He resolved never to let her interfere in his life again.

Aletha Carmody's titter scratched against his ears and he flinched. Swallowing another curse, he took a deep, resigned breath and dragged himself into the house.

Chapter One

October 1880

Rain came down in buckets. Rare shards of lighning cut through the night sky, followed by rumbling thunder.

Lily thanked the driver for the ride, then struggled out of the wagon, drawing her valise beneath her slicker to keep it dry. She watched the wagon lumber on, wondering how the poor horses could pull it through the mud. She'd been grateful for the ride, although she'd hoped to get farther than this. It had taken the better part of a week to get from San Francisco to this place, whatever and wherever it was. She was still near the coast; she often heard the crashing of the waves as they hit the rocks, and the air, though now filled with rain, still held the tang of salt.

Lightning flashed again, allowing her to read the sign on the outskirts of the town. TWIN HEARTS. In a futile gesture, she picked up her wet, muddy skirt and slogged through the muck, hoping to find some shelter from the storm.

Beneath her slicker, Lily was cold and miserable to the bone. She'd found refuge under a rickety lean-to on the edge of town. The rain had stopped, but the sky was still a dull slate gray, and the air was wet. Lily knew California weather well enough to know that it was only a brief reprieve.

She pulled off the slicker and shook it, sending sprays of water into the damp air. From her knees down, her skirt and petticoats were sodden and streaked with mud. Inside her shoes, her toes squished against the wet soles. She touched her hair and cringed; the tight curls were matted to her head.

Pulling in a cleansing breath, she straightened and looked around. Perhaps a few hundred yards beyond her was the main street of Twin Hearts. It was there that she would look for a job. The rancher who had given her a ride this far had told her there was a lumber mill outside of town. She hoped they needed a cook.

She glanced down at her clothes and her heart sank. How would she find a job looking like a rain-soaked, filthy urchin?

There was a brief break in the clouds, sending sunshine spraying through the watery air. A rainbow shone vividly against the green-spattered hills, the sight so lovely Lily's breath snagged in her throat.

Behind her, she heard the creak of a buggy. She turned to watch as it rocked toward her, feeling a sense of cautious surprise when it stopped beside her.

A young woman in a fur-trimmed bonnet poked her head out the buggy window. "Good morning!" She had one of those rare friendly smiles that lit up an already pretty face.

Lily swallowed and wiped her hands nervously against her dress. "Good morning," she answered.

"You're new around here, aren't you?"

Lily almost laughed. "Just arrived last night." By hitching rides and walking and sleeping under trees, she thought but didn't add. She was fortunate enough to have an innate sense of self-preservation, and she'd never accepted a ride from a man who was alone, no matter how harmless he appeared. The man who had given her a ride as far as Twin Hearts had had two young children with him. When she'd slept in barns, she was gone before dawn. All in all, her trip from San Francisco, though an adventure, had been without incident.

"Where are you from?"

"San Francisco," Lily answered simply.

The woman chewed at her lower lip, then narrowed her gaze at Lily. "You must be wet and cold."

"I most certainly am." Lily had never been one to mince words.

The young woman continued to stare at her. "I had my driver stop because I was nearly blinded by your wonderful coppery hair. It catches the sunlight like a bright new penny."

This time, Lily did laugh. "How very poetic! And a nice way of saying that my hair's so bright I could lead miners into a mine shaft without a lamp."

The woman merely smiled. A strange, secretive smile. "My name is Samantha Browne."

It was all so ridiculous. Two women conversing like they'd just met at a little soiree in San Francisco, nibbling finger sandwiches and drinking tea. "Lily Sawyer."

"Nice to meet you, Lily Sawyer. Get your things and come with me."

The invitation took Lily by surprise, and she stepped back. "I beg your pardon?"

"Surely you'd like to dry out a bit."

Lily swallowed a jaded retort. The woman was probably from the local bawdy house. She thought about it, aching for a chance to dry out. Maybe even have a bath. And a hot meal. Saliva pooled around her tongue at the thought of food. Bawdy house or not, she couldn't turn the offer down.

"Samantha Browne," Lily began, "you must be my guardian angel." Draping her slicker over her arm, she picked up her sodden valise and stepped through the mud to the buggy.

The house was lovely. And it wasn't a bawdy house but the home of Samantha Browne and her husband, Derek, who ran the logging firm on the far side of Twin Hearts.

Lily sat by the fire, wrapped in one of Samantha's plush, warm robes. She combed her fingers through her hair, fluffing it occasionally to help it dry. She felt like royalty; never in her life had she been treated so well.

Samantha entered the room from the kitchen carrying a tray

of coffee and scones, still warm from the oven. She placed it on the large round table in front of the couch, then glanced at Lily, obviously sensing she was being watched.

"You're wondering why I brought you here."

Lily chuckled. "That would be putting it mildly."

Samantha Browne arranged a scone on a plate and put it down in front of Lily. Lily's mouth watered and her stomach growled, but she forced herself to remember her manners.

"My . . . my family tells me I have a bleeding heart. My husband claims I can't stand to see anyone or anything suffer." A tiny laugh escaped her perfect mouth. "I guess a better way of putting it is that I'm constantly sticking my nose into things that aren't my business."

She put a cup of coffee down in front of Lily, then gestured toward the delicate pitcher of cream. "But when I see a lovely young woman standing in a vacant lot, drenched to the bone, my imagination gets the best of me. I can't conceive of any scenario that would have put you there. So you see, Miss Sawyer," she added with a smile, "I have to find out. And if I can offer you something to eat and a warm bath while you're here, so much the better."

Lily poured a tiny amount of cream into her coffee, then stirred. "It's Mrs., but please, call me Lily."

Samantha's head jerked up. "You're married?"

"Widowed, actually," Lily responded, picking up the warm cup and wrapping her fingers around it. She could have avoided this entire trip if she'd accepted Donald South's proposal. Sweet man that he was, he wasn't the man for her. She had no intentions of marrying again, anyway.

Samantha quickly turned away. "Oh, I'm . . . very sorry. I . . . I didn't mean to pry."

Lily appreciated the sentiment. "That's all right. It's been two years now. Seems like a lifetime ago."

They sat in companionable silence until Lily felt obligated to break it. "Do you always drive around after a storm rescuing drowned rats?"

Oddly enough, Samantha Browne blushed. "Of course not. Actually," she added as she sat beside Lily on the sofa, "I was coming from my cabin. My—" She stopped abruptly, put her hand to her mouth, then continued. "My parents owned a small cabin in the woods, and after they died, I couldn't find it in my heart to sell it. I drive up there occasionally to make sure it's in order."

Lily gave her a noncommittal smile, then turned to study the fire. "I'm looking for work."

"Oh? What do you do?"

"I've worked as a cook since my husband's death." No need to go into his history. It wasn't important; not to her, not to anyone else. "I cooked in a boardinghouse in San Francisco. Until it burned down." For a brief moment, she recalled the pain on Donald South's face as he watched his building go up in flames.

Samantha brightened. "You're a cook?"

Lily gave her shoulders a weary, sardonic shrug. "Now, don't tell me you're looking for one."

Samantha sat forward. "Well, not me personally, but the loggers are always wearing out the cooks. Why, that's perfect! You need a job?" Samantha nodded with finality. "You've got one."

Lily's weariness lifted slightly. "Now, if you can find me a room, we're in business."

"Oh, but I can do better than that," Samantha enthused. "How . . . how would you like your very own little cabin?"

Lily faced her, her mood lifting more. "Your cabin? Are you sure?"

"I'm positive. It's less than a mile from the logging camp. The kitchen is equipped for cooking large quantities. Someone from the camp will come by daily to pick up the food. There's a smaller cabin adjacent as well. Maudie Tupper, the previous camp cook, lives in it. She's not well." Samantha tapped her chest. "Lung trouble. Had to quit cooking when she started coughing up blood—Oh," she said, putting her hand over her mouth. "I hope that doesn't bother you."

Lily felt a wash of sympathy for the sick woman. "Of course not. It'll be nice to have the company. But . . . why doesn't she live in *your* cabin?"

Samantha's laugh sounded forced. "Oh, she refuses to. But don't worry, her cabin is snug and dry, and she'd love to have another woman around."

Lily couldn't believe her good fortune. She was wise enough not to question it. This was perfect. She didn't care if the whole cabin had fallen into decay, it was hers to use. She'd clean it up and make it shine. She'd make a home for herself, something she'd never had in her whole life. She and the late, not-so-great Black Jake Sawyer had lived in nothing but single rooms over saloons and taverns. Her luck was changing, and she knew better than to look a gift horse in the mouth.

Ross dismounted and stretched his aching back. The trip over the mountains into the valley was one he always hated. The valley was hot and dry, even in October; Twin Hearts had the blessed ocean breeze to keep it cool all year long.

He dragged in a breath of crisp air and glanced at the cabin. Thank God, he was home. Smoke chugged from the chimney. He grinned. Samantha's doing, no doubt. Before he left, he'd had an infestation of fleas in the cabin, so had moved his clothes and his bedding to Sam's for fumigation before they treated the place. Yawning, he hoped she'd returned them, but if she hadn't, he'd pick them up later. What he needed now was sleep. If it was on a bare mattress, so be it. He crossed to the lean-to and unsaddled his mount, brushed him down, and fed him.

The vegetable garden caught his eye as he trudged toward the cabin. It was free of weeds. Maybe Maudie had been feeling better. He hoped so. As he stepped onto the porch, he glanced at the sky. Morning fog clung to the tops of the Douglas firs. He'd risen long before dawn to get home, anxious to sprawl out in his own bed and sleep for the rest of the day.

Pushing open the cabin door, he barely glanced at the living room before closing the door behind him and heading for the bedroom. He yawned and rubbed his hand across his face, weariness oozing into his bones.

The bedroom door was closed. Ross shoved it open with the toe of his boot and stepped inside. The door slammed shut behind him, and before he could turn, he was hit from behind hard enough to cause him to stagger into the wall. He slid to the floor, shaking his head, trying to clear it.

He instinctively went for his bowie knife, but his hand was kicked away. He looked up and found himself staring into the familiar barrel of his own hunting rifle.

"Who are you?"

A *woman?* Attempting to focus his eyes, he shook his head again and saw a pair of pale, slim calves peeping out from between the edges of a frilly pink dressing gown.

His gaze slid up slowly, over rounded hips and a firm, generous bosom. Her hair, loose and wild around her face, was red as a firestorm, and her green eyes held not an ounce of fear.

"*Me?*" he roared. "Who the hell are *you,* and what are you doing in my bedroom?"

The woman looked momentarily surprised, then spat, "This is *my* bedroom. Get out before I blow your head off."

With a movement that belied his size, Ross grabbed the gun and leaped to his feet.

"Now," he growled, ignoring the fear that suddenly crept into her eyes, "I'll ask you again. Who in the hell are you?"

She recovered quickly. Moving away only slightly, she volleyed, "Who are *you?*"

This was getting them nowhere. "My name is Ross Benedict, and this is my cabin, therefore, my bedroom."

Her eyes narrowed. "That's a lie. I know who this cabin belongs to, and it surely isn't you. Now, what do you really want?"

Stupefied and angry, he continued to stare at her. "I want to know what in the hell you're doing in *my* bedroom. Is that so hard to understand?"

She returned an angry glare. "This is my bedroom and my cabin, at least for now. And . . . and stop staring at me, you ogling dolt."

Brows furrowed, Ross turned away, crossing his arms firmly over his chest. "I asked you before, who in the hell are you?"

"Why should I tell you? You're the one who's trespassing."

He spun around, catching her just as she tied the sash of her dressing gown, a movement that pulled the robe tightly over her generous bosom. As a thickness gathered in his groin, a thought wormed into his brain. He uttered a stream of curses that turned the air blue.

"Sam. Samantha put you up to this, didn't she? Damnit all to *hell!*" His fist slammed into the door—and it went right on through.

Behind him, the woman let out a shriek.

He turned on her, ignoring the wood splinters that dug into his flesh. One of her hands covered her mouth. The other clutched the lapels of her gown tightly at her throat.

"She did this, didn't she? Sam put you up to this."

She removed her hand from her mouth long enough to ask, "S . . . Samantha Browne?"

"Yes," he answered, his voice filled with silky understanding. "Samantha Browne."

The woman swallowed hard. "How . . . how do you know Samantha Browne?"

Ross was sick of the game. "You know very well how I know her."

The woman's demeanor changed. No longer cowering against the bed, she planted her fists on her hips and studied him. "No, I don't. Why don't you tell me? You come in here acting like a raging bull or a raving lunatic, frightening me half to death. I think I deserve an explanation. That is, if you're capable of stringing that many words together at one time."

Ross was momentarily surprised at her unusual tactics. After all, most women threw themselves at him. And no eligible woman, or any other for that matter, had ever called him an ogling dolt or a raving lunatic. Once, of course, Trudy had called him her raging stallion, but that was after a particularly satisfying night in her bed. It had been a compliment, not flung at him like pig swill. This red-haired witch was different from all the others, he'd give her that.

"She's my sister. As if you didn't know." He turned and studied the hole he'd put in the door. "And this is *my* cabin. I live here."

She gasped. "Your . . . your sister?"

Ross's temper was volatile, but after an explosion, he mellowed out quickly. "Now you understand. I don't know what little game Sam is playing, but this is *my* place. If the two of you thought this little ploy would work, well, damnit, think again."

"I don't believe I understand you," she said carefully. "If we thought *what* would work?"

"Ah, hell. Never mind. Just get dressed and get out of here. The little plan backfired, and I'm dead tired." He yawned, purposely emitting a loud, disgusting sound before pulling his shirt from his pants.

She didn't move.

They stared at each other, her gaze haughty and cool, his blatantly, purposefully sexual, while he unbuttoned his shirt. He pulled it open and scratched again, giving her a wide view of his naked chest. That usually frightened tight-assed women away.

Suddenly she shoved him, catching him off balance. He crashed into the wall again.

"Get out of here," she ordered. "You are nothing but a rogue. I'm renting this place from Samantha Browne, and if you have a problem with that, see her. *I'm not leaving.*"

Ross pushed himself away from the wall, feeling the knot of fury twist in his chest. He'd see Sam, all right, and he'd take her over his knee and tan her hide. Then he'd return and toss this flame-haired harridan out of his cabin on her backside.

Picking up his rifle, he stormed from the room. "This isn't over, woman. When I come back, I'd better find you packed and gone, damnit."

Lily closed her eyes and sagged to the bed, her heart pounding so hard she worried that it would crack her ribs. She allowed herself a moment to pull herself together, then hurriedly dressed and went into the kitchen to start preparations for the loggers' lunch.

As she worked, she thought of the man who had just left. Man? She forced a dry laugh. More like a bear. She was no small woman, but he was many inches taller than she. Shoulders so wide he'd had to turn sideways to get through the bedroom door. But he was a bear, in breadth *and* manners. He merely dressed like a man to cover his crude, beastly behavior.

Remembering his final threat, she stiffened. She was not leaving. She was *not*. She was curious to know, however, why Samantha Browne would rent her a cabin that was already occupied.

Chapter Two

Ross stormed into the house, catching Sam by surprise. When he slammed the front door, she visibly jumped. She looked up from the desk to see who had startled her and gave him a warm smile.

"How was the trip? I'm glad you're back." She bent over a ledger. "I've got to get the books done before Derek gets home. Did you bring the lumber order from Chico?"

Her calmness set his blood boiling. "Just what in the bloody hell do you think you're doing?"

She looked up again, mildly surprised. "Doing? I told you. I'm getting the b—"

"That's not what I mean and you know it, Samantha Mae Browne!"

Taking in a deep breath and expelling it slowly, Sam closed the ledger on the desk, then folded her hands in her lap. She managed a smile. "You've . . . you've been to the cabin."

"I want her *out!*"

"Oh, Ross, I can't do that." Sam's face was pinched with concern. "She had no place to go, and—"

"And you thought you could foist her off on me, is that it? Oh, no, you don't. I promised myself I'd never let you do this to me again, Sam, and I won't."

She rose from the desk, primly straightened the front of her blue flannel skirt, then stepped in front of him. "I . . . I don't know what on earth you're talking about. Her . . . name is Lily Saw—"

"I don't want to know her name, damnit!"

Samantha sighed, then spoke to him slowly. "Her name is

Lily Sawyer. She's a cook who . . . who came to me looking for a job. They need a cook at the camp, Ross, you know that as well as I."

Ross felt like punching a hole in another door, but he still had splinters in his fist from the last one. "What's she doing in my cabin?"

"There was nothing else available close enough to the camp."

"There still isn't."

Samantha turned away, disgusted. "Oh, quit bellowing. I've promised she can stay there until . . . until something comes available."

Ross tried to keep a lid on his temper. He didn't trust Sam. He'd discovered years ago that when his forthright sister hesitated in mid-sentence, she was up to no good.

"I don't believe this all came about out of the blue, Sam." He jabbed a finger at her. "No, you cooked this up, thinking that if you plunked some woman down in my cabin, I'd be too much of a gentleman to kick her out. Well," he continued, still bellowing, "you're wrong." He turned to leave.

"I'll never forgive you if you toss her out, Ross."

Stopping in mid-stride, he turned, giving her a suspicious glance. "What?"

There was no wicked gleam in her big, innocent brown eyes. "I said, I'll never forgive you—"

"I heard what you said," he interrupted. For all the times she'd tried to marry him off, she'd never threatened him this way before. It was unnerving. Unsettling. So damned unlike her. Suddenly he heard himself asking, "Where in the hell am *I* supposed to live?"

Shrugging expansively, she answered, "The cabin is big enough for both of you, isn't it?"

The thought staggered him. "Just how in the devil would that look?"

"Oh, for heaven's sake, Ross. We're not talking about Boston drawing room society. This is Twin Hearts, California.

Lord, it's on the edge of civilization. One more push and we'd all fall into the Pacific. Anyway, Maudie is there. She's so close, she practically lives in the cabin, anyway."

Ross moved toward the door again. "If this is your way of compromising her, forcing me to marry her because of it—"

"Oh, don't be foolish. I wouldn't do such a thing. And anyway, it . . . it won't be for long, Ross, truly."

Noting the tell tale hesitation in her voice, he flung open the front door and warned, "Damned right, it won't."

He was halfway to the cabin when he turned back. Because of his anger at Sam, he'd forgotten to pick up his clothes.

Lily finished cutting up the apples and tossed them with sugar and cinnamon. She set them aside while she rolled out the pie dough. She'd been amazed at the kitchenware that had been stored in a shed behind the cabin. And the kitchen was separate from the rest of the place. Well, a separate room, anyway. Samantha had told her that when her parents were alive, her mama had cooked for the logging crew, so the kitchen was not only a separate room but a very large one. After scrubbing every square inch of it, Lily had felt at home.

She draped a circle of raw dough over a pie tin and, with gentle fingers, pressed it against the bottom, then repeated the process until she'd covered the bottoms of six tins.

Memories of what had happened earlier continued to erode her self-control, and by the time all six pies were ready to bake, her hands were shaking. She glanced out the window, hoping the madman was gone for good. All morning, she'd been nervous and edgy waiting for the brute to return.

When she'd first heard noises outside, she'd been so frightened she thought her heart would explode from pounding so hard. She'd kept the rifle near the bed from the very first night, and her sense of self-preservation had always overcome her fears. But, she thought with a weary smile, he'd gotten the rifle away from her with ease. She just thanked the good Lord she'd heard him coming. At least she'd had time to throw on the dressing gown Samantha had loaned her. Otherwise . . .

She let out a whoosh of air. Otherwise, he'd have caught her without a stitch on. He could have . . . She shuddered and leaned against the counter, trying to keep her breath even, trying not to think about what he *could* have done.

Hearing a noise, she lifted her gaze to the window. Her heart sank. He was back. She slipped three of the pies into the oven, then picked up a knife and began slicing vegetables for the stew she was preparing for the logging crew's lunch the following day.

She would not let him toss her out. She would *not*. If he refused to leave, she would just make the best of a bad situation. At least Maudie was there as a chaperon, although Lily wondered what good the poor woman would be. Maudie hadn't left her own little cabin since the day Lily arrived. Lily had spent hours sitting with her watching her nap. She was sure a war could be waged in the next room and she wouldn't know it. No, she wasn't much of a chaperon, but no one had to know that.

She felt rather than heard the man behind her. The hairs on the back of her neck bristled.

He cleared his throat.

Attempting to compose herself, she turned, hoping her expression showed none of her inner turmoil. He was as big as she'd remembered. Bigger, perhaps. And he was a hairy beast. His dark hair was far too long, curling wildly about his ears, and she was certain his full, thick beard hadn't been trimmed in months.

They studied each other warily before he finally spoke.

"I guess I can tolerate having you here for a while. But just so you know, I made the frame for the bed myself, to fit *me*. I'm not giving up my bed for anyone, not even a damned woman. Stay out of that room. I don't want you fussing around, trying to clean it or straighten it. I'll give you time to get your things out of there, but from now on, I don't want to find out that you've set foot in there. Is that understood?"

Lily's blood boiled and she clutched the knife handle hard. "Let me get this straight, Mr. . . . Benedict, wasn't it?" she began, straining to contain her temper. "You're graciously allowing me to stay in your cabin, is that correct?"

He gave her an abrupt nod.

"But I'm not to expect to sleep in your precious bed or set foot in your bedroom."

Another imperious nod. "The bedroom is mine."

Still trying to restrain herself, she said, "I wouldn't dream of stepping into your domain. I'll have my things out of there as quickly as possible. The bed wasn't all that comfortable, anyway," she lied. The first night she'd slept in it, she'd thought she'd died and gone to heaven. But, then, anything was better than what she'd been accustomed to.

He turned to leave. "Good. Then, it's settled."

"Not quite."

He stopped at the door. "What do you mean?"

"I have a job to do here. I spend all day cooking for the loggers. I never allow anyone else in my kitchen. Nor do I have time to fix something special for you." She didn't add that she always prepared three meals a day for Maudie.

"I can eat whatever you fix for the crew," he answered almost congenially.

"I don't think so." Her voice was edged with iron.

"Well, sure I can," he answered eagerly.

She pulled in a breath, letting it escape audibly. "No, I don't think you understand." She placed her fists on her hips and stared at him. "The bedroom is yours? Fine. The kitchen is mine, and the same rules apply."

"*What?*"

She turned back to her vegetables, amazed that she could handle the knife without lopping off a finger. "You heard me, sir. You are not to enter my kitchen unless I invite you. Is that understood?"

He bellowed like a bull moose behind her, then finally retorted, "Ah, what the hell do I care? Your food probably tastes like bird shit anyway."

She allowed herself a small smile. "If you're familiar with the taste of bird droppings, Mr. Benedict, I'm sure you'll have no trouble foraging for your meals outside, like the other animals."

When she was certain he was gone, she expelled a long, shaky breath and leaned against the counter for support. She heard—and felt—the door slam and watched as he stormed to a tree stump, positioned a log on top of it, then proceeded to chop the wood into kindling with the ease of a child breaking up matchsticks.

She shuddered and briefly closed her eyes. Battle lines had been drawn.

An hour later, Ross was still chopping wood. He had enough to last the winter—maybe several winters. He tossed the last of the wood onto the pile, then flung the ax, carefully aiming for the tree stump. The blade hummed from the impact, and the handle quivered.

He was soaking wet. And exhausted. Wiping his forehead with his shirtsleeves, he started for the cabin. The smell of fresh-baked apple pie wafted toward him. His stomach rumbled and he swore. He hadn't had a thing to eat since four o'clock in the morning, when he'd begun his ride home chewing on the last of the biscuits he'd gotten in Chico.

Stepping to the cabin door, he shoved it open, letting it slam against the wall. Pie aroma was stronger inside the cabin, and he steeled himself against it, crossing purposefully to the bedroom.

As he walked past the bed, he saw her nightgown and dressing gown still lying across it. He grabbed them in his fist, intent on tossing them out into the living room. Instead, he brought them to his face and inhaled the fresh feminine scent that lingered on the fabric. Warmth transfused his groin, making him hard, and he tossed the garments onto the bed, cursing his weakness.

He grabbed a towel and soap from the washstand and stormed into the living room, crossing quickly to the front door. "Get your damned frilly things out of my bedroom!"

His angry roar nearly caused Lily to drop the pie she was retrieving from the oven. Juggling it carefully between hot pads, she placed it on the counter below the window with the others.

He'd stormed out again, slamming the door. With a wry smile, she wondered if he ever did anything by half measure.

Stepping away from the counter, Lily observed her mess. She would need plenty of hot water to clean up the stack of dishes and pots that cluttered the countertop and the sink.

With the pail in her grip, she went outside and crossed to the pump, praying there would be water. It had been hit and miss since she arrived. Sometimes the water flowed freely, other times she couldn't raise a drop. She primed the pump. Nothing happened. Uttering a mild oath, she picked up the pail and strode purposefully toward the river that ran swiftly by the cabin.

She was just leaving the footpath that ended in the clearing when she saw him. Her heart leaped in her chest and she quickly turned away, but not before she saw him standing in the knee-deep water bringing a soapy hand to his groin.

Pressing her fingers to her mouth, she stumbled up the path, her heart still hammering. She tried not to think about what she'd seen as she looked for another access to the river, but the vision would not go away.

Never had she seen so much body hair on a man. His chest was thick with it, as was . . . the place below. She refused to think about what else she'd seen in that place below. This man, with his delicious body hair and his immense size, made Jake look like a boy.

She tried to force another wry smile as she picked her way through the brush toward the river, but her mouth trembled instead. Sometimes she missed Jake terribly. Not that he'd been the perfect mate, for he hadn't. But they'd had some good times, and she'd always enjoyed their intimacy—until she learned of his unfaithfulness. She realized, to her consternation, that she still missed the part of her marriage that had led to the bedroom.

Spotting the river through the trees, Lily shook thoughts of Jake from her head and moved quickly toward the water. As she bent near the water's edge, her foot slipped on the wet grass and she scudded, rump first, into the river. Her shriek of surprise pierced the quiet air and she struggled to stand, only to find the current so strong she was unable to get her footing.

She looked up just as Ross Benedict came crashing through the trees, wearing nothing but a pair of jeans, buttoned only halfway to his navel. His chest hair was still wet. Hard muscles bunched in his shoulders and arms.

He reached toward her, and because she had no alternative, she allowed him to pull her from the water. His touch was firm and warm and surprisingly electric.

"What in the hell were you trying to do?"

She was becoming, accustomed to his bellow. "I was getting water and I slipped," she answered tersely.

He took in her soggy appearance. "What were you doing way over here?" he demanded, glancing at the slippery, muddy ledge she'd tumbled from. "The path is—" He stopped in mid-sentence and studied her.

She picked up the pail and brushed past him, unwilling to look at him lest he see the embarrassed bloom on her cheeks. "I can get water from any part of the river I please. I don't have to get it from . . . from the path."

He gripped her arm and she turned, surprised.

"Give me the pail." His dark eyes gave off a strange light.

Swallowing convulsively, she handed him the pail, then

trudged toward the cabin, holding her water-soaked skirts above her ankles.

Kicking off her wet slippers at the door, she went straight to his bedroom, picked up her valise, and crossed to the kitchen. She huddled near the stove and undressed, relieved that she'd finished cooking for the day.

Tossing furtive glances at the closed door, she changed into dry clothes, praying the bull had enough sense to stay out.

She was buttoning the last of the buttons on her dress when he knocked on the kitchen door. "What is it?" Her voice sounded shrewish. She didn't care.

"I've . . ." He cleared his throat. "I've . . . ah . . . got the water."

She opened the door and took the pail from him, thanking him with an austere nod. She noticed that he still wore no shirt, and she tried to ignore the unwelcome flutter of pleasure low in her belly.

Chapter Three

By late afternoon, Ross was so hungry he felt his stomach gnaw at his backbone. He shrugged into his buckskin jacket, saddled his mount, and rode to Twin Hearts to see Trudy.

The nice thing about Trudy, he thought as she pulled him into her kitchen was that she didn't expect anything from him. She was there when he needed her, and what he needed now, before anything else, was to be fed, even if Trudy wasn't the best cook in the world. He shoved aside thoughts of savory apple pie and hot stew, thick with chunks of venison and vegetables from his own damned garden.

"Poor darling," Trudy crooned, setting a plate of meat and cabbage in front of him. "You look absolutely worn out."

She sat down across from him and, as she always did, tucked her bare toes under his thighs. It usually readied him for what came later, but tonight it did nothing. Hell, he was probably too hungry to get horny.

Trudy was usually quiet, which he appreciated, but tonight she was full of chatter. As she blathered on, he studied her between bites of bland meat and sour cabbage. He'd always thought her reasonably attractive, but tonight, for some reason, her brassy, frizzy hair looked like it would spark dry tinder and her face appeared blotchy.

He pushed his plate away even though he hadn't finished eating. He was no longer hungry.

"Is that all you're going to eat?" Trudy rose and came to him, touching his forehead with the back of her hand. "Hon, your face is burning up." She ran her hand across his chest, then down over his groin. She gave him a not-so-gentle squeeze, then pulled away, surprised. "You aren't even hard, Ross." She busied herself undoing the buttons of his fly, but he removed her hand.

She gave him a questioning look.

He shoved his chair back and stood. "I'm not in the mood tonight, Trudy."

With nervous fingers, she clutched her dressing gown over her generous bosom and looked at him, her eyes filled with a strange fear. "Did I do something wrong, hon?"

Ross crossed to the fireplace and stoked up the fire. "It's not you, it's me." And he knew it was, although he sure as hell didn't know why.

He turned from the fireplace as she walked toward him, and when she pressed herself against him, he touched her back gently but didn't pull her close. The scent she wore was familiar, but he suddenly found it sweet and cloying and far too strong. Like she'd taken a bath in the stuff.

"You're scaring me, hon. I've never known you to pass on a toss in bed."

He gave her a pat on the rump, then turned away to stare into the fire. Trudy was a fine woman, although Ross knew that he wasn't the only man she saw. For want of a better term, he guessed she was a widowed housewife/whore. Her husband had been dead for two years, killed in a logging accident. She had no other means of support except for what men decided to give her for her services. She not only slept with them, she fed them and nursed them, listened to their complaints and soothed their sorrows. She had a good heart.

But he didn't want to crawl between her thighs. Not tonight, and maybe not ever again. It was the damndest revelation, but he simply couldn't imagine bedding her. "I'd still like to come by and talk once in a while."

"Talk? Just talk?" She sounded upset.

"Let's be honest," he said, his voice gentle. "I'm not the only man you see, Trudy. We both know that."

"Well . . . well, yes," she answered, "But—oh, Ross!" She flung herself at him. "I . . . always thought that . . . that maybe someday, we'd—"

He pushed her away as gently as he dared. Her eyes shimmered with tears, and streaks of mascara tracked her cheeks. "I'm never getting married. What we had was a damned fine time in bed. And you're a good woman, Trudy." He touched her chin, nudging her face up. "Remember that. Don't spoil what we had by pretending there was more."

She sniffed, wiping her tears with the sleeve of her robe, smearing her mascara further. "But you will still come to see me?"

He gave her a warm smile. "I said I would, didn't I? You'll have to feed me now and then." He guessed Trudy's cooking was better than bird shit, although not by much.

She stood on her tiptoes and kissed him. "I'll be right back." Her bounteous, dimpled buttocks shifted beneath her dressing gown as she retreated into her bedroom, and when she returned, she had his scarf in her hand.

"Here," she said, unfolding it and draping it around his neck. "You left this here last time. I've kept it in a drawer with my underthings."

It smelled generously of her favorite cologne—the very cologne she wore now. He tried not to make an unpleasant face. Bending to kiss her forehead, he said, "Thanks, Trudy. You're quite a woman."

"And you're a special man, Ross Benedict. But I'll admit I don't understand you."

He lifted his jacket off the coatrack and slipped it on. "That makes two of us." He'd come here tonight fully intending to do what he'd always done: enjoy Trudy's bland food, then have a good, lusty tumble in her bed. Instead, he'd found her cooking completely distasteful, and he honestly couldn't imagine sleeping in her bed ever again.

* * *

After checking on Maudie, Lily bathed and dressed for bed, then sat curled in a chair by the fire, planning the loggers' menus for the next week. Samantha had promised that tomorrow she would pick her up and they would shop for supplies.

And, Lily thought, one eyebrow arching skeptically, she must ask Samantha why she had rented her a cabin that was quite obviously already occupied. By her brother, no less.

Unable to imagine any sound reason for doing such a thing, Lily shook her head and went back to her list.

She found herself glancing up occasionally, wondering when the bellowing bull would come charging in. She had absolutely no interest in knowing where he was. It wasn't her business, anyway. She hoped he'd never come back.

But when she heard him ride up, she discovered that her heart was pounding hard and her palms were sweaty. She inspected her list, feigning an interest she didn't feel when he finally entered the cabin.

Her quick glance took in his appearance, and she had to admit she was surprised. In spite of the beard and unruly hair, he looked almost elegant in his snug jeans, white shirt, and tan buckskin jacket. A white scarf hung loosely around his neck.

"Evening." His voice was husky and deep.

She swallowed. "Good evening," she answered. She had almost formed a new opinion of him when she got a whiff of him as he walked past her on his way to the cabinet where she knew he kept his liquor. She wrinkled her nose and frowned. He smelled like a bawdy-house pimp, but why should she care? Where he spent his time was no concern of hers. Actually it didn't surprise her at all that he had to *buy* affection. How he and that sweet Samantha could be brother and sister still baffled her.

He was behind her, pouring himself a glass of something. Whiskey, no doubt.

"Can I . . . er . . . get you something?"

A small brandy would have been welcome, but she shook her head. "No. No, thank you."

With a glass half-filled with amber liquid in his hand, he took the only other chair in the room, which sat opposite hers, and stared at her.

She tried not to squirm under his scrutiny. The whole idea of them sharing this cabin suddenly became at the very best ludicrous and at the worst improper. She had known from the start that Maudie was a chaperon in name only, but that had never really bothered her before. Lily wanted to retire to the kitchen, but something kept her seated.

The silence stretched like a taut wire between them, vibrating with unspoken energy.

He set his glass on a round table next to him, then pulled out a small leather pouch. "Mind if I smoke?"

Shrugging nonchalantly, she answered, "It's your cabin."

"Nice of you to remember that," he muttered as he rolled a cigarette.

She pretended to study her list but occasionally glanced at him through the veil of her lashes. The firelight slanted across his face, casting the distinct planes of his features into bold relief. He had a patrician nose, and even with his beard, she could tell that his cheekbones were high and sharp. No doubt, he wore the beard to cover sallow, sunken cheeks. At least she hoped that was true, even though, for some reason, she knew it was not.

"Writing a letter?"

She jumped, unaware that he'd been watching her too. "What?"

He nodded toward the pad in her lap. "Writing to someone?"

"No. It's . . . it's a list of what the crew will eat next week."

He cleared his throat, then took a long pull on his drink.

The sickening scent of the whore's cologne still hung in the air, and suddenly Lily was anxious to remind him of the battle lines that had been drawn earlier.

"I can't decide if I should put ham hocks in the beans or just bake a ham and put a big, thick slice on each plate. With mustard sauce, of course.

"Then, on Tuesday," she said with a sigh, "maybe mutton pie or ham pie. Of course, I'll have ham left over from the day before . . . so I suppose I could make another stew. They seem to enjoy stew, and it's easy to make." She forced a small laugh. "All I have to do is prepare it, and it basically cooks itself all day long, and I *do* love the smell, don't you?" She affected a gasp and brought her hand to her mouth. "Oh, I'm sorry, Mr. Benedict. I do hope the smell of my cooking doesn't bother you."

He took another swig of whiskey and scowled into the fire.

"Then there's the dessert," she went on, hoping he was wallowing in misery. "They're getting apple pie tomorrow. I suppose I could make mince pies, but I think cake would be a nice change. I've got a recipe for a very good marble cake with rich chocolate frosting, or maybe an orange cake would be better. Oh, but that takes so much butter. I know!" she said with an innocent smile. "I'll make a sponge cake and drizzle sweet cream whipped with sugar over it. And fresh wild blueberries on top. What do you think?"

He downed the rest of his drink and slammed the glass onto the table next to him. His scowl deepened, shoving his dark brows together over his eyes. "G'night." The word came out of his mouth like a curse. He rose from the chair and stormed to the bedroom, slamming the door behind him.

With a satisfied smile, Lily turned out the lamp, banked the fire in the fireplace, and went into the kitchen. After unrolling her bedroll in front of the stove, she removed her robe and slid into her bed on the floor.

Sleep eluded her, and she knew why. This arrangement was not tolerable. Surely there must be suitable accommodations elsewhere. If Samantha Browne would not help her look, she would find a place herself. It wasn't that she minded sleeping on the floor. When she'd left San Francisco, penniless as a pauper, she'd slept anywhere, and she could do it again.

She hated to give that roaring bear the satisfaction of thinking he'd driven her out, though. That part rankled. Still, she had to leave because she was beginning to feel something else. Something she hadn't felt since before she'd discovered Jake's infidelity. And, Lord help her, she'd been alone with Ross Benedict for just one day. It would only get worse.

Ross lay on his side, staring at the door. Briefly rising onto his elbow, he punched his pillows, only to discover it didn't make him more comfortable at all.

He now knew why he couldn't bed Trudy, but he didn't understand it. Hell, he didn't even *like* this Sawyer woman, so how could it be because of her? He had to be wrong. Yeah, that was it. It couldn't be because of her. He'd been feeling a sense of restlessness with Trudy for months. Probably because he knew she was more serious about their relationship than he was. And he didn't want any entanglements.

Trudy was a good ol' gal. Hell, maybe he'd just had a bad night. The next time he went to see her, he'd take her to bed and make up for tonight. That would make them both happy. Yeah, that's what he'd do.

But as he flopped onto his back and studied the ceiling, he was puzzled that the very idea of it didn't make him horny.

Chapter Four

Borden's Chop House sat just back from a magnificent cliff from which one could watch the ebb and swell of the ocean. After their lunch, Lily and Samantha sipped coffee while they waited for the supplies to be loaded onto the buckboard. The ocean was hypnotic; their conversation had been sparse.

Finally Lily broached the subject of the cabin. "Samantha, if you knew your brother lived in the cabin, why on earth did you rent it to me?"

Samantha poured a dollop of cream into her coffee and gave it a dainty stir. As she tapped the spoon on the rim of the cup, she sighed. "I must have misunderstood my brother's intentions. I . . . I truly thought he was going to spend the . . . the entire months of October and November in the valley on the other side of the mountains." She took a sip of coffee, her big brown eyes innocent as she stared at Lily.

"I see," Lily responded. "Well, now that we know he isn't, perhaps I should find other accommodations."

Samantha's delicate fingers rested at her throat. "Oh, I don't think there's anything else available, Lily."

"Surely there must be *something.*"

Samantha followed the flowered pattern on the oilcloth with her fingernail. "But the kitchen at the cabin is equipped for cooking large meals, and it's so close to the camp."

"But your brother lives in the cabin," Lily answered, trying to sound reasonable.

"You like it there, don't you? Isn't it perfect for cooking for the loggers? There really isn't another place like it except at the—" She stopped and pressed her lips together.

"Except where, Samantha?"

"Oh, you wouldn't like it. Really you wouldn't," she said fervently. "Poor Maudie lived there briefly, before she moved into the other cabin on our property, but—"

"Why don't you let me be the judge of that?"

Raising her hands in a gesture of defeat, Samantha stood and pulled her black velvet cape around her shoulders. "All right, but believe me, you won't like it."

Lily rose, hugging her own much thinner cape tightly to her. She was actually anxious to look at the new lodgings. Surely anything was better than where she lived now.

Lily's heart sank when she saw the room. Although it was on land adjacent to the mess hall where the loggers ate, it was a poor excuse for a building by any stretch of the imagination. Dimly lit by one small window, it exuded the stench of dead mice and musty wood. And it had a dirt floor. Something scurried in a darkened corner, and both women jumped, automatically reaching for each other.

Lily swallowed hard and tried not to breathe through her nose. "You mean, the previous cooks actually *lived* here?"

Samantha covered her nose with a handkerchief. "Since Mama died, they've all been men. Until Maudie, and now you."

Lily lifted her skirt and backed toward the door, anxious to get outside. "But even so . . ."

Once out in the fresh air, they both inhaled greedily.

"Now you can see why the loggers love you, Lily."

She shuddered. Actually she really could. "If the former cooks kept the camp kitchen like they kept house, it's a wonder the men didn't die of food poisoning."

Samantha took Lily's arm and they walked toward the buckboard. "Now you know what I mean. The room is nothing more than a hovel."

With a shake of her head, Lily asked, "Is there nothing else?"

They boarded the wagon, huddling close for warmth against the cold, damp air.

"Nothing anywhere near close enough," Samantha said, her voice strangely cheerful. "As I said before, Mama used to cook for the crew. That's why the cabin is as close as it is."

They rocked and rolled down the rutted road that led from the camp. "Ross said he'd be there to help unload the provisions," Samantha said with a bright smile.

Just the sound of his name sent chaotic spasms through Lily's stomach. She didn't know what she was going to do, but suddenly she was angry. If Ross Benedict was any kind of gentleman at all, he'd move out and leave the place to her.

The last of the supplies were tucked away, and Samantha sat at the kitchen table, sipping a cup of fresh coffee. "I've always loved this room," she murmured, her eyes soft.

"Were you raised here?"

She shook her head. "Ross was, but when I came along, Papa insisted we live in town." She smiled. "But I always came with Mama when she cooked. I loved the smells." She inhaled deeply. "I still do. What are you cooking? It smells delicious."

Lily flushed at the compliment. "I'm cooking some mutton for meat pies. It's probably the onions that smell so good."

Samantha glanced at the corner. "What's that?"

Lily followed her gaze. "Oh, that's my bedroll."

Samantha turned quickly. "Your *what?*"

"My . . . my bedroll."

Samantha stared at her. "Where do you sleep?"

Lily gestured toward the stove. "Over there. It's always nice and warm."

"On the *floor?*"

Lily shrugged. "Of course," she said simply.

Samantha shook her head, clearly puzzled. "I can't believe Ross would make you sleep on the floor."

Lily had no intention of explaining their current arrangement. "Oh, don't blame him, Samantha. I've all but taken over the rest of the cabin. I couldn't very well take his bed too."

Samantha rose, tying the ribbons of her cape together before pulling the hood over her head. "But, Lily . . . the *floor?* Why don't I have Derek bring out a sofa. There's one in my parlor that we rarely use—"

"Nonsense," Lily argued. "It would be pointless, anyway. I won't be here that long. I'm not going to give up looking for another place, you know."

Samantha sighed and straightened the shawl on her cape. "No, I suppose you're not. But, Lily, Maudie will miss you if you leave." She sounded disappointed, as if she expected Lily would abandon her job.

Lily couldn't stop her smile. "Sounds like emotional blackmail, Samantha. Don't worry, I won't quit on you."

Samantha seemed distracted. "What?"

"I won't quit cooking for the logging crew."

"Oh. Oh, that's . . . that's good. Thank you, Lily, I appreciate that." She made her way to the door, then stopped. "I really had hoped—" She gave Lily a small smile and shrugged her shoulders.

"Yes?"

Shaking her head, she answered, "Never mind. I'm so happy we met. By the way. Derek and I are hosting a party next Friday night. Nothing fancy, just a gathering of some of our neighbors. Won't you please come?"

"How nice," Lily answered with a smile. "Thank you, I'd love to. Is there any way I can help?"

"Oh, heavens, I'm glad you asked. My housekeeper has gone to Sacramento to be with her daughter, who's expecting a baby. I'd appreciate any help you can give me."

Lily's smile widened. "Count on it."

With a distracted nod, Samantha turned away and opened the door. "I just wish—Never mind. I'll see you soon, Lily."

Puzzled, Lily watched her leave, then returned to the

kitchen. She was sampling the broth from the stewing meat when Ross cleared his throat behind her.

She turned, the big wooden spoon still in her hand. The sight of him still sent flutters into her belly. She would never become accustomed to his size. But one glance at his face and she knew something was wrong. "What is it?"

"It's Maudie," he answered. "She's coughing up blood. I think I—"

"Oh, my God!" Lily flung the spoon on the counter and hurried toward him. He caught her arm.

"I'm going to take her down the coast to Santa Rosa," he offered. "It's the closest thing we have to a hospital, and there's always a doctor available."

Lily's pulse hammered. "But . . . but isn't there a doctor in Twin Hearts?"

"Usually," he answered, "but he had to go to the mill upriver. There was a bad accident."

She pulled her arm free and grabbed her cape off the hook by the door. "I'm coming with you. You'll need someone to keep her comfortable."

"I doubt I could stop you," he murmured as he followed her out the door.

It was late when they returned, and Lily was exhausted. As Ross helped her from the buggy, he said, "I don't mean this to sound cruel or unfeeling, but under the circumstances, we'd probably better keep Maudie's hospitalization to ourselves."

She understood completely. The two of them, unchaperoned, would cause quite a stir. In fact, Lily had decided she would sleep in Maudie's cabin while she was away.

Lily went to the kitchen to finish up the chores she'd left undone while Ross unhitched the buggy and saw to the horse. She was putting away the last of the dishes when he came in.

Ross shifted nervously from one foot to the other. "I . . . I just thought you should know that I'm moving out."

Her heart lifted, then dropped, and she felt a shiver of fool-ish disappointment, even though it was the very thing she'd hoped for. "You . . . you are?" was all she could manage.

He combed his strong fingers through his hair. "I'll be next door, in Maudie's cabin, in case, well, in case you need me for something."

The pulse at her throat pumped hard and she automatically pressed two fingers against it. "I thought perhaps I should stay there."

He shook his head. "It's easier for me. I don't mind."

"Will you be comfortable there?" The words slipped out without a thought.

"There's a bed. I'll make do."

Lily repressed a shiver of guilt. He loved his bed, and he was willing to leave it. She hardly knew what to say. He was giving up a great deal of personal comfort for her sake, and quite frankly, it surprised her.

He slanted a glance at the stove, where the mutton and onions simmered, cleared his throat again, then left.

Lily was almost tempted to ask him if he wanted something to eat.

When she was sure Ross was out of the cabin, she stepped into the bedroom. A smile tugged at her mouth, for he'd straightened the bedding and fluffed the pillows.

Crossing to the wardrobe, she pulled it open and found his clothes hanging there. She'd often wondered why none of his clothes had been there when she'd moved in. She'd always meant to find out but never thought of it when someone was around to ask. She shut the doors and turned to study the room. It was big and masculine, like he was. The bed was enormous. How well she recalled sleeping in it those nights be-fore he'd charged in, regaining control.

She'd been too frightened at the time to dwell on the events of that morning, but now that she'd come to know Ross Benedict even a little bit, she realized how potent the situation could have been. If he walked in on her now, wearing only the flimsy borrowed dressing gown, what would happen? Would he pull it away and look at her? Would she let him, or, for that matter, would she encourage him to do so?

Suddenly feeling weak in the knees, she sat on the edge of the bed and took a deep breath as her heart clubbed her ribs. When she caught her breath, she stood and walked around to the other side of the bed, studying it as she moved. He was a big man. A normal-sized bed would probably make him feel as though he slept in a cradle.

His scarf was wrapped loosely around the bedpost. She picked it off and brought it to her face, drawing in the scent. With a sound of disgust, she hurled it away. It was drenched with the whore's cheap cologne.

Lily marched to the door, flung it open, and stepped through, pulling it shut soundly behind her. She realized that the whore had probably slept in his bed until she showed up, putting a crimp in Ross's wild lifestyle.

A gnawing hurt that she didn't understand gripped her stomach, and she went into the kitchen, busying herself with the crusts for the meat pies.

As she worked on the dough, she worked on her feelings as well. The man was one step up from an animal. He wasn't worth her hurt or her concern, and he certainly wasn't worth worrying about. If she were lucky, he'd spend every night with his whore. At least that way, he wouldn't be around, constantly annoying her. And to think she'd almost offered to feed him! Thank God something had brought her to her senses.

Maybe she could use his bed if she fumigated it first, but it would be just her luck if the whore's smell had already seeped into the bedding and the mattress to the point where she'd never get rid of it. No, she thought, mercilessly pummeling the dough, she wouldn't set foot in that room again. She'd pretend it didn't exist. She hoped mice nested in the mattress, producing offspring for many, many generations.

A little voice in her head tried to ask her why she was so angry with a man she barely knew, a man who had every right to live his own life. She soundly silenced the prying, snooping little voice. Somehow it felt good to feel something again, even if it was a foolish, inexplicable anger.

"You've moved out?" Sam sounded genuinely upset.

"I've moved out, Sam. So you see, your little plan didn't work."

"Oh, for pity's sake, Ross. You keep blathering about that, and I . . . I haven't the faintest idea what you're talking about." She folded the newspaper and put it on the kitchen table, presumably so Derek could read it in the morning. "Where are you staying, then?"

He spooned a generous serving of her rice pudding into a bowl, then doused it with cream to hide the fact that she'd burned the milk and rice, leaving it a dull shade of brown. Hell, he was so hungry he'd even eat his sister's cooking, which was worse than Trudy's.

"For now, I'm sleeping in the shed," he lied, downing the pudding quickly so he wouldn't have to taste it.

She made a sound of disgust. "Oh, Ross. That's an awful little shack."

"Well," he said, "if you have room here—"

"Of course I don't, and you know it," she interrupted. She began to pace. "I suppose that shed could be cleaned out and made presentable."

Suddenly she turned on him, her hands on her hips. "Did you know Lily sleeps on the floor?"

He'd suspected as much. Where else was there? He didn't even own a sofa. Shifting under her angry gaze, he answered, "Well, she won't have to now. She'll have my damned bed."

"Good!" She spun away and crossed to the window. When she turned, her expression was almost scathing. "How could you let her sleep on the floor, Ross? Mama and Papa taught you better than that."

Ross took a long slurp of coffee to wash away the taste of burned rice. What could he say? How in the hell could he tell her that this Sawyer woman made him do things he'd never thought of doing before. Made him act like an uncouth clod when he really wasn't. With the other women Sam had sent his way, he'd at least tried to be civil, even though he'd wanted to throttle someone. But Lily Sawyer made him forget his manners and his inherent love of women. Made him roar like a bear and stomp around like a wounded moose. She made him crazy!

"Do you know that she wanted to leave?" At his look of surprise, she nodded. "Yes. Why, she insisted on finding something else, and the only place available close to the camp is that awful, dirty room the other cooks used." She made a face and shuddered. "Fortunately she found it as loathsome as I did. If you hadn't moved out, I'm afraid she eventually would have."

"Christ," he muttered. "Now you tell me."

"That's not funny!"

"I didn't mean it to be! Hell, if I'd thought she was going to cave in, I'd have stuck it out."

Samantha unfastened her long braid from the back of her head and massaged her scalp. "For heaven's sake. If you act this way in front of her, it's surprising that she hasn't poisoned you."

He laughed in spite of his anger. "No chance of that," he said before he'd even thought about it.

"Oh? How can you be so sure?" Her eyes glittered.

"Because she refuses to feed me," he mumbled as he crossed to the door.

Sam's laughter slapped him in the back like a wet towel. "She *what?*"

"You heard me." He suddenly felt very put upon. His sister should have had more compassion.

"Good for her," she cheered. "I *knew* she had spirit the

minute I saw her standing, drenched to the bone, in that empty lot outside of town."

Ross frowned. "I thought you said she came to you looking for work?"

Sam whirled, her dressing gown swirling around her ankles. "I . . . I said that?"

"Yes, little sister." His voice was dangerously smooth.

She shrugged and skipped away. "What does it matter?"

He shook his head. "I said it before, Sam, and I'll say it again. It won't work."

She gave him a saucy look over her shoulder. "The important thing is that you've treated her terribly. You've been a perfect boor. I don't blame her for refusing to feed you."

Ross noticed Samantha's good table linens stacked on the counter near the door. "Why do you have those out?" His sister might not have inherited their mother's ability to cook, but she was an immaculate housekeeper.

"We're having a party on Friday." She took his empty bowl and put it in the dishpan, sloshing hot water from a teakettle over it.

"A party? And you weren't going to invite me?" He felt disappointed and betrayed.

"Why should I? You've never done anything but make fun of our friends."

"Well, yeah, but . . . you've always invited me before, Sam."

She lifted her shoulders and sighed. "Oh, come if you want to. I guess I can't stop you."

Her lack of enthusiasm stung him. Sure, he made fun of her friends, but he hadn't meant anything by it.

He turned toward the window. The wind had picked up and was blowing the branches of the fir tree against the glass. They scratched and clawed, as if trying to find a way inside. He shivered, thinking about the long, cold ride home. "The weather looks pretty bad, Sam. Mind if I sleep here tonight?"

She picked his hat off the coat tree and threw it at him. "I most certainly do."

At that moment, Derek stepped into the kitchen. "What's going on? I could hear you two shouting at each other from the den."

"Did you know this big boob makes poor Lily sleep on the floor?" Sam's fists were balled at her hips.

Derek backed up a step and put his hands up, as if to fend her off. "This has nothing to do with me."

"Aw, hell, Derek," Ross mumbled. "I didn't know she slept on the floor. I didn't *make* her sleep there."

Derek laughed. "Oh, no, you don't. I can't take your side, Ross."

Ross felt another jolt of self-pity. "You won't defend me? I'm innocent!"

Derek scooped Sam into his arms and nuzzled her hair. "And I'm not ready to sleep on the sofa, my man. I'd be a fool to argue with my beautiful wife."

Samantha gave Ross a superior nod. "See? Now, go. You can't sleep here."

He was stunned. "Why?"

She took his jacket off the tree and threw that at him too. "You don't deserve a warm place to sleep tonight," she insisted, shoving him toward the door. "Go sleep with your horse. It's where you belong."

Ross stepped out into the night, cringing as the door slammed against his back. Hell and damnation. Women. He'd never figure them out.

Chapter Five

Ross hitched his mount in the lean-to, rubbed him down and fed him, then trudged toward Maudie's tiny cabin. He was stiff from the cold, for although the wind had been at his back all the way home, it had gone straight through him. As he passed the kitchen window, he noticed the flicker of a lamp. He looked inside, then pulled away, feeling an intrusive wash of guilt and surprise.

Lily was in there, sitting cross-legged on top of her bedroll in front of the stove, brushing her hair. Why wasn't she in his bed, tucked snugly under his covers? What in the hell good did it do for him to sleep in the shed if she was going to insist on sleeping on the damned floor?

With a growling curse, he went inside and shoved open the kitchen door. She gasped in surprise, but when she saw it was him, she glanced away.

"You might try knocking," she scolded, continuing to pull the brush through her hair.

The lamp gave off enough light to make her hair look like fire. That he experienced a sudden urge to discover if the triangle between her legs was darker or lighter shocked him. That the thought could wangle space inside his head infuriated him. "What in the hell are you doing in here?"

She slipped her bare feet into the bedroll and pulled it to her waist, then rested on an elbow and stared at him. Her breasts swayed seductively against her nightgown, one resting on her arm. Although he could see only the plumpness against the fabric, his mouth went dry.

"I think it's quite obvious, Mr. Benedict. I'm retiring for the night."

"Why aren't you in my bed, damnit?" He realized as he spoke that the question held a double meaning for him, and that made him even angrier. The thought had come straight out of nowhere.

She held his gaze, and he almost flinched at the glittering fury he saw there.

"I prefer sleeping on the floor" was all she said, although he had a feeling she wanted to say more.

"That's plain stupid," he groused.

"I am *not* stupid."

"Well, you sure do stupid things," he informed her.

She sat up and put her fists on her hips, a movement that pushed her breasts forward against her nightgown. "Such as?"

His mouth continued to feel like cotton, and he tried not to look at the nipples that pouted against the cloth.

"Such as this," he answered, waving his arm around the room. "And . . . and such as trying to get water from any spot at the river other than the one I've cleared. Hell, you could have been swept downstream yesterday."

"I had no choice."

He should have left it at that, but he didn't. "Why?"

She turned away, but not before he saw her cheeks blooming with color. "You know very well why."

He had suspected that she might have seen him bathing, and the thought aroused him. "Did you like what you saw?" He enjoyed seeing her squirm.

Her gaze met his and she was quiet for a moment before she answered. "I've seen better specimens at the zoo."

He roared with laughter, then turned to go. "Hell, if you're not going to use my bed, I am."

"No, you're not." Her voice was deadly behind him.

Glancing back at her, he asked, "So, what are you going to do about it? Toss me out?"

"Oh, no," she answered, her smile as cold as a witch's heart. "I'll set a match to it while you're asleep."

He considered what she'd said, studying that icy smile,

sensing the strength and stubbornness behind it. "You would too."

"Count on it, Mr. Benedict. Now, get out of my kitchen. And next time, knock before you enter."

"Hell," he mumbled as he shoved open the door, "you'd think you were royalty rather than just a damned cook."

Lily let out a whoosh of air and cautiously positioned herself on her back. No gentleman would taunt her like that. A gentleman would not have brought up the subject of his bath at all, even if he'd actually caught her watching. But she knew that Ross Benedict was not gentle and he only bordered on being a man.

She shuddered as the memory of his nudity grew before her. Oh, he was a man, all right. And, remembering how his soapy hand had held his manhood, she sensed he was quite a man.

Quite a man with the whores. Yes, she thought, suddenly grateful for the little voice in her head. No doubt he was quite a man with his whores. They praised anyone as long as they were paid. Although Lily had only slept with one man in her life, she'd heard enough talk and innuendo to know that size had nothing to do with performance.

She heard the front door slam, then his footsteps as he walked toward Maudie's cabin. Did she feel guilty about not letting him use his own bed?

As she snuggled deep into her bedroll, only slightly uncomfortable as her hipbone dug into the floor, she decided she didn't.

Early the following morning, Lily hauled the tub outside, then stripped his bed and shoved the sheets into boiling water heavily laced with lye soap. She added some saltpeter for bleaching, then tossed in his whore-scented scarf, touching it only with the tips of her fingers. While the sheets boiled, she carried out the bedding and hung it on the line that was strung between two oak trees in the yard. Grabbing the paddle she used for the wash, she beat the bedding, sending dust into the air. It was quickly absorbed by the morning fog.

She had no intention of sleeping on the clean sheets, but she couldn't abide the fact that they had the stink of a whore's cologne. Any woman would feel the same way, and it had nothing to do with *him.*

"What are you trying to kill?"

Startled, she stopped attacking the quilts, her heart pounding both from exertion and from his sudden appearance behind her.

"The smell of your whore," she snapped without thinking. She cursed her tongue and refused to turn toward him.

"My *what?*" He sounded amused.

Trying to cover her blunder, she asked, "When was the last time the bedding was washed?"

"What the hell difference does it make if no one's going to sleep in it?"

"There was a smell to it that saturated every corner of the cabin," she answered sharply. "And . . . and that white scarf of yours too. Or," she added, turning slightly toward him, "does it belong to your whore?"

He gave her a lazy, irritating grin. "Oh, it's mine, all right. Kept warm for me between my sweet whore's thighs."

Heat raced to her cheeks. "Men. You're really such a despicable lot. There isn't a faithful one among you."

Taking the paddle from her, he asked, "Who have I got to be faithful to? I've got no wife. And even if I did, I doubt she'd satisfy me enough to keep me from straying. It's normal for men, you know."

She fumed, remembering those words. He was Jake Sawyer all over again. She watched him beat the bedding and wished she had the paddle, for make no mistake about it, she'd use it on him, and gladly too.

He handed her the paddle, then nodded toward the washtub.

"When you're ready to hang those, give me a holler. I'll be in the house, repairing the hole you made me put through the door."

She gasped. "The hole *I* made you—"

"If it weren't for you, it wouldn't have happened." He gave her a teasing smile, then sauntered into the cabin.

She watched him walk away, itching to go after him and smack him in the head. But truly, she was grateful to him. Every time she weakened and thought of how he affected her, he would say something stupid, which would harden her heart against him once again. Thank the good Lord for that. She didn't need to be interested in another man who, like Jake Sawyer, had the morals of an alley cat.

Ross forced a chuckle, assuming he'd feel a sense of well-being as he walked away. He didn't, even though everything he'd told her about the fidelity nonsense was the truth. Or at least it used to be. Damnit, anyway! What had she done to him?

Maybe she was jealous. He smiled, feeling warm and fuzzy inside. For some strange, inexplicable reason, the thought delighted him beyond words. He had to test the notion further, though.

He thought of Sam and Derek's party and gleefully rubbed his hands together. He wondered if Trudy was busy that night. The twinge of guilt that wormed into his conscience at the idea of using her was effectively squashed when he decided that the end always justified the means.

For Samantha's party, Lily wore the finest dress she owned, threadbare green faille that set off her hair and her eyes. She would be sorry when it was too worn-out to wear. She'd long since abandoned the cumbersome steel crinolette frame, taking comfort in the knowledge that the other women in this logging town had forsaken that too.

She stood near the kitchen, watching the other guests arrive.

Most were men who owned businesses in Twin Hearts, all accompanied by pleasant, sometimes pretty wives.

Lily had never cared much for parties and was grateful she'd agreed to attend Samantha's only if she could help in the kitchen. She had noted Samantha's visible sigh of relief and wondered why—until she'd tasted Samantha's cooking when she'd stopped by for lunch the day before the party.

As Lily replenished the spiced ale she'd heated for the men, the room, which had been filled with chatter and laughter, suddenly went silent. Two women standing next to her gasped and whispered. Lily looked toward the door to see what the fuss was about, and her stomach did that telltale little dipping dance it always did when Ross Benedict came into view.

He stepped inside, looking huge and handsome—with a woman clinging to his arm.

Lily's heart raced and her stomach hurt. She felt clammy, cold and hot all at the same time. She hated the feeling. Refusing even to look at the woman, she went back to her task and noticed that the container of warm ale she held actually shook in her hands. She retreated quickly to the kitchen.

She was attempting to still her racing heart when the kitchen door swung open and slammed against the wall.

"Oh! I could *kill* him!"

Lily's brief glance at Samantha took in her fury. "Who?" she asked, feigning only a slight interest.

"My brother, of course" was the terse answer.

"Why?" Yes, she really did want to know. She'd only known him a week and she'd already wanted to kill him herself.

"Because he brought *her.*"

Lily sliced through a loaf of cinnamon bread. "Who is she?" Her heart continued to pound.

"She's the town whore, that's who she is. We've always been very proud of the fact that Twin Hearts doesn't have a legitimate whorehouse." Samantha clucked in disgust. "We don't need one. We have Gertrude Harding. And to make it worse, many of the married men in that room have actually . . . used her services. Can you imagine how uncomfortable they must feel?"

Lily finished slicing the loaf of bread. So, it was true. The awful hurt continued to aggravate her stomach, rising up into her chest. She knew the origin of the feeling, for she'd felt it when she first discovered that Jake had been frequenting the local whorehouses. But she'd been married to him. It had made perfect sense for her to be angry, hurt, and yes, even jealous. But this? No. Lord, she didn't even *like* Ross Benedict. Why on earth would she care what he did with his private life?

"That's really their problem, isn't it? If they didn't choose to stray, they would have nothing to worry about."

"Oh, don't sound so logical, Lily. Everyone knows most men stray on occasion."

"Straying even once is one time too many," she answered. "But as for your brother, perhaps he actually likes the woman."

"Oh, no, he doesn't. He's doing this to get back at me for all of the times I tried to pair him up in the past."

She poured hot water over dirty dishes in the dishpan. "Every New Year's Eve, I'd get him together with one of the respectable single women in the area. *Every year,* I did this, Lily. And do you think he ever thanked me? Do you? Lord, no. He acted like I had a noose around his neck and was leading him to a lynching tree. But this . . . this takes the cake. He's never flaunted Trudy Harding in my face before. Never."

"Maybe he's trying to tell you something."

Samantha retrieved a large round tray from the cupboard and began arranging cookies on it. "Like what?"

"Maybe he's trying to tell you to stay out of his life."

"Oh, but I *can't,* don't you see? He's his own worst enemy. He *needs* me to . . . to get his life in order. That's why I—" She tossed Lily a guilt-ridden glance, then cleared her throat. "Oh, bother. I give up. If he wants to . . . to waste his life whoring around, then, I hope he burns in hell."

Lily couldn't stop her smile. "No, you don't."

"No," Samantha answered on a sigh, "I really don't. But, Lily, I'd so hoped—" She looked at her, longing stamped on her face.

"You'd hoped what?"

Samantha shrugged. "That you . . . that he . . . that you and he . . . Well, you know."

Lily was struck by an illuminating understanding. "Don't tell me you rented me the cabin knowing full well that your brother would be back."

Samantha was quiet for a moment, then answered, "I'll admit that I did. I really thought . . . I mean, you'd be perfect together." She fussed with the cookies, arranging and rearranging them on the plate. "How was I to know you'd end up hating each other?"

Lily felt herself redden. She didn't know what she felt for Ross Benedict, but she was beginning to realize that it wasn't hate. "Oh, I wouldn't say we *hate* each other, Samantha."

"But you refuse to cook for him, and that has to be because he's treated you like . . . like rubbish, which I don't understand at all, because he wasn't raised that way. Truly, Lily, Mama would turn over in her grave if she knew the way he's been behaving."

Lily chose not to talk about her relationship with Ross Benedict. Actually it would have been impossible to do so. How could she explain something to Samantha that she didn't understand herself?

Hearing furniture scraping across the floor, she turned toward the door just as Derek Browne pushed it open. He smiled and held out his arms to his wife.

"We always have the first dance, sweetheart."

Lily felt another ache in her chest, for the look Derek gave Samantha was filled with love and adoration. She would bet her last dollar that this man had never cheated on his wife.

"Oh, Derek," Sam scolded softly, "I should finish this tray of cookies—"

"Nonsense, Sam," Lily interrupted. "Go dance with the

man. I'll finish up." Lily was grateful to be busy in the kitchen, but when the tray was ready, she took it into the other room. It gave her an excuse to get a good look at Trudy Harding.

She and Ross were off in a corner, being completely ignored by everyone else in the room. Still clinging to Ross's arm, Trudy had the forced look of one trying valiantly to have a good time but failing miserably. But she was pretty. Perhaps a little plump, but she had a very pretty face. As she gazed up at Ross, her big brown eyes looked very much like a smitten puppy dog's. The knot of hurt twisted in Lily's stomach.

But she knew she couldn't dislike the woman if for no other reason than that every other woman in the room did. Ross bent his head to listen as Trudy whispered to him, and panic attacked Lily's insides when she saw him nod, then begin walking toward her. She wanted to escape into the kitchen but knew they'd just follow her there.

As they approached, Lily could smell the telltale cologne, and a war waged inside her. She was a fool to let the smell of some cheap scent bother her, but on a purely female level, it rankled.

They stood in front of her, so close she almost choked. It took her a moment to realize it wasn't the smell of the cologne that made her nauseous but the battle going on inside her because of it.

"Miss Sawyer? I'm Trudy Harding." She smiled and extended her hand.

Briefly Lily caught the look on Ross's face, one that dared her to be civil to his date when no one else would. He needn't have bothered. No matter what the woman did or was, Lily discovered she couldn't dislike her. She felt too sorry for her.

Lily took the hand, as calloused as her own, and answered, "It's Mrs., but please, call me Lily."

"Oh, then, you *are* a widow too?" Hope sprang into her eyes.

"Yes. Yes, I am."

"You hear that, Ross?" She playfully swatted Ross on the

arm. "I told you that's what I'd heard. Knowing that, I'm sure we can be friends."

Lily heard the expectation in her voice. She also sensed the loneliness and the quiet hysteria, for she'd felt them in herself often enough. Every other woman in the room could have sympathized if she'd had a mind to, but none of them would. Widowhood left a woman completely unprepared for the world. In some ways, Lily had been lucky. Jake's unfaithfulness had softened the blow of being alone when he died, for she'd shut him out months before. And her isolation had made her independent. Even before Jake's death, she'd been determined to find a respectable job. Obviously, perhaps through no fault of her own, Trudy Harding had not.

"I'm sure we could," she heard herself say. "Why don't you stop by and visit sometime?"

Trudy's puppy dog eyes widened. "Oh, you . . . you wouldn't mind?"

"Not at all." Lily discovered she meant it. In fact, she was looking forward to it—for a whole passel of reasons, not the least of which was to get a better understanding of the cad who would drag this poor soul to a party and subject her to such a miserable time.

Lively strains of "Oh, Dem Golden Slippers" announced the beginning of the dancing. Lily glanced at the fiddler, wanting to escape into the kitchen but not wanting to appear rude.

"Come on, Trudy, let's show 'em how it's done."

"Ross Benedict, you know I can't dance tonight." She looked at Lily and shrugged. "I twisted my ankle earlier this afternoon. That's why I've been hanging on to Ross's arm." She brightened. "Why don't you and Lily dance?"

Lily and Ross both voiced excuses, their words spilling out, jumbling together.

"Nonsense. I know how you love to dance, Ross."

Lily knew she was blushing, for her cheeks were hot.

"Well, it's a lively tune," he answered, his gaze lingering on Lily's face. "I suppose we could."

"Oh, no, I—"

"Ask her nicely, Ross." Trudy punched his arm. "What's the matter with you?"

He mouthed a curse, which Lily read clearly. "That's all right, Trudy, I should get back to the kitchen." She turned to leave but felt a hand on her arm. Instinctively she knew it wasn't Trudy's, for shivers played over her skin.

"May I have this dance?"

Had his eyes held even the slightest bit of derision, she'd have told him to take a flying leap off a cliff. But they didn't.

Pulling in a shaky breath, she told herself she could do this as long as the music was snappy and brisk. Unfortunately, the moment she stepped into his arms, "Oh, Dem Golden Slippers" became "I'll Take You Home Again, Kathleen," and Lily was forced to move slowly around the living room floor, cradled in Ross Benedict's very capable arms.

She wanted to speak, to diffuse the tension she felt at being so close to him, but she was suddenly tongue-tied. Whatever else she thought of him, she couldn't deny that he was a wonderful dancer. He led her over the floor, and she followed him as though they'd done this together a hundred times before.

With a subtle movement, he pulled her closer. She tensed in his arms but didn't draw away.

"We fit," he said against her ear.

His chest was hard and wide, and she forced herself to think of something else. It wasn't possible, for she'd seen it naked, and if she lived to be ninety, she'd never forget it. The vision swam before her eyes even yet. "Don't be foolish," she managed to say.

He chuckled, a deep, warm sound that teased her flesh. "Always contrary, aren't you, Lily?"

It was the first time he'd said her name. Her skin continued to tingle and she felt a breathlessness she hadn't felt since she'd been courted by Jake. She had to force herself to stay aloof, to keep her distance, if not physically, then mentally. Equal measures of relief and disappointment sifted through her when the music finally stopped.

She attempted to step away, but he held her fast. Her gaze shot to his, and she saw the hunger in his eyes, fearing he could see the same in hers. "The music has ended."

"I think our music has just begun, Lily." There wasn't a hint of amusement in his dark, dangerous gaze.

She swallowed hard. "You're being foolish again."

His hand was low on her back and he pressed her against him. She felt the hard ridge of him, even through the thickness of their clothes. Their gazes met again. His held a hint of laughter. "After the intimacies we've already shared, Lily, my sweet, I believe you should call me Ross."

That he would boldly mention their mutual hunger fed her anger. "I think I should call you a cad, Mr. Benedict. Have you forgotten that you brought a companion? How can you leave her at the mercy of these women?"

His gaze didn't leave her. "Trudy can hold her own against anyone. And we're just friends."

She snorted, rather indelicately. "Is that why your bedding is riddled with the scent of her cologne?"

He smiled, crinkly little lines fanning out at the edges of his eyes. "Why, Lily, I do believe you're jealous."

She gasped and pulled away, stunned by such a bold—and ridiculous—remark. "What surprises me, Mr. Benedict, is that your swelled head doesn't throw you off balance and send you toppling to the floor."

With a purposeful stride, she went into the kitchen. Once there, she sagged into a chair and listened to the thumping of her heart.

She stayed in the kitchen, busying herself with the chore of cleaning up. She wouldn't have set foot in the other room again even if the back door was on fire.

Chapter Six

Samantha insisted that Ross take Lily home. Trudy kept up a constant prattle all the way. Lily didn't know whether she was nervous at having Lily with them or whether her chattiness was normal. In either case, it made Lily uncomfortable even though she knew the arrangement made sense. The only other alternative had been for her to stay at Samantha's, but Lily had to set the sponge for her bread before she went to bed, then rise early in the morning to form it into loaves and bake it for the logging crew's lunch.

Much to her surprise, Ross dropped Trudy off first. To Lily's chagrin, Trudy threw her arms around Ross and kissed him. For some reason, the moment her lips touched him, he turned, giving her his cheek.

Lily almost sneered. If he had done that for her benefit, he needn't have bothered. For all she knew, he'd sneak back to Trudy's after he thought she was asleep.

They rode home, the sounds of the team's hooves on the hard-packed earth and the jingle of the bells on the harness the only noise in the quiet air.

As they rolled into the yard in front of the cabin, Lily quickly left the buggy and hurried inside. She had work to do; she couldn't concern herself with Ross Benedict, although she'd thought of little else all the way home. She should never have let herself dance with him. It was bad enough that she'd felt the stirrings of desire, but knowing that he'd felt them, too, made things worse. She'd been tempted to ask him why he'd purposely embarrassed Trudy by bringing her to a party where she was so obviously not welcome, but it would have meant starting up a conversation, and she'd thought better of it.

She'd just finished preparing the yeast sponge when she heard the spatter of raindrops against the kitchen window. By the time she'd undressed and crawled into her bedroll, the rain had become a deluge. Huddled in the darkness, she listened to the storm. The wind howled, sending great troughs of rain against the windows.

Behind her, where she'd stored flour and sugar, she heard a menacing *drip-drip-drip*. Struggling herself out of her bedroll, she lit the lamp and crept to the corner, cringing when she saw the water dribbling down the sides of the containers. She put the lamp down and dragged the heavy staples across the floor, shoving them under the table to keep them dry.

She hadn't been back in her bedroll for more than a few minutes when she felt the first drop of water hit her square in the face. Sliding from the covers again, she relit the lamp and took a turn around the kitchen, discovering many places where water was splattering onto the floor.

She stored everything in danger of getting wet under the table with the flour and sugar, then set a number of pots out to catch the water as it leaked through the roof.

Attempting to get comfortable again, she found that her bedroll was wet and her pillow soaked through. The smell of the wet feathers made her gag.

It went against every grain of sense she had, but the big, clean bed in the bedroom beckoned. She might be stubborn, but she wasn't stupid. It made no sense to sleep in a rain-soaked bedroll when there was an empty bed only a few dozen feet away. Leaving the kitchen, she crossed her fingers, hoping the roof over the bedroom didn't leak.

Stepping inside, she closed the door and listened. She heard no telltale dripping sounds, and although the room was cold, it felt dry. After draping the extra quilt over the bed, she quickly slipped between the flannel sheets and curled into a ball. A drowsy lethargy spread through her and she fell asleep.

* * *

Maudie's cabin leaked like a strainer. Ross cursed, finally so wet he couldn't even pretend to sleep. Hell and damnation, if she wasn't going to use his bed, *he* was. It made no sense at all for him to catch his death when there was a perfectly good bed going unused.

Dashing to the cabin through the deluge, he stepped inside, shut the door against the intrusive wind, and went directly to the fireplace to stoke up the fire. He sat close to the warmth until it seeped into his bones, then rose and strode toward the bedroom.

It was dark, but he didn't have to light a lamp; he knew his room by heart. He stripped out of his wet clothes, cursing again when he discovered that even his woolen drawers were wet. He unbuttoned them and slid them down his legs, kicking them off, not giving a damn where they landed.

Shivering, he lifted the edge of the bedding and quickly crawled into bed, releasing a luxurious sigh as the soft sheets molded around him.

He reached for his extra pillow—and discovered masses of soft, curly hair instead. "What the—?"

Lily had been dreaming, or she thought she had. His voice convinced her she was not. Coming fully awake, she scudded up from the bed before she rolled toward him, her heart bounding into her throat.

"Oh, God, oh, God, oh, God," she murmured, hurrying toward the door.

He got to the door before she did. "No." His voice rumbled out from deep within his chest.

Swallowing hard, Lily clutched at the neck of her flannel gown. "Get out of my way."

"No," he repeated. "I'll be damned if I know what's going on between us, but there's something there. There has been from the beginning, and we both know it."

The room was cold; she began to shiver. "I don't know what

you're talking about," she answered, trying not to let her teeth clatter.

"No?" He groped for her hand and pulled it away from her throat. "Here," he said, his voice barely above a whisper. "Touch me, then tell me I'm wrong."

Her hand splayed against his chest, the crinkly hair teasing her sensitive palm. She tried to pull away, but he held her fast. Unwitting desire pulsed through her and her knees felt weak. He moved her hand over the hard muscles that lay beneath his chest hair, and when she no longer argued, he took her other hand and drew them both lower, over his naval, then lower still.

She heard his labored breathing and realized she could barely breathe herself. When he brought her fingers against his thick, hard root, she felt her knees give way, and the place between her thighs, the place that had been dormant since she'd discovered Jake's whoring three years before, came alive like a sleeping lioness, ravenous with a terrible hunger.

Catching her to him, Ross lifted her into his arms and carried her to the bed. Once under the covers, they clung together, pressing tightly. Lily needed to be closer still, and when he moved his hand up her thigh, taking her gown with it, she encouraged him, lifting up off the bed, helping him remove the cumbersome object.

Mindless with desire, she reveled in the feel of his body against hers, rubbing her nipples against the hair on his chest, throwing one leg over his to bring him closer still.

His hand moved between them, down to her aching delta, and he touched her there but briefly, sending her soaring to a teeth-jarring climax. She lay against him, stunned at what had just happened. There had been release, but at what cost? She felt like a whore. Turning her face away, she felt tears run across the bridge of her nose, down her cheek, and into her hair. Ross pressed her shoulders to the bedding and began kissing and fondling her breasts. Arousal threatened again, and she caught her lower lip between her teeth to keep from crying aloud. She hated herself for needing him, despised herself for wanting him.

He was rigid and large against her thigh, but she fought the urge to touch him. A deep, private part of her still felt shame for the way her body had reacted.

"Ah, Lily, Lily," he murmured between kisses. "Your passion robs me of breath." He moved to her mouth, and she opened for him, taking his kiss, returning it with growing excitement that blotted out logical thought. His beard was soft; she'd never kissed a man with a beard before. She wasn't sure she liked it, but she did like the feel of his lips on hers, his tongue twining with hers. Her arousal grew, and she touched his arms, his chest, his stomach, allowing herself to stroke his thick root, moving the skin back and forth until he shuddered and shook beside her.

"Enough!" He pulled her hand away, brought it to his mouth and kissed it. "Do you want me to spend like a boy?"

"No," she whispered, coaxing him to her, spreading her legs to invite him in. He entered her, and the feeling was so exquisite Lily thought she would faint. "Oh," she whispered, close to tears, "it's been so long . . . so long . . ."

She put her legs around his back and drew him in as far as she was able while he rocked against her, his breath shaky and harsh in her ear.

She felt it begin again, that helpless sensation of pleasure, and she clung to him, reaching for the magic, feeling it spread through her like honey heated in the sun.

He stiffened, then rolled to his side, bringing her with him. She lay there, too spent to speak, or perhaps too uncertain to do so. She knew she should leave, but there was no place to go that wasn't wet and cold. And it was so warm in the bed. He was so warm. . . .

He curled around her, spoon style, and she drifted into sleep again, wishing she didn't have to face him in the morning.

* * *

Ross wanted desperately to sleep; he couldn't. How in the hell could a man sleep with a body like Lily's pressed against his chest?

Her breathing was even and deep. Certain she was asleep, he gently fondled her breasts, closing his eyes against the pleasure. He didn't know how to feel; his emotions disturbed him. He'd thought he would crow like a rooster at how she'd responded to him. Instead he was left shaken by the depth of her passion. And his own.

His hand wandered down over her soft, warm stomach to just above the soft thatch that covered her. He had no self-restraint, for one finger dipped lower, through the curls to the cleft beneath, then to the slick, wet flesh of her womanhood. Finding the swelling nub, he stroked her.

She made a sound in her throat, then gasped aloud, a telling sound that proved she had awakened. Curling her leg back over his, she gave him access. It wasn't long before she turned to face him and they came together again, their passions stirring like heady wine boiling over a fire.

Ross resisted the urge to stay inside her, although he wanted to fall asleep that way. He rolled to his back again, and when she turned to face the other direction, he felt a ridiculous, foreign sense of loss.

Lily awakened before dawn. Although she felt warm and supremely satisfied physically, dread and regret loomed inside her like an impending storm. Before her feelings for Ross could surface again, she inched away from his big, hard body and slid from the bed.

As she slipped from the room, she realized that what had happened the night before had happened because she'd allowed it to. She'd had no choice; her need had been building for years. But now it was over. She felt in control. She could keep him at arm's length.

Still, when she thought about what they'd done, a breathlessness stole over her that left her hungry for him again. Oh, damn! Men were such a faithless lot. Both her father and her late husband had been philanderers. She'd buried her feelings toward them a long time ago, but now there was Ross Benedict, bringing one woman to the party and sleeping with another. Though Lily guessed that probably made her no better than him, she resolved never to let herself be coaxed into Ross's bed again.

She fed the fire in the fireplace, then dressed, hoping the mountain of work she had to do would keep her from thinking of how wantonly she'd acted the night before. She could not understand how she had experienced an orgasm at the mere touch of his fingers. It had to have happened because she'd been in such need after so many years of abstinence.

Shaking away her thoughts, she entered the kitchen, and her heart plummeted. The pots she'd put out to catch the rain the night before were full, a few brimming over onto the floor. After emptying some of them into two large teakettles, she poured the rest into larger pots to use later. She had to get the bread started before she mopped and scrubbed the floor, but first she made a pot of coffee.

Just as she finished forming the bread into loaves, Ross knocked on the open kitchen door. "Permission to enter?"

The battle lines they'd drawn that first day seemed childish now. "Of course." She turned, and longing swept through her at the sight of him. Although he was dressed, she could imagine the body beneath the clothing, and she flushed. And his eyes . . . She'd never noticed how dark they were, like black coffee and just as hot as they swept over her. There was, however, a hint of anger—or something like it—in his gaze.

"I . . . I've made some coffee. Please, help yourself. And . . . there are some biscuits left over from yesterday in that tin at the back of the stove. There's butter and jam in the cupboard."

He nodded but said nothing as he helped himself. He bit into a warm biscuit, then glanced at the ceiling. "I guess I have my work cut out for me today."

"It appears to have stopped raining, at least for now." Their inane small talk grated on Lily's nerves. Needing something to do, she took some of the hot water from the reservoir attached to the stove and poured it into a scrub pail, then added shavings of hard soap. After it had dissolved, she filled the pail with rainwater.

She tried to keep her mind on her scrubbing, but just knowing he was watching her made her stiff and self-conscious. She sensed that his thoughts were the same as hers, but she knew she couldn't talk about what had happened the night before. What could she say? That it shouldn't have happened? That it would never happen again? She knew all that. She hoped he did too.

"Listen," he began. "About last night—"

"It should never have happened," she interrupted breathlessly.

Ross studied her as she dropped the brush into the pail and rested on her knees. For some reason he couldn't understand, he hated to see her this way, washing his floor like some dreary scrubwoman.

"No, I suppose you're right. It shouldn't have happened, but I—"

"It won't happen again. I . . . I have no excuse for my bold behavior. I'm sorry," she said contritely. "I don't know what came over me. Please . . . please, just forget it happened."

"Forget it happened? How in the hell am I supposed to do that?" He *was* angry now, angry at the words that told him so clearly how she felt. He stood, then walked around to face her.

Her head was bowed. "Please," she pleaded. "Don't make me feel any worse than I already do."

His anger turned to hurt. He hadn't been able to understand his feelings either, but beneath it all, he felt damned good. Never had he been so sure that something was right. And here she was, telling him flat out that it had been wrong.

She raised her hands to her hair and fussed with it, a motion that brought his gaze to her breasts, all snug and pressed tightly against her gown. The memory of how they'd felt in his hands and against his lips made his mouth dry. He'd thought of seeing them in the daylight, seeing all of her, naked in the sunshine. It fired the coals of his imagination and he deemed it only fair, for she'd seen him, bathing in the river.

"I'll pull my bedroll and pillow by the fire today. Hopefully they'll be dry enough to use tonight. I won't . . . intrude into your bedroom again."

Fury built up in him and he thought his head might explode. "Look at me and tell me you didn't enjoy what we did. I'm not that big a fool, Lily. I know when a woman is pretending, and I know when she's not. You weren't pretending. You were as anxious for it to happen as I was. Hell, you flew apart the minute I touched you."

Her head still bowed, she closed her eyes and uttered a shaky sigh.

"Now," he continued. "Look at me and tell me, straight to my face, that you didn't enjoy it."

Slowly she raised her gaze to his. The hardness he saw there shocked him. "I didn't enjoy it. I might have needed it, Ross Benedict, but trust me, I'm not proud of it, and I didn't enjoy it."

He felt a stunning wash of angry frustration. "I don't believe you." He left her, eager to put her cold, calculated answer behind him.

An hour later, he was patching the roof when he heard a buggy rattle into the clearing. He spat a curse when he saw Trudy alight from the conveyance and make her way boldly to the cabin door.

Chapter Seven

Lily ushered Trudy into the kitchen and motioned to a chair. "I apologize for the mess. The roof leaked in here, and I don't dare put anything away until it's mended." Lily poured her a cup of coffee, then turned back to the ginger cookie dough she was mixing.

"I've never been in Ross's cabin before," Trudy mused. "It's rather nice."

Cautiously surprised, Lily turned. "You haven't been here before?"

"No." At Lily's expression, she added, "You don't believe me."

Feeling foolish, Lily turned to her chore again. "I . . . I'm sorry. I guess . . . I just thought . . ."

"Well, you guessed and you thought wrong, Lily. The only woman ever allowed in Ross's domain, until you came along, was Samantha, that snippy little sister of his."

Lily felt a warmth around her heart. "Oh, Samantha's not such a bad sort, Trudy. She's really quite charming and likable."

Trudy snorted. "Not to me, she isn't. Of course, I know why. She and the other 'ladies' of Twin Hearts blame me for all the ills of the town."

Lily couldn't argue, so tried another tactic. "I thought it was very rude of Ross to bring you to the party last night."

She laughed. "Rude? Why?"

Lily rolled the cookie dough onto the flour-covered counter, cut large circles of dough with the lid of a canning jar, and slid them onto a baking sheet. "Surely he knew what kind of reception you'd get."

"Oh, he knew, all right."

Lily removed the last loaf of bread from the oven, then slid in the cookies. "And it didn't bother you?"

Trudy shrugged. "I knew he had a reason for doing it the minute he asked me. He's never invited me to one of his sister's parties before." She was quiet for a moment while she studied Lily. "I didn't know why he'd done it this time until I saw that you were there."

Lily's heart took a dip. "Me? Why me?"

"Obviously he wanted to make you jealous."

The comment stunned her, and she leaned against the counter. "Why on earth would you think that?" Damn! Why was her heart pounding so?

"I may not have an ounce of good sense when it comes to my own life, Lily, but I know Ross. We'd been . . . close for years. You've probably learned that what I do to keep body and soul together isn't the least bit respectable. Bluntly I've allowed many of the men in this town to support me, Ross among them."

Lily's stomach clenched like a fist. Gritting her teeth, she continued to roll and cut cookies, pretending nothing was wrong. Foolish as it was, it bothered her that Ross and Trudy had slept together.

"But not too long ago, about the time I learned there was a beautiful red-haired widow cooking for the loggers, Ross came by for dinner. Sadly for me, that was all he wanted. He said it wasn't me, that it was him. I knew then that someone had truly claimed his heart, and that it was probably you."

"But . . . but," Lily sputtered. "We don't even like each other. We haven't, I mean, we didn't—"

"Don't, Lily. Whether you have or haven't doesn't matter. I just know that eventually you will. When I saw the way he watched you last night . . ." She sighed. "He didn't take his eyes off you. If he'd ever looked at me that way, I might have thought I really had a chance with him. But he never did," she added wistfully.

It was all Lily could do to continue working. Her hands shook. Her knees were weak. Her pulse roared through her head, humming in her ears. What Trudy said was nonsense! It was pointless to dwell on it anyway, for Ross had said himself that it wasn't natural for a man to be faithful.

"I'm sorry if what I've said upset you, Lily."

Lily jumped at the sound of Trudy's voice. She'd all but forgotten she was there. "No," she said, shoring herself up. "It's not that, really. It's just that . . . that I think you're reading something into this that isn't there."

"I see." She sounded disappointed. "Well, I guess I should go—"

"Wait," Lily interrupted. "Don't go. I appreciate your company, Trudy, and your candor. I'd like to help you."

"Help me?"

Lily sat in the chair across from her. "It's none of my business, and you can tell me so if you wish, but . . . would you like to make your living another way?"

Clearly puzzled, Trudy stared at her. "Doing what? I'm not qualified to do anything. Gracious, I'm not even a very good cook."

Lily grasped her hand. "Oh, but everyone can cook. And what you don't know I can teach you. I need help. Badly."

Trudy's face crumpled and there were tears in her eyes. "You'd . . . you'd want *me* to work with you?"

Her expression left Lily feeling contrite. "I didn't mean to upset you. Really, it's none of my business what you do. And . . . and just because I wouldn't do it doesn't mean you shouldn't. I mean, I had no right to think you'd want to do something else—"

"You'd actually want me to work here, with you? Really?"

"I'm sorry. I shouldn't have presumed—"

Trudy put her face in her hands, sobbing quietly.

Lily felt awful. She went to the back of Trudy's chair and touched her shoulders. "I'm so sorry," she apologized again.

"I . . . c-can't believe you'd w-want me to work with you,"

Trudy stuttered between sobs. "You . . . you'd do that for me?"

Lily began to understand. "Of course. I asked you, didn't I?"

Trudy continued to cry. "No woman in this town has ever done anything nice for me before."

Lily bent and gave her a hug. "I'm not doing it just to be nice, Trudy. I really could use some help."

Trudy grasped her arm but couldn't seem to stop crying. "Oh, Lily. Thank you so much."

"What in the hell's going on in here?"

Both women looked up as Ross entered the kitchen, but neither spoke.

"What did you say to her, Lily? Why in the hell did you make her cry?"

Fury at his assumption made her flush. "I didn't. I mean, I did, but it's not what you . . ." No, she would not defend herself, not to him. "Oh, just shut up, Ross Benedict!"

His gaze went to Trudy's tearstained face. "Trudy? Did she upset you? Are you all right?"

Lily offered her a handkerchief, which she took and dabbed at her eyes. Sniffing loudly, she answered, "Just shut up, Ross. Why do you always jump to conclusions? That's one of your worst habits."

He stood in the middle of the room, stunned by their verbal attacks. Throwing up his hands in defeat, he demanded, "Why in the hell are you mad at *me?*"

"Oh, just never you mind," Trudy answered, gaining control of herself. "If you must know, Lily offered me a job."

Ross appeared puzzled. "A job? Doing what?"

"Why, helping her cook for the loggers, of course."

Lily saw the look of disbelief on his face before he quickly masked it. She knew what he was thinking: that she'd hired Trudy just to learn more about him. Oh, she thought, her fury mounting, he had an even bigger swelled head than she'd imagined.

"Trudy's going to *cook?*" He sounded incredulous.

"I'm going to help, aren't I, Lily?"

"Of course," Lily answered, still standing behind Trudy. "And I do need some help, Ross. If you see Samantha before I do, tell her the job is just too much for one person. If she doesn't approve of what I've done, then perhaps she should find another cook." Suddenly Lily was angry with Samantha for the way she and all the other women in Twin Hearts had treated Trudy. And the men, too, for that matter.

"You'd quit because of this?"

"Yes, Ross, I'd quit." She meant it too. "In the meantime, I imagine you're hungry. There's some leftover stew on the back of the stove. And eat the rest of those biscuits, please. I'd wait on you myself, but the way I'm feeling toward you and everyone else in this town right now, I'm afraid I'd dump the damned stew into your lap."

She hurried from the room, lifted her worn cape from the chair by the fire, and sailed from the cabin, leaving Ross and Trudy alone in the kitchen.

Lily couldn't stay away for long because she just had too much work to do. And she felt better after her little explosion. Years ago, Jake had compared her temper to a volcano, erupting quickly and leaving destruction in its wake.

When she returned to the cabin, she was dismayed to find Trudy gone.

Ross was waiting for her in the kitchen. "Trudy pulled out the sheet of cookies from the oven before they burned."

In her haste to leave, Lily had forgotten them. She put them on a rack, then rolled and cut more, sliding them onto the sheet.

"So," he said behind her, "what little scheme have you cooked up?"

A coldness settled around her heart. "Scheme?"

"Yeah. Why in the hell would you hire Trudy?"

"And why shouldn't I?"

He snorted a laugh but didn't answer her.

She clutched the mixing spoon in her fist and turned on him. "If you think I hired her just to find out more about you, then you're even more arrogant than I'd imagined."

He snorted again. "Is that what you think?"

She shrugged. "I can think of no other reason you'd disapprove."

"The fact that she can't make a decent cup of coffee might have crossed your mind."

Lily felt her first niggle of uncertainty. "Why, surely she can cook. What woman can't?"

"Let's just say it's not one of her more . . . endearing attributes."

His innuendo angered Lily further. "Has it ever occurred to you that she might need a friend? She's had enough snickers and snubbings from the lot of you to last a lifetime, I have no doubt."

"I've never laughed at her, Lily."

"Perhaps not. But you *did* bring her to a party knowing full well that she wouldn't be welcome. That doesn't show much respect for her, do you think?"

He studied her quietly. "I'm sorry about that. It was a mistake. I shouldn't have put her in that position. But you do know what she does for a living, don't you?"

Suddenly tired of the game, she said, "Yes, I know. She told me herself. But I know where she's coming from, Ross. I've been there. I'm a widow, too, remember? We're just different people. When I lost my husband, I'd already become quite independent, because, you see, he'd ceased to be part of my life at all. Of his own choosing. He found his . . . entertainment elsewhere. With good, old-fashioned whores. And not just one but many. I can't count the number of times he stumbled home reeking of some whore's cologne, expecting me to respond to—"

She stopped, angry that she'd revealed such a painful part of her life. "After he was killed, I had to do something to keep myself alive. I chose to cook because it was something I did well and enjoyed." She let that sink in before she parried again.

"Obviously Trudy knows what she does best. She enjoys the company of men, in and out of her bed. But, as I told you earlier, Ross Benedict, I might *need* that, but I certainly don't *enjoy* it." She was lying to herself as well as to him, for she *had* enjoyed it. Very, very much. She just wasn't proud of it.

He was quiet for a long, tense minute, his gaze never wavering from hers. "After what we did last night? Hell, there was pleasure on both sides, Lily, don't—"

"Will you stop reminding me of that?" she pleaded. "I will tell you just one more time. I did not enjoy it."

Another minute stretched, taut as a wire, between them. Finally he murmured, "I don't believe that's true for one goddamned minute."

She turned back to the counter, knowing his words held more truth than hers but unwilling to admit it. "Believe what you wish. I can't stop you."

In an instant, he was behind her, pulling her against his chest. His hands cupped her breasts; his thumbs rubbed her nipples through her clothing. She felt him, thick and hard, against the small of her back, and every nerve in her body responded. Still, she fought it.

"Don't," she pleaded softly as one hand dipped below her waist, inching toward the juncture of her thighs. "Please, please, don't." Even to her own ears, her request sounded feeble.

He turned her to face him, then bent to kiss her. She greeted him hungrily, without thought, for to think would make her crazy.

The kiss ignited their passion, and though Lily felt his fingers fumbling at the buttons of her dress, she couldn't have stopped him if she'd wanted to. His fingers on her bare breasts signaled the return of her sanity, and she pushed him away, her chest heaving.

"No." She held her bodice together, but he removed her hands, tugging her clothes apart.

"It's only fair, Lily," he coaxed.

"What do you mean?" Desire hummed through her.

"You've seen me bare," he reminded her, though there wasn't a hint of humor in his eyes.

The memory of his naked body rose before her, rendering her weak with a hunger that dissolved her resistance. Desire and humiliation fought for control within her. She remembered his feelings about devotion and fidelity, and her humiliation won. Shoving him away, she slumped into a chair and put her head on her arm, unable to keep from sobbing quietly. How could she continue this way? She wanted him. She needed him. She was falling head over heels in love with him. *Him.* A man whom she could neither trust nor respect.

Remembering all the nights she'd spent alone, waiting in vain for Jake to return to her bed, she knew, with a certainty, that were she to succumb to her feelings for Ross, she would suffer the same pains all over again. God, why was her taste in men so pathetic?

Her suffering was like a knife to Ross's gut. He wanted to comfort her but knew she wouldn't allow it. And why should she? He remembered telling her that he couldn't—wouldn't—be faithful. How could he prove to her it had only been words? Words to keep himself from feeling things he didn't want to feel. Words to get her ire up so he could watch her bristle. Words that he'd always believed before but that even then had suddenly sounded shallow and false. Words that made him sound exactly like the man she'd married and lost. Words that would separate them forever unless he could convince her he hadn't meant them.

He went to the door, bracing his arms on either side. "By the way," he said, remembering what he'd come in to tell her in the first place, "I checked up on Maudie. She's coming along fine, but the doctor wants to keep her for another week or so. I'm sorry, I meant to tell you earlier, but with Trudy here, I got kind of sidetracked."

She sniffed behind him. "Oh. I'm glad. Th-thank you for telling me."

Knowing there was nothing else for him to say or do, he left her alone to lick her wounds.

Chapter Eight

While Ross finished patching up the holes in the cabin roof and the roof of Maudie's place, Lily moved her bedroll and pillow closer to the fire. She fully intended to sleep in it come bedtime. Occasionally she crossed her fingers, praying it would be dry.

Trudy returned later in the day to begin learning Lily's routine, but when evening rolled around, Lily and Ross were alone again.

They sat by the fire, Lily preparing menus and Ross reading a newspaper he'd picked up in town. Were anyone to look in, Lily realized, they would appear to be a couple spending a quiet evening together before going to bed.

Bed. Even the word caused her to feel flushed, for Ross's bed was no longer merely a place to sleep but also a place where she'd found complete satisfaction.

"I want to apologize."

His words came out of the blue, shaking her from her reverie. "I beg your pardon?"

"For starters, I want to apologize for shouting at you the day I came home from Chico and found you in my bedroom."

She allowed herself a small smile. "You mean the day I hit you in the head with the butt of your rifle?"

He made a gruff sound and cleared his throat. "Yeah, that's the day. I thought you and Sam were . . . conniving to . . . well, to get the two of us together," he finished, sounding embarrassed.

Lily had already discovered that was exactly what Sam had planned. However, she wanted to hear his side. "Why would you think such a thing?"

"Well, hell. She's been trying to marry me off for years. Every New Year's Eve, she pairs me up with one of her unmarried friends, and I spend the whole miserable evening feeling like bait on a stick. Last year, I decided I'd had it. I wasn't going to let her lead me around by the nose ever again, and I told her so. It was my New Year's resolution."

Clearing his throat once more, he folded the paper and put it on the table. "I thought maybe this was her way of getting back at me."

Lily tucked her feet under her and warmed them against her robe. "I can assure you I knew absolutely nothing of her plan, if indeed she had one."

"Oh, she had one, all right. She knew damned good and well that I wasn't going to be gone more than a few weeks. You probably thought the place wasn't occupied, because while I was gone, she'd had the cabin fumigated for fleas. She took all my clothes and the bedding too." He gave her a lopsided grin. "She rented you the place knowing it was occupied. By me. And that I'd be back just about the time you started to feel comfortable. I guess she thought we might . . ."

Her face void of expression, she asked, "She thought we might—what?"

"You know," he murmured. "Get together."

"Well," she managed to say, "I think we can assure her that her plan failed. Miserably." She gave him a cold smile, then turned to her menu planning.

"Yeah," he reflected, rubbing his finger over his mustache. "The thing is, I just can't believe she's entirely wrong this time."

Lily's heart pounded hard beneath her robe. What he said was undoubtedly true. There had been something physical between them from the very beginning. There still was. And she might even wish things were different so it *could* be true, but he wasn't any better a man than Jake had been. Or her father. She'd rather have no man at all than one who couldn't be faithful.

"Physical attraction means nothing without fidelity, Ross," she said as her pulse thrummed at the base of her throat.

He frowned. "What in the hell is that supposed to mean?"

"It means," she began, her voice stern, "that Jake—my late husband—and I were quite compatible. Physically. But he was an unfaithful swine. I would sooner be celibate than be intimate with a man who cannot be faithful, no matter how much I'm attracted to him."

"Are you attracted to me, Lily?" His voice was as seductive as aged whiskey.

She squirmed, uncomfortable with his question. "I had certain needs the other night, and you . . . you were willing to slake them. That's all."

"Prove it."

"*What?*"

"Prove that's all it was, Lily. Prove you can kiss me without becoming aroused now that you're . . . *slaked.*" Clearly amused, he began unbuttoning his shirt. His chest hair was so thick it poked through the buttonholes.

Lily's mouth went dry, but she was indignant just the same. "I'll do no such thing."

"Why not? Afraid you might feel something?"

"Revulsion is what I'll feel," she snapped, having no intention of accommodating his ridiculous request.

"Tell me," she asked, "do your other women actually *like* all that hair on your face?"

His dark eyes danced. "My *other* women? Are you admitting to being one of my women, Lily-love?"

"Oh, don't be foolish," she huffed, throwing her notebook on the floor. "And I'm not your love. I'm going to bed."

For a big man, he was surprisingly agile. He stopped her at the kitchen door and caught her to him, pressing her hands inside his shirt, against his warm flesh. "A hairy man can keep a woman warm, Lily."

She clenched her teeth against the urge to rub her face against his chest, but she couldn't control the pounding of her heart or the lush weakness in her lower abdomen. "Let me go."

"One kiss, Lily. One little kiss to prove that's all you need. That you don't want what we had last night. Now that you're *slaked*," he repeated, "one kiss should be easy enough to part with."

He was baiting her. Teasing her. So sure she couldn't resist him. Oh, how she hated arrogance in a man! She wanted in the worst way to watch him tumble from his lofty, self-centered perch.

"All right," she said. "It won't be a problem at all."

Raising up on her tiptoes, she touched his mouth. She expected him to grab her and devour her: then she planned to stand limp and unresponsive.

He surprised her. She felt the tip of his tongue barely graze her lips, the flats of his thumbs circle her nipples, the front of his jeans press ever so slightly against her stomach.

Desire exploded like a bursting flower between her legs, and when his mouth opened over hers, she answered his kiss and threw her arms around his neck. Her self-control was gone.

Lifting her up, he wrapped her legs around his waist and pressed her buttocks with his hands, grinding against her. One hand snaked up beneath her gown and robe to her naked thigh, then to her bottom.

He stumbled with her to a chair, collapsing into it. She continued to straddle him, her desire so strong she flung all other thoughts aside as she reached for her pleasure. He opened her robe and unbuttoned her gown, freeing one breast. He kissed it. Licked the nipple. Nuzzled it with his beard, intensifying Lily's desire.

Her naked flesh pressed against the rigid fly of his jeans. She coaxed him to continue loving her breast while she rode him hard until the kernel of pleasure burst, sending her spiraling, rocking the world.

Her breath came hard, and she felt boneless . . . and ashamed at her inability to control herself.

Drawing her hand to his fly, he unbuttoned it with his other hand and urged her to touch him. Desire flared again, but she fought it, pulling her hand away, refusing to be coaxed.

His hands spanned her thighs, his thumbs nudging her cleft. "Don't be cruel, Lily," he whispered, his voice husky as a raw wind.

She allowed him to return her hand to his fly, and she reached inside, against his drawers, finding him still thick and hard. Quivering with unwanted desire, she stroked him until he stiffened and shuddered beneath her.

"Ah, Lily-love, let's go to bed."

She scrambled off his lap, buttoning her nightgown as she hurried toward the kitchen. "Just because I serviced you doesn't mean I'll sleep with you."

She shut the door behind her, crossed to her bedroll, and fell upon it, angry tears stinging her eyes. She couldn't imagine what was wrong with her. She wanted him fiercely. She could love him easily. She probably already did. But he was all wrong for her. His kind was wrong for any woman who wanted a loving, faithful mate.

The next morning, Ross was nowhere around. Lily began working, and shortly after, Trudy arrived. They worked well together and time passed quickly. When the clock on the mantel chimed eleven times, she heard the wagon from the camp stop out front. She and Trudy carried biscuits and apple fritters to the wagon, and she ordered the driver to retrieve the rabbit pies from the counter in the kitchen.

He returned with the meat pies and placed them in the wagon, his gaze raking Trudy. "Whatcha doin' here, Trudy?"

"I . . . I'm . . . um—"

"She's working with me," Lily intervened.

He doubled over with laughter. "Working in a *kitchen?* Lost yore way, did ya?"

Trudy actually blushed. "It's an honest living, Lou."

He wiped his eyes with his sleeve and tried to stop laughing. "Tell me it ain't nothing permanent, Trudy. The boys'll be disappointed if it is."

Lily pushed him toward the wagon. "Will you please get this food back to the camp before it gets too cold to eat?"

"Sure, sure," he murmured amicably. He hiked himself onto the wooden seat and snapped the reins over the team. But as he rode away, the women could still hear him laughing.

Lily put her arm around Trudy's waist. "Ignore him."

"This isn't going to be easy, Lily."

"Nothing worth having is come by easily, dear."

They went into the cabin, and Lily fixed lunch. "Have you ever considered marrying again?"

"There isn't a single man within miles. Except for Lou and a few of his cronies, and I don't like any of them. And, of course, there's Ross."

Lily's stomach pitched downward. "He . . . he never asked you?"

"No. At one time not too long ago, I really wanted him to, Lily."

"And . . . and now?"

"Now he's so crazy about you that no other woman matters."

Lily's feelings were all jumbled inside her. "Do you think there's a man alive who can be faithful to his wife?"

"Oh, yes," Trudy answered. "My Roy was."

"How did you know?"

"It's just one of those things I knew. We were so close. Not only was he my husband and my lover, he was my best friend. I could tell him anything."

Lily chewed on that, thinking about Jake. He'd been her husband and her lover, but her friend? She'd never thought of him that way. There were things about herself that she wouldn't have dared tell him.

They'd just sat down to eat when there was a knock at the door.

When Lily answered it, she gasped in surprise. "Donald!"

Donald South grinned his famous dimpled grin and hauled Lily into his arms, squeezing her tight. "You look good enough to eat, Lily-girl."

Lily allowed the embrace from her last employer, then pulled away. "What on earth are you doing here? And how did you find me?"

His hands stayed on her shoulders as he gazed at her. "You're as beautiful as ever. Will you marry me?"

Lily laughed, then took one of his hands and drew him into the cabin. "You haven't changed an ounce. How did you find me?" she asked again.

"Wasn't hard," he answered. "I just kept going from town to town asking if a gorgeous redhead had moved in."

"We were just sitting down to lunch. Please, join us, Donald."

He hesitated. "I didn't know you had someone with you. I don't want to intrude."

"Nonsense." They entered the kitchen and Lily introduced him to Trudy, who actually blushed when he gallantly kissed her hand.

"What have you been doing since the boardinghouse burned down?" she asked.

"Trying to decide what to invest in next," he answered, sitting across from Trudy. "That's what brought me north, in fact. I'm tired of San Francisco."

Lily studied him. He was handsome, in a blond, Nordic kind of way. And he'd proposed marriage once before, only then he'd been serious. As much as she might have wanted to, she couldn't have said yes. Yet, any woman who caught him would be profoundly fortunate. Lily sensed he would be a faithful husband. But for her, there was no spark. She felt she was better off alone than with a man she didn't love, no matter how faithful he was. Just as she was better off alone than with a man she loved who couldn't be faithful.

After lunch, Lily and Donald reminisced while Trudy

washed the dishes and cleaned up the kitchen. Lily noticed that Donald's gaze often went to Trudy as she bent over the dishpan, and Trudy was uncommonly shy as she cleared his plate away. Perhaps a fresh start was all that Trudy needed, after all.

"I've missed the sight of you, Lily Sawyer." Donald reached across the table and took her hand in his. "I wish you'd stayed around."

"There was nothing left for me there, Donald, you know that. First Jake died, then, two years later, the boardinghouse burned down. I'd wanted to leave before that, but the fire gave me impetus."

Donald looked around the kitchen. "And you came here. Whose place is this, anyway?"

"It's mine," came the gruff answer.

Everyone turned toward the door. Lily's jaw dropped when she saw Ross, and she quickly removed her hand from under Donald's. "Ross? Is that really you?"

He stepped into the kitchen, his dark eyes holding not one ounce of pleasure as they examined Donald South.

"I can't believe it." Trudy's voice was filled with the same disbelief Lily felt. "You've shaved off your beard *and* your mustache."

Lily couldn't believe it either. She was weak and puzzled and filled with longing at the sight of him. He was as handsome as his sister was beautiful. His cheekbones were high, his lips just wide enough to be sensual, and why she'd never noticed the thick, curly lashes that rimmed his eyes before now, she'd never know. His hair had been trimmed and capped his head in deep, coffee-brown waves.

"It's only hair," he answered tersely. "It'll grow back." His gaze still hadn't wavered from Donald's.

Donald stood and extended his hand, which Ross took, albeit reluctantly. "Donald South."

"Ross Benedict." The handshake was brief.

"Is there anything worth investing in around here?" Donald asked.

"Logging mills all the way up the coast," Ross answered. "There's one in trouble up near the Oregon border. They'd probably be happy to see you."

Donald studied him for a moment, then gave him a sly smile. "Nothing around here though, huh?"

"Nope. Nothing around here."

His smile widened, and his glance swiveled from Ross to Lily. "I believe you're right. There doesn't seem to be anything for me around here." He lifted his jacket off the back of the chair. "Trudy? How would you like a ride home?"

The light in Trudy's eyes faded as quickly as it had lit up. "Oh . . . oh, I can't leave yet. There's—"

"There'll be plenty of time to do what you have to do in the morning," Ross interrupted. "I'll help Lily finish cleaning up the kitchen."

Lily stared at him. Why, he was jealous! He couldn't get poor Donald out of the cabin fast enough. She felt a breathless surge of hope.

Donald gave Ross a quick look, then bent and kissed Lily full on the mouth. His eyes twinkled when he let her go. "Remember my offer, Lily." He turned and pulled Trudy's arm through his. "Come, lovely lady, your carriage awaits."

Lily watched them go, then fussed with the pots Trudy had washed, stacking them neatly on the shelf near the window.

"What kind of offer?"

Lily's hands shook, but she continued straightening up.

"What kind of offer, Lily?" His voice held a threat.

"I don't think that's any of your concern," she answered.

"I think it is."

She spun around and faced him. Hoping to deflect his question, she said, "I hope you didn't shave for my sake, Ross. I might have said I preferred a man without a beard, but with or without one, that man is not you."

"Is it *Donald?*"

She ignored his snarling tone. "He . . . he once asked me to marry him. He asked again today." Although she knew full well he would have fainted if she'd said yes.

His expression was stoic, his eyes hard. "Who in the hell is he, anyway?"

She wiped off the table. "He owned the boardinghouse where I worked. It burned down. That's why I left."

"Why didn't you marry him the first time he asked?"

She took a deep, shaky breath. "Because . . . because I didn't love him."

"And do you love him now?"

She shook her head. "No."

"Marry me, Lily."

Her heart took flight, nearly breaking free from her chest. "I . . . I . . . I . . . can't do that."

"Why in hell not?"

Finally able to gather the ragged edges of her feelings and bring herself back under control, she answered, "Why should I marry you, Ross? Donald's offer is safer. I might not love him, but at least I know he'd be faithful. I . . . I'd always thought I'd marry once in my life, for love. Even before Jake died, that foolish illusion was shattered. Jake wasn't a faithful husband. I won't marry another man who isn't."

Slumping into a chair, he rubbed his fingers over his smooth skin, then dug the heels of his palms into his eyes. "Damnit. What makes you think I wouldn't be faithful?"

"Because you told me as much." When he started to interrupt, she put her fingers against his mouth. "You told me it wasn't natural for a man to be faithful to just one woman."

He enclosed her fingers in his and held them. "Do you love me, Lily?"

She tried to tug her fingers away, but he pulled her onto his lap. "I might, but . . . but that isn't reason enough to marry you."

"What if I told you I loved you too?"

Her heart zinged with hope again, but she cautioned herself

against it. "It . . . it still wouldn't be enough, Ross. Love without trust isn't enough."

"*Damnit.* I'm not your bloody Jake!"

"But that day when I was washing your bedding, you sounded just like him."

"I was trying to get a rise out of you, that's all."

"You did. And I'll never forget it." She pushed herself off his lap.

He stood, his hands in his back pockets. "What can I do to change your mind?"

"At this point, nothing," she answered, fighting tears. She couldn't succumb. She just couldn't. But marriage to Ross beckoned, for she knew it would be a heady, satisfying, fulfilling life—if he didn't feel the need to stray.

Chapter Nine

Ross stormed from the cabin, went to the shed and grabbed the ax and the scythe, then strode angrily toward the brush he should have cleared weeks before.

Every time he'd ever spouted off about a man's inability to be faithful to a woman, it had come back to haunt him. There was no way in hell he could convince Lily he would be faithful. But that wasn't going to stop him from trying, damnit. The very thought of someone coming along and taking her away from him ate at him like acid. Never before had he cared enough about a woman to want her for his own. He wanted Lily and only Lily. He knew he wanted to spend the rest of his life with her.

He loved her. He loved her for befriending Trudy when no one else would. He loved her wit and even her sharp tongue, for he knew that beneath it all, she was vibrant and passionate. The idea that she would be even more fervent if she trusted him made him weak.

Paying little attention to his menial task, he imagined all the places he wanted to make love to her. In the river, with her legs wrapped around his waist; on the floor in front of the fire, with her astride; outside on a bed of leaves in front of God and the world.

Suddenly he heard a crashing noise, and the next thing he knew, he was on the ground. . . .

Lily heard him scream. Terror reached into her throat, and she instinctively grabbed Ross's rifle, fled from the cabin, and ran toward the noise. She faltered, only briefly, when she saw Ross on the ground, grappling with a black bear.

Raising the rifle, she shot it into the air, praying the noise would scare the animal off. At the sound of the gunshot, the bear released Ross, lifting her head long enough for Ross to roll away and scramble to his knees. Lily shot again, and the bear lumbered off into the brush.

She flung the rifle to the ground and rushed to Ross. He was still on his knees, blood dripping from his chest and forearms.

"Oh, Ross! Oh, dear God!" She grabbed him under one arm and helped him to his feet.

"I was . . . thinking about you," he mumbled. "Not . . . not paying attention—"

"Hush," she soothed, trying to be strong though she felt so weak. "Come on, now. Help me get you to the cabin."

They struggled to the porch, where Ross had difficulty making it up the steps. "Chest . . . like fire and . . . and raw blisters."

He stumbled inside, and she could barely keep him from slipping to the floor. "Oh, my poor dear. Just a little farther, darling. Just a little farther."

It seemed like an hour before they got to the bed, but once there, she willed her hands to stop shaking and examined his wounds. A wave of fear coated her stomach. He needed a doctor. Badly. But she couldn't leave him.

She rushed into the kitchen, grabbed the teakettle, some dish towels, and her darning kit. Once back at his side, she cut his shirt away and dabbed at the wounds, cringing at the appearance of the ragged flesh.

His face was pinched with pain, but he grabbed her fingers and brought them to his lips. "You . . . you called me dear. Darling."

A blush stole into her cheeks. "Don't talk, Ross. Save your strength, please."

"I . . . I would be . . . faithful, Lily. I knew . . . the minute I saw you that . . ." He coughed, gasping against his pain. ". . . that I'd never want another woman."

Tears welled up in her eyes and slid down her cheeks. "Shhh," she whispered, working at a frantic pace to clean his wounds.

She heard the sound of horses outside, and in a moment, Sam was beside her.

"Oh, my god," she whispered, her mouth quivering. "What happened?"

Lily continued to dab at his wounds, for they still bled. "He disturbed a black bear's den. She attacked him." She turned to Sam. "He needs help, Sam. Go. Please. Bring a doctor."

Sam hadn't taken her eyes off her brother. She backed away, toward the door. "The . . . the doctor is over at the camp right now. I . . . I just came from there."

"Please, Sam. Hurry."

Sam rushed out, and Lily prayed she'd return with the doctor before Ross bled to death.

Sam walked the doctor out, then returned to the bedside. Lily sat slumped in a chair by the bed.

"He'll be all right, don't you think?"

Lily rubbed her eyes. "He's lost a lot of blood, but the doctor seemed to think he would."

Sam sat on the edge of the bed, her fingers touching Ross's cheek. "He shaved his beard and his mustache. I'd forgotten how handsome he is."

Lily could only nod quietly. She remembered her harsh words and his softer, seductive ones: *A hairy man can keep a woman warm, Lily.*

There was a sudden catch in her throat, and she felt a wealth of tears press against the backs of her eyes. Oh, why had she been so nasty? If he should . . . should die, he'd never know how she really felt about him.

"That's funny," Sam said wistfully.

"What?"

"It's odd that he would shave. He's been proud of his beard for years."

"Perhaps . . . he was just tired of it."

"I don't think so."

"Why not?"

She gave Lily a little smile and shrugged. "Last New Year's Eve, I teased him because his date—a woman I forced him into asking to my party—complained about all his facial hair. We made a wager." She pulled a handkerchief from her dress pocket and blew her nose. "I bet him that he'd shave off his beard and mustache if he met the right woman and she asked him to."

Lily's heart expanded and she felt so much love for Ross, mingled with shame at how she'd spoken to him, that she had to turn away.

"I didn't ask him to do it, Sam."

Sam continued to watch her brother. "Maybe you're right. He probably just got tired of it."

Lily gave her a wobbly smile and shook her head. "No."

"What?"

"I . . . I didn't ask him to shave, but I did tell him I didn't like his beard." She swallowed the lump in her throat. "He asked me to marry him, Sam."

Sam gasped and brought her hands to her mouth. "He did? And what did you say, Lily, what did you say?"

Lily's tears came freely now, and she hunted for her own handkerchief. Unable to find it, she brought her apron to her face and wiped her eyes. "I told him I wouldn't marry a man I couldn't trust."

At Sam's crestfallen look, she added, "He'd admitted to me that it wasn't normal for a man to stay faithful to one woman. My late husband was like that, Sam. No matter how much I love Ross, I can't bear the thought of him being with someone else. I guess I'm just selfish that way."

The clock on the mantel chimed five times.

"Oh, dear. I have to pick up Derek at the camp." Sam stood. As she swung her cape over her shoulders, she studied Lily. "Will you be all right here alone?"

Lily gave her a reassuring smile. "Of course. Go. Take care of your husband."

"I'll come back in the morning." Fresh tears spilled down Sam's cheeks. "Oh, Lily . . . I'd so wished the two of you . . ." She pressed her hand over her mouth and ran from the room.

Once Sam was gone, Lily turned her gaze on Ross. The doctor had given him something to kill the pain and help him rest. He was asleep.

She left the chair, sat on the edge of the bed, and studied him. Had he really shaved for her? Did she dare believe that he really loved her enough to be faithful?

Lily watched him into the night. She soothed his face with a cool, damp cloth. She checked his bandages to make sure he wasn't bleeding.

If he'd been thinking about her when he was attacked, then, it was her fault. Tears stung her eyes again, and she swiped them away with her sleeve.

They'd gotten off on the wrong foot, that much she knew. And all because sweet, meddlesome little Samantha had wanted a wife for her brother.

Lily wiped his face again, letting her fingers linger on his skin. His beard was already a rough stubble. She bent and kissed his forehead, nose, his mouth, his chin.

She sat back and rubbed her shoulders. She was tired, but she couldn't leave him. She continued to watch him, her mouth curving into a sly smile.

She left him just long enough to bank the fire, then hurried to the kitchen and grabbed her nightgown. Back in the bedroom, she undressed and slipped into her gown, turned down the lamp, and slid into bed beside him, careful not to lean against his bandaged forearms. She justified her actions by telling herself that if he woke up, she'd know it.

She dozed lightly, in tune with his every movement and the changes in his breathing. Toward morning, however, she fell into a deeper sleep.

Awakening with a start, she opened her eyes and found herself looking into his. They were warm as fresh-brewed coffee.

"I'd like to wake up this way every morning, Lily-love," he said with a drowsy smile.

She swallowed the emotion that swelled in her chest, threatening to erupt into her throat. "I . . . thought it best to be close, just in case you needed me." She attempted to scoot to the other side of the bed and get out, but he tugged her back.

"Don't go."

Without an argument, she settled next to him, then hiked herself up on her elbow. "How do you feel this morning?"

He grinned, sporting a deep, lovely dimple in his left cheek. Lily's self-control was slipping fast. "Like I've been attacked by a bear."

She let out a shaky breath. "Ross, you could have been killed."

He continued to smile at her. "Would you have grieved for me, Lily-love?"

She gave him a gentle smack on the shoulder. "Don't tease about this."

"But would you have?"

She bent and kissed him, thrilling as his mouth responded. "Yes," she admitted. "I would have grieved for the rest of my life."

"Do you love me, Lily?"

She returned his smile. "Yes," she answered simply.

"Will you marry me?"

She wasn't even tempted to ask if he'd be faithful; somehow she just knew he would. "I guess I'd better. There are too many women out there who would take my place in a minute."

He was suddenly serious. "There's not another woman alive who could ever take your place, Lily."

She kissed him again, careful not to touch any of his numerous bandages. "Samantha will be delighted that her plan worked."

He stroked her hair. "Samantha deserves a good spanking. I'll have to talk to Derek about that."

Lily chuckled. "Be careful, she just might enjoy it."

He laughed out loud, then coughed and groaned. "Why, Lily Sawyer, I'm surprised at you."

She snuggled against him briefly. "Life is full of surprises, darling."

With a clumsy motion, he reached over and touched her breast. "I can't wait."

Warmth spread through her at his touch, but she forced herself to get out of bed. "The doctor and Sam will both be here soon. Trudy, too, I suspect. It wouldn't do for them to catch us in bed together."

"It would just force me to make an honest woman of you."

As she unbuttoned her nightgown, she said, "You'll do that anyway once you've healed properly." She picked up her clothes and walked toward the door.

"Lily?"

Turning, she smiled at him. "Yes?"

"Dress in here." His gaze was hot, his request bold.

Pausing only briefly, she put her clothes on the chair by the bed and pulled her nightgown off over her head. The room was cold; her nipples tightened immediately.

His gaze was almost reverent. "Pink nipples. My favorite kind," he added with a smile.

She blushed, feeling the heat from the roots of her hair to her womanhood. "Seen enough, you dirty old man?" she asked, her voice soft and loving despite the harsh words.

His gaze raked her, settling on the thatch of hair between her legs. "Red. My favorite color." He held out his hand. "Come here."

She moved toward him. "Ross, someone will be here any minute—" She gasped as his fingers touched her, then felt her knees go weak when he slid a finger inside. With all her strength, she pulled away and started to dress, noting the tent over his groin.

"One day soon, I'm going to make love to you and watch you when you come, Lily. If I'm not too far gone myself."

His words intensified her hunger, but she forced herself to finish dressing, surprisingly comfortable having him watch her. "I'll make you some oatmeal before I start cooking for the crew." She crossed to the door.

"Lily?"

She stopped, her hand on the latch. "Yes?"

"I love you," he said simply. "The bedroom is ours."

With tears of joy in her eyes, she hurried from the room, allowing his words to nudge her heart. It opened like a flower, and Lily knew she'd found her future husband, her lover, and her friend. She also knew they would be together until the end of time.

Epilogue

New Year's Eve, 1880

From a distance, Ross watched as Lily hugged Trudy, who had just returned from a trip up north to visit Donald South. She gave Trudy a final squeeze, then sat on the sofa to visit with a recuperating Maudie. Under Lily's care, the old woman had done remarkably well and was still able to live independently in the tiny cabin just behind theirs.

Ross's heart swelled with love and pride every time he looked at Lily. He couldn't believe she was really his wife. Who would have thought that love could do such things to a man? Last year at this time, he'd been completely unaware of the power of love, easily spouting platitudes about infidelity, strutting around like an arrogant rooster. Then Lily entered his life, and all that changed.

He was pouring himself another glass of applejack when an obviously pregnant Samantha sidled up to him.

"Kind of a different party than the one we had last year, isn't it?" Her eyes were filled with merriment.

He gave her a half smile. "I was thinking the same thing."

"You lost the bet, you know," she reminded him.

He tweaked her nose. "One bet I was happy to lose, Sam."

"Are you ever going to thank me for meddling?"

"You deserve to be spanked," he said with a growl. "You can't just throw two people together and expect them to fall in love."

"But I did, didn't I?" She gave him an innocent smile.

"That was dumb luck," he answered.

She sighed. "Maybe, but you *are* happy, aren't you, Ross?"

His smile broadened. "Yeah, Sam, I'm happy as hell."

She sighed again, sounding contented as she studied Lily. "Lily looks . . . different."

Ross cleared his throat. "She looks beautiful, as always."

"No," Sam answered with a shake of her head. "She sort of glows." With a tiny gasp, she grabbed his arm. "She's pregnant, isn't she?"

Ross wasn't sure how to answer. Lily had gotten pregnant the very first night they'd been together, which was a full six weeks before they got married. They'd hoped to keep it a secret awhile longer.

Sam tugged at his sleeve. "She *is,* isn't she?"

"Yeah, she is."

She studied him. "Aren't you happy about it?"

"I'm so happy I could crow, but don't advertise it." And he was. He couldn't wait to start a family with this woman who had so completely stolen his heart.

"Why not? What's the big secret?"

He shrugged. "We just want to . . . to wait awhile before we announce it."

"Uh-oh, the famous Benedict telltale mid-sentence hesitation. Why, Ross Benedict. I do believe you're not telling me the entire truth. When is the baby expected?"

"The baby is due in early July," Lily answered, offering Sam a patient smile.

Samantha pulled her close and gave her a hug, which she returned.

"July?" Sam counted on her fingers, then looked at the two of them, her mouth open in surprise. "Why, that would mean—"

"That would mean, Samantha Mae," Ross interrupted, "that whatever you're thinking, you'd better keep it to yourself."

She grinned, her smile nearly splitting her mouth. "So. I wasn't wrong about you two after all."

"Oh, Lily! Our babies will be so close in age they'll be play-mates." Her eyes filled with happy tears. "Isn't that wonder-ful?"

"Yes, Sam, it's wonderful. And, darling," Lily added, giving Ross a squeeze, "Sam actually deserves all the credit for bring-ing us together, don't you think?"

Ross chuckled. "We can't deny it. We can return the favor by naming our first child after her."

Sam's smile wobbled. "Why, that's so sweet, Ross. Thank you. I'd be honored."

"Yeah," Ross said, "Samantha the Snoop, or Meddlesome Mae. Which do you prefer?"

She gave him a mock insulted look, then swept graciously into the waiting arms of her husband. "Ross is picking on me, Derek, darling."

Derek kissed her full on the mouth, then asked, "Shall I give him a sound thrashing, my love?"

She snuggled against his chest, tossing Ross a devilish look over her shoulder as Derek whisked her away. "I think some-one should."

"We *do* owe her a lot, Ross."

"I know, but it wouldn't do to let her know how much we really appreciate it. She'll be a doting aunt as it is."

Lily rested her head against her husband's shoulder. "And I don't imagine you'll be a doting uncle at all."

"Oh, I fully intend to be. But," he said, bending to kiss her, "I'll be an even more doting father."

Lily closed her eyes, wonder filling her. "I never believed I could be this happy."

For a brief moment, Ross remembered the New Year's reso-lution he'd made the year before, vowing never to let Saman-tha meddle in his life again. He pulled Lily close, loving how she felt in his arms. Hell, everyone knew that New Year's reso-lutions were made to be broken.

Please turn the page for
a tantalizing peek at
PURE SILK
by Susan Johnson,
coming in January 2004 from Brava.

On his passage to the grotto, fatigue suddenly overcame Hugh in a wave. Perhaps his weeks of drinking had finally taken their toll or maybe the warmth of the brazier had been too much after not having slept for so long.

The bath house was steamy and warm, the hot water heavenly after their long, cold journey. The tray of food left for him beside his bed was superb.

Hugh was surprised to find himself housed in the same room as the princess, but fell onto his mattress beside hers without undue contemplation. The grotto was small. Perhaps the abbot was beyond issues of desire and temptation. It didn't matter in any case; Hugh was asleep in seconds.

The secret chamber had been built by a pious noble of the Heian era who would retreat from the world on occasion to meditate and pray. In his search for nirvana, however, he preferred worldly comforts and the small apartment beneath the temple of Amida was rich with ornament executed in the finest of materials—coffered ceilings in gold leaf, exquisite screens painted by the great artists of the time, colorful lacquerware chests and tables fit for a potentate, all the architectural detail and carved friezes picked out in shimmering gilt, marquetry and niello work. When Hugh had first seen the rooms two years ago, he'd been dazzled and amused and remembered hoping the Amida didn't take points off for ostentation when considering which souls to guide in the true path to salvation.

But no luxury was as blissful as the soft silk mattress and quilts in which he was cocooned. For the comforts of this bed, his weary soul might have given serious thought to reciting 'I call on thee Amida Buddha,' the salvation-by-faith-alone phrase that made Amida Buddhism so popular. The pleasure of uninterrupted sleep was indeed paradise.

Some time later, deep in slumber, swathed and muffled in her quilt, Tama rolled in a languorous flow from her futon to the one beside hers. Meeting the solid warmth of the captain's body, she unconsciously pressed closer to the blissful heat.

In a dream-state detached from substance and reality, Hugh felt the small form drift into his back, curve along the contours of his spine, melt into his body. Shifting minutely, he sought to heighten the pleasure.

His dreams were of the princess, her image floating whimsically in and out of his imagination—as she looked last summer, elegant and refined, a princess in silken garb . . . or as she had tonight, wet and muddied, her delicate beauty fresh scrubbed and pure despite her drab attire. And she would smile in his dreams from time to time and laugh.

He stirred in his sleep, wanting to reach that illusive smile.

And she purred in response, a hushed, breathy sound.

After years of playing at love, his senses were attuned to dulcet murmurs, his receptors alert to female longing. He came awake. Lying utterly still, his nostrils flared at the scent of a woman, and a smile slowly curved the corners of his mouth. Perhaps paradise was being offered him in this hermitage at Amida's feet. Perhaps he was being rewarded for his kindness.

Under normal circumstances he would have known what to do. He would have rolled over, wakened her with a kiss and taken what Buddha offered. Under any other circumstances he wouldn't have hesitated.

So why was he now?

There was no one here to stop him. No one to hear. No one who even cared if he did what he wanted to do to her. And surely, when a woman purred in that flagrantly voluptuous way, ethical issues of morality ceased to exist. Right? "Damn right," he muttered inadvertently.

Her hand came up in response to his utterance and she gently stroked his shoulder—as though to comfort him.

It did the exact opposite, of course, and he silently cursed every god in creation for putting him in this untenable position. If he acted on his impulses, he'd be sorry as hell the second after he climaxed. If he didn't act on his impulses, he'd be even more afflicted.

In some misguided attempt to act the gentleman, he eased away, putting a small distance between them. Perhaps she wouldn't notice and he could slip away and sleep in the other room.

She did, though.

Clutching his shoulder, she pulled close once again, slid the quilt from his shoulder and nestled against his naked back. Clenching his teeth, he silently counted to ten backwards in every language he knew while her breasts burned into his flesh.

All he could think of was mounting her and plunging deep inside her over and over and over again . . . until he couldn't move, until she couldn't move, until every urgent, ravenous desire scorching his senses was sated. His cock was so hard his spine ached up to his ears and if he knew any useful prayers he would have prayed like hell for help.

Don't, he kept telling himself. Just don't.

You'll live if you don't fuck her.

Maybe.

He wasn't sure of anything right now.

Then he felt her move again, felt the quilt slip down further, felt her soft silky mound against his buttocks and any further gentlemanly motive fell victim to lust. Rolling over, he took her face in his hands and kissed her gently. He intended to woo her softly, but sharp-set lust wasn't so easily tamed when they lay flesh to flesh. His kiss deepened with feverish haste, ravenous need and opportunity fierce stimulus.

She came awake—but not in fear . . . lazily as though intrigued by the violence of his passions and tranquil and yielding, she uttered the smallest of sighs.

"Hello," he whispered, his breath warm against her mouth.

"Konnichi-wa." She half-smiled.

As they lay side by side, he felt her smile under his hands, the inhalation of her breath, the inherent acquiescence in her quiet greeting. But he wanted sanction too, or perhaps only the pretense. "Do you know what you're doing?" he whispered. "Yes . . . no . . ." She shivered faintly as a streak of longing quivered through her senses. "It doesn't matter."

He wasn't about to ask for clarification. "You're cold . . ." he murmured, pulling up the quilt.

"No." She stopped him. "I'm warm; you're too close." Or her dreams had been too graphic.

"Should I move?" He already knew the answer, the scent of female arousal pungent in his nostrils.

"I should say yes . . ."

"But?" His voice was assured, impudence in his gaze.

He was too confident; she should refuse. "I don't usually—I mean—this is . . . very—disconcerting," she stammered, trying to repress the ravenous desire coursing through her blood. "Do you suppose the food was drugged?" she blurted out.

"If it were, I'd have an excuse," he gruffly replied. If he were sensible he'd leave her alone.

"We shouldn't," she said, as though reading his mind.

"You're right." Abruptly sitting up, he stared off in space as though some remedy to his frustration lay just beyond the lantern glow.

"And yet."

His gaze snapped around. "And yet, what?"

"Never mind."

He was about half a world past "never mind," his throbbing erection immune to practicalities. On the other hand, did he really want to get involved? Or more to the point, what would she expect of him afterward? "Perhaps we could work something out," he heard himself saying as though he were negotiating the price of rim-fire cartridges. "It depends," he said.

Coming up on her elbows, her gaze took on a sudden directness. "On what?"

And please enjoy an excerpt from
DRIVE ME CRAZY,
a sensual treat from Nancy Warren
coming from Brava in February 2004.

Duncan Forbes knew he was going to like Swiftcurrent, Oregon when he discovered the town librarian looked like the town hooker. Not a streetwalker who hustles tricks on the corner, but a high class 'escort' who looks like a million bucks and costs at least that much, ending up with her own Park Avenue co-op.

He loved that kind of woman.

He saw her feet first when she strode into view while he was crouched on the gray-blue industrial carpeting of Swiftcurrent's library scanning the bottom shelf of reference books for a local business directory. He was about to give up in defeat when those long sexy feet appeared, the toes painted crimson, perched on do-me-baby stilettos.

Naturally, the sight of those feet encouraged his gaze to travel north, and he wasn't disappointed.

Her legs were curvy but sleek, her red and black skirt gratifyingly short. The academic in him might register that those shoes were hard on the woman's spine but as she reached up to place a book on a high shelf, the man in him liked the resulting curve of her back, the seductive round ass perched high.

From down here, he had a great view of shapely hips, a taut belly, and breasts so temptingly displayed they ought to have a 'for sale' sign on them.

He shouldn't stare. He knew that, but couldn't help himself—torn between the view up her skirt and that of the underside of her chest. He felt like a kid in a candy store, gobbling everything in sight, knowing he'd soon be kicked out and his spree would end.

Sure enough, while he was lost in contemplation of the perfect angle of her thigh, the way it sloped gracefully upward to where paradise lurked, she looked down and caught him ogling. Her face was as sensual and gorgeous as her body—sleek black hair, creamy skin and plump red lips. For that instant when their gazes first connected he felt as though something mystical occurred, though it could be a surge of lust shorting his brain.

Her eyes went from liquid pewter to prison-bar gray in the time it took her to assimilate that he hadn't been down here staring at library books. What the hell was the matter with him acting like a fourteen-year-old pervert?

"Can I help you with something?"

Since he'd been caught at her feet staring up her skirt, he muttered the first words that came into his head. "Honey, I can't begin to tell you all the ways you could help me."

The prison bars seemed to slam down around him. "Do you need a specific reference volume? A library card? Directions to the exit?"

The woman might look as though her photo ought to hang in auto garages reminding the grease monkeys what month it was, but her words filled him with grim foreboding. He was so screwed.

"*You're* the librarian?"

A ray of winter sunlight stole swiftly across the gray ice of her eyes. "Yes."

"But you're all wrong for a librarian," he spluttered helplessly.

"I'd best return my master's degree then."

"I mean . . ." He gazed at her from delicious top to scrumptious bottom. "Where's your hair bun? And bifocals? And the crepe-soled brogues and . . . and the tweeds?"

If anything, her breasts became perkier as she huffed a quick breath in and out. "It's a small mind that thinks in clichés."

"And a big mouth that spouts them," he admitted. God, what an idiot. He'd spent enough time with books that he ought to know librarians come in all shapes and sizes, though, in fairness, he'd never seen one like this before. He scrambled to his feet, feeling better once he'd resumed his full height and he was gazing down at her, where he discovered the view was just as good. He gave her his best shot at a charming grin. "I bet the literacy rate among men in this town is amazingly high."